Secrets of

Savannah

The Entire Series

By:

S.M. Donaldson

Dear Reader,

This series started honestly, because I wasn't quite ready to let go of my Temptation characters although I felt like their stories were complete. When I started Fighting Temptation (Cade's Story) and came up with the story line I found my "in" to continuing the series without continuing the series.

I also wanted to approach the subject that not all New Adult Romance should be set in college. I feel like at times when you say New Adult people assume it means a college romance. Not everyone goes to college, some people even though they are technically still a new adult are already living an adult life and have a career etc.

I picked Savannah as a setting because I wanted the world to see a glorious depiction of the South. Savannah is a beautiful place filled with Southern culture and tons of history.

I really hope you enjoy these characters as much as I've enjoyed bringing them to you.

Love,

SM Donaldson

The South:

In order of priority. It's God, Family & Football. Juke Joints, Cotton Fields, Sweet Tea, Southern Hospitality, Good Ol' Boys & Fireflies. BBQ & Cold Beer, Front Porches, Fast Cars and Always Blessing Somebody's Heart.

 XOXO

SM Donaldson

Secrets of Savannah- The Entire Series

Editing by Chelly Peeler
Cover by: Sharp Designs

Secrets Behind Those Eyes

Book 1

For my Crazy Friends with their Crazy lives.

Introduction

- Due to mature subject matter this book is for readers 17+.
- This book is written in a true southern dialect, from a true southern person. Therefore, it is NOT going to have proper grammar.

Secrets Behind Those Eyes

Prologue

Scarlet

How could I be so dumb? I bust my ass to graduate a year early so I can start at the Savannah College of Art and Design in the fall and now I'm sitting here in a holding cell. He wasn't worth this.

"Scarlet Johnson. Come on. You're bein' released."

I nod. "Yes, sir."

Walking out into the front lobby of the police station, I see my brother, Gable. "Hey, kid. What in the hell happened?"

I hug him. "I'll fill you in once we're in the car."

Once we are in the safety of our car, Gable looks at me. "Okay, so tell me."

"Well, when we got back from meeting Cade last week, I felt like something between Dustin and I was off." Cade is our brother that we've just met for the first time.

"Okay?"

"So this morning I decided to surprise him. I stopped by our favorite coffee shop to grab us some coffee and bagels. When I pulled up to his house, I noticed an Audi sitting in the driveway, but I thought it was one of his frat brothers or something. I walked in his apartment and I heard them. Walking back to his bedroom, I shoved the door open and I saw them."

"Who was he with?" My big brother with the murderous glare on his face says looking at me.

I shake my head. "Him, his friend, Brandon, and my friend, Kelsie. They were in the middle of some weird shit. I screamed and they looked at me. That dick Brandon asked me to join in. Kelsie started blubbering and telling me she was sorry. Dustin's naked ass jumped up and tried to talk to me, but I shoved him away. I took off running out the door, and he grabbed me from behind. Then he had the audacity to ask me not to tell anyone."

"Wow that took balls. That still doesn't explain how you ended up in jail."

"Well, when he asked me that, I saw red. I grabbed some sort of handle. I think it was from an ax. I swung it at him until he backed up. I was just so angry. So embarrassed. It was like a switch flipped and I lost it. The first lick to his car was pure accident, but that one felt so good that I couldn't stop."

"Holy shit, little sister."

"Yeah, well, the neighbors called the cops about all of the screamin' and car bashin.' When they got there, who were they going to believe? Me, part of the working class society around here, or three blue bloods? Three blue bloods who don't want their parents or any of the town to find out they were having some kind of weird sex fantasy shit going on. Oh, and that two of the town's most beautiful blue-blooded men have gay tendencies."

"Whoa, what? I thought they were with Kelsie?"

"Yes, but Kelsie was on the bottom, Brandon was on top, and Dustin was *in the middle*." I get grossed out just thinking about it.

"Oh shit!"

"Look if he'd just came out and told me he's gay or bi whatever, we could've went our separate ways, but he embarrassed me. Then, to see my best friend involved. Not one of them said a word when the police put me in the car."

"So what are you looking at?"

"They said probably probation and community service."

"Well, that's good. I mean, I know Mom would worry about trying to come up with money."

"Yeah, I know. All I could think about was the fact that they may take my scholarship to SCAD."

*****

Looking out the window of the museum, my mother works as she demands my attention. "Look, young lady, you should be glad they just gave you probation and community service. You did enough damage to that car to constitute a felony."

"I know, Mom. It's just... If everyone knew the truth of why I flipped-"

"You will not tell anyone his business."

"I'm the one being looked at like the crazy ex-girlfriend."

"Young lady, I raised you to be compassionate to people. You couldn't tell he was confused when you were together?"

"No. How would I know about being confused anyway?"

"Well, I just assumed since you two had been seeing each other for so long. I guess I just thought you guys had been having sex. You know how I feel about sex and all."

"Yes, I know you are completely casual about sex most of the time. But no, we never had sex; as a matter of fact, I've never had sex."

My mom stops in her tracks. "Really?"

"Yes, Mom, really. Oh my God, why am I discussing my non-sex life with my mother?"

"Hey, I've always told you. Sex is an expression with our bodies. I'm okay with you discovering that. As a mother, I would prefer it be someone who you've been with a while. But the free spirit my parents raised says go for it."

"Jeez. I'm going to do my community service."

Ryder

"Son you're nineteen years old. It's time you get some direction in your life." My dad spins around. "And by direction, I mean a plan other than living off your inheritance, booze, and whores."

I run my hands through my hair in frustration. "So you're sayin' you won't talk to Judge Griffin about throwing out my community service? I mean, shit, I could pay all the fines for probation and shit. Hell, I'll even pay that old asshole restitution for the damages."

"No, son. You need to pay with your sweat and hard work. It's time that you learned money will not get you out of everything in life. You can't go around bein' hotheaded wreckin' cars and tearin' other people's shit up. Also money isn't going to be all you need in your life. Having friends, family, and people you can trust; that's what matters."

"So you keep sayin.'"

My dad makes his way across the room and puts his finger on my chest. "Let me explain something to you. I loved your momma with every breath I had in me. I was an incomplete person when she came along. There isn't a day that goes by that I don't wish that she was still here and not a day that goes by that I can't wait to see her again. But sometimes, I can't help but wonder if she'd be disappointed in me for how I've let you turn out." He turns and walks out of the room.

Feeling like the biggest douchebag in the world, I make my way out of the house to my community service.

*****

Sometimes it's hard for me to remember my momma. I was only nine when she died. So there's been a lot of shit since then. Plus, those last couple of years, she wasn't herself. She was sick from the chemo and radiation. She wasn't the momma who would take me pond swimming. Her long sandy blonde hair had fallen out; she looked frail, but she always tried to put on a smile for me. She always made me chocolate chip cookies, even when the smell of something cooking made her vomit. I haven't eaten a chocolate chip cookie since. The taste, the smell, they make me nauseous.

I park at the address given to me for my community service. I'm going to help build a Habitat for Humanity house. I figured doing this would be better than scrubbing toilets or picking up trash on the side of the road. Plus, I get more out of it. I can actually see what I accomplish and I'll be able to finish up my time sooner than picking up trash every Saturday.

I walk up to the big guy with a clipboard in his hand. "Hey, I'm Ryder Abbott. I'm doing some community service here."

He huffs. "Good, I'm Gus. I was hoping I'd get some good, strong guys. They sent me that girl over there and I can tell she's going to be a hard worker, but the southern man in me says I can't have her hauling lumber over her shoulder. My granddaddy would roll over in his grave and come back to haunt my old ass."

I push my shades up on my head, laughing. "Yeah, I can see that. So where do I start?"

"Go over there where I've got Scarlet handing out hard hats and tool belts and she'll give you the info."

"So Little Miss Blondie over there got community service?"

"Yep, smashed the shit out of some guy's car or something. What did you do?"

"Um, kinda the same. Except, well, I smashed up my car doing about 110. Taking out some guy's barn and a cow."

"Wow, it's a wonder that man didn't kill you over that cow. The price these days." He walks off, shaking his head.

I step up to the table where Blondie is handing out everything. "Hey, I'm Ryder. Gus sent me over here to get some information and stuff from you." She has her blonde hair up in a messy bun. She's wearing ripped up jeans, a white tank top that accents the gorgeous set of tits she's got, and a pair of cheap mirrored sunshades. Damn. She's fucking hot.

"Yeah. I'm Scarlet; nice to meet you." She sticks her hand out to shake mine. I take her tiny hand and shake it. She smiles. "Here's your hard hat, your tool belt, a set of daily instructions and the OSHA guidelines."

"So what did a pretty little thing like you do to get community service?" I flash her my signature get a girl into bed smile.

Pushing her shades up on top of her head and putting her hands on her hips, she looks at me. "I took an ax handle to my ex's car. You?"

"I was stupid racing a car. So he was stupid enough to dump you? He deserved it."

"No, I dumped him."

Flags fly up in my head. She's a crazy ex. We all have one. The one you half expect to come home one day with a rabbit boiling on your stove *Fatal Attraction* kinda crazy. "So then, what exactly did his car do to you?"

"Look I'm not going into this. I'm here to do my time. I don't need to deal with another blue-blooded, conceited, spoiled rotten, selfish bastard. So just stay out of my way."

I put my hands out defensively in front of me. "Hold on, sweet tits. What gives you the right to think you know a fucking thing about me?"

She turns to walk off and glances back. "I don't and I'd like to keep it that way."

I spin around, walking away from her. *Damn. She's a crazy bitch. But the crazy ones are always the hottest in bed. Self- challenge accepted.*

Chapter 1

Scarlet

Burning up in the Georgia humidity isn't exactly how I wanted to spend the last few weeks of my summer, but its better this than trying to come up with the eighteen hundred dollars' worth of damage I did to Dustin's car.

Truth being told if his parents found out that I didn't just find him screwing Kelsie, but that I found him being drilled in the ass at the same time by one of the city council member's son they might think differently. I can't though; I know what would happen to those two boys. Their families would blacklist them and, after that, they might as well be dead. Because one thing is for sure. If you are raised up being a blue blood, if you rock the boat, they can make your life a living hell.

So here I am, working off my time. It's been cool, though, to watch a house being built pretty much from start to finish. Most of the framework was done when I got here, but today I'm helping paint the interior walls.

"Hey sexy. You need some help with those paint cans?"

Dealing with this obnoxious jerk may kill me before this week is over. "No. I still don't need *your* help with anything."

"I was just trying to be nice. We finished up the landscaping outside and Gus told me to come in and help you paint."

"Fine," I tell him. "Just grab a roller and start on the other side of the room."

"Sure." He shrugs and walks over to the other side and starts painting.

After an hour of blissful silence, it's time to wait for the paint to dry a little before we start the second coat. He walks over and hands me a bottle of water.

"Thanks." I sit down on a bucket.

"So what do you do normally? Like are you in college or whatever?" he asks.

"I graduated high school a year early so I could start SCAD this fall."

"Which program are you doing at SCAD? Wait, let me guess. Something in fashion or, with a name like Scarlet, art history."

"No. My mother works for the Telfair Museum so art history has been crammed down my throat for most of my life. I'm kinda scattered right now. I'm doing some sculpture, some painting, sketching, and graphic design. "

"Wow, that's kinda all over the place."

"I have an interest in all of them and I'm good at all of them so I just really can't decide. Sculpting and painting are passions. The feeling of creating something is awesome. But I'm also realistic enough to know that it isn't going to pay the bills. I already do some graphics stuff for my brother's band, so I figure why not look into doing some of it professionally."

"So you have a brother. Older or Younger?" he asks.

"Older. I have two actually, but I just met my oldest brother, Cade, a few weeks ago. My brother Gable plays in a local band."

"Did you just find out about this other brother?"

"No, I knew about him for years. Well, after the fact that my dad had two families came out anyway."

"Holy shit. That's wild. I don't have any brothers or sisters. My mom died when I was young and my dad never found anyone else."

"I'm sorry," I tell him. "That's so sad. My dad going away wasn't so bad; he was a jackass most of the time. But my momma, I don't think I could live without her. As crazy as she is."

"So your mom works down at the Telfair, huh? What's her name? I used to have to go down there all the time to deliver stuff for my dad."

"Her name is Whisper Johnson."

"Yeah, I've met her; she's really nice. Seems really into art." He waves his hands around.

"Her parents were like true to the word hippies. So she's all free love, art, don't hate people. The only thing she has done differently was try to be married once and live in one place with us, rather than floating around like gypsies."

"Damn. So how are you not so much free love then?"

"You're an ass. As soon as I start thinking you're a normal person... I should've just ignored you."

"I'm just saying you put off all kinds of frosty vibes. No wonder you and the ex had hard times."

"Shut up; you don't know a fucking thing about my ex. Mind your own damn business and leave me the hell alone." I storm back to the other side of the room and start the second coat.

We go back to our silence. I can't wait to get off work today. It's Friday and my best friend Annabelle is taking me out for my birthday finally. My birthday was actually a month ago, but I wanted to go to meet Cade and then all the shit with Dustin happened, so I never got the chance to go until now.

We are finally finishing up for the day. At five o'clock sharp, Annabelle pulls up in her new Camaro. She's a blue blood but you wouldn't think it. She steps out of the car, pulling off the ultimate Southern Belle sex appeal. She's in a pair of cut off shorts and a bandanna tank top. "Hey girl, you ready to go get our barhopping on?"

"Yeah, just a minute; let me go make sure that I closed up all the paint and stuff."

She follows me into the house. "Wow, this is really neat. I can't believe you helped do this."

"She didn't do this painting all on her own, you know," Ryder says.

Annabelle rolls her eyes. "So, is this Sir Douchebag you told me about?"

"Yep," I say, popping the p.

"Sir Douchebag, huh? Does that make you Queen Frosty?"

I ignore him, but Annabelle just can't. "Hey, didn't I go to high school with you? When you weren't doing some stupid shit to get suspended?"

"Probably. School isn't really my thing. Never has been." He says with a slight grin.

"Abbott Cotton Company. No wonder you don't have to like school," Annabelle scoffs.

"Hey, I'm ready to go," I interject. "I need to go by my place and grab my clothes."

"Great! I'm ready to get our barhopping on." We walk out, not even bothering to give Ryder a goodbye.

Two hours later, I'm showered, shaved, and buffed. My hair and makeup are done, and I have a killer sexy outfit. Annabelle and I walk out of her place dressed to kill. I have on my new Miss Me jeans I'm so proud of because I busted my ass and saved to buy them, a hot pink, sparkly, strapless top, and some killer hot pink cowgirl boots Annabelle got me for my birthday.

Once we get in her car, she laughs. "Okay, so this is the second part of your birthday gift." She pulls out a bottle of Parrot Bay. "Now we'll swing by Sonic and grab a couple of slushes to add this to so we can pre-game."

"Are you going to be able to drive us all the way to Swampy Tonk and back? Or like usual, am I driving home?"

"No, I got it covered tonight. Since we'll be so close to Richmond Hill, we'll crash in a hotel room down there."

"Okay, sounds cool."

Forty-five minutes later, I have downed my route 44 blue coconut slush along with half the Parrot Bay. Annabelle has downed her slush with the other half. We're feeling tipsy walking into the bar. We chose the Swampy Tonk because they don't really check the IDs of pretty girls. Since she's the only person besides my mom and Gable that know the truth about my break-up, she's buying my shots tonight. Our plan is to get buzzed good here and then head to some of the other small bars. No one really knows us down here and there are always hot soldiers here from the base. They are always willing to buy pretty girls drinks.

"You are getting on that mechanical bull tonight, Scarlet," she says.

"Hell, no, I'm not."

She giggles. "We'll see."

Chapter 2

Ryder

Just when I thought I was going to be having a boring Friday night...

I figured I'd be sitting at home or hitting up some local bar, but my buddy Judd just got stationed down at Ft. Stewart and he got a pass for the night. We're going to hit up some little bars down in Richmond Hill. It'll be good to have a few beers with him. I think he's going to be deployed soon and he's like a brother to me. Good thing we both had some great fake IDs made two years ago.

When we pull my Jeep Wrangler into the parking lot of the Swampy Tonk, I can tell tonight is going to be interesting. I look two spots over and see the bright red Camaro that picked up Scarlet today. *Hmm, so this is where they started their night off.*

We walk into the bar and I see her across the room, dancing with her friend. "Judd, I may need you to keep that little raven haired beauty on the dance floor busy tonight."

"Damn, bro, I don't think that'll be a problem for me."

A nice slow song pipes up just in time for Judd to make his way over to Scarlet's friend and ask her to dance. Scarlet makes her way to the bar and so do I.

"Can I buy you a drink?"

While turning her head, she smiles. "Sure." Until she sees that it's me offering. "Ugh, damn, just my luck. No, I'll get my own drink, thanks."

"I just want to buy you a drink to say sorry."

"Fine."

I motion for the bartender to give her another and I get a beer for myself. "Didn't think I would run into anyone I knew down here."

"We came here to get away from the locals and celebrate my birthday." She has a cute little slur going on.

"So it's your birthday?" I ask.

"No, it was a few weeks ago, but I've been kinda busy."

"Wow, well, I'll buy you another drink for your birthday then."

"No thanks. We also came down here for the cute military guys. See? My friend's already found one."

I laugh. "That's my best friend, Judd. He's who I came here with tonight."

"Great," she says.

"Just be careful who gets you drinks, okay? You can't be too safe these days."

She throws her hand over her shoulder as she walks off. *Damn, her ass is hot as fuck in those jeans.* I sit at the bar for a little while and watch her get hit on by every guy in the place except for Judd; he's so wrapped up with her friend. Shit, I may be sleeping in the car tonight. *Hell, I get him to help me and he's the one who's probably going to get laid.* A little while later, I notice that Scarlet is well on her way to being drunk. That's when she climbs on the bull. Fuck, that is a girl tell-all. If you're drunk enough to want to make an ass out of yourself on a mechanical bull, it's time for you to go home.

My phone vibrates. It's a text from Judd.

JUDD: Hey, man, I'm leaving with Annabelle for a little bit. Thanks for the hookup BTW.

ME: Fuck you, man. Did you play the whole "I'm being deployed and I may never see you again card?"

JUDD: Hope, she just thinks I'm sexy. Good luck yourself. Meet you back at the hotel; they are staying at the same place. So if you'll just alert me when you're on your way back, that would be great. Oh and Annabelle said can you make sure Scarlet makes it back. I told her I didn't think you'd have a problem. But she did say if you put your hands on her or let anything happen to her, she'll cut off your balls.

Great. I now get to go convince a drunk girl that possibly hates me that I'm her ride back to the hotel and *Oh yeah we need to hang out for a little while because our friends are hooking up.*

I watch her fall on the air mat under the bull. Now is as good a time as any. I walk over.

"Hey Scarlet let me help you up and get you back to your room."

She shoves me. "No. I don't like you."

"Too bad, I'm your ride since our *friends* ran out of here to go hook up."

"Shit, I told that bitch I'd have to be the DD."

"No, I'm the DD; she wanted me to make sure that you made it back. Judd and I are staying at the same place so it works."

"Okay, I guess." She slumps her shoulders.

We start making our way through the now thick cloud of people. As we get to the door, she tenses up. Then she shakes her head. "As if tonight couldn't get more fucked up."

I look at her, confused. "What?"

"My ex and his *best friend*."

I recognize these two assholes. I went to school with them. Maybe she had the right to fuck up either one of their cars.

Dustin stops, looking me up and down. Then he looks over to Scarlet. "Scar, baby, what are you doing here with him?"

"I'm not here with him; he's giving me a ride. Plus who I'm here with is just as much none of your fucking business as it is mine that you are with him." She says, pointing to Brandon.

Dustin touches her arm. "Come on, let's go outside and talk."

"Hey, you need to take your hand off her," I say.

"Yes, take your hand off of me."

Brandon reaches for Dustin. "Man, don't waste your damn time with her; she always was trash. We just know it for sure now."

That's when the punch happened. Brandon stumbles, holding his jaw. "Scarlet, you are one fucking crazy bitch. You know, maybe I should talk to the judge about your obvious anger issues. With your probation I'm sure he'd like to get you some help."

I'm about to knock him on his ass when she steps up, jutting her perfect chest forward. "Yeah and maybe I should talk to everyone I know about your *issues*. Wonder how Mommy and Daddy would feel about that? Don't fucking push me, Brandon. I'll ruin you."

He grabs her arm. I step toward him. "Take your fucking hand off of her or I'll break it."

"Come on, Brandon; let's just go grab a drink. They were leaving anyway. I guess those two years of no sex with her is paying off for Mr. Cotton over here."

Scarlet steps at Dustin. "For your information, I never wanted to have sex with you; it didn't feel right. I guess I know why now. As for Ryder and I... Not that it's any of your business, but that's not going to happen. You kinda turned me off guys for a while. Maybe you guys can help me out with those issues, huh?"

Dustin spins around and grabs Brandon's arm. "Come on."

I look down at Scarlet. "You ready to go now, Rocky?"

"Yeah."

As we walk out of the bar, I look over at her. "Okay, so I won't ever give you shit about bashing his car again. He's always been a dick."

"I don't know; he was always nice to me. Brandon always seemed off, like he hated me from afar but I don't know why."

"Um, because he's always been in love with Dustin."

She stops, almost making me slam into her. "Why do you say that?"

"Well, let's just say I'm not totally dense to the conversation you just had and I had my own suspicions when we were in school. Brandon was always possessive over Dustin like a jealous boyfriend."

She shakes her head. "How did I miss it?"

She stumbles and I catch her waist. "Let's get you to my jeep. I think those shots are finally catching up with you."

I have to help her up in the jeep and I get to touch her ass. My dick starts to stiffen and I have to shake it off. Once I'm in the jeep, she reaches over, rubbing the stubble on my face, and giggles. "You know, Ryder, if you weren't such an asshat, I'd think you were cute."

"Well, thanks, Blondie."

She passes out on the way to the hotel and I have to carry her in. I go to the room number that Judd text me, but there's no answer. I beat on the door again with a passed out Scarlet draped over my shoulder. Finally, my phone chimes. It's another text from Judd.

Just give me another hour, man. Please, I'll owe you.

I respond. *Look, just crash there. Scarlet is passed out anyway she can stay with me.*

A minute later he responds back a quick. *Awesome.*

I make my way to my room down the hall and put her on the other bed. I pull off her boots and place her under the covers. The next thing I know, her pink top is flying off, revealing her amazing tits and she shimmies her jeans off under the blanket. She pulls the blanket up on her and passes back out. Fuck, this is going to be fun to explain in the morning.

Chapter 3

Scarlet

Oh, damn, my head hurts. I think something died in my mouth. I roll over to see a male figure covered up in the other bed; he has his back to me. Looking down, I realize that I'm in nothing but my lacy panties. I can feel the heat creeping up my face. All of a sudden, there is a grunt from the other bed.

"Hey."

I look back over to find Ryder staring at me. Well, to be honest, at my boobs, which I just noticed aren't covered. I pull the blanket up, covering myself. *How did I get out of my clothes? That son of a bitch.* I pick up my boot off the floor and throw it at him.

"You asshole. How could you?"

He puts his hands up in defense. "What?"

"You stripped me practically naked. What the hell am I doing in the room with you anyway? When we left the bar, you were giving me a ride to my room."

As I'm picking up something else to throw, he put his hands up again. "Whoa. That was the plan. You passed out after we left the bar. Then Judd and Annabelle were still *busy* when we got here. So I brought you here, put you on that bed, and took off just your boots. You did the rest there, sweetheart." He motions up and down my body.

I put my head in my hands. "I'm going to kill Annabelle."

He stands up, walking to the bathroom in a pair of boxers. Grabbing a cup of water, he returns and hands it to me with some aspirin. "Here, take these. We'll go grab some breakfast and see if our friends can tear themselves apart from each other."

"Did Judd go to school with you and Annabelle?"

"No. Judd's daddy worked for my dad. His dad runs a couple of our farms. So Judd and I grew up together. He tries to keep me straight and out of jail."

I try to relax. He's trying to be nice. This has obviously been a weird twenty-four hours. So I try to make conversation. "He seems nice. Well, the five seconds I got to talk to him before he and my best friend started sucking face. Will you hand me my top and my jeans? I gotta walk down to my room and grab my bag."

Handing me my clothes, he goes back to the bathroom. "He's a great guy," he says through the bathroom door. "I'd trust him with my life. He likes me for who I am, not how much money my family has."

"You know, if you hadn't come on to me like some kind of sleaze ball, I might have liked you for who you are, too."

He steps back out into the room. "Hey, I just feel that it's important to be upfront. You're the one who was telling me how cute I was last night when you were drunk."

"I did not," I argue.

"Yes, you did. Well, in your defense, we'd just ran into the two douche nozzles. So I think, looking at me, you just said what felt natural."

I stand up after pulling on my boots. "Whatever. But I do appreciate you giving me a ride and not leaving me with those two. I vaguely remember seeing them anyway."

"Like I said, I go way back with those two and I can't stand them."

I touch his arm as I grab the door. "Well, thanks anyway. I'm going to grab my bag."

I walk down the hall to my room and bang on the door. Annabelle answers with a towel wrapped around her. She has "I just got fucked all night long" hair. "Hey," she says.

"I need my bag. If you can pull yourself away from GI Joe long enough to hand it to me."

"Yeah, sorry about last night, but that was just too good to pass on, trust me. Here's your bag. We were thinking about going next door to that Waffle House to grab some food. What about you and Ryder?"

"We were talking about some food. I'm going to take a shower and we'll meet you over there in, say, forty-five minutes?"

"Sure."

I walk back down to Ryder's room and knock on the door. He answers in a towel. *Damn, he's got some killer abs.* He motions for me to come in. "Do you mind if I use your shower?" I ask. "Annabelle said that they'll meet us next door in forty-five minutes for some breakfast."

"Sounds good; I'm starving."

I walk into the bathroom and shut the door, leaning back against it. Reaching over, I turn on the shower, letting the steam fill the room. I slip back out of my clothes and step under the hot spray. I scrub last night's make-up off and then get to work on the mess I call hair. I hear the door open. *I know he didn't just come in here.* "Um, hello. Still in the shower here."

"I'm going. I forgot to brush my teeth. Shit, it isn't as if you didn't show me plenty last night."

"You're an asshole. Do you know that?"

"Yes, I know I'm an asshole. Don't be so defensive. I don't want to sleep with you. So can't we just be civil to one another?"

That asshole! "What do you mean you don't want to sleep with me? You'd be lucky to get to sleep with me. I don't want to sleep with you, either, so get the fuck out of the bathroom."

"What the hell? One minute I'm an asshole because you think I want to sleep with you and now I'm an asshole because I said I don't want to sleep with you?"

I find myself standing with my hands on my hips like I'm arguing face to face with him. I shake my head. "Just get the fuck out."

He slams the door, walking out mumbling something.

Ten minutes later, I'm out of the shower and dressed. I finish drying my hair and walk out into the room, where Ryder is propped against the headboard of one of the beds watching TV. *Why does he have to be so fucking sexy?* He's left his shirt unbuttoned and I can see the top of his boxers poking just out of the waistband of his jeans. *Pull it together, Scarlet; he's a rich boy with entitlement issues.*

"You ready to get some food?" I ask.

He turns the TV off and sets the remote down. "Yeah." He reaches down by the bed and pulls on his boots. "Let's go."

"Do you need to check out or anything?"

"Nah, I'm staying another day to spend some time with Judd," he says, buttoning his shirt.

I shrug and we head out the door. I text Annabelle to let her know that we're walking over to the Waffle House. She texts that they'll be over in just a few minutes.

"Annabelle says they're on their way and for us to grab a table."

We walk in to the typical "Welcome to Waffle House" chorus among the waitresses and cooks. I slide into the booth and Ryder slides in next to me. I look at him, about to argue, when Annabelle and Judd walk in and slide into the other side.

An older lady walks up to wait on us. "How're y'all doing this morning?" We all nod and mumble fine. She chuckles. "Sounds like y'all laid out with the dry cows last night."

Ryder laughs. "That sounds like something my nana would say. Yes, we did, and it was fun."

She smiles and laughs. "Well at least you're honest. Now what can I get y'all?"

Judd looks up. "I'll have coffee and the All American Breakfast. Eggs over medium, with grits, bacon, and a pecan waffle."

Ryder looks up. "I'll have the same."

Annabelle laughs. "Well, make that three except give me a Coke instead of coffee." She looks over at a shocked Judd. "Hey, I burnt off a lot of calories last night. I'm starving."

We all chuckle. I look up. "I'll have a Coke, two eggs scrambled, hash browns, covered and chunked. Bacon and toast."

Ryder grins. "Nothing like some good ole' Waffle House grease in your belly to make you feel better after getting trashed huh?"

Judd shakes his head. "Yep it's one of the things I'm going to miss about home that's for sure."

We spend the next forty-five minutes making general conversation with Ryder and me being total smart asses to each other.

We finish our food and walk out. Annabelle and Judd exchange goodbyes. I look over at Ryder. "Thanks again for the ride last night and not leaving me."

He pulls his shades down. "No problem. So you're finished with your hours now?"

"No, I've got a couple of days this week and I'll be done. What about you?"

"I've got another week." We both look over at our friends sucking face. "Damn, is he gonna let her come up for air?" he asks.

I shake my head and chuckle. "I'm beginning to wonder about that myself."

They finally break apart and Annabelle grabs her keys. I pull my shades down over my eyes and climb in her car. She smiles at me. "Ready?"

"Yeah, I wasn't the one sucking face."

"You so could've been."

I look at her like she's lost her mind. "You're crazy."

"Come on, I wasn't even around you and Ryder that much but you guys have some serious sparks going on."

Trying to play off how nice he actually was to me. "Um, yeah, sparks of anger, hate, loathing each other. We've just moved past the urge to kill each other."

She laughs as we get on I95. "Whatever."

Chapter 4

Ryder

Watching the girls leave, I just shake my head. "So, lover boy, do you think you'll spend a day with me now?"

"Hey, you asked me to keep Annabelle busy and I damn sure did," he says with a cocky grin.

"Dude, spare me the details. I've hit a dry spell since the night I got arrested."

"You had that hot little spitfire all night and did nothing?"

"I don't know that I've ever met someone like her before. I think she fucking hates me."

"No way, man; you two are one hot argument from tearing each other's clothes off."

"Whatever. What about you and Annabelle?"

He shrugs. "We had a good night, nothing serious. She knows I'm probably leaving on a deployment so we exchanged numbers. We plan to keep in touch, but until my schedule gets figured out, we are just keeping things fun."

"I remember Annabelle from school; she was kinda cool. Hey, I also figured out whose car Scarlet bashed up. That asshole, Dustin Winston."

"The dude who was a closet case gay guy? He had that dickhead friend, Bobby or Brandon, right?"

"Yep. As a matter of fact we ran into those two dicks as we were leaving. It got interesting. Scarlet punched Brandon in the jaw. Let's just say I think the reason she and Dustin broke up is because he and Brandon aren't doing such a great job of keeping it all in the closet anymore. She didn't really elaborate," I tell him.

"Damn. Some people. Well, enough of the Bay Street Soap Opera. What do you want to do today?"

"Let's go shoot some pool or something."

"How about we go to one of the ranges and shoot some rounds?" he suggests.

I shrug. "Works for me. Let's go."

~*~*~

Pulling up to the worksite, I see Scarlet walking across the front yard. I call out to her. "Hey, nice hat."

She smirks. "Thanks. Usually I don't do the color yellow but since the inspector was coming by, I figured why not."

"Has he already been and gone?"

"He's in the house with Gus right now doing the walkthrough," she says.

"So what's on the agenda for the rest of the week?"

"Well, tomorrow is my last day, but I think just finishing up landscaping and cleaning up the inside."

"So you'll be out of my hair after tomorrow, huh?"

"Yep."

"What are your plans for the rest of the summer?" I ask.

"I have to get my crap together for SCAD. I really need to find my own car and I've got a bunch of graphics work to catch up on for my brother's band. Oh, yeah. I also need to find a new job because I can't work for Dustin's family anymore."

"What did you do for them?"

"I helped out in his Dad's office doing invoices and general paperwork. I'm going to need something in the evening anyway with school."

I shrug. "If I hear of anything, I'll let you know."

She smiles. "Thanks I appreciate it."

I watch her walk back across the yard into the house. *Damn. I could watch her ass all day long.*

~*~*~

After leaving my last day at the jobsite, I head to visit my Nana Pearl. She's probably the coolest eighty-year-old I know. She smokes Pall Mall's like a chimney and drinks a shot of homemade moonshine every night before bed. She cusses like a sailor and keeps a .45 revolver in her chair side table.

Turning off of the pavement onto her gravel driveway, I look at the gorgeous cotton fields across the property. Her plantation style house was built in the early 1900's, but the land it's on has been in our family since the early 1800's. My dad and I only live just a quarter mile down the road from her but I haven't been taking much time to stop and see her. She is going to crawl my ass when I walk through the door.

I don't even make it up the back steps before I hear her. "Damn a' mighty, look what crawled out from under a rock."

"Hey Nana." I lean over to give her a hug and kiss. "How've you been?"

"Well, I woke up this morning. So that's a plus when you get to be my age. Then down at the senior center Thomas Fitzgerald and William Beck want to court me, but I don't know if they can keep up with me. They are nearly ninety."

"Nana, you're eighty; that's not too far from ninety."

"Honey, when you get to be my age, ten years seems like twenty. None of us know if we'll reach breakfast tomorrow and the older they are, the less chance they have of reaching it. I might be crazy, but I'm not accepting a date from a gentleman caller who may not make it to see daylight with me."

I laugh, shaking my head, and flop down in a rocking chair. "You are crazy, Nana. I'm not sure I like the idea of gentlemen callers staying with you until daylight." I start rocking slowly. "Sorry I haven't been by lately. I had to do some community service."

"I know; your daddy told me. I was wondering if you'd lost your damn mind driving that fast. Then I figured out you were just that stupid. I wish you'd find a nice girl like me and settle down."

"I'm only nineteen; it's not time to settle down. I'm not even ready to move out of dad's house and, considering you are wanting callers to stay with you until daylight, I'm not sure I'd consider you a nice girl."

"You're full of shit, Ryder Grayton Abbott. I know you don't date nice girls; hell, your business is all over this town. Don't think I don't know about that little hussy Lacey Whitfield being in the car with you that night. The cops got there and she was still topless, drunk, and passed out." She shakes her head. "I'm not so old fashioned that I think you should wait 'til marriage. Hell, your granddaddy and me didn't wait, but I knew it was him; he was the one. Now there have been a few gentlemen since then."

I throw my hands up. "Damn, Nana, I don't want to know about your sex life."

She grabs my arm. "Do you really think I want to hear about yours every time I go to the beauty parlor? Hmm. The latest conquest's mama or grandmamma telling me how you're a male whore. Hmm?"

"I get it. I get it. I'm sorry if you've been embarrassed by my craziness. I seem to be the failure and disappointment in this family," I say.

"You're not an embarrassment or a disappointment. I just wish you'd pull that beautiful head out of your ass. As for being crazy, honey, this is the South; we're all a little crazy and we don't hide it down here. We parade it around and offer it a glass of sweet tea."

I chuckle and sit back in my chair. "Next time you're down at the beauty parlor and those ladies start talking, tell them if I weren't so good at it, they wouldn't be talking about it."

She pops me on the arm and we both bust out laughing. "Damn you, boy."

"I'm just telling the truth and you know it."

"Just like your granddaddy was."

"Awesome?" I ask.

"No. A cocky bastard. But I loved him just like I love you."

Chapter 5

Scarlet

The sun is setting when I walk into Bay Street Blues Bar to talk to my brother. As I walk in, I'm greeted by a couple of the regulars, as well as Dottie. She's been the bartender here for over twenty years. "Hey guys," I say.

Dottie smiles. "Hey, college girl. You waitin' on Gable?"

"Yes, ma'am. He asked me to meet him here, said he needed to talk with me about something."

"And I'm here," Gable calls out as he walks through the door.

I spin around. "Hey, big brother."

"Hey, kid. Come over here. I've got some stuff to go over with you."

"Okay." I walk over and sit down at a table. "Shoot. What's going on? You're kinda freakin' me out."

"Well, a guy came in here and offered my band the opportunity to go on a small tour with some other up and coming groups. I'm going to be leaving for a little while."

I sigh. "How long is a little while?"

"Six months. I'll have a few days off around Christmas and then go back to touring."

"Six months? Gable, we've never been apart from each other for more than a week. What am I going to do?"

"Scar, you are going to be so busy with school and work that you'll hardly notice."

"What did Dottie say?" I ask.

"Well, she cussed a little but overall, she's happy. I've also talked with Mom about it and she's happy, too."

I nod, fighting back tears. "So I guess I was the one you were the most worried about?"

"Yes."

"I'll be fine; don't worry about me."

"Look at it this way. You'll have full access to the car while I'm gone and you'll have more time to save toward your own."

"Yeah, I guess."

He puts his hand on top of mine. "Hey, you are going to be fine. Are you still planning on going to visit Cade and Daria when their new baby gets here?"

"Yes. Daria keeps me posted on her doctor appointments and stuff. It'll probably be around fall break in October."

"Is it strange how we hit it off with Cade?" he asks.

I shake my head. "No, we have something in common besides DNA. We both got screwed over by our father."

He nods. "True. Oh, I did want to say that the guy who recruited us for the tour loved your artwork."

"Really. Wow, that's kinda cool."

"Maybe if we hit it big, it'll get your name out there."

"Yeah, that would be cool. So when are you leaving?"

"The end of the week," he says.

"Damn, that's soon."

"I know it is kinda soon. But I'll be back before you know it. So have you found a job yet?"

"Um, yeah. I'm going to be waiting tables."

"That's cool. Where at? The Pirate House or Moon River? Some place like that?" he asks.

"No, none of them had any openings. I'm working just outside of town. Between here and Richmond Hill."

"What restaurants are between here and Richmond Hill? There's just bars." He throws his hands up. "Wait, no. You are not waiting tables in a dive bar."

"It's just until something at one of the restaurants opens up. It's one of the more decent bars. It's not like Swampy Tonk or anything. It's called Silver Moon. It's clean and the bouncer walks all of us to our cars at night." I'm lying to Gable about how nice and clean the place is, but he'd shit if he knew how dumpy it was.

"Just until something around here opens up, right?"

"Yes. I promise."

He nods. "Okay, then. Just be careful. I love you, kid. I don't want to see anything happen to you."

"I know. I love you, too." I give him a big hug. "I'm going to miss you."

~*~*~

The past week has flown by. Gable left yesterday and now I'm getting ready for my first night at my new job. Looking at myself in the mirror, I check out the little denim shorts and tight black t-shirt with *Silver Moon* strategically written across my chest. I'm not totally excited about the uniform but it's only temporary. I've got to find something closer anyway.

An hour later, I walk into the bar and Danny, the owner, looks at me. I feel his eyes roaming over my body. I feel nauseous. "Looks like I did a good job picking out the new waitress."

The other bartender, Lana, slaps him on the arm. "Shut up, Danny. You'll freak her out and I'm not ready to train another girl. She's at least had some waitress experience." She puts her bar rag down. "Hey, Scarlet, how are you doing? Don't let this asshole worry you. He just owns the place; I run it."

"Okay. So how long before it picks up in here?"

"A couple of hours. Tonight is quarter draft night, so it'll be crazy around here from eight to ten. Then it'll slack back off."

I nod. "Okay." I put my apron on around my waist. "Just point me in the right direction."

By nine-thirty, it's packed like sardines in this place. The smoke is so thick it feels like I could cut it. As I lean over clearing off a table. I feel a hand on my ass, "Hey, baby. I need another beer."

I pull away. "Sure, that was a Miller Lite, right?"

"Oh, yeah."

"Is there anything else y'all need?" I ask.

"Not unless I can talk you into going home with me tonight."

"Sorry. I'm in a relationship."

"Aw, come on now, honey. He doesn't have to know."

"Yeah, but I would." I turn and walk off to grab his beer. He needs to keep his damn hands off of me. If I didn't need this damn job, I would've punched that asshole. I get his beer and walk back over to him. "All right. Here ya go."

He slaps me on the ass again, and then grabs and squeezes it. "You sure you won't cheat on that boyfriend of yours?"

A deep voice comes from behind me. "I don't think her boyfriend would like that." I spin around to see a familiar face and he gives me a wink. "Hey, Scarlet, baby. Is your shift about over?"

I smile. "No, hon, I have a couple of hours left."

"Okay, well, I'll be over there waiting on you."

I look back down at the drunk and he shakes his head. "Damn lucky son of a bitch."

As I turn to walk away, he grabs my hand again. "Hey, if you ever want a real man, let me know."

"Yeah. Thanks but no thanks."

Chapter 6

Ryder

I've been out at one of our farms all day helping Judd's dad work on some of the equipment, since Judd's not here. When I decided to stop in at Silver Moon to cool off and grab a beer, she was the last person I expected to see. My pants instantly tighten as I watch her move in those little shorts and that top.

Why is she working at a place like this? I see men watching her like a damn fox in a hen house. She hasn't realized I'm here and I'd really like to keep it that way. Well, until I see that drunk asshole putting his hands on her.

I make my way over and I hear her diffuse the situation by telling him she's in a relationship, so I'm gonna stay back. Then the guy grabs her ass again. I'm close enough to hear what he's saying now.

"You sure you won't cheat on that boyfriend of yours?"

I step up behind Scarlet without letting her know. "I don't think her boyfriend would like that." She spins around and I wink. I almost see relief wash across her face. "Hey, Scarlet, baby. Is your shift about over?"

She smiles. "No, hon, I have a couple of hours left."

"Okay, well, I'll be over there waiting on you."

I hear the drunk as I'm walking off. "Damn lucky son of a bitch. Hey, if you ever want a real man let me know."

I have to smile when I hear her say, "Yeah. Thanks but no thanks."

I walk back over to the corner I was standing in and watch. Soon she makes her way over to me. "Hey."

I nod. "Hey," I say, trying to ignore the uncomfortableness in my pants.

"Thanks for your help over there. I really don't want to punch someone and lose my job on my first night."

"No problem. I'll be over here when you're ready to go. You know, to keep up appearances."

She looks back over her shoulder and smiles. "Oh yeah. Thanks."

I'd only planned on being here for a beer or two but I can't leave her. Just watching her does something to me. I can't seem to shake her from my mind. Why do I care if guys hit on her? Why did I want to rip that guy's head off for groping her? Why am I still standing here waiting for her to get off? I watched that asshole's friends carry him out of here over an hour ago. But I have to stay and talk to her, which watching her take off her apron, tells me it'll be soon.

Never mind I need to go. I gotta get out of here. I start making my way to the door. I make it out the door and almost to my jeep when I hear my name.

"Hey, Ryder."

Shit. I turn around. "Hey."

"Thanks for helping with that guy tonight."

"Yeah. You definitely need to be careful working in places like this."

"Well, it's only temporary until I find something else. It shouldn't worry you anyway. I could've taken that guy. I just didn't want to get fired on my first night."

"Bullshit, sweetie. You were nervous with that guy and it showed."

"No. I. Wasn't."

I move toward her. "Oh, so when he grabbed your ass like this, it didn't make you nervous?" *Oh fuck! Her ass. I gotta stop thinking or my dick is never going to recover.*

She looks up at me, full of piss and vinegar. "No, it pissed me off! There is a difference. Why? Does it make you nervous when I grab your ass like that?"

Sure enough, she grabs my ass and I know she feels the bulge in my pants pushing against her stomach. She's going to be the death of me. "No, it doesn't make me nervous." I lean down by her ear. "But it does make me hard as hell and it make me want to do this." I push her back against my jeep and slam my mouth down on hers.

I have one hand on the side of her face. I run the hand that's on her ass down her leg and grab behind the knee, lifting it. She automatically brings her other leg up around my waist, tangling her fingers in my hair. I can feel the heat radiating between her thighs, and my dick feels like it's about to explode. I start working my lips and tongue down her neck. A small moan escapes her lips and suddenly, I know I have to hear that noise again, preferably with my name following it.

Running my hand from her face down her stomach and then up her shirt, I pull the cups of her bra down and feel her nipples tightly pebbled against my fingers. I slide one hand back down to her legs and slide back up, rubbing against the crotch of her shorts

I hear a gasp. "Oh, Ryder."

I quickly open the door of my jeep and sit her on the passenger seat. Her calling my name will be my undoing. I take no time working the button and zipper of her shorts, sliding them and her panties down just enough to get my fingers into her wetness. I hear another gasp escape her mouth as soon as I slide my fingers into her.

"Oh, shit, Ryder."

"Fuck, Scarlet, you feel so good."

I feel her hand brushing against my jeans while she fiddles with my zipper. Her hand reaches my throbbing cock right as she comes apart in my hands. I feel like a fucking teenager when I come right in her hand because I've been hard as hell for the past three hours watching her. I lie across her on my seat. "Shit, Scarlet. That was fucking amazing. I think that is probably the quickest I've come without actually having sex."

"Why?"

"Well, because you are so fucking hot, that's why. Plus those little noises you make..."

"No, I mean, why me? Why do you want me? I mean, we normally can't stand each other. What the hell was that?" she asks.

"It's called sexual frustration."

She pushes me up off her and starts pulling her shorts and panties up. "Fuck. I can't believe I just did that. I've never done anything like that in my life."

I tuck myself back in my pants. "You've never gotten caught up in the heat of the moment and had awesome foreplay? Most of the time, it leads to awesome sex."

She adjusts her shirt. "No. Never. I mean, when I was with my ex, we played around, but it never got too far. I've never..." She fiddles with her shirt some more, looking more nervous than I've ever seen her.

I pull her chin up to look at me. "Scarlet, are you telling me you've never had sex before?"

She looks down, shaking her head. "No."

Crap, my dick just started getting hard again. "Hey, that's nothing to be ashamed of. It's probably the sexiest thing I've ever heard someone say. Also, I know all of my suspicions about that douche you dated were correct. If he couldn't appreciate this." I run my hand down her body. "Then he's just plain damn stupid."

She looks at me weird. "Um, thanks, I guess."

"I'm serious."

"I'm serious, too. What is going on here? You hung out here even after those guys left; you keep saying the sweetest things to me. I'm just not sure I can handle another rich boy. That day I met you, I wasn't kidding."

I pull her to me. "I don't know what this is, either. Trust me, relationships and sweet words aren't usually my game. I don't know what it is about you, but I can't get you out of my head."

"So what now?" she asks.

"Well, I haven't taken a girl out on an actual date in a very long time, but how about I take you out one night? Just casual and we'll see how it goes from there."

She nods. "Okay. I guess that works."

Chapter 7

Scarlet

"Wow. That is some crazy shit, Scarlet."

I look over at Annabelle from the lounge chairs we are in beside her pool. "I know, right?"

"So, what did you do then?"

"I just kinda said, 'sure' and gave him my number. It was weird. I mean I'm normally so in control. How could I let that shit happen?"

"Hey, you got all hot and bothered with a smokin' guy. That's normal. You don't have to be in control every moment of your life, just because your mom is-" Annabelle says.

I stop her. "It's not just about my mom. I mean, I don't want him to think I'm easy. Plus, I mean, most of the time we can't stand each other," I remind her.

"Oh, come on! He knows you aren't easy and hell, Judd and I have both been saying that you two are one good argument away from tearing each other's clothes off anyway."

"You and Judd have talks about me and Ryder?" I ask.

"Yeah. We still talk. Well, we Skype and text anyway."

"So, are you guys like pen-pal lovers now?"

"No. He's a nice guy we had a great night, but we both know it can't work. We're just friends." She looks away. "And, if we happen to have sex a few times when he's in town, then great."

"I'm guessing he's gone? I didn't ask Ryder."

"Yeah, he left last week. He's made it to his 'destination' and they have internet, so that's cool."

"Sooooo. You guys are just friends?" I tease.

"Yes. We had an awesome time, but we both have too much going on for anything else. He's cool, though, and I don't mind talking to him."

I shrug. "Okay." I can tell she's not interested in talking about this anymore. Annabelle's never been one to talk emotions or feelings. She'll shut down if I don't stop. "Should I go out with him if he calls or not?"

Her face lights up. "Hell, yes. See if we can finally turn in that v-card of yours."

"Seriously? Annabelle, is that all you can think about?"

"Hey, you got further the other night than you ever have. Maybe you just needed that chemistry. There was more than Dustin's sexual preference that held you back."

"Oh, my God. I can't believe I'm even thinking about this."

"Why not?" she asks.

"It's just... Ryder is so much to take in."

Her eyes get as big as dinner plates. "He's that big?"

I shake my head. "What the fuck? Get your mind out of his pants. I'm saying personality wise, he's a lot to take in."

"I was just wondering. You did have your hand on his dick."

I burst out laughing. "Well, I guess he is pretty big, but that's not what I was talking about, you girl perv." I lie back on the chair, still giggling. "I do have a serious question, though."

She smiles. "Okay."

"Since you went to school with all of them... do you know what happened between Ryder, Dustin, and Brandon? They hate Ryder and he hates them. All Ryder would say is that it was a long time ago."

"I don't really know. I know they were all best friends until we were like fourteen or so."

"Fourteen? That long ago?"

"Yeah. I was gone most of that summer to North Carolina and, when we got back, Ryder was absent the first couple of days of school. He was at a juvenile center. After that, they weren't friends anymore. I just figured that Brandon and Dustin's parents said they couldn't be around Ryder anymore. Especially since, after that, Ryder started hanging out with older kids. Drinking all the time. Becoming Sir Douchebag and fucking anything that walked by him."

"Did you and he ever...?" I ask.

She shakes her head. "Hell, no. I went out with a few of the older guys he was friends with. You know my rule about guys my own age."

My alarm goes off on my phone. "Shit, I've gotta go home and get ready for work."

"All right, be careful and have fun. Oh.., and when he calls, say yes."

~*~*~

A couple of hours into my shift, I realize that I really have to find another job. This place is so much more disgusting than I'd ever thought possible. I knew it was a dive bar and not the greatest, but the deals I've seen going on in the back room freaked me the fuck out. Earlier, Danny and the guy who grabbed my ass the other night were out there, snorting a few lines of cocaine. I just acted as if I didn't see anything; I got what I went in there for and walked back out, although my heart was pounding like it was going to explode. Gable would have an absolute shit fit if he knew.

Once Danny and that guy return from the back room the guy keeps watching me. It just feels creepy. After another hour, I tell Lana I'm stepping out for my break. Stepping outside, the air still feels like summer and the humidity hits me in the face. Taking my phone out of my pocket, I discover missed calls and texts. I scroll through them; they're all from Ryder.

Are you at work tonight?

Since you haven't answered me back, I'm hoping you are and that you aren't just trying to avoid me. ;)

I text him back. *No, not avoiding you. I'm at work. There you go again, thinking everything is about you. ;)*

I get a chime back immediately.

Whoa, I'm wounded. Do you mean it's not? Well, since you're at work, I'll leave you be for tonight. But I still want to go out on a date. Be careful, pretty girl. I really hope you find something different soon.

I reply again. *Since you asked so nicely, I'm off tomorrow night. I'm always careful and trust me, I want out of this place faster than anyone else.*

:D Until tomorrow then. Text me and let me know you've made it home safely.

I take a few more minutes to catch my breath before heading back into what I'm starting to call the seventh circle of Hell. I've still got a couple of more circles before I can go home. I've already been groped and grabbed so many times tonight it's absolutely insane. Then I had a couple of drunks try to fight each other. Try being the appropriate word. I ended up having to mop up from where one of them hurled on the floor after being hit in the stomach. All with the creepy guy eyeballing me.

The last couple hours pass quickly. The band starts back up and the drunks who think they have dancing skills and a lady old enough to be my mother get up on stage. She flashes us.

Words to know and live by. At a certain age, no matter how skinny you think you are, Lycra is only appropriate inside your clothes, not as clothes.

I get in my car, dreaming of my date tomorrow night. At least I have that to look forward to. I smile and begin my drive home.

Chapter 8

Ryder

After a long day of sitting with a few cows waiting without luck for calves to be born, I'm finally driving home and it's damn near 1am. I smile thinking about my conversation with Scarlet earlier. I can't believe I'm this excited over a date. I haven't been on a real date since…I don't think I've ever been on a real date. Fuck I'll have to get up with Judd, he'll tell me some cool shit to do. I guess I really never cared enough to impress a girl.

Looking up ahead, I see a car up against a tree. Slamming on brakes I stop and run over to the all too familiar looking car. I quickly call 911 and run over to the car. *"911 What's your emergency?"*

"Yes, I just drove up on an accident on Hwy 17, it's only one car." *"Is there anyone in the car?"* "Scarlet, her name is Scarlet Johnson." *"Sir. Can you give me a cross roads you are near or something near your location?"* "Um. Yeah I'm about three miles north of Richmond Hill. Close to Andrew Jackson Trail." I leaned down in the car to check on Scarlet, placing my fingers on her neck. *"Sir. Is the person moving or awake?"* "No ma'am, she's not awake but I can feel her pulse." *"Ok is she bleeding anywhere that you see?"* "She has a few cuts, nothing major." *"OK can you stay with her until EMS arrives?"* "Yes ma'am, I won't leave her side." I hear the sirens before I actually see them. "I hear them now, so they must be close." I step back as EMS pulls up trying to give them room to get her out of the car.

A few minutes later one of them steps over to me. "Sir. Do you know her?"

I give a gentle nod. "Yeah. She's a- she's a friend. Is she going to be okay?"

"Yes sir I think so, I can't confirm anything just yet. We are going to take her to the hospital now. You can follow if you like. She doesn't have an emergency contact listed with her driver's license so if you know her immediate family, you may want to call them."

"Thank you. I'll be right behind the ambulance, I'm just going to find her phone and see if there is anything else in the car she may need."

The EMT nods. "Okay look, you seem to be pretty worried about this girl." I nod. "Okay, I'm not supposed to do this but give me your name and I'll give it to the girl in the ER. I'll tell them you're her family so they'll let you back. Okay?"

I shake his hand. "Thanks man. My name is Ryder. Ryder Abbott. I'm going to try and get in touch with her mom now." He nods walking to the ambulance.

A state trooper steps over. "You didn't happen to actually see what happened did you?" I shake my head no. "Do you know if she has a company she'd prefer to come get her car? I'm pretty sure they are going to total it, but we like to send it somewhere that the owner likes."

I shake my head. "No. But I have a guy I trust." I scribble his number on paper and hand it to the cop. "Here's his number, tell him Ryder asked you to call. That I'll be in touch tomorrow."

I dig through her car and grab her phone and purse. Also, a little cash she had in the center. Opening her contacts on her phone as I'm walking to my jeep, I find her mom's. Her phone rings with no answer, no voice mail set up either. I scroll through until I find Gable's number, his phone goes straight to voice mail. *"Hey you've reached the love master leave me a message."* "Hey, um Gable, this is Ryder a friend of Scarlet's, she's been in an accident. I was trying to get in touch with your mom. If you could give me a call back, my number is 987-425-6549. Thanks man."

Walking into the emergency room I find a young girl at the desk. "Can I help you?" She purrs. She looks at me like she wants to tear my clothes off. I know that look, I've been getting it since I was fifteen. After that when they figure out I have money, they're even faster to try and tear my clothes off. Maybe that's one of the things that attracts me to Scarlet so much. She was completely turned off by my money.

I snap back to here and now. "Yes, Scarlet Johnson was just brought in by ambulance, I'm here for her."

She looks back at me almost disappointed. What in the hell does she think people come to the emergency room for in the damn middle of the night. She looks down at some paperwork and then back up at me. "Yes, right this way."

I follow her into a treatment room and Scarlet is actually awake. She looks up, "Hey what are you doing here?"

"I drove up on the wreck. I called 911. You kinda scared the shit out of me, by the way."

She chuckles. "Sorry about that. Certainly didn't mean for that to happen."

"So what the hell did happen?"

She shakes her head. "I'm not really sure, some asshole came flying up behind me and then bumped me. They had their headlights off so I have no clue who it could've been. Next thing I knew I was waking up here."

They spend the next hour or so looking over Scarlet. She speaks to the police about the wreck. There isn't really much she can tell.

The doctor finally comes through the doorway. "Ms. Johnson, everything seems fine, you're basically just a little bumped and bruised. I would like for you to stay with someone tonight just in case you have a concussion. You need to be woken up every couple of hours."

A few minutes later, I'm pushing Scarlet out of the hospital to my jeep. I put her in the passenger side. After I get in the driver's side, I turn to her. "Where is your Momma? I tried to call her and Gable."

"She's at a spiritual retreat. She can't have her phone. Gable was probably still on stage." She looks around as we drive. "Where are you taking me?"

"To my house. You can't be by yourself."

"Um, no. You can just take me home."

"No, the doctor said I have to wake you up every few hours to make sure you don't have a concussion," I tell her.

"No."

"Look, it's already almost morning. Get a few hours of rest and then I'll take you home."

"What about my car?" she asks.

"They said it was probably totaled. I had them call my tow guy so we'd know where it was at. I'll give you his number and stuff."

"SHIT!" She leans her head back against the seat and closes her eyes. "Gable is going to kill me."

I reach across to her and grab her hand. "Hey, it'll be okay. Just relax. I'll take care of you. "

I drive slowly up the long gravel drive to my house. When I look over, she's asleep. My phone buzzes as I'm stopping, I answer it. "Hello." *"Hey, this is Gable is this Ryder?"* "Yes. Hey Scarlet's fine." *"Man I was freaking out. I just got back to the bus and got my phone. Are you sure she's okay?"* "Yeah man. Look she's worried because your car is probably totaled. I think she's more worried about that than anything else." *"Tell her I said don't worry about the fucking car. What happened anyway?"* "She was on her way home and she said someone tried to run her off the road. I'll tell her to call you in the morning and give you more info." *"Okay thanks man."* "Hey anytime. I'm just glad I drove up on it." We hang up and I look back over at the beauty of her face sleeping. I walk around and gently lift her in my arms. I love the way she sighs when she's against my body.

I carry her in the house and straight to my room, lying her gently on the bed. I slide her shoes and shorts off and tuck her under the covers.

I hear her whisper. "Hmm, Ryder, you can be so sweet."

I strip off my clothes, down to my boxers, and settle in on my side of the bed, setting the alarm on my phone so I can check on her. She moves closer and wraps her body around mine, settling her head against my chest. I softly stroke her hair and press a soft kiss against her head.

What in the hell is going on with me? This feels so natural; she feels natural. I can't be feeling like this. She confuses the hell out of me.

I wake up a few hours later when my alarm goes off. Scarlet is still snuggled against my side. I brush her hair back from her face. "Scarlet. Hey, wake up a little for me, okay?"

"Shh, I'm trying to sleep, dickface."

I laugh. "Okay, that's good enough."

I settle back in, quickly drifting to sleep with Scarlet wrapped around me.

Chapter 9

Scarlet

I wake up to my head pounding. I feel something heavy wrapped around me and what I'm pretty sure is an erection poking me in the ass. Last night comes flooding back to me and I shiver. Ryder pulls me closer. I smile and giggle. Yes a giggle actually comes tumbling out of my mouth. Probably completely inappropriate since I was just in a wreck, but I can't help it, this guy makes me giggle.

I feel the hot air of his breath against my ear. "Good morning. How are you feeling?" he asks.

"Like I've been hit by a truck."

"Here," he says, "let me get you some ibuprofen. You're probably going to be pretty sore today."

He gets up, heading into his bathroom. I notice he's in his boxers and I look down to realize that I'm missing my shorts. "Ryder, how did my shorts get off?"

He hands me a glass of water and two pills. He smiles and shrugs. "I thought you'd be more comfortable without them on."

"Oh really. How sweet of you. Such a gentleman."

He brushes his knuckles against his chest. "You're just now noticing this?"

"Ha ha, very funny."

He sits down on the bed. "I'm serious, hey you even told me I was sweet when I was putting you to bed last night."

"Yeah, well, I can't be held responsible for what I said under the influence. I'll probably wish I was still under the influence of something when my brother finds out I totaled his car."

"I talked to Gable last night, he's cool."

"You what?"

He's about to say something when his phone rings. "Hey.-I don't know. - Okay. Okay. I'll see you in a few minutes. Umm. I have a guest with me... Ugh. Yes. See you in a few."

"Do I need to go?"

He laughs. "No, but you may want to shower real quick and I'll give you something to put on. That was my Nana Pearl. She has breakfast ready and is expecting us in a few minutes."

"O- Kay. I really can go if you need me to?"

"No, just get in the shower."

I stand up and walk over to the bathroom. Looking around, his bathroom is very neat for a guy. You can tell everything has a place. I'm tempted to move stuff around just to screw with his head.

Getting in the shower, I have to be careful of my cuts. I laugh when I see that Ryder, who is totally masculine, doesn't have the typical manly body wash. He just has regular scented Dial body wash. He totally struck me as an Axe body wash kind of guy.

"Hey, Scarlet?" he calls.

"Yeah?"

"I put some clothes on the counter. Sorry I don't have a clean bra or panties for you to wear. I did put a small pair of boxer trunks here for you."

"Thanks. I'll be out in just a minute. I'm not sure I'd know how to take it if you had a bra and panties for me."

I step out of the shower a few minutes later. A t-shirt, pair of wind pants, and what I'm guessing are boxer trunks are sitting on the counter.

They are just like boxer briefs but shorter. They look like what girls call boy shorts. I quickly dress and walk out into the bedroom.

When we walk outside, he leads me over to a Polaris Ranger. "Come on, we'll take this." As he sits down, he laughs. "I always wondered what it would take for you to get in my pants."

I smack his shoulder. "Shut it. I always thought you wanted to get in my pants." I look around. "Where does your Nana live?"

"Just down the road."

I nod and sit in the passenger side. We take off through a pasture and, within a few minutes, we are parking in the backyard of what I'm assuming is his Nana's house.

I whisper. "What is your Nana going to think? I mean, I'm in your clothes and I was obviously there when you woke up."

"Hell, she'll probably be proud I let a girl stay for breakfast." I gasp and he laughs. "I'm just kidding. I don't bring girls back to my house. You're the first."

I stop and look at him hard. "Really?"

He smiles. "Yes, really. Come on. Nana is waiting."

When we step on the back porch, I hear someone whistling a tune inside. He swings the screen door open and we walk inside. "Hey, Nana."

She pulls his cheek down to her and kisses him. "Sweet boy. Who is this pretty young lady you have with you?"

"This is Scarlet. She's a friend. Scarlet, this is my Nana Pearl."

I give a soft wave. "Nice to meet you. I'm sorry for barging in like this."

She smiles. "No, honey, it's no problem. Call me Nana. Now, what on Earth happened to your pretty face?"

"I was in a wreck last night. Ryder came to pick me up from the hospital and made me stay with him."

"Well, that was sweet of him. Are you sure it was Ryder?"

"Come on, Nana," he says. "I can be nice. Plus they asked me to wake her up every few hours to make sure she didn't have a concussion."

Nana Pearl puts her hand on her hip. "Well, come on. I got you two some grits, eggs, bacon, and biscuits ready. Scarlet, honey, are you sure you're okay? Do you need some headache medicine or anything?"

"No, ma'am. Ryder gave me some this morning."

We sit down to the table and Ryder automatically starts inhaling his food. Nana pops his arm. "Ryder, act like you got some raising, boy. You don't have to swallow your food whole like it's your last damn meal. There is a lady present."

I chuckle. "It's okay. My brother Gable eats the same way."

"Damn boys." She shakes her head, laughing. "So, Scarlet what do you do?"

"I go to SCAD and right now, I'm working as a waitress."

"That's wonderful. You know, Ryder's mama was an artist. That girl could sketch or paint dang near anything. I don't know how my bumbling son was lucky enough to turn her head but he did. I'm glad, too, because she was a wonderful daughter, a great mama, and she gave me this beautiful little devil right here."

"She sounds like a wonderful lady." I look over at Ryder and notice his solemn expression on his face.

Nana smiles. "Oh, she was. So, what kind of art do you do?"

"Well, my loves are painting, sketching, and sculpture. I know that really doesn't pay bills, though, so I'm also doing some graphic design. I also do all of the artwork for my brother's band."

"Wow, that's quite some ambition you've got there. So, your brother is in a band?"

"Yes, ma'am. They're on tour right now. Some of the people he's met in the music business loved my artwork and want to talk more about it with me."

"Well that's just wonderful. You really do remind me of sweet Lillian."

Once again I notice Ryder's solemn expression and I figure we've talked enough. We finish the rest of our breakfast in silence.

"Thank you again for breakfast, Nana."

"It was my pleasure, honey. Now don't be a stranger. Bring some of your work by here for me to see. I don't get out as much anymore, but I love to look at pretty things."

I smile. "Yes ma'am."

We head out to the Ranger after Ryder gives her a hug and kiss.

Chapter 10

Ryder

"So it seems like you and my Nana hit it off."

"She's sweet. But she gives off that whole 'don't screw with me' vibe. I love it."

"Yeah, she's definitely a tough old lady."

"Thanks again for being such a good friend to me last night," she says.

"It was nothing. What are you going to do today?"

"Getting ready for the hot date I'm supposed to have tonight."

"Oh, so do I know the guy?" I tease.

"You might. At first, I thought he was a complete douche nozzle. But now I think he's kinda nice. Anyway, can you give me a ride to my house? I can call Annabelle to come and get me if it's easier."

"I can give you a ride home. Let's just go inside and grab my keys and stuff."

She smiles. "Okay, thanks."

My dad's car is in the driveway when we get back. He must be home from his business trip. He's standing in the kitchen when we come in.

"Who is this pretty thing?" he asks.

"Dad, this is Scarlet. Scarlet, this is my dad, Greer."

Scarlet sticks her hand out to him. "Nice to meet you, Mr. Abbott."

"Please call me Greer. Nice to meet you, too. What have you guys been up to?"

I fill him in on last night's events and our visit with Nana.

Dad laughs. "So Scarlet was lucky enough to meet the famous Pearl Abbott?"

Scarlet smiles. "She was very sweet."

Dad and I both laugh. I tug her arm. "Come on, let me get you home."

The drive to her house is quiet. She turns to me as we get close to her house. "Sorry we talked about your mom so much at breakfast. I could tell it made you kinda sad."

"No, it's okay. It's just I haven't heard Nana talk about her in years. She really loved my mom, as if she were her own. Nana always wanted a daughter. When my mom came along, she fell in love with her as much as my dad did."

We pull into her driveway. "That's so sweet," she says. "Thanks again for everything. So what time do I need to be ready?"

"I really want you to rest. How about I pick you up at six?"

"Sounds great." She steps out of the car. "Oh, how should I dress?"

"However you want. Comfortable."

She smiles. "Okay."

~*~*~

I make my way back home and find my dad in his office. "Hey, how was your trip?" I ask.

He looks up from the paperwork he's staring at. "It was somewhat enlightening."

"Sounds interesting."

"Yes. While we are on the subject, we need to discuss our business and your plans."

"I really don't want to," I argue.

"Son, it's not about what you want. This is part of growing up. I can understand if you don't want to live the day-to-day office life. I really can. But you need to at least have an idea as to what's going on. So you'll know if your money is being taken care of or stolen from you."

"Why? Is something going on?" I ask.

"Well, this last trip to Atlanta was very interesting. Let's just say I had to let a vice-president and his secretary go. He was doing a great job; technically, he did nothing wrong. His secretary, whom he was diddling on the side, however, got ahold of his company credit card and was living a rather lavish lifestyle on our dime."

"Damn. Are you pressing charges?"

"Against the secretary, yes," he says. "She admitted he knew nothing about it. So he was only fired for fraternization and basically not keeping up with company funds. But I'm sure he'd probably rather be in jail. Now he's got a hell of a lot of explaining to do to his wife."

"That's some crazy shit. Look, Dad. I promise I'll try to take more of an interest in this stuff with the business."

"That's all I'm asking. I'm trying to protect you, but I won't be around forever. I know you'd rather work with Nelson on the farms and believe me, I respect that and I'm proud of you for it. But I would really like for you to think about taking some classes in business and learn a little more about this side of the farm as well. Okay?"

I know he's right, as much as I hate the business side of things. "Yes, sir. I gotta go help Nelson move some of the equipment around here today. Then I have a date later, so I have to get a move on."

He smiles and nods. "Sure. By the way, Scarlet seems like a lovely young lady. Where did someone with your ugly mug find her?"

"We met when we were both doing community service at that Habitat house. She pretty much told me to F off within the first five minutes of meeting her."

He barks out a laugh. "Well. Now I know I like her. What on earth did she have community service for?"

"Um, well, Dustin Scott is her ex and she bashed up his car with an ax handle. I don't know all the details, but I know he deserved it."

"I guess she'd have no trouble keeping you in line. Are things serious?"

"Dad, it's just a date." *Of which I hope that there will be many more of. What the hell am I thinking? Why in the hell do I want her so much? Maybe it's just the challenge. Maybe it's the fact that she's a virgin or that she never gave it up to Dustin. Yeah, that has to be it.*

"All I'm saying," he continues, "is I saw the way you were looking at her. Not to mention that my mother liked her, which is... well, you know how Pearl is."

"I know. Nana even said she reminded her of Mom."

My dad has a shocked look on his face. "Really? So what else do you know about her? I'm intrigued now."

I laugh and start to tell him about Scarlet. I don't realize until I'm done talking how much I actually do know about her, but then how much I don't.

"She sounds like a headstrong hellcat. That's good for you. You can be a pain in the ass sometimes. You need someone who's a challenge. Someone who will call you on your bullshit. But now that you talk about her mother, I do remember meeting her at the museum. Kind of a free spirit but overall, a nice lady. "

"Again, it's just a date. You have us married already."

"I'm just saying I've seen that look before," he says. "I remember it all too well, staring me back in the face from my mirror when I met your mother. It's a mixture of fear, lust, admiration, love, and adrenaline."

Damn. Holy shit, he might just be right. I find myself wondering what she's thinking, what she's doing. I can't get her out of my head and every time I think of her, my pants tighten almost uncomfortably.

Shaking my head and trying to clear my thoughts, I go out to the barn to help Nelson.

Chapter 11

Scarlet

Annabelle puts her hands on her hips. "What do you mean you were in a wreck last night? You didn't call me."

"I didn't call anyone. Ryder drove up on the accident. He tried to call my mom and Gable, but they didn't answer."

"I'm just glad you weren't hurt really bad. What about Gable's car?"

"They said it's totaled."

She chuckles because she knows my brother all too well. "He's gonna be pissed."

"I talked to him this morning after I got home. He was just glad I wasn't really hurt. Especially since I was ran off the road and the person didn't stop."

She looks at me with fear written all over her face. "Do you know who it was?" she asks.

"No, it was late and they turned all their lights off so I couldn't even really get a good description of the car. I couldn't see their tag, plus it all happened so fast."

She walks over and pulls me into a hug. "I'm just glad you're okay, but I really hate the thought of you driving that far at night by yourself." She pulls me down on the edge of the bed. "So did you call Cade?"

"I called and talked to Daria because I'd promised to come after the baby is born and if I don't find a car by then, I can't."

"Don't worry about that. If you need a way to get to Alabama to see the new kiddo, just let me know. I'll get you there." She claps her hands together. "Now, let's find you something casual sexy to wear on your date."

I just shake my head. At this point, trying to argue with Annabelle would be pointless. She likes to use me as a dress-up doll. Plus it's her own way of coping with what I just told her about my wreck.

I walk out of my bathroom in my panties and bra after my shower and she takes one look at me. "Oh, hell no, you don't."

I look at her I'm sure looking confused. "What?"

"You have to wear matching underwear and preferably not cotton."

"Seriously, Annabelle. He's seen me in my panties a couple of times now, both of which I don't remember. I really don't plan on him seeing them tonight."

"You never know and you should always be prepared. Speaking of prepared, did you shave your-"

I cut her off. "Look, Annabelle, I've been dressing myself for several years now. I don't think he will kick me out of the jeep for having on panties and a bra that don't match. And my lady business is just that. *My* business." She looks at me, defeated, which makes me feel bad. I reach and grab the lime green lacy bra and panties she laid out for me and stomp into the bathroom to put them on. I walk back out and she smiles and claps.

"Are you happy now?" I ask.

She smiles and claps again. "Yes. You are freakin' hot. I wish I looked like that in my underwear. If I had a body like yours, I'd probably walk around naked."

I roll my eyes. "I'm sure you would. Now what else?"

"Here." She shoves some clothes in my hands.

Thirty minutes later, I'm looking at myself in the mirror. She picked out a denim skirt that ends just above the knee, brown cowgirl boots, and a chocolate and cream peasant top.

"Damn, you look good."

"Thanks, Annabelle."

~*~*~

I hear someone knocking on my front door and open it to find Ryder standing there, looking completely delicious. He has a pair of biker boots on with jeans and a plaid button up shirt with the sleeves rolled up to his elbows.

He smiles. "You look pretty."

"Thanks." He pulls my hand out the door. "So where are we headed?" I ask.

"I was thinking we could ride out to the island."

I nod. "That sounds great." I stop and look at the Honda Goldwing sitting there. "Who's Goldwing?"

"Mine."

"Wow, I didn't know that you rode a bike. I shouldn't have worn a skirt."

"I won't peak. I promise." He winks a me. "I thought it would be a nice night to ride. Before it gets too cold out."

"Yeah." I'm sure my nervousness is showing.

"Have you ever ridden a motorcycle before?" he asks.

I smile, embarrassed. "No."

"Well, come on. I promise you'll have fun." He turns back and winks. "I'm glad to be your first." We climb on the bike and ride off.

Boy, was he right. It's exhilarating. The breeze and the salt smell the closer we get to the beach. When we pull up to the lighthouse on Tybee Island, Ryder gets off his bike.

"We're here."

"Isn't this place closed?" I ask.

"Yes. To the public, but I have a friend."

He reaches into the side compartment on the bike and pulls out a blanket. Taking my hand, he leads me toward the lighthouse. He stops and opens a door to a small room on one of the small buildings, grabbing a basket. Then we continue around the lighthouse until we can see the ocean. He spreads the blanket and pulls me to sit down.

"Wow, this is really beautiful," I tell him. "I've never been out here at night before."

He sets out containers of food on the blanket. "It's one of my favorite places. I hope you like picnic food?" he asks.

"What exactly is picnic food?"

"Fried chicken, potato salad, macaroni and cheese, with rolls and sweet tea."

"Did you cook all of this?"

He laughs. "No. There's a small grocery store close to my house with a deli. They cook the best damn food. I love their chicken."

"It smells delicious."

"Yeah the funny part is I'll only order when one lady is there cooking. I call to see if she's there," he says.

I burst out laughing. "That is funny. It also says you eat out a lot."

"I do. But Dad and I grill. I can only handle Nana so many times a week. Hell, even Nana orders her chicken from this place."

He hands me a plate and a Solo cup with tea. "Thank you." I take a bite out of the chicken. "Holy shit. This is awesome. I need the name of the store and the lady's name."

He smirks. "It's Tom's Market and Deli, and her name is Miss Phanie."

I laugh. "I'm writing that down."

Chapter 12

Ryder

I really wasn't sure what to even do on a date. I had to Skype with Judd to figure out what a girl would like. Most of my "dates" have consisted of hooking up at a bar and sex somewhere close by so I could drop them back off at their cars. I don't bring girls home.

We've just finished our picnic dinner and she's packing up the basket.

"So you like the lighthouse?" I ask.

Her eyes light up. "I love it. It's one of my favorite places to visit. It's seriously more beautiful here at night than I could've ever imagined."

"Great. I was kinda nervous."

She laughs. "You nervous?"

"Yeah I don't... Well, I've never really taken a girl out on a real date before. To be honest, I really wasn't sure what to do."

She laughs again. "So, let me get this straight. You've never been on a real date before?"

"I'm glad you find this amusing."

"I'm sorry, it's just funny. So how did you come up with this perfect date? Did you Google it?" she asks.

I laugh. "No but that is an awesome idea. I Skyped with Judd."

She falls over on the blanket, holding her stomach. She's laughing so hard she can't catch her breath. "I'm really glad you find this funny. Just remember I'll pay you back for laughing at me."

She sits up, wiping her eyes. "I'm sorry. It's just you always seem so cocky and confident. It just threw me for a loop that you'd have to ask someone like Judd for advice on women. You and Judd have done a wonderful job tonight."

I pull her in between my legs. "Look at that ship," I say, pointing to the tanker moving along.

"I know. I think that's probably one of the coolest things about living here. We get to see so many different parts of life. We have history, art, boats, ships, beach, sand, food, and the coolest thing of all. Ghosts."

"Really? Ghosts top your list?" I ask.

"I know it sounds touristy but every year on Halloween, I do the ghost tour. I love it. I eat at Moon River all the time, hoping I catch a glimpse."

I laugh. "Wow, you really are a ghost nut, huh?'

She smacks my arm. "Sounds like you're a big chicken."

"No, I love chicken. I thought we just covered this."

"Hey, did that friend of yours manage to leave us a way to get into the lighthouse?" she asks.

I smirk. "Well now, what would a date to the lighthouse be without going up the stairs?" I pull her up and grab her hand. "Come on, let's go see something pretty."

We start up the stairs in the lighthouse and it sounds full of creaks and moans of an old building. She laughs. "Gonna run on me?"

I smack her on the ass. "I'm no chicken."

She stops in front of me, making me run into her. "Oh really. Hmm, we'll see about that."

I grab her waist, spinning her around and pressing her against the wall. Leaning against her, I can feel her heart pounding in her chest. "Your heart is the one racing. You sure you aren't scared?"

She exhales. "Not of ghosts." I lean down and take her lips and she lets out a soft moan.

I pull back with my nose still touching hers. "So what scares you then?" I ask.

She lets out a soft sigh. "You."

I pull back a little bit, still not letting her go from the wall. "Sweetheart, you have nothing to be afraid of with me." I dive back into her lips and rest my hands on her waist, pulling her tight against me. My tongue works effortlessly in her mouth. I pull away from her a little and kiss her just below her ear. She shivers a little. "Are you cold?"

She shakes her head. "No. Just nervous."

"About me?" She nods. "Baby, do you even know how much you undo me? I can't think straight around you."

"This is just all a little much. It's so fast. I swore, after Dustin, I wouldn't get in over my head again."

"Over your head?" I ask.

"Well, over my social class."

I take a step back. "Scarlet, this may come as a shock to you, but I could not care less about your social class."

She turns around and walks the rest of the way up to the top of the lighthouse without saying a word. Looking out over the water, she finally speaks. "You say that now. You say it doesn't matter. Trust me, though. Eventually, it will."

"I don't know what all that little insecure bastard Dustin put in your head, but I can assure you I am *nothing* like him."

She looks so lost. "It didn't matter, not until the past few months. When we started going to functions together or his parents' dinners, though, they would make snide comments about *how well I was trying to fit in.* They always dismissed me. Not just his parents but their friends. Then they found out that my mom works at the museum."

I put my hand on hers. "First of all, you know I don't care about money. Judd is my best friend. Second, my father would rather die than make someone feel uncomfortable about how much money they do or don't have. As far as Dustin's parents and their friends, they're just as big of dickheads as he is."

"I know it sounds stupid to you, Ryder, but the way they looked at me... When I got arrested, it was like, see, she's crazy white trash, just like we always said. Crazy like her mother."

I chuckle. "Sorry, but I wouldn't worry so much about what those people think."

She spins around. "But I do. Don't you understand? I still hear them whisper when I walk by that I'm crazy or I should go back to the trailer park."

"They like to talk about me, too. I had to stop giving a shit a long time ago. Those little shits talk about me all the time. From the sounds of things, the whole *town* talks about me. I would've either had to move or just let it go. So I ignore it."

She looked up at me with sad eyes. "Why would they all talk about you? You're one of them."

I knew these questions would come up eventually. I hear thunder in the distance and see lightning. "We'd better go. Looks like we're about to have a storm come in."

She doesn't say anything, but she starts down the stairs ahead of me. Once we are back outside, I feel sprinkles of rain. Shit.

"It's starting to rain," she says.

"Yeah. I can feel it," I snap and dig in the side compartments of my bike. "Shit! I guess I left my rain suits in the mudroom at the damn house."

It starts to rain harder. I grab her hand and the blanket, taking off toward the building I had Ed leave unlocked for me.

Chapter 13

Scarlet

What the hell did I do? I snatch my arm away as we enter the small storage room. "What the hell? What the fuck did I do? You tried to snatch my fucking arm off."

He runs his fingers through his hair. "Sorry. It's just I can't believe I left the rain suits at home. Plus I always get tense talking about Dustin and Brandon. I'm sorry I pulled on you so hard. I would never hurt you."

I know he's telling the truth. I've never felt in danger around Ryder. "Just tell me why you hate them so much."

He sits down on a stool. "You aren't the only one who's been hung out to dry by those two. When we were fourteen, I introduced a girl I went to school with to Judd. She seemed to really like him and he was over the moon for her. One night we were all hanging out, and she and Judd went off to make-out. Well, in the meantime, I guess she, Dustin, and Brandon had cooked up this situation to embarrass Judd. I figured it out and ran to get Judd but it was too late. They had already busted some windows and spray painted some shit. Judd was just standing there. He had tried to talk them into stopping, but they did exactly what they'd planned and ran off, leaving him to get the blame. I told him to get the hell out of there. He ran off and before I could leave, the cops showed up. I got sent to juvenile detention for the summer. Judd felt bad that I got the blame. Dustin and Brandon laughed about it. When I came back to town, their parents had told them I was a bad influence and they couldn't hang out with me anymore. Dustin's mom even said that maybe if my mom had been alive, she would have raised me right." He shakes his head. "My dad believed us when we told him what really happened, but that didn't really do any good. So see? I do know what it's like to deal with those two and their parents."

I put my hand on his. "I'm sorry Ryder. Who was the girl?"

"A girl named Kelsie Carlisle." My mouth falls open. "Do you know her?"

"Until recently, she was one of my closest friends. I met her and Annabelle when I was working downtown at a clothing store."

"What did she do?" *Hmm, that's a loaded question.* He was honest with me, though, so I take a deep breath.

"I've only told my mom, Gable, and Annabelle this."

He leans back against a shelf. "Shoot."

I launch into the story and, after I finish, he laughs. "What the hell? You laugh at my story?"

"I mean, my thoughts were always right on those guys. I can't believe..." He has to stop because he's laughing again. "So you walked in on that? Did they even offer an explanation?" He puts his hands up. "I really am sorry for what happened to you, but you have to realize how funny this all sounds."

I can't help but laugh, too. "No explanation. I told you Brandon asked me to join. Kelsie was crying and Dustin chased after me. Well, until I took that axe handle to his car. Then the three of them started screaming."

"I really hate you had to go through all of that, but I have to say, it sounds like something straight off of *Cops*. Were y'all saying stuff like, 'He took my cigarettes' or 'But I love him?' Did anyone have curlers in their hair?"

"Um, they really didn't have much on to start with. So no. No curlers." I look out the small window on the side of the building. "Damn, it's really coming down out there."

Ryder stands up behind me. "Shit, yeah. I may have to call someone to bring me my jeep so we can go home."

My heart races as I realize how close we are to each other. The nerves in the pit of my stomach flutter and ache, all at the same time. "Why? I think we are fine right here."

He cocks an eyebrow and leans into me, pushing my back to the wall next to the window. "Oh, really. You think we are fine here?"

"Yeah, unless you're scared there might be a ghost or something."

He places his lips on mine, nipping at my bottom lip and getting me to open and give his tongue access. His hands slide down under my ass. "I don't think ghosts are what we should be worried about."

I smile against his lips. "Oh really? What should I be worried about?"

"I'm really trying to be a standup guy when it comes to you. But I don't know how much I can control myself. When I'm around you, I feel this overwhelming sensation to wrap you up and own you," he says.

"Maybe I don't want you to stop."

He lets out a groan. "Shit, Scarlet. You can't say things like that."

I don't know what happens, but when he let out that groan, my panties flood. I put my hands on his chest and push him to a small chair, making him sit down. I straddle him, kissing him and running my tongue down the side of his neck.

"Fuck, Scarlet." My skirt rides up my hips.

Still nibbling at his ear, I whisper, "Hmm?"

Lightning pops and the lights go out. I scream and wrap my arms around his neck.

"Scarlet, baby, I can't breathe."

I giggle. "I'm sorry. That kinda took me by surprise."

"Me, too." He lifts me up. "Here, let me find a light or something. I think I saw one on the little table." I hear him bumping around. "Ah, here it is. Let's see if it works."

Sure enough, there is a light. It's just a small flashlight but he stands it up. At least we aren't in the dark. He looks over at me and I shiver. "Are you cold? We both got pretty wet," he says.

I nod and he motions for me to sit with him. He takes our picnic blanket and pulls it over both of us. I smile. "Maybe this rain will blow over soon."

"Maybe so," he says. "I'm not complaining about the company I'm with, though."

I tip my head down and snicker. "Good. I wouldn't want to burden you or anything."

He runs his hands down my side. "Oh, it's far from a burden." Pulling me closer, he starts kissing down my neck. "Did I tell you that I think those boots are sexy as fuck?"

I smirk. "No, you didn't, but I'll take whatever you give me."

"Oh, baby, don't say that. But I will say this. Those boots are sexy as fuck and I would love nothing more than to watch you ride the fuck out of me. I do have one question though. Are you wearing panties? Because I'm pretty sure I didn't feel any earlier when my hands were on your ass."

I giggle. I've never giggled this much in my life. I put my lips right by his ear. "Yes, I have on panties. They are just very, very tiny."

He flops his head back. "Are you trying to kill me? You know, if you are plotting this, it could be considered first degree murder."

I've never felt like this in my entire life. I feel the dull throb between my legs, an ache that needs to be touched. I rub my hand down the front of his pants. He's hard, so hard. Kissing his neck, I start down his chest. "Not even close."

Chapter 14

Ryder

"I think you are going to kill me." I lean down and take her mouth to mine. The kiss starts slowly but it's needy. She slides down a little, pulling me over her. I'm lying to her side with my torso over hers. My hand glides up under the edge of her shirt and rubs her side and stomach. She startles me when she lifts up and pulls her shirt off. Her tits are about to spill out of her lime green bra. I kiss down her neck, reaching the front clasp of her bra and opening it up. I kiss, lick, and suck on the most beautiful boobs I've ever seen.

Running my hand up her thigh, I suck on her nipples. She lets out a moan that almost sends me over the edge. She starts fiddling with my shirt, trying to get it off. I slide one of my hands under her skirt, moving her barely there panties to the side. I slide two fingers into her wetness, using my thumb to rub her very sensitive nub. She starts panting and working on getting my pants undone.

"Scarlet, slow down. If you get my pants off, I don't know that I'll be able to stop without doing permanent damage to my manhood."

She giggles. I love her giggle; it is so intoxicating. "Ryder, I don't want you to stop."

I brush a little piece of hair back from her face. "What are you saying?" I ask.

"I want you. Right here. Right now."

"Are you sure?" She nods. "Look at me. If you decide you want to stop, you tell me. I will. I may damage my balls but I will." She nods and begins sliding her skirt down, along with the lime green thong that matches her bra. "Oh God." When she reaches her boots and tries to slide them off, I stop her. "Don't. Leave them on."

"Ryder. I'm ready."

I slide down my pants and boxers, kicking my boots off. I take out a condom and, as I tear the package open, I look at Scarlet's beautiful form, lying there in front of me. "Damn, is this for real?"

She nods. "Yes, very real." I notice her glance down at my dick. Her eyes grow wide. "Is that?"

"Yes, I have a piercing," I chuckle as I roll the condom on.

"Oh, sweet Jesus."

I spread her thighs and I can't help myself. I have to taste her. I lean in and lick her sweet wet pussy. She squirms and gasps. "Mmm, this is beautiful. So wet, so sweet. Tell me, Scarlet. Have you ever been this wet before?"

She shakes her head and sighs. "No." She shudders. "Oh God."

"Has anyone ever been lucky enough to do this before?"

Her hips are rocking and I can tell she's close. "N- no. N-no one. Oh God!"

I crawl up her body to hover over her. Brushing her lips with mine, I ask, "Do you have any idea how sexy you are? I'm so glad I'm the only person who's ever had the pleasure of tasting that sweet pussy. I hope to God I'm the last one."

I place my cock at her soaked entrance and tease her a little.

"Oh God, Ryder, please," she begs.

"Has anything ever been in here before?" I circle the entrance with my cock.

She looks at me. "Just my vibrator. Nothing or no one else."

I start to enter her and I can see her tense up. "Baby, relax. Do you want me to stop?" She shakes her head no. "Okay, this is going to hurt but since you've used a toy, it shouldn't be too bad."

She nods. "O- Okay." I slide in little by little until I'm buried deep in her pussy.

"Fuck, baby, you're tight. I'm going to wait a second for you to adjust." She nods, but a few seconds later, she starts to move her hips a little. I start moving in and out, a little at a time. "Oh shit, Scar. You're beautiful."

"Oh, Ryder."

I move a little faster. I can feel my release creeping up on me.

I lift her legs to rest them on my shoulders. This gives me the access to go deeper. "Oh Shit. Oh God. Fuck. RYDER! Oh God. Harder!"

I grab around her legs, and start slamming into her harder and faster until she's rambling some incoherent gibberish and I'm spilling my load into the condom.

~*~

We lie wrapped in each other's arms, under that picnic blanket, with her head resting on my chest. My stomach suddenly growls like I haven't eaten in weeks.

She smirks and looks over at me. "So I guess you worked up an appetite, huh?"

"Well yeah." I reach over and grab the picnic basket. "I'm glad we still have a little food left. I may have starved before this storm blows over." I glance over at her, lying there in just her panties and bra.

She glances up. "Yeah, we wouldn't want you starving to death. Could you give me a little of that sweet tea?"

"Of course. I'm a growing boy. Hey, are you okay? I mean, not just physically."

She nods. "Yeah. It's just funny. When I was getting ready for tonight, Annabelle made me go back and put on this panty and bra set. I wasn't going to. I told her that you'd already seen me in my underwear and I really didn't intend for that to happen tonight." She sits back against the wall. "Funny how things don't always go like you plan."

I sit next to her and pull her into my side, as I bite into a piece of chicken. "Hey, are you sure you're okay? I mean, trust me, it wasn't my fantasy to take your virginity right here in this storage room. But I'll never regret being your first."

She looks up at me and bursts out laughing. "You have chicken crumbs all over your face. Are you really that hungry?"

I start laughing. "What can I say? You really make me a starving man."

We laugh and talk for a couple more hours. When the rain finally decides to let up, I glance down at the now empty picnic basket. She looks as well and we both start laughing again.

As we walk out to the bike. "Ryder, I'll never regret you being my first."

I pull her to my chest. "I don't know what to do with you sometimes. You stormed into my life with a ton of spitfire and took over my every thought."

She giggles again. "Well, if you don't know what to do with me, I can definitely ask you to keep doing what you were doing earlier. You can do that with me."

"I think I can manage that."

"And as far as where it happened... Sometimes the best things in life aren't planned."

We settle on the bike and head off to her house. She holds me tight as we drive through the night from Tybee Island. Once we get to her house, as we are getting off the bike, she grabs her phone and we both hear it chiming. She opens the message and looks angry.

"Damn it. What in the hell are they thinking?" she asks.

"Is everything okay?"

"Yeah just pain in the ass. Look, I'm kinda tired and I'd really like a hot shower. I'll explain this later. If that's okay?"

I really want to know more, but I'm not going to push. "Yeah sure. But if you need me, let me know. I don't know what this is about, but I care about you. If you need help in the shower, I'd be more than willing to help there, too."

She pops me on the arm. "I'm sure you would. Thanks for a wonderful night. I really had a great time tonight, it's been awhile since I could say that."

I press her back into the door frame. "Good. I hope it's the first of many." I take her lips with mine. "You have to be the sexiest creature God ever put on this planet."

She smiles, turning and opening her door. "I'm going to go take a hot, soapy shower."

She did that shit on purpose. "Well, I guess I'm going home to take a shower and think about your shower, while I beat off like I'm in ninth grade."

She looks back at me serious before she shuts the door. "Ryder, thank you for a great night."

"Anytime."

She shuts the door and I text Judd.

Hey man. Date was a success. Thanks again for your help. But I think I'm in trouble. I think I'm falling in love.

I shove the phone in my pocket and take off for home. I know it'll be a while before he reads it with the time difference. I wish he were here.

Chapter 15

Scarlet

What in the hell are Cade and Daria thinking? I read over their texts again.

> **Cade: Hey so Daria told me about your wreck and that you were worried about coming here for the baby to be born. I want you here and I don't want you going back to work so late at that bar. ---Yes I talked to Gable and I did some research on the place. So in the morning my old car will be sitting in front of your house I'll have the keys dropped in the mailbox. Don't argue with me about this, I've already put it in your name. I'll see you when the baby is born. I mean it call and quit that bar, the insurance is paid for the year and you have an unlimited gas card in the glove box. I want you to go to school.**

> **Daria: Sorry my husband can be a bit of a bully when he's trying to protect people. But I do want you to take this offer. He's just found you and he loves you. That is just Cade he couldn't be your big brother growing up so he wants to be one to you now. Trust me one day I'll get a chance to tell you our story and you'll understand just how protective he can get. Can't wait to see you when the new baby gets here. Be careful We Love You.**

I guess I should respond to them, but I'll wait until the morning when I see exactly what kind of car Cade sends over here. If he sends some brand new expensive car I'm going to kill him.

I climb in the shower and wash the evidence of my night away. It doesn't make sense to me how I became so comfortable and open with Ryder. I dated Dustin for a long time and never felt like this with him. Never felt this much attraction. But after just a few weeks I can't get within ten feet of Ryder Abbott without wanting to take my clothes off and rub our bodies together.

I hate that I acted that way toward him about it but Cade's text caught me completely off guard. I've never had someone even be able to think about giving me something of this magnitude.

I was so overwhelmed. I mean the only time someone has given me something like this was when I got my scholarship and I could accept it because I worked so damn hard for it. My mother never got much from my father when he left. She was always happy with us getting by on her job at the museum and the craft fairs and shit she did. It always aggravated me that she never got much from my father. Then again how much money can someone send you from prison? Hell even after he was released from prison his ass just ran off, none of us have ever heard from him again. He's probably making a new family somewhere since he seems to be so great at that. Fuck he's probably got two or three by now. The water starting to run cold pulls me out of my thoughts.

Looking at myself in the mirror and seeing my flush cheeks, I think about Ryder again. I should text him. I walk into my bedroom and grab my phone and see a text from Gable.

> **Gable: I know you are probably pissed about Cade sending you a car. Shut up about it. Also since he did some investigating and found out what that bar is really like I'm going to beat your ass when I get home. You told me it wasn't that bad. So Quit. Don't worry about my car I'll have enough money to get something when I get home off tour, plus I'll get a little insurance money from it. I mean it Scarlet quit that place. Also where the fuck was mom in all of this? Love you little sister just looking out for you.**

I guess I'm going to have to text a bunch of people in the morning. Right now I'm texting Ryder and apologize for how I acted.

> **Me: Goodnight. Sorry I was kinda a bitch after that text. Please come see me in the morning and I'll explain. I had a wonderful time tonight and I can honestly say I thought about you quite a bit while I was in the shower. ;-) LOL**

My phone dings right back.

> **Ryder: I can't be there in the morning I have to help Judd's dad around here we are still waiting on some calves to be born. But can I come by tomorrow afternoon? I had a wonderful time with you too and I'm glad you thought about me in the shower;-D**

Me: That's fine just text me. See you then. XOXO

Ryder: Can't wait. <3

Wow. I gotta get some sleep I have a bunch of housework to catch up on tomorrow. I also have a bunch of return texts to make tomorrow.

~*~

Waking up this morning I step outside to see a black four door Infiniti. I'm going to kill Cade. Yes this car was a few years old but it was a freaking Infiniti. I retrieve the keys from the mailbox and climb inside. There is a note on the dashboard. I open it.

Scarlet,

This is yours, I don't want to hear shit about this. I may not have been there for you when you were younger, but, I'm here now. Our Dad shit us all. I just happened to have a mother who came from a little money. I talked to Gable about this, he is pissed that you were working in a place like that and agrees that this is what you need. If you want to work a few hours a week that's fine but not in a bar and not late though. Your job is school right now. Once you get finished and start making big bucks doing artwork for all kinds of musicians you can pay me back. Maybe. You may have just found me, but you are my little sister and I will always take care of you. Taking care of family is what I do. Not something I get from our father. Take Care.

I love you.

Cade

I wipe my eyes. Okay so maybe I won't kick his ass. If Gable and I had ever had the money like this we would have probably done these same things for each other.

My momma finally pulls in the driveway. Once she gets out she looks at me in the car.

"Scarlet, who does this car belong to?"

"Um well while you were gone, I was in an accident and Gable's car got totaled. Cade sent me this car."

"Cade? As in your dad's child from his first marriage?"

"Yes momma, you know Gable and I met him. This is his old car, he's helping me out because he doesn't want me waiting tables at the bar I was working at."

"So you were in a wreck and no one thought to get ahold of me?"

"Momma, they tried to get ahold of you, but um, hello, your phone was off. You were at a spiritual retreat. Remember?"

"Well what happened?"

"I was on my way home late after work the other night and someone ran me off the road."

She shook her head. "Honey, I'm sure they didn't do it on purpose."

"ARH! It was on purpose. Everything isn't all peace signs and happiness."

"So negative."

Ugh I can't handle her 'love the world shit' this morning. "Mother, it was on purpose, there is proof. Anyway. Ryder drove up on the wreck and called 911. I had to let Gable know about his car and I called Daria, Cade's wife. I needed to let her know that I wouldn't be able to come for the baby to be born."

"You're going for their baby to be born, you don't even know these people."

My momma is obviously having a hard time with the fact that I went looking for my brother. "Yes Mother, I told you this when we came back from meeting him. We hit it off. Cade is a good brother. He's nothing like our douchebag father. Anyway he sent me this, paid the insurance for a year and gave me a gas card. He wants me to go to school and not be working somewhere that I get felt up every five minutes or witness people snorting lines of cocaine in the backroom. Whatever beef you have is with the asshole who was married to a couple of unsuspecting women at once. Not Cade, so get over it."

"I loved your father."

"Well he didn't really love anyone. But Cade loves Gable and I both, so lay off. You are always talking about free love and being good to people. Well don't just say it. Do it. Now I have some errands to do, before I come back and catch up on laundry and stuff."

"Scarlet. I'm sorry. It's just hard you know. I'm glad you've found someone else that you can count on, I know it takes a lot for you and Gable to trust people. So did Ryder think to try and call me or Gable?"

"Yes, I did, but I couldn't get anyone to answer the damn phone. So I took care of her myself."

We both turn startled at Ryder's voice.

Chapter 16

Ryder

I walk up on the end of a heated conversation where her hippie ass mother is actually defending their father, or her love for him, rather. She's pissed that her brother sent her a car *that I am still a little confused over*. But when her mom questions why I didn't get up with them, I hit protective caveman mode.

Scarlet runs over to me. She kisses me on the lips. "Hey I thought you weren't coming by until later."

I smile down at her. "Well, we had a calf born this morning, now we are only waiting on a couple more, so I told Nelson I'd meet him around 1. I wanted to come surprise you and take you to breakfast."

She gives me a smile that I hope I always make her have. "That sounds great." She pulls me by the arm. "Whisper Johnson, meet Ryder Abbott. I believe you guys have met at the museum."

Her mom nods. "Yes, he used to come in and drop off paperwork and things for his daddy. You have certainly grown into a handsome young man."

I smirk. "Thank you." I look over to Scarlet. "You ready to go?"

She bounces. "Yes just let me grab my purse and I'm driving."

As she turns to run I grab her arm. "Babe not that I don't like seeing your cute polka-dotted jammies, but you may want to change before we head out to breakfast."

She starts laughing. "Oh come on, I was trying to make a fashion statement."

I shake my head as she runs in the house. Her mom looks at me. "She seems happy."

"I hope she is." I turn to her. "Look, I'm sorry I popped off like that, but I've never- I mean never had someone affect me like Scar. So I'm a little defensive when someone questions that."

She nods. "Well I'm sorry they couldn't get in touch with me. I guess it's one of those things you just don't think about until it's too late." She leans against her car. "I'm sorry my questions came off like that, it's just I've always taken care of my kids myself. So to find out one of them got hurt and they couldn't get in touch with me, it's just hard on me."

"I can understand that. Trust me, I tried to call you several times. Gable and I did talk when he finally got back to the bus where is phone was that night."

She looks at the ground. "Did you know that was the kind of bar she was working in?"

"I knew it was not the place I wanted her working. As a matter of fact, I sat there one night just to keep her safe. Is she planning to quit? I've been asking her to."

"Yes, Cade and Gable asked her to after all of this."

"Oh, Cade is her other brother, right? The one she just found?"

Her mom nods as the front door opens and Scarlet comes bouncing out. She smiles. "Ready?"

I grin. "I guess."

I sit down in the passenger side of the Infiniti. "So who does this car belong to?"

"Well me now, I guess."

"Ok I'm a little lost. Your mom also said something about you quitting your job. I'm happy but also a little lost on that one too."

She smiles and starts with the text from last night. Once she's finished explaining we are pulling into the Waffle House for breakfast. I laugh. "Oh I bet you were pissed about the car. You get all pissy about people paying you compliments or giving you stuff."

"What do you mean I get pissy about compliments?"

"Look how you treated me when I first gave you compliments."

She punches my arm playfully. "You were being a chauvinistic ass."

After we get out, I walk around to her side and press her against the car. "I can say, however, that I am very excited that you will no longer be working at the bar." I kiss her hard on the lips.

She pulls away for a second. "I think I can feel just how excited you are."

"If you look at me like that much longer I'll be eating for breakfast but it won't be Waffle House."

"Well I'm hungry, and not for tube steak, so let's go eat."

~*~*~

An hour later we are driving back to her house. "So when are you going to let them know that you're quitting?"

"Well I'm not due to work again until Wednesday, but I'll probably go by or call tomorrow."

"I'd prefer that you call. After the other night and what you witnessed in the back room, I can't help but feel it's connected. If you decide to go, promise me you'll make sure it's when I can go with you."

"It shouldn't be a big deal if I go in broad daylight."

"Please don't." My phone starts ringing. "Hey Nelson, what's up? - Oh yeah, I'm sure I can, hang on."

I look over to Scarlet. "Hey can you swing by the FRM store and run me by my house? Nelson needs a couple of things for the new calf."

She gives me a huge smile. "Yes! As long as I get to see the new calf."

I go back to Nelson on the phone and chuckle. "I'll be there in twenty minutes."

Twenty minutes later we are driving down my driveway. "Here, pull up to the house and I'll load this stuff in the Ranger and we'll take it out to the barn."

"This is so exciting." She dances in her seat.

"Let me guess. You've never actually touched a brand new calf before?"

"I only petted one once at a petting zoo."

I laugh. "Okay, well I tell you what, you can help me feed some of the new babies. I have a couple that have to be bottle fed."

"Oh my Gosh Really?"

I shake my head as I'm loading powder mix in the ranger. "Yes REALLY!" I act silly like a teenage girl.

She play punches my arm. "Ass. I'm excited."

I pull her to me and kiss her. "Okay. Come on, let's go make your calf feeding dreams come true."

She jumps in the ranger and kisses me. "This is so exciting!"

We drive out to one of the barns and Nelson comes out to meet us. "Hey Nelson, this is Scarlet. Scarlet, this is Judd's dad, Nelson."

Scarlet smiles. "Hey nice to meet you. Judd looks just like you."

"Well that erases my thoughts that he might belong to the milk man." Nelson chuckles. "But it's nice to meet you too. I've been looking forward to meeting the young lady who not only Judd, but Greer has said has our Ryder smitten."

She blushes and I laugh. "Thanks Nelson, I was trying to play it cool."

He gives us a belly laugh and Scarlet starts laughing too.

"Okay, enough laughing at my expense, I promised her she could help me bottle feed some calves. So let's get to it."

Scarlet takes off in the barn like a kid. Nelson looks at me. "I like her, kid. She could love you for the rest of your life or break you in half if she had to. A true Southern Belle."

Damn he's right and that scares the hell out of me.

Chapter 17

Scarlet

Lying here in my bed, I think today has been an awesome day. I've never had so much fun in my life. I loved helping Ryder out on the farm. The calves are so damn cute. Growing up I've never gotten to spend much time on a farm or anything.

It hits me "SHIT." *I never texted Cade.*

I'll text Cade first.

> ME: *Thank you for all you've done. I don't normally do well with gifts like this. It's really taken me a little while to calm down about it. But I see now that this gives me a great opportunity for school. I will definitely not be as stressed and I really did hate working at that bar. So thank you and I know you are NOTHING like our father.*

I get an immediate response back.

> Cade: *I'm glad you're happy. I really did this to make life easier on you. I never got to grow up with siblings like I said before Gabby and Anna are the closest things I've ever had and even though I know they would kill for me, it's different knowing you share blood with someone. Now get some rest you have class tomorrow.*

How did I luck up and get not one, but two wonderful big brothers?

~*~*~

Waking up this morning to go to class, I feel like I have a new lease on life. I'm not stressed about work or a ride. I'm good. Ryder makes me happy. As I'm walking out the door for class my cell rings. "Hello. – Hello." Then a hang-up. I guess it was a wrong number.

Walking into to my advanced sketch class, I smile. I feel so at home in this class. I love the rush that drawing gives me. It's like my own personal nirvana. So I'm stoked when our teacher gives us our next project assignment. I have to sketch a scene from nature and I know where I'm heading to do that. The rest of the day seems to blur by. Annabelle texts me she wants to get together for coffee after I get finished for the day.

We meet up at Lulu's for dessert and coffee. I walk in to find her already at the table. I sit down across from her. She looks at me. "So. I can only guess how your date went the other night since your ass hasn't called me."

"Sorry it's been crazy. Let's just say the date was awesome, I'm no longer carrying around that v-card as you love to call it, I now have a car thanks to Cade, my mom is back from her retreat and I spent yesterday bottle feeding calves at Ryder's farm."

She flops back in her chair and lets out a snort laugh. "Okay. Well that's a hell of a way to catch me up on the past few days there friend. I'm not even sure where to start asking questions."

"Just start where ever."

"So you had sex."

I bark out a laugh. "How did I know that would be where you would start? Yes."

"So much for planning not to show him your panties that night, huh?"

"Shut it. It's not like it was planned. We got trapped by a rainstorm at the lighthouse. One thing led to another."

"So did you get off?"

"What the fuck? Damn Annabelle, can't you give me a few minutes here? I haven't told anyone and you've started grilling me."

"I'm your best friend and I better be the first person who knows besides you and Ryder."

"Oh my gosh. Whatever, don't get jealous." I lean back and look around. "Look, I do need you to give me the name of your doctor. I would like to go on the pill and I don't just want to go to some clinic. I'm nervous about it and I want, I don't know, some sort of tranquility when I go."

"Fuck Scarlet, I thought you'd been on the pill."

"No, I never really had to think about it. I mean we used a condom the other night, so I'm okay there. Look, I'd just like to have the peace of mind and you have always seemed to like your doctor, so I just figured you could give me his name and stuff."

"Sure, and Scar, I am really happy for you. Now on to this car business."

We spend the next hour catching up on everything else.

Once we walk out to my car she smiles. "Damn this is a nice car."

"Yes it is. I'm still kind of in awe over the whole thing. But I need to go, I'm doing a nature sketch for class and there is a cute little calf that has his name all over my project."

She smirks. "Oh, and I'm sure the guy who owns the calf has nothing to do with your sketch, huh?"

I sit down in my seat. "Shut up."

She blows me a kiss and I blow her one back.

~*~*~

Twenty minutes later I'm pulling up to the barn where the calves are. I jump out with my pad and charcoal set. Nelson is coming out of the barn. "Well if it isn't Miss Scarlet."

"Oh wow, Nelson, like I haven't heard the *Gone with the Wind* references my entire life."

He chuckles. "Well, Ryder isn't out here. He's gone over to Waycross for the day. I needed him to go check some stuff over there."

"Oh, I just need to do a nature sketch for one of my classes and I want to sketch one of the calves I fell in love with."

He shakes his head. "You girls. I remember Lillian falling in love with new animals, too."

"She must've been a really great person. I mean everyone talks about her so wonderful."

He sits down on a stump. "Lillian was a wonderful person. She made Greer the happiest man alive. Pearl had the daughter she'd always wanted. Lillian didn't come from much and at times all of this was a little overwhelming to her, but she loved with her whole heart. When Ryder was born she fell in love all over again. She took care of that boy even when she was too sick to walk."

"She died from cancer, didn't she?"

"Yes. Bless her heart she suffered. Greer and Ryder suffered right along with her. You know Ryder didn't talk for months after his Momma died. Judd spoke for him, he was the only person that Ryder would talk to."

"That's awful. When did he finally decide to start talking?"

"Well he started talking some about six months later, but he was still quiet. A few years, later a local woman from town decided all of a sudden that she was smitten with Greer and had her sights set on him. Well, she also had a thing for Ryder, who was now 11. She started touching him and getting him to do things to her. He wouldn't say anything for a long time because he wanted his daddy to be happy again. He finally talked to Judd about it, who talked to me, and I talked to Greer. Needless to say that woman was run out of town. Greer made Ryder start going to counseling but he's never trusted women much after that. He's always had, shall we say an *active* lifestyle, but he figured either they just wanted that or they were after his money, so he's never trusted a female. Well, until you."

"You really think he trusts me?"

"I know Ryder as if he were my own boy, he's over the moon for you. Now go sketch that calf. If you want you can help me bottle feed a few in a little while."

I smile. "Yes!"

He walks back out to check on some fence and I go to catch a glimpse of Button. Well that's what I'm naming the calf I fell for. Well I think I've kinda fell for his owner too.

Chapter 18

Ryder

I can't help but be excited when I pull up in the yard and see Scarlet's car at the barn. I walk into the side door and see her bottle feeding a small calf. "Hey looks like you're making friends."

She smiles. "I came to sketch Button and his mommy for my art project. Nelson told me I could help feed."

"Button?"

"Yeah. I gave him that name in my mind because he's cute as a button."

I step over to her and pull her close. "Well I could say the same for you."

"Mmm really. Are you sure that I'm really that cute, or is it just because you've seen me naked?"

"Oh Baby. Cute isn't what I would describe you naked as. Hot as Fuck is you naked. Cute is when you are here feeding calves."

She starts kissing my neck. "Oh really. Well I think you're pretty hot too."

"Baby I need to take a shower. I stink, I've been at one of the farms all day."

She looks up through her eye lashes at me. "Well, would you like some help in that shower?"

Fuck. "Yep, right in here." I lead her into the mud room shower at the barn. As soon as we walk in the small room I turn the shower on. I start kicking my boots off, she tears at the buttons on my shirt. I slip the sundress she's wearing over her head as she kicks off her flip flops. We start kissing as she's pushing my jeans and boxers down. I flip the clasp on her bra and tear her panties. Picking her up we step in the shower.

She breaks away. "Condom."

"Oh shit, sorry." I step back out and grab one from my wallet.

I pick her back up and thrust into her. "Shit Ryder."

"Oh sorry, was that too much?"

"Fuck no. Just right."

She grinds against me and I start slamming into her pussy. "Shit Scar you have the sexiest pussy. I would leave my dick in here forever if I could."

She giggles. "People might look at me funny." She draws in a deep breath as I start moving faster. "Fuck Ryder harder. Don't stop."

I can feel her tightening around me. "Baby I'm almost there." I slam into her again. "Fuck!" Spilling into the condom, I feel her shiver as she says something I don't understand. I lean against her on the wall. "Shit girl you are going to kill me. You make me do things and fuck like a mad man. It takes all I can do not to blow my load as soon as I see you."

"Well that's attractive." She giggles.

I gently let her legs down and step back. I pull off the condom, disposing of it in the trash. "Sorry, you make me feel crazy. I can't explain it."

She starts washing my body with soap. "I think I can understand. I've never felt like this before either."

A few minutes later we both step out of the shower. I hand her a towel and as she dries off, she starts picking up our clothes. She puts my jeans and stuff on a chair. She picks up her now shredded panties and looks at me. "Really you couldn't give me the opportunity to slide my panties down. You had to tear them off."

"I would have torn more off than that had we not moved fast enough."

She slips her dress over her head sans panties. As I reach over in the closet I keep a few clothes in. "I've got a couple of extra pair of boxer trunks in here. I know how you like wearing my underwear."

"Nope I think I'm going without panties just to torture you. I may even stop by the grocery store on the way home."

"Um no. You can run around here with no panties all you like, but you are not stopping anywhere on the way home."

"Well I might take your argument more seriously if you weren't standing there half hard and butt ass naked."

"Oh I can be completely hard in just a second thinking about you with no panties under that dress."

"Come on. Get dressed you perv, I have to finish my sketch."

I finish getting dressed and walk out where she has picked up her sketch looking over it. "Wow that is an awesome sketch."

"It's Button and his momma."

"Baby that is beautiful."

"Well I still have some shading to do and a few corrections here and there."

"You are so talented." She shades and sketches for a little longer.

Then she looks over at me. "I have a strange question. Why is there a bathroom out here?"

"Well. We get really nasty some days out here. Like if we have to help a cow give birth or when they are sick. Things like that, so it's easier to shower and change out here than me going all the way back down to the house or Nelson having to ride home that way."

"Oh, well that makes sense. I figured it was something like that, but I didn't know."

I hear the barn door open. "RYDER!"

"In here dad!"

"Well hey Scarlet." She waves back to him. "Here, I need you to take this down to Nana."

He hands me a brown grocery bag full of fresh cut okra. "What the hell dad? Where did this come from?"

"Mr. Beck ran into me at the post office and wanted to make sure she got this."

"Oh yeah, he's got the hots for Nana."

"Ryder." Dad sneers as Scarlet snickers.

"Hey I'm just telling you what she told me. At least the okra is better than the homemade hooch that Mr. Fitzgerald sent her the other week when I ran into him at the feed store."

He shakes his head. "Good Lord. That woman, I swear." I start laughing. "Just take the damn okra to her house." He turns to walk to the door. "Scarlet did you do this sketch?"

She smiles. "Yes."

He smiles. "It's beautiful." Then walks to the door. "Good to see you again Scarlet."

She waves. "Good to see you too Mr. Abbott."

"Did you get all you needed for your assignment?"

"Yeah I can do the shading and stuff at home. But I am going to take you up on the underwear offer after all. Because I can't go see Nana commando."

I laugh as she goes back in the bathroom to slip on a pair of my underwear. She steps back out into the barn. I grab her hand. "Ready to go?"

She smiles. "Yep."

"We'll take the jeep."

Chapter 19

Scarlet

Pulling up to Nana Pearl's house, she's sitting in the rocking chair. She's the definition of a true southern lady. *I'm going to sketch her one day on this porch.*

"Well. What do I owe the pleasure of having you two come by?"

Ryder sits the bag on the porch. "Mr. Beck ran into dad at the post office, he sent this to you."

"That man just won't take no for an answer."

I sit down in the rocking chair next to her. "Are you playing hard to get Nana?"

She laughs. "Honey it's like they said in a movie one time. At my age we don't play hard to get, we play beat the clock."

Ryder leans back against the porch railing. "Nana I don't want to hear this stuff

"We've had this discussion boy."

He laughs. "I know. I know. I'm changing my ways."

She smiles. "I hope so. I like this little girl right here."

"Hey Scar go get that sketch you did and let Nana see it."

I draw in a deep breath. "It's not really finished yet."

"Baby it looks awesome. Go get it please."

I finally give in. I run to the jeep and grab my pad. Stepping back on the porch I show the sketch to Nana.

"Sweet girl this is just beautiful. It looks so real."

"Thank you." I feel a blush creeping up on my cheeks. "Button is really cute."

Nana looks up. "Button?"

"Yes she named the calf Button."

Nana laughs. "He is cute. Y'all want some sweet tea?"

Ryder stands up. "No thank you. I plan on taking Scarlet out to dinner tonight."

I look up. "Oh really you do? Well I don't think you've asked me."

Nana chuckles as she lights her cigarette up.

Ryder looks back at her. "Nana I thought you were going to try that vapor cig I got for you."

"I did, I don't like it, and I figure I got to be this damn old by doing whatever in the hell I wanna do, I might as well keep doing it. Also, I figure you need to ask this lady, out on a date not tell her she's going."

He smiles over at me. "Scarlet, would you go out to dinner with me tonight?"

I put my finger against my chin like I'm thinking. "Hmm I guess I will."

We wrap up our visit with Nana and he takes me back to my car. He leans in the window after I'm in and kisses me. "I'll pick you up at 6 okay?"

I nod. "Sure. Now where are we going? So I know how to dress."

"How about the Tapa's Bar?"

"Sounds good."

~*~*~

Looking down at the pencil skirt and blouse I'm wearing, Ryder smiles in appreciation. "You look nice."

I feel the blush of my cheeks. "Thank you."

"You ready to go?"

"Yes." I follow him out to his jeep. After he gets in his side I laugh. "So did you ask Judd for advice on this date too?"

"Nope I did this one all on my own."

"How sweet." We just make casual talk until we get to the restaurant.

Making our way inside and finding a table, we sit down and order drinks. "You look really nice tonight. Have I ever told you that I love your smile?"

"Thank you."

A couple of sleazy looking girls stroll up to our table. "Hey Ryder." They purr.

He nods. "Lacey. Bethany Sue. How are you guys doing tonight?"

Lacey winks. "Doing good now that I've laid eyes on you."

"Well, we are kinda in the middle of a date so if you'll excuse us." Ryder says with a sweetness dripping from his tongue.

They wave as they sashay off.

"Well they seem nice, I guess."

He shakes his head. "They are catty bitches."

I know I'm going to regret asking this. "Did you sleep with either of them?"

"No, I almost did though. The night that got me community service. I was headed to Lacey's, she was passed out topless when we wrecked."

"Oh." Suddenly feeling nervous.

"Look, I'm being honest with you. I want to always be honest with you. Yes, I just about made a damn stupid mistake with her. Trust me, the entire town was talking about it. Nana crawled my ass because the ladies at her beauty shop told her."

I laugh. "I bet she did. If you'll excuse me I have to go to the ladies room."

He nods and I make my way to the restroom. As I'm finishing up in the stall, I hear the door open and two girls come in giggling. I hesitate before walking out.

"So did you see Ryder with her?"

"Yes I guess since she struck out with Dustin she's moved on to bigger and better."

"Well that won't last long. Ryder will get over his little revenge case soon enough and I'll get to finish what I started a few months ago."

"She's pretty cute you know. Do you really think this is about revenge with Dustin?"

"Why else would it be? Dustin never screwed her. He's trying to fuck her because he and Dustin still have this damn hatred toward each other. It's really stupid. It's all over that poor friend of his. Kelsie told me about that guy."

Finally I've had enough. I step out the door and they both freeze, I walk to the counter and wash my hands. I don't say a word to them, I just turn and walk out the door.

I make my way back to the table Ryder smiles as I sit down. I look up, "Ryder, I'm not really feeling well, do you think we can go?"

"Sure. Are you sure you are ready to go?"

"Yeah I just think I'm just tired."

He pays the bill and we drive back to my house making small talk. Once we get to my house he looks over at me. "Scarlet what's going on?"

"Have you been screwing me to get even with Dustin?"

"What the fuck? How can you even think that?"

"I overheard Lacey and Bethany Sue in the bathroom. They seem to think so."

"Look at me. Do not ever listen to anything those catty bitches have to say. They are jealous you have me, don't you realize that? You have every part of me, so much that it fucking scares me. Don't you see that?"

I can even seem to form words. "I'm sorry. They just brought out all of my insecurities. This is a lot to digest for one night, my emotions are all over the place. I just need to go in and get some sleep I think. I'm sorry again."

He winks and smiles. "It's okay, I know I'm a lot to take in."

I bark out a laugh. "You always have a way of turning things into sex, don't you?"

"Yes. But I'm serious, you trust me, don't you?"

I think for a second. "Yes I do. I just need a little bit of time."

He leans over the console and kisses me deep. "Just think about that. I'm giving you a day to think and then I'm coming back for more."

I nod. "Okay."

Once I get to my room I sag against the door.

Do I really trust him? How do I know that he's real, that this isn't some kind of game to him? I can't be embarrassed like that again.

My phone beeps that I have a text message.

Cade: Daria's blood pressure is off the charts. They are going to do a C-Section in the   morning. She wanted me to let you know that if you can't make it here tomorrow she understands. We know you have school.

I grab my overnight bag and start packing. Maybe a couple of days is what I need.

Me: I'm leaving now. I'll be there in a few hours.

Cade: It's too late for you to be leaving.

Me: It's only 7 here I can be at your house around midnight your time. I'm coming I'll call you along the way.

I grab my duffle bag, leave mom a note and head out the door.

Chapter 20

Ryder

Waking up this morning. I know I'm never going to make it the full day I gave her. I've got to see her. She's got to know just how much I care for her, I want her.

I'm going to take her to breakfast. "Dad, when Nelson stops by, tell him I've got some things to do today. I won't be back until later."

"Okay. You taking Scarlet out for the day or something?"

"Gonna try to."

He chuckles. "Good luck son."

I drive to her house and knock on the door. No answer. "Come on Scarlet, open up." I notice her car isn't here. Maybe she's at class already. I call her phone no answer.

I wait an hour, call again, no answer.

I wait another hour, still no answer. I text *Call me please,* no response.

I make it back home and I'm beyond pissed. Dad sees me come in.

"So I take it you didn't go to breakfast."

"I can't fucking get up with her."

"Okay son. Slow down tell me what all this is about."

I sit down and tell dad about our date last night and our conversation in the car. I probably talk to him more in that afternoon than I've talked to him in the past ten years.

"Son. You do know that your reputation with women has a lot to be desired. Having someone from your past show up like that and her hear those things would make anyone uneasy. Especially when someone has been treated the way she was by Dustin. You should understand the whole trust thing."

"I just want to talk to her dad. She won't return any of my messages or calls."

"She needs time son. Give her a little space to cool off."

"Okay. I'm going outside to get some air try to calm down."

He nods that he understands as I walk out the front door.

~*~*~

I wake up feeling like hell. I sat last night and got drunk in the barn with Button. Yeah. I'm calling the calf Button now too.

While I'm in the shower I decide I'm going to talk to her mom. I need to see her.

Walking into the Tel-fair museum, I ask for Whisper and she walks out a few moments later in a fluster. "Hey I've been trying to get up with Scarlet, but she won't answer my calls or anything."

She shrugs, trying to motion to some workers about moving items around. "She left me a note that she was going out of town. She'd call me and let me know when she got there. She called me, she's fine."

"Do you know when she will be back?"

"No. She didn't say. Sorry hun I really have to go before they break something."

I slump my shoulders. "Okay thanks."

She left town and didn't tell me. What in the hell do I do? It's been almost 48 hours since I've laid eyes on her and I can't handle it.

Fuck this, I'm calling Gable. Once the phone starts ringing, I realize its 8am where he is and he's probably still sleeping last night off. Shit, he's gonna be pissed.

"Hello." He sounds groggy as hell.

"Hey man its Ryder. Where is your sister?"

He lets out this big yawn. "She's over in Tuscaloosa man. Are you drunk or something?"

"No. She won't answer my calls or texts. Dude I'm lost."

"Chill out. I'll text you the fuckin' address dude, I'm trying to sleep."

"Thanks man."

Good to his word, Gable sends me an address. I throw some stuff in a bag and head out. It takes me almost 7 hours to get there. Driving into a very upscale suburban neighborhood, I see her Infiniti parked outside the house.

Getting out of the car I take a deep breath. *Okay here goes nothing.*

I knock on the front door and a big ass guy answers the door. "Yeah."

"Um is Scarlet here?"

"Yeah. Who are you?"

"Ryder."

He turns around. "Scarlet there's a guy here to see you. His name is Ryder."

She opens the door and smiles. "Hey what are you doing here?"

I'm angry that she seems so casual. "What do you mean? You tell me you need a little time and you leave fucking town without saying a word. I'm freaking out. I sat out there the other night and got drunk with your damn calf."

She puts her hands on my chest. "Ryder stop, calm down."

Big guy is back at the door. "Everything alright Scarlet?"

She turns. "Its fine Cade, he's a friend of mine." He turns and walks back in.

A little relief hits me. "Cade. As in your brother?"

She laughs. "Yes, my brother. What did you think, I ran off to some random man's house? How did you find me anyway?"

"I called Gable. I didn't know what to think. I couldn't find you. You wouldn't return my texts or calls. I knew you were upset the other night and I really couldn't handle the thought of you being mad with me. I needed to hear your voice, see your face and I couldn't."

"Calm down. Cade's wife had to have an emergency C-Section. I left not long after you dropped me off the other night. When I got here I crashed, we went straight to the hospital the next morning. My phone fell in the toilet at the hospital and quit working. I didn't have anyone's numbers, I had already called to let Mom and Gable know I'd made it here. I was going to call you today when my new phone came in. I'm sorry."

And I feel like a dumbass.

"Ok now I feel stupid. I'm sorry I over reacted. I've never felt this attachment to another person. I got scared."

She moves to the side. "Come on in and I'll introduce you."

We walk into the kitchen and a little girl is dancing around the table. She looks up at me. "Who are you?"

Scarlet steps in. "Madison, this is my friend Ryder. Ryder, this is my niece Madison, my brother Cade and his wife Daria. The new little fella is sleeping."

Madison looks up at me and Scarlet. "Is he your boyfriend?"

Scarlet turns red like her name. I speak up. "Yes I'm her boyfriend." She looks at me like I've lost my mind for a second then smiles.

Cade steps over and shakes my hand. "Hey."

I look at him closer in the face. "Wait, you're Cade Johnson."

He chuckles. "Yeah last time I checked."

"You played some awesome college football. I always figured you would go pro, with your buddies. But none of you did."

"No man we all decided to live a little more low key life."

"Wow. Do you still keep up with them?"

About that time I hear two loud guys coming through the back door. "No way man. Gabby needs rest. She's big, ill, and pregnant. I'm not messing with her, get nookie-."

Daria looks up laughing. "Guys this is Scarlet's boyfriend Ryder. Ryder these are the two bozos you asked Cade about a few minutes ago. Linc and Russ Addison." I shake their hands.

Cade looks at them. "Seriously guys watch what you do and say when you come in here. Maddie told her teacher the other day that Mommy and Daddy take really long showers together and that it must be because Mommy is so big with her baby belly. That I must get soap in her eyes because she screams a lot. So we are trying to guard little ears."

Linc and Russ have to sit down they are laughing so hard. Cade looks at me. "So Ryder what do you do?"

"My family owns Abbott Cotton and we have several farms. I mostly work at the farms with the animals."

He looks at me a little harder. "Now just exactly what possessed you to come all the way here and get huffy with my little sister?"

Scarlet steps up. "Cade it was all a misunderstanding."

"No Scarlet I should explain myself to him. I showed up at his house acting like an ass."

I sit down and explain to them what all had transpired in the past 72 hours. Once I'm finished, Daria laughs. "Well Cade, you damn sure can't be pissed about him tracking her down, you would have done the same thing had I left you a way to."

Everyone except Scarlet and I laugh, I guess it's something we don't understand.

Daria looks at Scarlet. "That's the story I told you would be for another day."

Scarlet laughs. "Oh okay."

Cade looks up at me. "Ryder come out back and have a beer with us. I'm putting some burgers on the grill for tonight. Anna and Gabby are on their way over with some stuff so we'll just have a dinner party."

I nod. "Okay sounds good." I step out back with the guys. "Man this is a nice place, seems kinda private but in the city. I'm used to living on a thousand acres, my nearest neighbor is my Nana Pearl."

"Yeah it's nice. So are you serious about my sister?"

"Well, she's the first person I've ever cared this much for. She's the most beautiful girl I've ever laid eyes on, she's smart, quick witted and sometimes a pain in the ass."

Russ holds up his beer. "Son, go ahead and pick you out a ring, you've found the real deal."

Cade pops up. "Dude don't go trying to marry off my kid sister. I just found her."

Linc looks up. "Cade describe Daria."

"Shut up asshat."

I laugh. "Look, we haven't been dating that long. I just put a label on what we have a few minutes ago. I've been afraid to. The first five minutes I met her, she put me in my place."

They laugh and Cade looks at me. "Did she quit that bar?"

"She was supposed to. She was going to call them, I told her not to go without me."

"That place sounded pretty rough."

"It was the first time I saw her working there I stayed the rest of the night to watch out for her."

Cade puts his hand on my shoulder. "Thanks man. I appreciate it."

Chapter 21

Scarlet

Not long after the guys go outside Anna and Gabby show up. Daria pulls them over to the kitchen window to look at Ryder. Anna pipes up. "Ooh he's hot."

Daria laughs. "You should have seen him when he came to the door. He was like half unsure of his self, half pissed off. It was sexy. But I think when Cade's big ass answered the door he about pissed his pants."

I laugh. "Well, we had a little issue and I didn't think to let him know I'd left town, plus all the stuff with my phone, he couldn't get ahold of me. He panicked a little and called Gable to find me."

Gabby laughs. "Oh so he went all caveman on your ass."

I laugh. "I guess so. But he did admit to sitting in the barn and getting drunk with my calf. Even though it's not my calf, it's his, I just named him."

"So how did you guys meet?" Anna asks.

"During community service."

Anna laughs. "Oh yeah, the ex's car. I have to say, you might be Cade's little sister and not mine, but I was very proud of you that day. It was like something Gabby would've done."

"Anyway. He hit on me, I shot him down. Like shot him down bad. He kept kind of stalking me until I said yes to a date. He took me on an awesome first date and I guess, according to him, now we are boyfriend and girlfriend."

They all laugh and Daria speaks up. "Caveman style. Honey go ahead and figure you are going to marry that man. Only two people who love each other can act that crazy to one another and that guy is over the moon for you."

The guys come back inside with the burgers and we begin to eat. Madison, Marshall (Gabby and Linc's son) and Emma (Anna and Russ's daughter) have all fallen in love with Ryder. I can't really say as I blame them.

After dinner Daria and Cade invited Ryder to stay with me and follow me back home tomorrow. As we are lying in the bed I turn to him. "So what did you really think I had done?"

He shakes his head. "I honestly didn't know. I just knew I was scared to death that you'd given up on me."

I brush my hand down his chest. "Ryder I'll never give up on you. I just needed a little time to think and then it all got crazy. I should have texted you on my way here, before I killed my phone."

"It's okay, I shouldn't have flipped out so bad." He kisses my lips. "I'm sorry again."

I start kissing down his neck. "You're forgiven."

"I'm not having sex with you in your brother's house. Plus you could've told me that your brother was the Cade Johnson."

I giggle. "I'm sorry. It's not that big of a deal to me. I didn't really watch football that much and at that time I never knew Cade. So the only thing I know about his football days are the things I've read and the stuff he's shown me."

I run my hand over his stomach and down to his erection. He grabs my hand. "I told you no. No means no."

I laugh. "Oh really. I consider that a challenge."

"Shh. Your big ass brother will come in here and kill me."

"We could be really quiet."

He turns over to me and starts kissing me hard. He starts making his way down my belly and works my panties down my legs. "Now if you're really quiet I'll give you a treat until we get home tomorrow."

I giggle and whisper as his tongue swipes my clit. "I promise. I'll be quiet."

~*~*~

"Are you guys sure you don't need me to stay a couple of extra days to help you with the baby?"

Cade laughs. "We are sure. Don't worry, Anna will be over here all the time and its a few months before Gabby has their new addition. Plus, if I don't let you go, I think Ryder over there is going to have a coronary."

I laugh and hug him. "Yeah I guess so. But I'll be back to visit and get baby cuddles."

Still hugging me Cade chuckles. "And for God sakes, the next time you decide to blow out of town, text the boy and let him know. I've done the crazy over the girl you love thing. It's not fun."

I step back a little. "You think he loves me? Really?"

"Sure do kiddo. Nobody follows a piece of ass 7 hours from home. I don't care how good it is."

I smack his arm. "Damn Cade. Don't say shit like that, it grosses me out."

"Be safe going home and call me when you get there."

Driving back from Tuscaloosa I take some time to think about Ryder and me. The things Cade said. That Ryder loves me or else he wouldn't have almost lost his mind trying to find me. He got drunk with Button because he missed me. I pull off the interstate and pull into a hotel parking lot.

He pulls in behind me. "Baby what are you doing?"

I step out of the car and walk over to him. "Did you really start calling that calf Button?" He nods. "Did you really sit out there and get drunk with Button?"

"Yeah."

"Did you really call him my calf?"

"Yeah. Baby what is this all about?"

"Stay right here, I'm going to get a room, we are staying here tonight because I'm going to screw your brains out." His mouth drops open as I turn and go in to get a room.

Ten minutes later we barely make it in the hotel room. We are both breathing heavy. "Fuck Scarlet this is some wild shit. You are so fucking hot."

I reach and grab the hem of my shirt and snatch it off over my head. I unhook my bra and throw it off. We are a tumble of clothes flying and finally he has my ass in his hands with me pressed against the door. "Ryder, condom."

"Shit." He reaches down and grabs one out of his pants and puts it on. The next thing I know he has his hands on my ass again drilling into me against the door.

I bite his shoulder and let go. "Fuck Ryder, harder. Oh God. Oh God don't stop."

"Baby, I don't know how much longer I'm gonna last, your pussy is like a vice grip on my dick."

"Oh shit. I'm coming, I'm coming."

He slams into me one last hard time. He leans against me and the door. "Shit baby. That was crazy, but sexy as hell." He kisses my lips hard as he starts to let my legs down.

I start to the bathroom and fall down. I start laughing. "Damn I was going to screw your brains out and you fucked me til I can't walk."

He leans down and picks me up. "Here, I'll help you walk and then once you catch your breath, I'll let you screw my brains out."

So we do just that. We've tried out the bed, the floor, bent over the desk, in the desk chair, on the bathroom counter and in the shower. Needless to say I think we've both been thoroughly fucked.

Checking out this morning he looks at me. "Hey are you ready to go home now or do we need to stay another day?"

"I'm ready to go home now. I have a calf to check on."

He kisses the side of my forehead as I'm getting in my car. "I love you."

I think I just stopped breathing. "I- I love you too."

Chapter 22

Ryder

It's been six weeks since Scarlet and I came back from her brother's house. Six weeks since we first said I love you to each other. Six weeks since I drove her to that bar so she could quit. She pretty much stays with me all the time when dad is out of town. He wouldn't care if she stayed while he's here, but she feels weird about it. It's not like he doesn't know what's been going on between us, but she says it doesn't matter. However she does come by every day to check on Button. That cow loves her, she has this magical way with anything or anyone she comes in contact with.

Thanksgiving is coming up next week. Since her mom is going on *another* retreat, Gable is still on tour and Cade is going to his mother's, she is coming to my house. I told her even though Dad is home she is going to be staying with me. She agreed, but not happily. My Nana is so excited about me bringing Scarlet to a family dinner that you'd think I was announcing our engagement or something. We aren't there yet though. If I was to ask Scar right now, she'd probably punch me in the face and leave town. I'm going to one day though.

When I look into her eyes, I see my forever. I see living on this farm with her. Staying right here was not something I cared to even imagine before her. I see little blonde headed kids running around, I see the entire picture. Shuddering I put that shit in the back of my head.

I pull in her driveway on my motorcycle. She bounces out the front door. "Hey sexy, what brings you by?"

I grin. "Well, I came into town to grab this beautiful girl I know and take her for a drive. Maybe go to my cabin for the weekend."

"Oh really. Without even calling her to make sure she wasn't seeing someone else?"

"Call me confident."

She shakes her head and laughs. "Okay let me grab my jacket and a bag."

"Wait. Here I got you this." I hand her the riding jacket I got for her.

She kisses me on the lips. "Wow this is sweet." She slides it on. "How do I look?"

"Sexy."

Before jumping on the back she runs back inside to lock-up, grab her purse and an overnight bag.

"Okay now I'm ready. Now where is your cabin?"

"It's at my farm in Waycross. It's an old fishing cabin." I kiss her cheek. "But it's quiet and it's very private."

Her eyes light up. "Private huh?" She winks. "Let's go."

We drive for a couple of hours, making great time getting to my farm. Pulling up to the old cabin, she smiles. "This is really a gorgeous place. How old is this cabin?"

"The land has been in my family since 1926, best we can tell the cabin was built in the 1940's. Nana remembers my granddad's brother building it. We've done a little remodeling and upkeep to the inside. We added indoor plumbing and rewired it. Stuff like that."

"Well thank God for indoor plumbing." She laughs. "Let's go inside."

"I came by the other week and opened it up, but it may still smell musky from being shut up."

She walks in and smiles. "This is really cute." She looks around at the simple one room cabin, with a small bathroom added in the corner. There is a small couch and chair, a fireplace, small kitchenette and a full size bed. "It's cozy. I love it."

"I brought some groceries out the other day when I came by. I keep a little stuff out here anyway, since I'm out here working sometimes. It's a lot easier than trying to run back into town just to grab a sandwich."

"Yeah I bet. So what do you want to do now?"

"Well I'd love to throw you down and make passionate love to you, but I'm going to gather a little wood for tonight because it's supposed to get chilly tonight. Then I thought we might try and catch a few fish for supper. What do you think?"

She jumps up and down. "I haven't been fishing in forever. Gable and I used to go when we were little. It's probably been almost ten years."

"Well it sounds like a plan. Why don't you grab our little bags and I'll gather up some wood. Then we'll do some fishing in the pond."

She smiles. "Sounds great to me."

~*~*~

An hour later we are on the dock of the pond. She looks over at me. "So what kind of fish are we trying to catch?"

"Well there are mostly catfish in here."

"Good I like catfish."

"On the chance that we don't catch anything, I made sure that there is some meat in the fridge."

She sits down Indian style on the ground like a kid. "So you really have been planning this huh?"

"Sure have. I wanted to get you all to myself for a weekend."

"I think it's really sweet."

I sit down beside her. "Oh you do, huh?"

She sits her rod down on the ground and kisses me. "Yes, Mr. Abbott, I do."

I drop my rod on the ground and pull her close. "Oh so it's Mr. Abbott now?"

She nods her head into my neck as she kisses the vein that runs up the side. "Mmm hmm."

I glance over at her rod and jump. "Oh shit you have a bite."

She shrieks. "Oh crap. Ryder help me."

Grabbing the rod we fight the fish for a minute before her line snaps. We fall back onto the ground laughing. She rolls off of me. "You are way too distracting to go fishing with. That could've been like a sixty pound trophy fish and I'll never know now."

I laugh. "I doubt it was sixty pounds. He was probably just a fighter and we had crappy line."

"Nope I say he was huge and I lost out."

"Baby, this is a small fish pond, and I hate to break your heart but Moby Dick doesn't live in here."

She looks up at the sky. "Whatever helps you sleep at night buddy."

I roll over on top of her. "I think you help me sleep at night."

"For some reason I don't think we'll be having fish for supper tonight."

I kiss down her neck to her collar bone. "I think you might be right."

She grabs my shirt and snatches the buttons open. She giggles. "Good thing those are snaps, huh?"

I grab the bottom of her shirt and pull it over her head. Staring down at the rise and fall of her chest over the cups of her bra, I reach down and flip the clasp exposing her beautiful tits. She reaches for my belt, and what feels like seconds, her hands are pushing my jeans and boxers down. I flip the buttons on her jeans and slide them, along with her panties down her legs. All of a sudden she stops me. Putting her hands across her chest, she looks embarrassed. "Ryder someone may see us, it's still light outside."

I smile. "Baby there is no one here but you and me. No workers. No one. So relax."

She gives me an evil grin and pulls me on top of her.

I duck my head down and pull her nipple into my mouth and she arches her back up off the ground. I slowly kiss down her body, dipping my tongue into her navel, working my way to her warm wet core. As my tongue flicks her swollen nub, she cries out. I work my way back up her body and thrust into her.

"Oh God Ryder!"

I slowly pull back and slam back into her. I start pumping in and out of her faster and faster until I explode inside of her. I barely hear her come again, over my own sounds.

As I pull out I realize I just screwed up big time. "Oh shit Scarlet. I forgot a condom."

She smiles. "It's okay sweetie. I've been on the pill for a little over a month now. I know that's not a hundred percent or anything but, I'm pretty sure we are okay."

I let out a huge sigh. "Are you sure? I mean I've never had sex without a condom before."

"It's okay. It's not even my ovulation time, we are okay."

I grin. "Well, in that case, can we do that again? That felt fucking amazing."

Chapter 23

Scarlet

Sitting on the couch watching a shirtless Ryder work in the small kitchen, I smile. Standing up, I walk over to him and put my arms around his waist. "Hmm there is something sexy about a man in the kitchen."

"Babe I'm just making hamburgers."

"I know, but I've never had any guy, except Gable or Cade, cook anything for me. Also, let's face it, you're sexy without even trying." I kiss his back.

"Are you trying to seduce me or tempt me, you vixen?"

I pat his ass. "Maybe."

"Well let me finish these burgers and you can have your wicked way with me all night."

Wearing only his snap button shirt I'd torn off of him earlier, I feel a chill run down my spine. I shiver. "I'm glad you brought in that firewood, it's starting to get chilly."

"I promise I'll keep you warm." He kisses me as he puts the last hamburger on the plate. He grabs the plates and pulls me to the couch. "Here cover up with this throw." He spreads a small blanket over my legs.

I smile and laugh a little. "Thanks."

"What's so funny?"

"Just the fact that you aren't anything like that guy I met over the summer. He was cocky and arrogant. He was only thinking about himself. This guy is so sweet, takes me for weekend getaways in the woods and plans romantic dates. Oh, and he is a very, very generous guy in bed."

"Oh crap I'm going to have to meet this guy who is so nice."

"Hmm maybe I can introduce you two."

He smiles as we eat. "So how are my culinary skills measuring up?"

"I'd give you an 8."

"Hey, I'm good with that. Burgers and steaks are about the only things I can do. I am, however, a master at takeout."

He reaches over and wipes the corner of my mouth. I smile. "What?"

"You had a little ketchup mixture on your face."

"Thanks." I sit my now empty plate down. "So what are we going to do now?"

"Hmm." He moves closer to me. "I can think of a few things." He kisses me. "But first I'm going to build a fire, because it is starting to get pretty chilly in here. Especially since I turned the stove off."

I stand up and wrap the blanket around me. I walk around the cabin while he starts a fire. I find a deck of playing cards lying on the counter in the kitchen. I pick them up. "So do you want to play some cards?"

He grins as he pokes the fire. "Play maybe some strip poker?"

I smile and lie. "I've never played poker before."

He grins. "Well, I'll teach you."

~*~*~

An hour later Ryder is sitting naked in front of me. "I think you hustled me." He shakes his head. "Can't play poker my ass. Babe, if you wanted to get me naked, all you had to do was say so."

I giggle. "Yeah but it's so much more fun to beat you at something."

"Are you saying I'm a sore loser?"

I stand up and start cleaning up. "Well you did throw your shorts at me. Then you slung your cards on the floor." I shrug my shoulders.

He jumps up. "Oh you are going to see whose sore in the morning." He runs up behind me and grabs me.

I squeal as he throws me on the bed. He starts to kiss my neck. "So I'm a sore loser huh?"

I nod. "Yes." He starts tickling me and I squeal. "Okay you aren't a sore loser."

"You have entirely too many clothes on Miss Scarlet."

I look up at him. "Oh I do? Well why don't you be a gentleman and help me out of them?"

He works the buttons on my shirt slowly, kissing me as each one is undone. By the time he finishes sliding my panties down my legs, he has literally kissed my entire body. I'm so fucking wet and I think I'm going to die if he doesn't take me right now.

"Ryder I may explode if you don't fuck me right now."

He chuckles. "Oh I plan on making you explode, just I want it to be around my dick."

In one swift movement he buries himself inside me. I scream. "Oh Shit!"

He starts kissing me again slowly and torturous. "Scarlet I love you."

"I love you too. But if you don't start moving I'm going to kill you."

He chuckles and starts moving faster. Suddenly pulling out. I feel empty. "What the?"

He stands up at the edge of the bed and pulls me over there by my legs. He lifts me by my legs burying himself inside me and starts pounding harder.

"Oh shit Ryder! Harder! Oh God Oh GOD!" I explode. Before I can think twice he flips me onto my stomach putting my ass in the air as he slams into me again. Grabbing my hips he pounds into me, he slaps my ass. "Oh God!!!" I explode again at the same time he comes inside me.

We fall on the bed and he smiles at me. "Holy shit baby that was fucking awesome."

I giggle. "Yeah it was." I feel the goose bumps pop up on my body and I shiver.

"Damn it got chilly, let me throw some more wood in the fireplace and we'll get in bed."

I nod, standing up and pulling the blankets back on the bed. He stokes the fire after putting some more wood on it.

We both snuggle under the covers. I roll over to face him. "I can't believe you slapped me on the ass."

He starts laughing. "Babe, your ass is fucking hot. I just went with it and admit it, you liked it, you came within seconds after that."

I feel the blush creeping up on my face. "Yeah I guess I did."

"Scarlet. I want you to know this is all serious for me. I know you said earlier that I'm a lot nicer than the guy you met over the summer. I've never felt these things before, I never would have dreamed that I could feel this way about anyone."

"I know. You know I dated Dustin for a long time and I never felt this way. I never felt so comfortable. You make me feel emotions I never thought I could. My dad really screwed up my ideas on men. Maybe deep down that's the reason I dated Dustin for so long. I knew I would never completely fall for him. I guess deep down I knew it would never work."

"Baby you will never have to worry about me walking out and leaving you."

I feel my eyelids growing heavy. I sigh. "I know."

He rolls onto his back and I place my head on his chest. Soon the soft rise and fall of his chest makes my eyes too heavy to keep open. I feel myself drift off into a warm sleep.

Chapter 24

Ryder

Being that it is the night before Thanksgiving and she's helping nana with lunch tomorrow, I've talked my girl into spending tonight with me. Originally she only agreed to Thanksgiving night because of my dad being home. After we spent last weekend at my cabin I could go to sleep and wake up with her every day of my life.

She's still nervous though. Little by little she's shared more and more about her dad with me. He left her really screwed up. It would be one thing if he'd been a dickhead forever, but she says when she was small he was a great dad. He was always out of town working they thought, now they obviously know he was with Cade and his mom, but when he was home she was his princess.

We are standing in my nana's kitchen. I'm washing collard greens and Scarlet is mixing up dressing for tomorrow. She smiles and looks over at me. "You know, this is exciting for me. The last time I had a real family Thanksgiving, I was like seven or eight. So this is great."

"Well I'm excited and so is my family. Nelson and his wife Naomi are coming too, since Judd is deployed they don't feel like being in their house all alone."

She nods. "I can understand that, I miss Gable, Cade and my mom. I know it's not the same as being deployed but Gable and I haven't ever been apart as long as we have now."

I lay the last of the greens in the dishpan. "Well, maybe he'll be home around Christmas."

She shrugs. "Yeah he's supposed to be." She looks sad.

She doesn't know that I've talked to Gable and they are playing a gig up in Hilton Head this weekend. I've worked it out with him for us to come up and see him play. I'm going to tell her tomorrow at dinner. It's just about killed Gable and I both to keep this secret. She's missed him so much and Gable constantly keeps in touch with me checking in on her.

I wrap my hands around her waist. "Hey, do you know how sexy you are?" I move her hair and start ravaging her neck.

She squeals. "Stop. That tickles."

"Ryder, leave the girl alone, she's trying to work. Did you get them collards washed up?"

I turn around to see nana standing there with her cigarette in one hand and her other hand on her hip. "Yes ma'am, they're right here in the dish pan."

She nods. "Okay well now you can start getting these pumpkins ready for cookin'. We ain't got no time for you to be playing Casanova of the damn Kitchen." She pops my arm as she walks out on the back porch.

Scarlet is laughing. I pop her on the ass. "I'll spank you for laughing at me later."

She giggles. "Oh I'm so scared."

I pinch her side and she leans over giggling. "You better be."

"Ryder! Get your ass out here now boy." My nana calls out from the back porch.

Scarlet chuckles as I walk out the back door. "Yeah Ryder, get your ass out there."

I duck my head and walk out the back door to help nana.

~*~*~

After spending the day helping my nana get the food prepped for tomorrow, Scarlet wanted to go check on Button. So needless to say, I'm tired by the time we get in the house. I look over to her as we sit down on the small couch in my room to watch a movie. "I'm tired babe. I think hanging out with you and nana today was more work than working on the farm all day."

"Are you saying you can't handle two women, Mr. Abbott?"

I shudder. "Don't say shit like that."

She giggles and then smiles. "Come on, I'll draw you a bath and if you are nice, I might join you." She's pulling me from the couch.

"I think you deserve a bath, too. I mean you did a lot of prep work at nana's today. By the way, did I tell you what she said to me when we were on the back porch?"

She shakes her head as she's filling the tub. "No. Do I want to know?"

"She asked me when I was going to move you in over here permanent."

"She cracks me up. We've been dating what, almost three months now? Nana is ready to have me move in. Wait, did she mean get married and move in or just move in? I never can tell with her."

I slide down in the tub and watch her while she undresses. "I don't know. With Nana some days she all *rebel without a cause* and then at times she *that's not what a good Christian girl would do.*"

She steps over into the tub, sitting down with her back on my chest. "She's funny, she told me today that she couldn't wait to see me big and pregnant in the kitchen with you."

I choke for a second. "Pregnant."

She laughs. "Yeah imagine my surprise too. I told her that was a long time away."

We both laugh and lay back relaxing in the tub. It's only later when the water gets cold that I realize we both dozed off. I kiss her shoulder. "Babe we gotta get in bed." She turns on her side and mumbles something against my chest. I kiss her forehead. "Hey beautiful, come on. I need you to lean up and then I'll carry you."

She finally leans up so I can take her and myself to bed. Placing her gently on my bed, I slide in next to her and she cuddles against my chest. My heart feels like it is going to explode. *I love her and I really do want to go to sleep and wake up like this for the rest of my life.*

~*~*~

I hear my Nana's voice from the porch. She's talking to Scarlet and Naomi while Dad, Nelson and I watch the turkey. "I don't know why they didn't come up with frying turkey's sooner, at least this way men would've been helping out longer. Give them something with fire outside and all of a sudden cooking turns into 'doin' man shit.'"

I chuckle. "Nana I'd be happy to let you take over out here if you'd like."

"No I'm good up here. I don't want to get all sweaty before my company shows up."

"Who in the hell is your company?" My dad asks.

"Well, Mr. Beck and Mr. Fitzgerald are going to be having dinner with us."

"Nana, really, two guys at once! And you always talked about me."

Scarlet looks at me and points. "Ryder, it's really none of your business. If Nana wants to invite half of the damn town out here."

Naomi and Nelson are both snickering and my dad is just standing there with his hands in his pockets. Nana looks at me with a death glare. "Ryder Abbott, I am 80 years old, and I didn't say that they were my dates. I said they were my company. Now, they are both widowers who have children that have moved off and left here. I know that they are both sweet on me and I can't help that, but I'll be damned if that stops me from feeding them. When you get to be my age, companionship and friends can be your lifeline."

"Nana, I'm sorry, it's just weird sometimes. Dad and I go out into town and these two old men are sending you everything from vegetables to homemade shine."

"I know sweetheart, but when you get old you like to give stuff to the people who mean the most to you. You like to do nice things for them. I have you, your daddy, Judd, Naomi, Nelson and now the lovely Scarlet to do things for. But those two old men don't have anyone but me and the rest of our senior citizens group. So they share with all of us, they share vegetables and moonshine with their buddies at the VFW just like they do me." She sits back in her rocking chair. "Now I know I'm a catch, but really I just think they are being friendly more than anything else." She slaps her hand on the chair arm. "And speaking of doing things for people that you love. Naomi I made some peanut brittle to send to Judd."

I shake my head. Naomi smiles. "That's sweet, Nana. I'm getting his Christmas package together now. I vacuum sealed some cookies and banana nut bread already."

I tilt my head up to the porch. "Momma N. I've got some stuff to put in that package too. I'll give it to you tomorrow."

The mood has suddenly shifted. I can tell that everyone is thinking about Judd. I miss him so much. Growing up without siblings he was the closest thing that I had to one and with all the other weird shift that happened in my life he's always stood by me. This year will be the first Christmas that we won't be seeing each other.

"Ryder! Did you hear me boy?" I didn't realize that I'd spaced out.

"Sorry Nana, I kinda zoned out for a minute. What were you saying?"

"I was saying that when you take the stuff to Naomi tomorrow I have some canned fruit to send him."

"Nana, this canned fruit. It wouldn't happen to be homemade wine, would it? You know he can get into trouble for that."

She sits there rocking in her chair, laughing like rules don't apply to her. It's according to the jars look like actual canned fruit. If they do look close enough, then he might get away with it. If I look at them and think he'll get into trouble then, I'll never tell her I didn't put it in there. I don't want him to get into trouble.

Chapter 25

Scarlet

Watching Ryder interact with his family and talk about Judd makes me miss Gable. I feel bad because I know that there is no comparison to what Judd is doing, but I still miss him. Spending yesterday and today with nana has been the greatest time, even without Gable being here. I hope I get to spend more time like this. As much as I never wanted to admit it, I was never this close to Dustin's family. They saw me as more of an employee, which was technically true, but in the same respect, I was their son's girlfriend, too. I was never invited to family functions like this.

After the guys finish the turkey, we come back into the house. Naomi and I start setting the table. I really like Judd's momma, she is so sweet and caring. She treats Ryder like he's her son. Nana's friends have arrived and are currently arguing about some show on T.V., they are funny. After we get everything on the table, Mr. Abbott calls everyone in there. Ryder grabs my hand motioning for me to sit beside him.

Mr. Abbott sits down at the head of the table. "Before we eat let's bless the food." We bow our heads, Ryder and I hold hands as his father speaks. "Dear Lord thank you for the many blessing you have given this family, thank you for wonderful friends. Help us remember the loved ones who have gone home to be with you Lord. Be with Judd as he protects this great nation we call home. Please bless the food we are about to eat and the people who helped to prepare it. In Jesus name Amen."

I look up to see Nana and Naomi wiping their eyes. Mr. Abbott looks at everyone and says, "Alright y'all, let dig in."

As everyone is wrapping up with their food, Ryder suddenly stands up. He looks down at me. "I have a surprise for you."

I can feel the heat creeping up on my face. "Okay." Everyone is staring at me now.

Nana speaks up. "Ryder son, you are making her nervous."

"Oh sorry. I didn't mean to. It's just I can't wait any longer to tell you this."

I'm really freaking out now.

He puts his hand on my shoulder. "Scar it's okay. I know that you've been missing Gable a lot lately. So he and I have been texting each other. The band is playing up in Hilton Head this this weekend and we are going to see them."

I jump up out of my seat and wrap my arms around him. I'm crying big tears. "Oh My God! Ryder I love you. I have missed him so much, I can't believe you two have been working on this together." Suddenly I remember the rest of the people at the table. "Oh I'm sorry."

Naomi smiles. "Don't be. It's sweet how much you love your brother, and Ryder, that was so sweet of you." She stands up and walks over to him and hugs him. "I'm so proud of you and the man you're becoming."

~*~*~

Ryder and I have spent so much time together over Thanksgiving break. He's convinces me to spend every night with him, or he keeps me there so late that I fall asleep. I'm so excited that we are leaving this morning for Gable's show. I'm curious to see how Gable is doing, he's been so quiet on the phone lately. There is something going on and I intend on getting to the bottom of it when I see him.

My phone alerts that I have a text from an unknown number. "You should have learned by now to keep your mouth shut." I don't know who it's from, but my phone dings again with a pic of Gable's car after the wreck.

I'm scared. I've been having a bunch of hang-up phone calls lately from unknown numbers and I've tried to play it off. The other day on my way out to Ryder's I swore I thought someone was following me and now this text that I know for a fact was sent to me. But what would I need to keep my mouth shut about?

A knock at my front door startles me. I look through the window and see Ryder. I open the front door and hug him. He chuckles. "Hey I could use greetings like that all the time. You ready to go?"

"Yes!" Maybe while I'm out of town I can figure out who sent me that message.

I read my kindle most of the way to Hilton Head because Ryder is on the phone with Nelson trying to figure out why some of the smaller cows are sick.

We arrive at the hotel the band is staying in. I knock on Gable's door expecting him, Stoney or Keeg to answer the door, but it's Ivie the bass player and Gable's singing partner. She's in one of his t-shirts, I know it's his shirt because I bought it. What the hell? She smiles. "Hey Scar, Gable's in the shower." As if she can sense I'm trying to figure this out, she looks back at me. "The hotel was short on rooms last night so Gable bunked with me. Normally he and I both get rooms to ourselves."

"Oh okay." She's trying to steer clear of something. So I'm just going to leave it for now. About that time Gable comes out of the bathroom in a towel and Ivie slips by him with her overnight bag into the bathroom.

He tightens his towel acting a little uncertain I can tell, but he steps over to hug me. "Hey baby sister, I've missed you so much."

I smile hugging him tightly. "I've missed you too."

I point to the bathroom door where I can hear the shower running, "You wanna explain more about that?"

He shakes his head. "No, we are in the same band, we crash in the same room sometimes." He shrugs his shoulders. "Hotel was out of rooms, normally we get three because I'm not sleeping in the room with Keeg and Stoney. Neither is Ivie. They are always dragging some skanks back to the room and they both are messy as hell."

I laugh thinking about the kind of women those two would bring back. I also notice that although both beds look like they've been messed up, only one looks slept in. I shake my head, I'm not going to pry anymore. I know Gable is private, but damn he knows Ivie has issues. I mean don't get me wrong, she's been in their band forever, she's an awesome singer and bass player, but she has this way of finding crazy. I've only heard stories about her exes and her parents, but it's enough.

Gable slides on some boxer briefs under his towel, pulling the towel off he steps over and shakes Ryder's hand. "Hey man how was the drive up?"

"It was good man. Didn't get much time to talk to Scar because I had to deal with some business calls, but she got some reading done."

Gable flops down on the bed. "So, what do you guys wanna do today?"

I flop down next to him. "I don't care, I'm just excited to get to spend some time with you."

"Well I have to be at the venue by three so we can go grab some lunch and just hang out." He stands up to slide on some jeans. "I wish I had more time, but I'll see you in a few weeks at Christmas. I'll be home for a few days then." Walking over he taps on the bathroom door and Ivie cracks it open. He steps inside and shuts the door. I hear them speak in hushed tones. He steps out and she closes the door back.

I look over at him with a cocked brow. "What was that all about?"

"Nothing I was just telling her where I'd be, in case the guys ask."

"Oh alright, well let's go." I have a feeling that is utter and complete bullshit but my thoughts are interrupted by my phone ringing, I look down at it. Unknown again. I ignore it for now. I'll talk to Ryder about this later. Right now I want to spend time with Gable.

Ryder looks at me. "You good?"

I smile. "Yeah guys, let's go, I'm starving. You didn't feed me this morning."

"You said you weren't hungry."

I push his shoulder. "Whatever. Let's go dill weeds."

Gable pulls me into a somewhat headlock. "Why are you calling me a dill weed? This is the first time you've seen me in months and I'm taking you to get some food."

I hug him around his waist. "You're not. Let's go."

He kisses me on top of the head. "I'm glad you're here kid."

"Me too."

Chapter 26

Ryder

Scarlet seems to keep staring at her phone. She's keeping something from me. I can see it in her eyes. They always say that the eyes are the windows to the soul, hers are definitely the windows to whatever is going on with her.

"Sir what can I get you?" The waitress breaks me from my thoughts.

"Oh you two go first."

Gable laughs. "We already did."

"Oh shit. Sorry. I'll have a sweet tea and the French dip with steak fries."

Gable laughs. "Dude, are you here with us?"

I chuckle. "Yeah, just thinking about work."

Scarlet grabs my hand. "Is Button okay? Is he one of the cows sick?"

I shake my head. "No baby. I'm sure Nelson would have told me."

Gable looks at us. "Who is Button?"

Scarlet gives her big beautiful smile. "Button is my baby cow. Well kinda anyway."

Gable looks at me with confusion on his face. I explain. "When some of my cows had calves a few months ago, Scarlet fell in love with one that had to be bottle fed. So I gave him to her."

Gable rolls his eyes. "So you gave my sister a cow? I guess steak is a pretty awesome gift."

Scarlet looks at him like he just told her that Van Gogh was a two bit hack. "Excuse me. My Button isn't steak. He will never be steak. He is going to die from old age."

Gable shakes his head. "Man she's got you over a barrel on that one."

"Hey, I don't care as long as she's happy. I'd give her twenty cows to keep as pets."

Gable shakes his head. "Never thought I'd see the day."

Scarlet looks up at him. "What day?"

"The day my little sister actually fell in love and had some poor guy all in knots about her."

"Hey man I never thought I'd see the day that a girl even had me near in knots, but there is something about Scarlet. She has this power over me."

Gable laughs. "Obviously. You followed her ass all the way to Cade's place. How did that meeting go?"

I laugh. "Well I have to admit when his big ass answered the door, I was a little intimidated. But he's a cool guy and his friends were awesome."

Scarlet smiles. "They hit it off. Don't let him fool you though, he drooled over Cade and his friends once he figured out they were some kind of football Gods or something."

Gable laughs. "Yeah, Cade's pretty cool and his friends are awesome. We didn't know him during all the football stuff so I guess it's weird for us how people think he's some sort of star."

"Dude, a star? No, people thought he and his friends were all going to be first round draft picks. I can understand why they decided not to be though. So yeah, they were awesome."

Gable and Scarlet laugh at me getting so worked up.

We wrap up lunch later and head to the hotel so Gable can get to the venue on time and we can get checked into our room.

~*~*~

As Scarlet and I get ready for the concert, her phone goes off again. She looks at it and tosses it on the bed.

"Scarlet what's going on? You have been staring at that phone all day."

"I was going to wait until we were back home but I keep getting these unknown number hang-up calls and I thought nothing of it. But this morning I got this text." She pulls it up on her phone and hands it to me.

When I read the text I'm beyond pissed. "Who in the hell do you think is sending you this stuff?"

She looks scared. "I don't know. I don't know who would think I'm saying stuff about them. I mean I really hadn't thought much about the phones calls. The wreck freaked me out, but I was really starting to think that maybe it was just someone who was too drunk. But now I'm really starting to freak out. The hang up calls were creepy, but now with that text it's just-."

She's starting to cry. "Baby I know and we are going to figure out who is doing this. What about the bar? You know the wreck did happen after work. Maybe some of those guys thought you saw something."

"Well I saw the owner and one of those nasty guys doing lines, but I never said anything."

I pull her into my arms. "It's okay baby we'll figure it out. Let's just go to your brother's concert and worry about all of this crazy shit after we get home. It's obvious whoever is doing this is from Savannah so we don't have to worry about them here."

She nods. "Okay just let me get my purse."

~*~*~

On the way to the concert I look over at her. "Hey so what's up with your brother and that chick in his room?"

She shakes her head. "I don't know, you heard him today. He says they are just bandmates, but I think there is more to it. But the way Gable is, if he doesn't want to talk about it, he's not going to."

"What's so bad about her?"

"Nothing. Well I mean she's a good person, it's just drama follows Ivie where ever she goes. Her parents were crazy, like my life seems tame compared to hers. Her mom ran off when she was in elementary school, with a pit boss from Biloxi or something. Then when she was around 15, her dad got locked up for smuggling drugs, money, people. Whatever he could in and out of the ports at home. She had to go live with her Aunt, that had like five kids already and Ivie was always considered a pain in her ass. But she brought some of it on herself. Any guy who was covered in tattoos, had been picked up for something by the cops. Basically anything she could do to drive her aunt insane, she did. When she was like 18, the guys met her at a party. Her aunt had just kicked her out for the final time, they started talking music, invited her over to listen to them and within a few weeks she was part of the band. She moved in with Stoney for a little while until she met some guy and it's been that way ever since. She moves in with a guy, when she moves out she stays at Stoney's."

"Yeah but I mean most of that was her years ago. What about now? I mean she doesn't seem to have a boyfriend now. Maybe she's outgrown some of that."

"Maybe but last account I had she was dating some blown up gym rat or something. The boys wouldn't say but I'm pretty sure he was running around on her and knocking her around."

"Damn that's sad. Seems like she's had it pretty rough."

"Yeah and I like her. I just worry about her being with my brother, that's all."

"Hey he's probably just being a friend to her, which it sounds like she could use a few of them."

"Yeah I guess you are right. It was just weird walking in that room today and her there like that." She shakes her head. "Whatever. Let's just go enjoy the concert."

"Sure, we can deal with all of the drama later."

She leans over and kisses me. "Sounds like a plan to me."

Chapter 27

Scarlet

Gable's concert last night was awesome. I know it won't be long before his band hits it big and are headlining their own shows. People were going crazy. They opened for Razor's Edge and they've had billboard chart toppers. So I know being around them has helped their publicity, but that place was balls to the walls crazy. I've never seen so many girls trying to get my brother's attention, hell there were some who even wanted Ivie's attention.

Now I'm heading back to my real world. I'm sad, I know I'll see Gable in a few weeks but I'll still miss him. That in combination with the fact that I have to go back home and figure out who in the hell is basically threatening and harassing me.

"Hey what are you in such deep thought about over there?"

I jump a little. "Oh I was just thinking about how crazy good Gable's show was last night."

"Yeah babe, they were pretty great. I think it won't be long and they'll be selling out venues all on their own. Don't get me wrong, Razor's Edge was great, but I actually liked the sound Gable's band had better. I like more of the old school rock sound they have, but with a sexy edge. Ivie's voice is like amazing."

"Yeah it is. So how do you think I can go about finding out who this is harassing me?"

"Well first of all I think we need to get your cell changed, but also I'm going to talk to the bastard that owns that bar."

"Please don't cause yourself any trouble. I mean both of us probably wouldn't look too favorable in the judge's eyes right now, if we got into trouble."

"Yeah well I'm not going to let someone threaten you or hurt you. Do you understand me?"

"Yes I do. I just think we need to be smart about this."

He takes my hand. "We will, I promise."

The rest of our ride home is quiet, I nap, while Ryder, bless heart, talks to his dad and Nelson on the phone about farm stuff.

I wake up as we are pulling down the drive to Ryder's house. "Babe I needed to go by my house and get some clothes, my car. I have stuff to do tomorrow."

"Yes I know, which is why your mom packed some of your things and dropped them and the car off at my house. Plus she's going out of town again, and until this mess is sorted out, you are not staying alone."

"Did she say where she was going? Hell she tells you more than she's ever told me."

"Well I actually ask her. She's going up to Augusta, something about a meeting with some of the people from her retreats. She knows I don't like you staying alone so we have an understanding. She lets me know when she will not be in town and I always have an emergency contact number for her. I think your wreck scared the shit out of her, more than she lets on. She wants to know that someone is taking care of you."

"I've been doing a fairly decent job of taking care of myself for years. Why now is she so concerned?"

"Like I said, I think the wreck, and the fact that Gable is gone, and she depended on him more than she realized when it came to you. Plus, she knows that I love you and would never let anything happen to you. Now come on let's go inside. I know you are dying to go check on your cow."

I smile. "Yes I do."

My phone dings, I almost dread it until I see it's a text from Annabelle.

Has Ryder talked to Judd lately?

I look over to him. "Hey Annabelle is asking if you've talked to Judd lately."

"He told me their base would probably be on blackout for a few days, something to do with a sand storm coming in and some high rank officials coming through. Tell her don't worry they can continue sexting or Skype sex or whatever they are doing soon enough."

"Ugh." I text her back.

Ryder says that he told him his base would probably be on blackout for a few days because a sandstorm was coming in and high officials coming through. That you'll be able to continue whatever the hell it is you two are doing soon enough. LOL

My phone dings right back.

Okay it just worries me when we go on radio silence like this. Tell Ryder to get his damn head out of the gutter it's not like that between us. We had our fling, but he's my friend.

I text back.

Will do. We should do lunch this week I miss you.

K. Will do.

"She said get your mind out of the gutter, they are just friends, she was just worried about him. Which is true, she was going out on a date the other night. I guess he's been seeing someone in his unit from what she told me, he told her."

"I think he's killing time with someone in his unit. But whatever. Let's go out and check on your cow."
I clap like a little girl. "Okay. I know you think I'm silly because I love that damn cow so much."

He shakes his head. "No I don't." He kisses me. "I think it's cute."

~*~*~

We walk out to the barn and check on all the babies and their mommas. I check on Button who will still eat straight out of my hand. Nelson and Ryder talk about the cows that got sick. It seems they are all fine now and that it was narrowed down to one shipment of bad feed that was delivered.

I'm rubbing Button when Ryder walks up behind me and puts his hands around my waist. "Hey you ready to go inside and settle in for the night? I'm kinda tired and I have to meet Nelson out here at 4 in the morning."

I lean back into him. "Sure, let me get Button his treat and I'll be ready."

He laughs. "Okay, get him his treat."

After getting Button a treat and closing the gate, Ryder and I make our way back to the house.

As we enter the bedroom, Ryder turns quickly and picks me up, I instinctively wrap my legs around his waist. "What are we doing?"

He grins. "Shower. Because you are a very dirty girl."

He carries me in the bathroom. "Oh I'm a dirty girl? Well I think you are a very dirty little boy."

He grins as he sits me on the counter. "Baby you know there isn't anything little about me."

I slide off the counter and strip out of my clothes while I watch him strip. As soon as his boxer briefs come off I drop to my knees and take him in my mouth. That damn piercing does it for me every time.

"Shit babe. That feels awesome." He pulls me up and I let go with a pop sound. "But before I blow I want to fuck you in my shower."

I squeal as he turns the water on. It's so cold my nipples automatically perk up until they almost hurt. He takes one of them in his mouth roughly as he thrusts into me. "Oh God Ryder." I feel his piercing inside me. It always drives me right to the edge as soon as it hits the spot. "Ryder I'm about to come."

"Good because I'm so fucking turned on this won't be my best time. This is definitely going to be a quickie."

We come together, he sits down on the shower bench. I'm still straddling his lap. "I love you Ryder."

"I love you too babe."

Chapter 28

Ryder

"Damn boy you look rough." Nelson chuckles when I walk through the barn doors at four in the morning.

"Thanks, you look like one big freakin' ray of sunshine yourself."

"Hey. You should be in a good mood if you're tired for the reasons I'm guessing you are tired from."

I laugh. "Thanks Nelson." If he only knew that I got about two hours of sleep because we couldn't seem to get enough of each other and when my alarm went off I really could've went another round with her, but I didn't have time.

I spend the morning going around with Nelson to our different farms. We are checking the feed shipments to see if any are from the same group that caused the cows at home to get sick.

Which I can't stop worrying about Scarlet and whoever is threatening her.

We pull into a small café to grab some lunch. Once we sit down he looks at me. "So are you going to tell me what's goin' on in that head of yours? I see the worry all over your face. Your daddy gets the same look."

"That obvious huh?"

"Yeah. Look, I know Judd is who you normally talk to. I know that you don't trust many people, and truthfully son, I can't blame you. But why don't you give me a shot at the job until Judd gets back home?"

I nod. "Okay." While we eat our blue plate special I explain to him all that's happened to Scarlet.

"I agree son. We need to figure out some way to get to the bottom of it." He looks at me curiously. "I do have one question. Do you think whoever is doing this might be involved in the cows getting sick?"

I shake my head. "No, it seems like that was narrowed to the one shipment of feed, plus you know there is so much security footage of the farm, I think we'd have caught something."

He nods. "I get your point. So what are you going to do about Scarlet?"

"Well, we are going to change her phone number and I'm going by to talk to that asshole she used to work for."

"Don't get yourself in trouble Ryder. The judge may not be so lenient next time."

"Yeah I know. She said the same thing."

"Well listen to her. I'll tell you a secret son. When it comes to common sense, women are mostly right. After twenty-five years of marriage, I'll admit that."

I laugh and shake my head. "Thanks Nelson. For the record, you listen and give out advice like Judd."

"Huh, I taught him everything he knows."

~*~*~

I pull into the parking lot of Silver Moon. It's still kinda early so I know there won't be many people in the bar. As I walk in I see the older lady working that I remember working with Scarlet. "Hey, is Danny in?"

Lana looks up. "Yeah, he's in the back, we aren't open yet, though."

"Well, I need to speak with him. It's a private matter."

She tosses the bar towel on the counter and takes off toward the back. "Fine."

A few minutes later Danny comes out from the back looking pissed. "So what can I do for you?"

"Well it seems my girlfriend Scarlet was ran off the road after she left work here one night. Also she's been getting some very harassing phone calls and texts. You or maybe your "clients" know anything about that?"

"What exactly are you getting at boy?"

I lean onto the bar. "I think you know exactly what the fuck I'm getting at."

"I think you might want to get the fuck out of here before you have to be carried or the ambulance needs to be called."

Lana steps in. "Hey, look here, Danny might be a dickhead, but he'd never hurt that girl."

"What about that asshole who groped the shit out of her one night and then she saw him cutting lines with Danny here? What about him?"

Danny braces himself on the bar. "Look you tell her to forget she saw that and I'll check with that guy to make sure he leaves her alone. Another piece of advice son. Don't waltz up into a place like this with that attitude or they may have to search to find your body. You get me?"

I flip him off as I'm walking out the door. "Yeah. Yeah. I fucking get you, I'm just not scared."

I storm out to my jeep, never looking back at the bar. I tear out of the parking lot throwing gravel everywhere.

I decide to stop at a small jewelry store on the way home. The lady behind the counter stops me. "Sir Can I help you find something?"

"I don't really know what I'm looking for yet. I want to get my girl something special for Christmas."

"Like perhaps an engagement ring?"

"Ugh no, we aren't quite there yet. Don't get me wrong, we will get there, but I don't want to scare her off."

"Well. Have you thought about maybe an open heart necklace or a promise ring?"

"What exactly is a promise ring?"

"Well it's kinda like a pre-engagement ring. It's basically saying that you want to commit yourself to her and her alone, but that you guys aren't quite at the engagement stage yet."

"That sounds perfect. Let me look at those."

I look around at some small rings. I pick one finally that is a simple infinity band with our initials inside of it.

I'm so pumped from ordering her ring that I decide to stop by a small local florist and grab her some flowers. I know she's gonna be pissed with me when she finds out that I showed my ass like that, so call it a little extra.

I walk in looking at the small bouquets of spring flowers. She's not a rose's kinda girl.

As I reach in the cooler to grab another bouquet to look at, I hear someone snicker behind me. "Well well well, if it isn't Ryder Abbott, boyfriend of the year."

I turn around to see Kelsie. "I'll take that title."

She puts her hand on her hip and sneers. "So how exactly does a guy go from being one of the biggest whores I know to being head over heels in love?"

"I guess it's all about finding the right girl."

"Yeah well Scarlet certainly seems to find the right guys with the right amount of money every time."

"She doesn't care about my money."

"Yeah, well trust me, I think she's killing time with you until Dustin gives her a chance again."

"I don't think she'd give him the time of day."

"Hmm I guess you never know."

I grab the bunch of flowers and turn for the counter. "Here's the thing, I think I do."

After paying, I go out to my jeep and make my way across town to the small campus she is at today.

I find a spot close by her car and wait for her to come out of class. I spot her walking with a guy. A guy that just happens to be Dustin. I almost explode when I see them hug and he kisses her on the cheek.

They smile and wave to each other as they are parting ways and I'm at my boiling point by the time she makes her way to me.

She walks up smiling and I can't help it. This whole situation just pisses me off.

"What the fuck was that about Scarlet?"

Chapter 29

Scarlet

Needless to say Dustin was the last person I expected to be waiting for me outside of my class but here he is.

"What do you want Dustin?"

"Look Scar I don't want anything. I just have a few things to say."

"Yeah well I really don't want to listen to them."

"I'm sorry."

I spin around and throw my hands out. "You're sorry. That's all you can come up with."

"Just stop for a second so I can say what I have to say."

"Fine but you are walking with me I have shit to do. This better be damn good."

He looks terrible I notice for the first time since he stepped in front of me. "Look I will never be able to apologize enough for what you walked in on. I never meant for you to find out that way. The Kelsie part was all Brandon. In case you haven't heard by now, Brandon has pretty much always called the shots in my life. He's upset with me right now because I decided to come out to my parents."

"You what? Your daddy will cut you off."

"I know, but I'm tired of living like this. Anytime I get pissed off with Brandon he threatens to out me to my parents. I'm tired of the way he treats me and treats people I care about. At least if I tell them how I feel then he has nothing over me. I can walk away."

I stop him and touch his arm. "Are you sure about this?"

"Yeah I am. Mostly I wanted to stop and talk to you today because I know I should have said something to keep you out of jail. Don't get me wrong I was pissed that you took your anger out on my car. But I kinda get it and I really should've said something."

"It's a little late but thank you."

"I'm sorry you almost lost your scholarship and that you had to do community service and all."

"Well. The scholarship I was pissed over. The community service wasn't bad. I got to help a great family have their own home. I also met the love of my life."

"Ryder?"

"Yeah. At first I thought he was a huge prick. Now I can't imagine my life without him."

"Wow. We dated for a long time and I never heard you talk about me with that tone of voice and the light in your eyes. I'm glad you've found happiness."

"Thank you. I hate to cut this short but I really do need to get going call me soon and we'll do coffee or something."

He leans in and give me a hug and kiss on the cheek. "Sure thing, but after I tell my parents you might have to buy the coffee."

I smile. "Can do. We'll talk soon."

I make my way to my car and I see Ryder's jeep parked by it. I smile and almost start running to see him. You'd think after the love fest we had going on last night that I'd be tired of him. But I'm not. As I approach him I notice the look he has on his face.

"What the fuck was that about Scarlet?"

"What was what about?"

"Your ex-boyfriend."

"It was nothing. He was apologizing for everything."

"Oh he was apologizing. I saw you hugging him, what are you going back to him now?"

"What the hell are you talking about? We were having a civilized conversation. Which is more than I can say for the one you and I are having."

"I guess Kelsie's warnings were right about you."

That is a deep cut. "Why in the fuck are you talking to Kelsie about me anyway?"

"I stopped to get you these fucking flowers and ran into her. She told me if Dustin ever came around again and gave you the time of day you'd go running back."

I feel like my body is on fire I'm so pissed. "You know what, Ryder? I know that woman fucked you up when you were young and you don't trust women, but I've never given you a reason not to trust me so you can go to hell."

"What are you talking about my issues with women?"

"Nelson told me. He told me about the lady that dated your dad."

"That was none of your fucking business."

"Well you know what? It's obvious you don't trust me, you are acting like I had sex with a man, who is gay by the way, outside of school and I have to get to an art lecture at the main campus tonight. So just leave me alone."

He growls but I don't hear a word he says because I slam my car door and fly out of the parking lot.

I see flowers flying all over the parking lot in my rearview mirror.

How dare he think that little of me? I wasn't the one who was the whore he was. What the fuck was he doing talking to Kelsie anyway?

I call Annabelle on the way to campus and fill her in on the events that just happened minus the part about the lady molesting Ryder. That's his business. She's furious like me. We decide to meet for lunch tomorrow as I reach the main campus.

This is a big art lecture and anyone in my program has to attend so the parking lot is slammed. I finally find a parking spot, and knowing I'm going to be a few minutes late, getting in there I rush out of my car and start walking fast toward the lecture hall.

My phone starts ringing and I see its Ryder. I ignore it I'm not in the mood to talk to him tonight. I'm going home to a nice bubble bath when I get done here.

I finally reach the door to the hall and it is locked. I notice a sign stating that the door is broken go around to the emergency exit.

As I round the corner my phone starts buzzing. I throw it in my bag and suddenly someone grabs my arm.

I look up half expecting it to be Ryder. But it's not and it's not someone I expected to see.

"What in the hell?"

After the words came out of my mouth I felt a dull ache in my head and I start blacking in and out. I overhear him saying. "You should've kept your mouth shut you fucking cunt."

My head feels so heavy. I can't seem to stay awake as he throws me over his shoulder. Then I'm out.

I wake up tied to a chair in a simple loft apartment from the looks of it. It's all very confusing.

"Ah I see you're awake."

I refuse to answer him.

"Are you going to ignore me or are you going to talk to me. Since you obviously like to run your mouth so much about matters that don't concern you."

"Go to hell."

"Now Scarlet that's not nice. I was hoping that it wouldn't come to this. I thought maybe your accident would make you see things in a new light or kill you I was okay with either."

"Fuck you."

A slap cracks across my face. "You have ruined my life you whore."

I spit some blood out. "I'm not the whore here you are, so you can go to hell Brandon."

Chapter 30

Ryder

Why in the hell won't she at least answer her phone and argue back with me? I caught Dustin as he was coming out of the coffee shop next door to SCAD and I punched him in the face. That's when he stopped me and explained that what I saw was exactly what Scarlet said it was. I'm so fucking stupid how could I not listen to her and listen to Kelsie. I lost my damn mind when she brought up what Francis did to me as a child. I shiver as I remember my first betrayal by her.

"Ryder you want your daddy to be a happy man don't you?"

I looked at the rug in my room. "Yes ma'am."

"Well if I stay your daddy will be happy. Now I need you to do something for me. Will you do that Ryder to keep me happy so I can keep your daddy happy?"

"Yes ma'am."

She sat on my bed. "Come here." I walked over and sat down she ran her fingers through my hair. "You are going to break hearts someday." She ran her hand down my chest and to my eleven year old penis. She started rubbing me through my pants. "Do you feel funny Ryder?" I nod, because I do. "Well good. Now give me your hand." She takes my hand and puts it under her skirt. All of a sudden I'm dizzy and my penis shoots stuff out in my pants. She smiles. "Good job now this is our secret. Go get cleaned up." I nod and make my way to the bathroom.

Bringing myself back to the matter at hand. It's freaking 10 o'clock at night, I know she said she had a thing for school, that's why I tried to get her before she went in but she should be done by now. I really pissed her off this time. I'll just text her and hope she forgives me.

Baby I'm so sorry please give me a chance to say this in person. I had a lot going on today and Kelsie fucked with my head. When I saw Dustin touch you I just went crazy. I should never have even spoken to her. I'm so sorry. I love you, please forgive me. I'll let you rest tonight but I'm coming to see you tonight and we are going to talk about all of this. I am going to beg and you are going to feel sorry for me. I love you. I love you I love you.

I get nothing back. I go into the den and make myself a scotch and water. My phone rings. I snatch it up thinking its Scarlet, but its Judd.

"Hey man."

"Hey you don't sound so happy to hear from me asshole."

"I just had a really shitty day and I need to talk to Scarlet, but she's not answering my calls or texts. I think I really fucked it up this time man."

"Man what the fuck did you do?"

I start explaining to him the events of the day up to me talking to Dustin.

"Dude you really fucked up. You know better than to listen to that bitch Kelsie. Why would you even think to let her get inside your head like that?"

"I know I'm fucking stupid."

"Yep you are. Have you talked to Annabelle lately?"

"Yeah she asked me had I heard from you, but that was when you said your base would be on blackout for a few days so I told her not to worry. Why what's up?"

"I don't know man. We are friends and I know we agreed to stay that way, but something about knowing she's going on dates and talking to other guys makes me angry."

I laugh. "Dude you have a thing for her. But you can't be pissed with her. You already told me you're hooking up with some random girl in your unit."

"I'm not fucking talking about that right now. I don't have enough time on the phone. Just make sure she's okay for me. She hasn't really been in touch much."

"Sure man, I'm sure before this is all over with between me and Scarlet she'll be over here to kick my ass. So I'll let you know."

"Shit look man I gotta go, we are pulling out for a mission. I'll be out of touch for a few weeks probably till closer to Christmas. My mom is going to be worried so look in on her."

"Will do man. Stay safe. Keep your head down and all that shit."

"Roger."

I have a few drinks and finally head to bed. Maybe the alcohol will help me sleep. Sliding into my bed it feels so lonely without her. I went from never having a person besides myself in here to having to have Scarlet in my bed. I start to realize my drinks are catching up with me. I roll over to her pillow and smell the coconut scent of her hair.

~*~*~

Waking up this morning I feel just as alone as I did when I went to sleep. I walk into my bathroom and I smell her again. I see her hair crap all over my vanity. I grab some aspirin and take a shower. I'm going over to take her to breakfast and we are going to talk. She's going to let me grovel and apologize. Then she's coming home with me and I'm probably not going to let her leave my house again.

After I slide some jeans and a shirt on, I grab my phone off my dresser. Still no text or calls from her. After I put my boots on I jog out to my jeep and head over to her place.

Pulling up I notice her car isn't in the driveway. Shit this is like before. I wonder if she went to Cade's again. But I know she has projects due, she wouldn't leave town with those due.

I call Annabelle.

"What do you want, fucktard?"

"Have you talked to Scarlet?"

"Yeah I talked to her yesterday right after you basically called her a slut."

"I didn't call her a slut."

"Anyway, we are supposed to go to lunch today."

"Well, I can't find her this morning. She's not at home and she won't answer her phone or even a text. Do you know where she is?"

"No she's probably just avoiding you."

"Thanks Annabelle, you've been so much help." I say with sarcasm dripping from my tongue.

"For the record, I hope you can make it up to her because you guys are good together when you don't have your head up your ass."

"Thanks Annabelle. I appreciate it. By the way Judd called me last night he said that we wouldn't hear from him until closer to Christmas."

"Okay thanks for the info." Her voice sounds hollow as she hangs up.

I pull in at the florist I bought flowers at the other day. I buy two bouquets of spring flowers and drop them on her door step with a note.

Scar- I love you. When you are ready to talk I am too. Love Ryder

I need to head home and look in on the cows. Nelson had an appointment today.

Now it's 3 in the afternoon and she still hasn't called me, I'm starting to get a little pissed off. You'd think she'd at least call me and tell me to go to hell.

My phone rings. It's Cade, probably telling me to quit harassing his sister.

"Hey Cade."

"Hey I can't get ahold of Scarlet and campus security is calling me. They said her car has been there all night and it's had tickets issued. They've tried to get in touch with her to let her know it's about to be towed, but she hasn't been in class either. I asked them to wait until someone can get there to check it out. "

"Why in the hell is her car still there?"

"I don't know genius that is why I'm calling you. Where is she?"

"I don't know, we had an argument yesterday. I've been trying to talk to her but she won't answer my calls."

"Well go down there and check the car see if something's wrong with it. Maybe that is the reason it's still parked there."

"Okay. I'm already in my jeep driving that way. I'll call you when I get there."

Ten minutes later I'm pulling into the campus parking lot and see her Infiniti. As I walk around the car I can tell it's been here overnight. I walk toward the big lecture hall and start calling her phone. As soon as I round the corner I hear my ringtone *Ladies Love Country Boys*. I keep looking for her until I see her phone in a hedge by the door.

I call Cade back.

My heart starts racing as he answers. "Hey Ryder you talk to her?"

I'm already running back to my jeep. "I think we have a problem. Her car looks fine, but I just found her phone in a hedge by the lecture hall."

I hear him slamming things in the background. "Call the cops NOW! I'm heading that way. I'll call Gable, you call Whisper."

I start up my jeep and start circling the campus just in case she's walking somewhere. "Okay."

I don't even realize the quiver in my voice until Cade speaks. "Ryder. We are going to find her man. Stay calm. I've been there man."

I wipe a tear that I didn't realize was running down my cheek. "Thanks."

Chapter 31

Scarlet

I wake up with a pounding headache. As I try to open my eyes I realize they are almost swollen shut. Then yesterday comes flying back to me. Last night.

"I'm not the whore here, you are, so you can go to hell, Brandon."

"You are such a stupid bitch Scarlet."

"I'm not scared of you. If you were a real threat to me, you wouldn't have to tie me up. You know that if I'm not tied up that I can kick your ass."

"No, you can't kick my ass. You are psycho and will grab something like an axe handle to assist in your efforts. I remember, I was there."

I chuckle. *"I'm psycho? Says the person who kidnapped me and has me tied to a chair, just so he can try to intimidate me. Because he can't beat me up otherwise."*

He draws back and punches me in the face. *"I fucking hate you. When Dustin started seeing you to cover for himself, I told him you were a mistake. He just planned to use you as a cover for a while and keep his parents from finding out. Then you actually became a friend to him."* He's pacing around the room. *"Here's the thing Dustin has always been MY best friend. I've always helped him cover up for his preferences. I always filled his needs so he didn't pick up any random townies to screw. Now all of a sudden after you went to jail he decides he wants to come out to his parents. What did you say to him Scarlet? Who were you going to tell? How did you blackmail him?"*

"I didn't say anything to him about it. Until today I haven't seen or heard from him since that night at Swampy Tonk."

"You're lying." Another crack to my face.

"No, I'm not, did you ever think he just wants to be honest about who he is? So that maybe he can have a real relationship with someone

other than you? Because if someone is using someone here, it isn't Dustin using you, it's you using him. It's your way of controlling him."

He punches me again. "YOU DON'T KNOW SHIT ABOUT IT! Now he's planning on coming out to his parents, they will tell my parents and we'll both be cut off. So Scarlet I'm going to ask you again. What are you threatening him with? Because he wouldn't come to this decision on his own."

"I told you nothing. You're sex life or love life has nothing to do with me."

"YOU LYING CUNT!" Then the lights went out.

~*~*~

"Ah so you decided to wake up." I look up to see Brandon and Kelsie standing there.

"What were you hoping I wouldn't?"

Kelsie shrugs. "Maybe."

I try to smirk. I won't let them break me. That's what they want. "Well you're probably too late because when I saw Dustin yesterday he had planned on coming out to his parents last night."

I see a look cross both of their faces. "Shut up you skank." Brandon sneers.

I'm going to either drive them crazy or they are going to kill me but I'm done with this. "So Kelsie, what's in all of this for you? Why do you need a relationship with two gay guys?"

Brandon glares at me. "I'm not gay!"

"Okay, bi-sexual, whatever."

"I'm not bi-sexual either, you dumb bitch."

I chuckle. "Oh I'm dumb. You drill another man in the ass and that doesn't qualify you as bi-sexual? Whatever."

Kelsie chimes in. "Brandon is going to marry me. Our two families are going to own this town. I'll keep his secrets and he'll keep mine. We'll have an open marriage and all of the money we want."

"No wonder Dustin is sick of the two of you. You guys are both real pieces of work."

Brandon's face turns red. "Dustin isn't sick of me! He worships me."

"So that's what it takes to be your friend, blackmail and worshiping you? Glad I never made the cut then."

He grits his teeth. "No you were always just temporary. We were almost done with you anyway, when you walked in that morning. So you just sped up the process and made us out to seem like victims of a crazy girl."

My head is still pounding. "Look, as you can well see, I don't want Dustin. I have a real man, who cares for me and loves me."

Kelsie laughs. "Oh really. Ryder Abbott care about someone other than himself. That would be a first. Oh wait he always cared about that poor boy he's friends with."

"Judd is serving our country, you need to shut up. Also I know what you chicken shits did and how Ryder took the fall."

I see Brandon throw his phone at the couch. "IT'S ALL FUCKING OVER!!!! Dustin did it. He actually came out to his parents last night. I just got several messages from my dad and his." He storms over to me and hits me so hard the chair flips over.

"We are both fucking cut off."

Kelsie looks at him. "You better figure out a way to fucking fix this Brandon. Call Dustin and make him tell them you weren't involved."

I see Brandon pick up his phone and dial. What the hell I'm gonna make sure he knows I'm here. "So Kelsie I guess this puts a damper on your plans huh?"

"Yeah well, if this doesn't work out, I can always go after Ryder. Like you said, he's a real man."

I'm going to get louder so Dustin might hear me. "Hell Dustin's a real man! He told the truth to his parents! YOU GUYS ARE FUCKING SELFISH SORRY EXCUSES FOR HUMANBEINGS!"

Brandon looks my way as he's speaking to Dustin on the phone. "No man." He looks at Kelsie and whispers. "Shut her up."

"WHY DO YOU WANT TO SHUT ME UP BRANDON?"

He slings the phone across the floor and storms over to me. He uprights the chair I'm in and stares at me. "I'm fucking done playing games with you. I fucking hate you and you've ruined my life."

"I didn't ruin your life. You're really fucking delusional."

He hits me hard, once again the chair goes over, but this time I land different and I hear a snap in my arm. Pain radiates through it, I see his foot coming at my face and then everything goes dark.

~*~*~

Sometime later in the distance I hear people screaming, but I just can't bring myself to care.

I'm tired and I hurt. I try to move but pain shoots up my arm and my head feels like it weighs a hundred pounds. I just want to sleep, sleep will be good.

Chapter 32

Ryder

I have looked all over this town for Scarlet. Annabelle and I have talked to the police, but since it hasn't quite been long enough for her to be considered a missing person. I thought it was crazy since her phone was found but they say that isn't enough to go on. Whisper and Cade are on their way here. Gable called me but they are in Seattle and he can't get a flight out because of fog. Cade and I both told him to just wait and we'd figure something out.

My phone starts ringing. I look down to see Dustin's number. Why in the hell is he calling me? I ignore it and Annabelle's phone starts to ring, she answers it.

"Yeah Dustin. Hold on."

She looks at me. "He says he has to talk to you right now, it's an emergency."

I grab the phone. "What?"

"Ryder have you talked to Scarlet?" There is a panic in his voice.

"We are trying to find her now. Do you know something?"

"I think Brandon has her. I called him earlier and I thought I heard someone screaming in the background and it sounded like her. Brandon is pissed because he can't control me anymore."

"Where does he have her?"

"I'm on my way there now. He has a small studio apartment just outside of town. I'll text you the address."

"Okay I'll meet you there." My heart is pumping so fast it's about to explode. "Annabelle get in the jeep. Dustin thinks Brandon has Scarlet."

She nods and starts raising all kinds of hell, but I can't pay attention, I have to get to Scarlet. I get the address for the apartment and I manage to pull up at the same time as Dustin. We get out and I see

Brandon's Audi. I start beating on the front door of the apartment. Dustin speaks up. "Brandon open the door!"

I hear Brandon behind the door. "Fuck you, Dustin!"

I look at Dustin and motion that we are going to knock the door in. I whisper for Annabelle to get at the bottom of the stairs and be ready with her phone. Dustin and I back up and slam into the door a couple of times before the hinges finally give. Brandon is on the other side still trying to keep us out.

As we finally get inside it's all a blur, I feel so much rage. I see Scarlet tied to a chair that has been knocked over on the floor. She's a bloody mess. I hear Annabelle scream.

I scream for her to call 911. I turn to see Brandon and Dustin having words. Words aren't going to cover this. I walk over to Brandon and start beating. I don't stop until the police and the paramedics are pulling me off of him.

I look around the room to see Dustin crying holding Scarlet, I guess he's untied her from the chair. I see the cops holding Annabelle. She's panting in anger. I see Kelsie's had the hell beat out of her and I can only imagine it was courtesy of Annabelle. The paramedics look at Brandon and determine he can see the doctor at the county jail for the few stitches he's going to need and to set his broken nose. I honestly think they just didn't want to deal with him. I run over to Scarlet. "Baby, I love you, please open your eyes. Let me see those beautiful eyes."

"Sir, she took quite a beating over several hours it sounds like. Let us just get her to the hospital to get checked out."

I nod. "I have to go with her."

He nods. I look over at Annabelle. "Here's my phone and the keys to my jeep. Call Cade, Whisper and Gable, tell them what's going on and to meet us at the hospital."

She nods through tears. "Okay. Do I need to call your Dad or anything?"

"No, he's out of town. Call Nelson, ask him to meet me too."

She nods. I look over at Dustin who looks lost and scared. "Dustin ride with Annabelle please." He nods as they are shutting the ambulance doors.

~*~*~

The ride to the hospital felt like it took forever. Once we got to the hospital, I was shuffled to a waiting room while they checked Scarlet out.

I'm worried because I couldn't get her to wake up the entire ride here. I talked to her, but she was beaten so bad, I'm worried. Her eyes were damn near swollen shut. The paramedic said her arm is broken they just don't know how badly, they had to have it x-rayed. I am so angry.

I look up as Whisper comes running in the waiting room door. Tears are pouring down her face. "Annabelle, Ryder what is going on?"

Annabelle hugs her. "We are waiting to find out. They said her arm is broken they just don't know to what degree."

Whisper walks over to me. "Oh Ryder you know I'm not for violence, but I hope you beat the hell out of that boy."

"Oh I did. I'm pretty sure that Annabelle took care of Kelsie too."

She sits down and shakes her head. "Why would they do this to her?"

Dustin sits down beside her and starts to explain the last few years. Which is a good thing, it makes time pass a little faster. We have found out they are doing surgery on her arm along with her nose. She has a cracked cheek and a couple of cracked ribs.

A few hours later Cade comes bursting in.

"Ryder. What the hell is going on man? Where's Gable?"

I stand up and do the guy hand shake half hug. "She's in surgery."

Whisper looks like she's seen a ghost. She stands up and walks over to Cade putting her hand on his face. "Your face looks just like his."

"Well I damn sure can't help that. I would if I could. You must be Gable and Scarlet's mom."

"Yes I am. Gable is still stuck in Seattle, they are fogged in but I told him just to stay put since we know now that she's not in critical danger. He's coming home in a few days anyway."

"What about the son of a bitch who did this to her?"

I put my hand on his shoulder. "I beat the shit out of him, until the cops and EMT's pulled me off of him. Little Annabelle over there did a number on the girl that was helping him."

"So was this the asshole who ran her off the road and had been harassing her?"

I nod. "Yeah, best we can put together."

Annabelle stands up and walks over. "So you are the brother I've yet to meet. Wow you're even more handsome than Gable." She giggles and then sticks her hand out. "It's nice to meet you. I'm Annabelle. Scarlet's best friend."

"Good to meet you. Glad you took care of a little girl justice on that other bitch."

She smiles. "Thanks."

"Trust me, one day you'll get to meet my wife and my step-sisters and you'll understand."

Suddenly the door opens and a doctor comes in. Whisper and I make our way over to him. "Ms. Johnson. I'm Dr. Hagan. I've reset her broken bones. She's going to be asleep a little longer. Even when she wakes up we'll probably give her some more meds to put her out for a while. She's going to be in some pretty bad pain. All the inflammation from the beating she took, along with the pain from surgery is going to hurt like the devil when she wakes up."

I look at him. "Thank you. What about her arm? Will she have full motion of it, I mean she's an artist? I've watched her sketch and paint with both hands but I know she's prefers the hand that is attached to the broken arm."

"With physical therapy and time, yes. Luckily she's young and that will help."

"Thank you so much." Whisper hugs him.

"If you would like to go visit her now, a couple at the time will be fine."

I look at him. "Where can I stay tonight? I'll be staying with her."

The doctor looks at Whisper. She smiles. "Yes I'm sure Ryder will be staying with her as well as myself."

I look at Nelson. "Will you please let Cade follow you out to the house and show him inside to the guest room?"

Cade steps over. "You don't have to do that man. I can grab a hotel room."

"No it's no big deal. The house is big and empty without Scar and I there."

He nods. "Okay I'm gonna go check on Scar. Then I am kinda tired so I'll take you up on your offer. But I'll be back first thing in the morning."

We make our way into her room and Whisper starts crying when she sees Scarlet's face. She brushes Scar's face. "Oh baby."

I walk over to her. "Whisper, you are exhausted. Why don't you let Annabelle take you home and I'll stay here. Come back tomorrow after some rest."

She looks into my eyes and nods. "Okay, I guess so."

After everyone visits I sit down beside Scarlet. "Baby I know I fucked up, please wake up and forgive me. I love you and I need you. Open those beautiful eyes and let me see them."

Chapter 33

Scarlet

I feel like my head is going to explode, I feel someone rubbing my hand. I try to move my arm and I can't move it. It hurts. "Ouch."

"Baby."

I try to open my eyes, but it's too hard. "I can't see. Ryder?"

"Yes baby your eyes are swollen pretty bad, just get some rest. The doctor said some of the swelling will be down tomorrow."

"Did they get him?"

"Baby, I beat the shit out of him and Annabelle kicked Kelsie's ass. I'm so sorry. I love you." I feel him kiss my face. "I love you so much. I was so scared when Cade called me."

I try to clear my throat. "Cade called you."

"It's a long story, the nurse is here to give you some meds. Get some rest, I'll be here when you wake up."

"You will?"

"Baby, after everything from today, I may never let you leave my sight again."

"I love you, too." I drift back off to sleep.

I wake up and am actually able to open my eyes a little. I can see Cade, my Mom and Annabelle standing there. "Hey." I keep looking for Ryder.

My mom smiles. "I made him go downstairs with Dustin and grab a bite to eat. He was worn out, but he wouldn't admit it."

I'm confused. "With Dustin?"

Annabelle chuckles. "I know you're confused, but Dustin is who led us to you yesterday."

Cade steps over to my bed. "Little sis you have to quit scaring the shit out of everyone like this."

"What are you doing here?"

"I'm here for my little sister. Yesterday was one of the scariest days of my life. I have to say one of because Daria's damn near given me a heart attack a few times."

A sudden movement from the door catches my attention. I look up to see Ryder. He crosses over to my bed. "Hey pretty girl. I'm glad to see you awake and able to open your eyes a little."

I nod. "Yeah. I feel kinda lost about the past couple of days."

"Don't worry, we'll get you caught up in time." My mom says from the corner of the room.

Ryder smiles at me again. "Right now all you need to know is that you are safe. Brandon and Kelsie are in jail. Now just focus on getting better."

I look around the room. "Um can I have a minute alone with Ryder?"

Everyone nods.

Ryder looks at me with fear and uncertainty in his eyes. "Baby if you are going to break up with me, now is not the time. I may just turn into a stalker."

I chuckle even though it hurts my tender face. "No. I just want you to know I understand we both said some things to each other and we have some talking to do, but right now I don't want you to leave my side."

He smiles. "Oh thank God. I was afraid you were going to wake up and say 'Get out of here dickhead and never look my way again' because I know that would be what I deserve after how I treated you the other day."

"Hey, we both got wound up and if I'd seen you talking to an ex and then hugging them, I would've probably lost it, too. I'm sorry I brought up your past. I shouldn't have done that."

"It's okay. I should've given you a minute to explain rather than just blowing up. I would want someone to give me a minute to explain and the benefit of the doubt. As far as my past goes, I wish it had been me that told you. But truth being told I probably would've chickened out and Nelson knew that. I know he would never tell someone I didn't trust."

"I know but I shouldn't have thrown it at you like that. We both just have insecurity issues we need to deal with. I think we both have some abandonment issues. While I was in and out during the time that Brandon had me tied up, all I could think about was that I might never get to see you again. That I may tell you how sorry I was. How much I love you."

He leans over me and kisses me gently on the lips. "I would give you a lot sexier kiss but your lips are pretty bruised. I'm going to let everyone back in here so I don't risk your safety."

I look up. "Risk my safety?"

"Because if we don't get some people in here, I'm going to try all of the positions that hospital bed offers. I will fuck you until everyone in this hospital knows you're mine. But right now you have guests and you are bruised. I'd be afraid I would hurt you. But just so you know, I want you."

Fuck, now I'm turned on and wet. My mother, brother and friends are about to walk in here. I have to find a way to calm myself down. Too late, my mom is walking through the door, just a talking. "Well Scarlet, the doctor says you can get out of here in the morning."

I smile. "That sounds great."

Ryder steps up. "She's coming to stay with me. Y'all are welcome to come see her anytime, but there are more people out at my house. There is me, dad, Nelson, Naomi and Nana Pearl. So she won't be alone."

My mom looks up at him. "I'm not sure about that Ryder."

He looks at her. "I am. You have to work, Gable is touring for another week, Cade has to go home and Annabelle has school. At my house there are people in and out all the time, and with Brandon being arrested, there is probably going to be press hounding her for a statement. I can control security at the farm."

"Momma, it'll be okay. I'll stay at Ryder's. He's right, there is someone there all the time without even trying. Plus that way I can be near my Button, I miss him."

My mom shakes her head. "Leave it to you to try and show reason for your argument with a pet cow."

"Look, the farm is beautiful so while I'm recovering, I can sit out back and sketch all day, with my good hand."

She nods. "I understand and I didn't think about reporters. But I'm going to be out there daily to check on you."

"I'm counting on it." I am really hoping. My mother has always been kinda flighty when it came to Gable and me. She was more about free love and doing whatever we want. Sometimes you just want a real mom.

Ryder smiles. "Well Nana is going to be excited, she'll be up there to take care of you. She has called me non-stop since Nelson told her about you being in here. She also threatened to beat my ass when she found out about our argument."

I laugh. "I bet she did. Nana's got my back."

Everyone chuckles.

I realize that I need to talk to Cade a little he has a life to get back to seven hours away.

"Alright guys I wanna hang out with Cade a little, before he has to head back. As much as I love him being here, I know Daria needs help with those babies." They step out the door.

He steps forward. "Hey she's okay. I'm here as long as you need me."

"I need you to go be home with your wife and kids. I'm safe and I have the distinct feeling that Ryder isn't going to let me out of his sight." I see Ryder stalking outside the door.

He laughs. "Yeah, I can totally see that and I like it. Being an overprotective, caveman bastard myself, I understand it."

I smile. "Thanks Cade. I'm so glad I threw a fit with Gable like a five year old to go meet you."

He smiles and shakes his head.

Cade and I spend a little while longer talking. We set up a visit in our near future and I send him on his way, telling him to be careful and call me when he gets home.

The rest of the day is filled with Annabelle's craziness. Ryder's overprotectiveness. My momma's concerns. Dustin's apologies. A visit from Nelson, Naomi, Greer and Nana Pearl. The highlight of my day, a phone call from Gable telling me he would be home within a week.

After the crazy day has passed, I'm exhausted, Ryder slides in the chair next to my bed. I look over to him. "Ryder?"

"Yeah?"

"Will you lay with me?"

"Are you sure babe? I don't want to hurt you."

"I'll be fine. Just get up here."

He winks. "Yes ma'am."

I turn on my side so that my arm with a cast is draped over him and fall into a secure peaceful sleep.

Chapter 34

Ryder

It has been two weeks since Scarlet came home from the hospital. She is about to go crazy to get her cast off or at least get it changed. She says that it itches like crazy and she's afraid it smells. She feels like she can't take care of herself. Although one of the perks for me is that I have to help her take a bath since we have to keep her cast wrapped up. Thank God most of her soreness went away after a few days because we have definitely been making up for any lost time that may have occurred in the sex department.

I can't wait until tomorrow, it's Christmas Eve. I have invited her mom, Gable, Ivie, Annabelle, Naomi, Nelson and even Dustin. Dustin and I have come to have a new respect for each other. I can't be angry for the rest of my life with him. He was just a scared little boy deep down inside, just like I've been. He wanted acceptance and Brandon was the only person who would give it to him. Even though his acceptance came with a price and some emotional damage.

I can honestly say my dad would always love me no matter what I've done to embarrass him. Actually he's already proven that time and time again. I don't understand how Dustin's parents could just turn their back on him. Which his coming out and Brandon's arrest churned up a huge shit storm of press for their families. I let him hide out for a week or so at the cabin in Waycross. Nelson and I have had to have more than a couple reporters thrown off the property trying to catch a glimpse of Scarlet.

I had my attorney contact SCAD about her turning in her assignments and making sure she got full credit for the semester. Considering if they hadn't been holding a mandatory lecture in a building that forced students to walk around to a dark side entrance, she probably wouldn't have been as easily caught off guard by Brandon. They gladly accepted her assignments and gave her full credit. I also made sure they got a nice donation for better lighting on all their campuses. I know her and she's going to want to go back. I can't handle the thought of her or any other woman getting attacked like that.

My dad called me in his office the other day to inform me that he was going to have to go stay in Atlanta for six to eight months to get the mess straightened out up there. I am going to have to do more of my part with the business side down here. I'm not looking forward to it, but I understand it. Plus, in talking to Dustin, I found out that Scarlet is really good with financial books and organization. He said when she worked for his dad, she did a great job. That was one reason his dad was angry with him when they broke up. He had to find a new assistant. Not that his dad would've ever accepted her as more than an assistant.

So that brings up the most exciting part. Tomorrow night, when I give Scarlet her promise ring, I'm asking her to move in with me. I know she is going to flip out, but I really want her here all the time. I thought maybe I was just getting ahead of myself a few weeks ago, but after her attack and being with her these past two weeks, I can't live without her.

~*~*~

Waking up this morning, it's like I believe in Santa all over again. I'm so excited to have my first Christmas with Scarlet. I roll over and kiss her behind her ear.

She giggles. "Didn't you get enough last night? I think you've broken my vagina."

I laugh into her neck causing her to squirm. "Just for the record I can never get enough of you."

She sits up in bed. "I have to get up. I have to help Nana with the food for tonight. Now come on and help me in the shower and if you're a good boy, I'll let you check my vagina to see if it really is broken while we are in there."

I jump up out of bed and meet her in the bathroom. She holds out her arm while I use the small garbage bag to pull up over her cast and tape it to her arm. She laughs. "This is super sexy huh?"

"Babe if I had to wrap your entire body in a garbage bag, it'd still be sexy as hell."

I smack her on the ass as she steps in the shower. She giggles. "I guess it's time for you to check my vagina, Dr. Abbott."

I smirk. "I guess so, Ms. Johnson."

After spending a little while in the shower giving each other physicals, we get dressed and make our way down to the kitchen where Nana is baking a cake.

"If you two don't stop spending so much time undressed in that bedroom, I'm going to be a great-grandmother before you know it."

Scarlet and I glare at each other. She shakes her head. "Nana, it's okay trust me, I'm not pregnant, I take my pill every morning like clockwork and I'm on the one that you take for three months straight, so I can't even ovulate but like three times a year."

Nana shakes her head. "Well y'all just be careful. You have your whole lives ahead of you and you need time to be with each other."

I hug her. "We know Nana, that is the reason we are so careful."

She chuckles. "Alright. I love you both and I just want y'all to be happy."

Scarlet hugs her. "Thanks Nana, I don't know what I would've done without you guys."

"No problem baby." Nana says as she hugs her back.

I open the refrigerator to grab our steaks and shrimp for tonight. I need to get them in the marinade. We don't do your normal southern Christmas dinner with several meats, a thousand sides, bread and twenty different desserts. We do steak, shrimp, baked potatoes, salad, fresh rolls and my Nana's famous seven layer chocolate cake.

Scarlet looks over at me as I'm getting all the steaks out. "Jeez Ryder, how many damn steaks are you guys gonna eat?"

I'm still trying to keep it hidden how many people are coming. "We just do a bunch at one time babe."

She smiles. "Oh okay, I was wondering."

~*~*~

A few hours later everyone starts arriving. The doorbell rings and I get Scarlet to answer it. She screams when she opens the door. "Gable!!"

I hear Gable. "Is mom here yet?"

"No. Not yet."

I step into the foyer to see Gable and Ivie standing there, with Scarlet wrapped around his neck. I step over. "Hey guys, how's it going?"

Gable steps over to shake my hand. "Good man. It has been a long trip."

"You wanna come out back with me? The steaks are about ready to take off the grill. My dad, Nelson and Dustin are out there."

"Sure man. Ivie, you wanna come out with me or do you want to hang out with Scarlet?"

She speaks softly. "I'll go with Scarlet."

He smiles. "Okay good."

Scarlet and I look at each other. Ivie seems distant, not like the girl we saw in Hilton Head. You can tell Gable doesn't want to leave her side, but he trusts Scarlet.

After Gable and I step out back, I hand him a beer. "So is Ivie okay?"

"Yeah this is just a bad time of year for her. Her mom took off at Christmas and her dad was locked up right before Christmas. So you know it just sucks."

"Ah yeah. I don't eat Chocolate Chip cookies. Ever. My mom used to make them for me. Even when she was so sick from her treatments. After she died I just could never eat them again."

He nods. "Well I'm glad you've been there for Scar. She looks great. Cade told me what she looked like. I was trying my damnedest to get on a plane here even after they told me not to. Ivie kept my ass on lockdown."

"So what's up with you and Ivie, are you a thing or what?"

"Man, it's complicated. Not a topic for Christmas."

I laugh. "Okay man, lets go get these steaks."

Chapter 35

Scarlet

Sitting around the dinner table, we are eating some of Nana's cake. When Ryder sits small box in front of me I look up at him with huge eyes.

"Scarlet, it's not what you're thinking, calm down."

I laugh. "Okay."

"First I want you to know that you are my forever." He opens the box. "But this is a promise ring, I want to show you this is my promise of forever."

I feel the tears welling up in my eyes. "Thank you. It's beautiful. I love you so much."

Greer stands up and walks over to me. "Now Scarlet, I have to say I'm proud of my son. That is one beautiful ring for one beautiful girl. I'm glad that you've hung in there with my son while he gets his shit together." He steps back. "Everyone, let's go sit in the den."

We all get up and go to the den. My mom sits down by me and across from Gable. "Kids I want to talk with you about something. I've been seeing someone up in Augusta. I met him on one of my retreats. He's a very nice man, the first man I've been interested in since- well your father. I think it's time that I move on. He's asked me to move in with him."

"Oh wow mom. That is great." Gable stands up to hug her.

I smile. "Mom that is awesome. I'm so happy for you. It is time that you moved on."

Ryder stands up and gives my mom a hug. "Well that kinda works out for me too. I wanted to ask Scarlet to move in here. Dad is going to be in Atlanta for most of the next year and this big house gets lonesome. Plus I really don't like the idea of her staying in town by herself." He looks up at Gable. "Man, you are welcome to stay here, too. I'm tired of this house being so empty."

Gable smiles. "Well I was going to wait to tell you guys this, but they have asked us to join in on the USO shows overseas at the end of this tour. So I was going to let you guys know I'll be in and out of the country for the next year."

My mom smiles. "That is wonderful Gable, congratulations."

I hug him tight. "That is awesome. I will miss you like crazy, but I know this is a great opportunity for you."

Ryder leans over and shakes his hand. "Hey man maybe you'll be able to get up with my buddy Judd."

"Yeah man maybe so."

Naomi jumps up and hugs my brother, who she barely knows, with tears in her eyes. "You be careful over there. I know you guys are supposed to be safe, but just take care, your sister needs you back here. If you happen to run into my son, you tell him I said the same to him."

Dustin stands up. "Well, I guess since we are all sharing, I've decided I'm moving down to Florida. I need a fresh start and I have some friends down there." He shakes Ryder's hand. "Thanks for letting me stay out at your place and inviting me over here. I'm gonna head out now and try to talk to my parents before I leave town."

We all nod and say our goodbyes. Gable, Ivie and my mom head home. Nelson and Naomi leave, dropping Nana by her house on the way out. Greer excuses himself to his study. That just leaves Ryder, Annabelle and me.

Ryder looks over at Annabelle. "What's really going on with you and Judd? You guys are both vague and giving bullshit answers. I saw how you were with his parents tonight. You wanted them to like you, but you wanted to keep your distance."

"It's nothing, Ryder. We are just friends and I've been worried about him, that's all."

"I told you he'd be out of touch for a little while." Ryder says.

"I know, it is just a feeling." She says sadly.

I sit down by her. "Annabelle, are you sure you're okay. You've been acting distant from me, too. You've been looking so sad and kinda pale. I'm worried."

Annabelle stands up. "Look guys, I'm fine, but I do need to get home. Santa still runs at my parents' house, you know."

I laugh. "Give them my love."

She gives me a hug. "Good night you two, and Merry Christmas, I'm happy for both of you."

After Annabelle is gone, Ryder looks at me. "I'm going to talk to dad for a few minutes before bed."

I smile. "Well that works for me, I need to go upstairs and get your gift ready." I wink.

He grins. "Mmm sounds like I've been a good boy this year."

I throw my arms around his neck and kiss next to his ear. "You've been a very good boy."

I run upstairs and change into the red nighty that I bought with the Santa hat. I'm giving him his normal gift tomorrow like we originally agreed but he decided to surprise me tonight.

I pose myself in the bed to look as sexy as I can with this damn cast. He whistles when he walks in the room. "Merry Christmas to me." As he jumps on the bed with me.

~*~*~

I roll over this morning to find Ryder staring at me. I chuckle. "Okay that is kinda freaky."

He smiles. "I'm just so glad I know I'll be waking up next to you every day."

I snuggle into him. "Hmm that does sound nice." I kiss him. "So let's go downstairs, I want you to open your present."

We get dressed and head downstairs. Nana and Greer are already up and eating breakfast.

I smile at Greer when he hands me a cup of coffee. He speaks softly. "I'm glad you are staying here with him. He loves you and you're good for him."

"Thanks Greer. He's good for me and I love him, too. Now come on you two, I want to give y'all your gifts at the same time."

After we are around the tree I hand them all their package. "Now open them."

Ryder stops as he tears the paper off his. "Baby this is- I don't know what to say."

"Do you like it? I was nervous about it."

"Baby I love it. It makes me love you even more."

Nana looks at it. "Oh my word. It is a beautiful picture of Lillian." She says as she looks at the picture of Ryder and Lillian together that I drew.

I look over to see tears on Greer's face. "Scarlet, this is the most beautiful thing I've ever seen." He's holding the picture I sketched from an old wedding photo of he and Lillian.

Ryder looks at Nana. "So Nana, what did you get?"

"She sketched a picture of me, sitting on the porch watching the sun go down and my house, it's just wonderful."

Ryder pulls me into a tight embrace. "Scarlet I love you. This is the most wonderful gift anyone could've given me. You make me a happy man every day that I'm alive knowing you."

I smile with tears in my eyes. "Ryder Abbott you are the most wonderful, amazing, smartass I know. I love you forever."

He gives me a knowing look. "Come help me find a spot to hang this picture in my room."

I hear Nana as we make our way up the stairs. "There they go again. I swear Greer, you better be ready to be a grandfather."

We both laugh as he shuts his bedroom door and we start tearing each other's clothes off.

He looks at me serious for a moment.

"Scarlet, when I met you, I could see that you had hurt hidden in those eyes. I'm so glad that when I look there now, I don't see so much hurt."

I smile. "Ditto."

Epilogue

Four Months Later

Ryder

Living with Scarlet for the past three months has been great. We have both been busting our asses to make sure that the farm and the business side of it are ran good while dad is gone.

She is a freaking whiz with numbers. I'm beginning to wonder if there is anything she can't do. She's been going to SCAD and she even talked me into taking a few general business classes.

So when I knew spring break was coming up, I really wanted to do something special for her. Gable had also confided in me he'd be in town that week and wanted to surprise her. I called up Cade and he planned a trip for us all to go to his wife's beach house in Destin.

So we drove down yesterday and met everyone at the house. She was thrilled to see Gable and Ivie. She's come to be a peace with whatever is going on with them. No one actually knows, I'm not even sure if they do.

I hear the bathroom door open. "So what do you think of my new swimsuit?"

I turn around to see her beautiful body in a skimpy hot pink bikini.

"I think it's still not as gorgeous as the girl wearing it, but I don't want other men looking at it." I pull her tight against me. "See, it does things to me." I grope her ass.

"Why are you grabbing Aunt Scarlet's hiney like that?" Madison asks with a grossed out look on her face.

We both look at each other lost as to what to say. All of a sudden Daria comes to our rescue. "Come on Madison, let's go get bubba's sunblock on and then we'll get some ice cream."

She turns and runs. "Yay!"

Daria looks at us. "I'm sorry, we've been getting on to her about just opening doors."

Scarlet shakes her head. "It's okay."

Daria smiles. "See you guys down at the beach."

We both can't help but laugh when they leave.

Scarlet smiles. "I'm so glad I take my pill every day. I don't think we are ready for those kinds of interruptions."

I laugh. "Yes, please keep taking that pill, for a little longer anyway. Now come on, I want to show you something."

As we make our way down to the beach I've made a picnic for us. We sit down and I pull a small box out of my pocket.

"Scarlet Leigh Johnson, will you marry me?"

She looks at me with huge eyes like I've grown another head. She covers her mouth and screams. "Oh My GOD! Yes. Yes. Yes. Oh My God!"

I stand up and pull her up with me hugging her, she wraps her legs around me as we spin in pure bliss.

<u>Secrets In The Lyrics</u>

For every girl who ever felt like she wasn't enough…
In the words of one of my oldest friends,
"Some will, some won't. So What, Next!"
~ TRM

Introduction

- Due to mature subject matter this book is for readers 17+.
- This book is written in a true southern dialect, from a true southern person. Therefore, it is NOT going to have proper grammar.

Now with those two points out of the way. I will say that this is probably one of the darker books I've written. Ivie has a lot of problems with self-esteem, self-respect and self-worth, to work through. She's been dealt a crappy hand in life and she has to learn to work through these things.

To females of all ages self-image is something we all deal with. After life has beat you down, it takes years to learn that beauty comes from the person you are inside.

Trust me on this one, I was always the chunky best friend. I always wondered what was wrong with me. In the end, I figured out that some people are just going to be catty bitches and that people now have way more respect for me than those catty bitches I worried so much about.

I guess I'm saying Love Yourself, treat yourself with Respect and tell the rest of the world to take a flying leap.

Eight Years Old...

I hope my mom made macaroni and cheese tonight. She and my dad have been fighting a lot lately about her going out of town so much. I hear all the girls at school talking about how their moms fix supper and they pack them lunch every day. I'm lucky if my mom remembers what time I get home off the bus. My dad is always in his office talking business.

I walk in from school and start to panic because our living room is a mess. I'm scared someone broke in so I run and hide in my closet. I stay here until I don't hear anyone but my dad. My tummy is growling. "Daddy? Daddy?"

"What, Ivie? Where have you been?"

"I came in from school and it was a mess. I was scared so I hid. I'm really hungry."

"Fine, I'll go fix you something quick, then you need to get ready for bed. I have business partners coming over and I can't have you in the way."

When we sit down to the table to eat, I look up. "Where's mommy?"

"Your mother is nothing but a two-bit whore who just ran-off with a loan shark from Biloxi."

I stutter. "Is- Is she- c-c-coming back?"

"No, and we are better off without her."

I nod. "Okay Daddy, but what about Christmas? She said she'd tell Santa that I want a Holiday Barbie."

He looks at me with sadness. "I'll make sure he knows. Now eat up."

Fifteen Years Old...

I sit down on my side of the visitation glass. "Hey, Dad."

"Hey, sweetheart. How are things going at your Aunt Stella's?"

I shrug. "They are going. I'm pretty sure she hates me."

"She doesn't hate you. You're her sister's kid."

"Well hell, Dad. I mean her sister didn't stick around for me, so why should she?"

"Ivie, your mother...look, I only have a few minutes to talk to you and I don't want to waste it talking about Jenna."

"Fine. So how come you thought criminal life was more important than your only child?"

"Ivie-." He looks defeated. "I was trying to provide a good life for you. Now do me a favor, get better grades, go to college, and make something of yourself."

I stand up. I have had wonderful grades, I couldn't get any higher, but he wouldn't know that. He's always been too busy with his 'business deals' to pay attention. "You know what, Dad? If you knew me, you'd know that I have colleges already asking about me. You know what would have made me have a good life? Having two parents that gave a shit." I turn and walk out.

Seventeen Years Old...

"Ivie Butonelli, get your ass in this house! Where have you been all day?"

"I was at school."

She smacks me across the face. "You're lying, the school called me. Don't think I don't know that you were at that thug boyfriend of yours house. Smoking your wacky weed and playing on your little guitars."

Damn, how did she know what I was doing? "What I do is none of your business. The state gives you money to let me stay here."

"Yeah well, your money is supposed to run out when you turn eighteen in two months, but the school told me today that you are expelled for non-attendance and the drugs they found in your locker, so the state is cutting off your money. So get out. Pack your shit and get out you ungrateful little bitch, you are just like my damn sister."

I go to the small room that I have and throw my crap in a bag. I wasn't allowed to keep much from my house since most of it was seized, so I only have a few things to pack. I leave the house without saying goodbye and make my way back to my boyfriend Aaron's house.

Three weeks later...

Yeah, living with Aaron has lasted all of three weeks. When I came home a couple of hours ago from my shift at McDonald's, I found some bitch blowing him and another bitch smoking my weed. I grab my shit and my guitar and leave. I walk around for hours trying to figure out where I'm going to go. I remember one of my friends is having a party tonight, so maybe I can go hang there for a little while and maybe crash there.

As I walk into the party, there are people from wall to wall. There is a small band on stage playing that is pretty good. I walk closer to listen to them better. As they finish up, I walk over and talk to the guy that is playing the drums.

I step out in front of him. "Hey, you guys were awesome. I'm Ivie."

He shakes my hand. "Hey, I'm Stoney, this is my buddy Keeg and our lead, Gable."

My body quivers as Gable shakes my hand. "Hey, nice to meet you guys. Well I just wanted you to know I love your sound."

Stoney smiles. "Thanks. I see you carrying a case. Do you play?"

"Yeah, I do a little and I do some vocal stuff."

He grins. "Come to the garage with us and let's jam a little. The rest of the crazy people at this party won't even know we left."

Unsure about going off with three guys, "I don't know" must show on my face. Gable steps up. "Hey, we are nice guys and there is generally more people out there than just us. I understand your skepticism about being alone with us, you don't know us. I hope my kid sister is as smart as you."

I smile. "Well, as long as there will be more people out there."

GABLE

Ten Years Old...

My mom sits down across from Scarlet and me. She's been crying. I wonder what my mean dad has said to her now. He was always saying ugly stuff to her. He's only here a day or so a week anyway, I wish he would just go away. I just stare at her. I can't feel sorry for her because she would be fine without him. She should just tell him to get lost.

Scarlet looks at her with a trembling lip. "Mommy, what's wrong? Where is daddy?"

She clears her throat. "Well, Daddy probably won't be coming back for a little while. He's gotten into some trouble. See, it seems Daddy has another family. I guess he has so much love that one family just wasn't enough and he got into trouble for having two families."

I look up at her, something she's saying makes no sense. "So. What do you mean a little while? He's always gone for a little while."

"Well, probably a few years. But he's promised me that as soon as this is all cleared up, he'll be back and help raise you guys. We are going to go and visit him if it's close enough."

Scarlet crawls up in my mom's lap and starts crying. "I'm going to miss Daddy."

My mom sighs. "I am, too."

I look at them. Are they crazy? I stand up and go to my room to do my homework.

Fifteen Years Old...

I look across the dinner table at my mom who is crying, once again, because she's been trying to find my dad since he was released from prison but she can't locate him. "I'm sorry Gable, I know you don't like seeing me cry but I just can't help it. I still love him."

"Why? I gave up loving him, or even caring about him, a long time ago."

"Look, I know you don't understand."

"No, to be quite honest I don't. The man married you and had two kids. This whole time being married to another woman first and having another kid. I think you and that lady should get together, hunt his ass down, and string him up by his balls."

"Gable, don't talk about your father that way. He is a loving man, he just loves too much."

I grit my teeth. "He's not a father, he's a sperm donor. That is it. Hell, he's probably got another family out there already. Hell, two wives and families aren't enough, he's probably got like four wives and families by now."

"Gable!" Scarlet screams at me. "Stop it. Mom is upset."

I stand up. "Look, you know by now I don't sugar coat things, and I know in the hippie commune life you grew up in, it's probably ok, but for me it's not. Scarlet, quit babying her about him, he's an asshole, plain and simple." I grab my guitar case and jacket. "I've got band practice. See ya."

I storm out the door, heading down the street to Stoney's house where we practice. As I walk in the garage, it's already filled with people waiting to hear us.

My rage fuels my performance as we finish a couple of hours of practice. I sit my guitar down and turn off my amp. Keeg steps up beside me. "Hey man, don't know what had you going tonight but you were on flipping fire."

"Yeah. Just bullshit stuff, you know."

He laughs. "Well that little chick, Eva, is standing over there looking like she's just dying to suck your dick, so you should probably go check on that."

I've been with Eva a couple of times and she's a lot of fun. She's seventeen, but I'm the youngest member of our band and I don't think she knows, or maybe she doesn't care, that I'm fifteen.

I pull her into Stoney's house and find an empty room. Once I shut the door, she smiles. Pulling herself to me, she licks the salty sweat from my neck. "You did a great job tonight."

"Thanks." I'm not much for words and she knows that.

She drops to her knees and pulls my dick out of my pants. Once she slides her mouth over it, I reach around and grab the back of her head. I literally fuck her face until she swallows every last bit of cum I shoot out. She stands up and wipes her mouth as I tuck my dick in my pants. "Thanks, that was good."

She throws her hands on her hips. "What about me? I need to get off, too."

I roll my eyes. "Fine. But it won't be with my dick, he's down for a little while."

I push her back on the bed and sink my fingers into her damp folds, rubbing her clit until she cries out. I stand up without saying a word and go to the bathroom to wash up.

Seventeen years old...

What in the hell are we doing jamming in the garage with a girl named Ivie? When she stepped out in front of us in the house I thought she was another groupie, but as it turns out, she's a bass player. When I shook her hand, I could have snatched her up and fucked her right there on Stoney's drums.

She doesn't look like the normal girl who follows us around. She has a rather small waist but big tits and a plump ass.

Keeg pipes up after a few minutes. "Damn girl, you rock that bass."

She smiles shyly. "Thanks."

Stoney speaks up. "Hey, let's hear some vocals. What's a song you do?"

Her voice almost trembles when she looks up to see my face. "Do you know *Underneath it All* by No Doubt? I know it's pretty old but I like the beat."

Stoney nods and starts to tap out the beat. As we join in, I don't expect her to even start singing as her fingers tremble playing her bass. But her voice never falters when Gwen Stefani's lyrics come out of her mouth.

Damn, she's good. Once we finish jamming, I snatch a regular groupie up and take her to a back bedroom and knock the freakin' bottom out of her trying to get thick Ivie off my brain. Her freakin' voice almost did me in, it was like velvet. After I walk back out into the main room, I see Stoney leaving with Ivie and I start to get pissed. I don't know why I'm getting pissed but I want to know why in the fuck she's leaving with him.

"Hey, Stone! Where you guys off to?"

"Oh, Ivie got kicked out of her place so she's gonna crash with me for a little while. I need a roommate to help with expenses, she needs a place to crash, and she's got a job." He shrugs.

I jam my hands in my pockets. "Okay. See ya."

They both throw up a short wave.

Eight Months Ago...

Twenty-One Years Old

I have gotten used to blocking out Chad's yelling at me. "Don't fucking think for a second that I don't know that you are fucking one, if not all three, of those guys in your band."

I shake my head. "Shut the fuck up, Chad. I'm not fucking anyone in my band."

He's never understood that those guys pulled me from the depths of Hell. One of the worst places I was in my pathetic existence, I was headed straight to a drug overdose or being homeless. When Stoney let me move in, I got clean and went to work and came home every day. I have to make this relationship work though. I can't keep running back to Stoney's place every time I break up with someone. I feel like I'm an inside joke.

What Chad doesn't get is I'm not those guys' type and they don't see me that way. They see a girl with great bass skills and a set of pipes. Keeg and Stoney see me as a little sister they have to protect. Gable has a great little sister, so he doesn't see me as that. He sees me as a chunky chick side kick.

Look, I know I'm not that fat. I have curves and I'm solid through the middle. I've never been one to have my shit hanging out for the world to see, so I'm normally wearing clothes that are a little big for me. Plus, on stage I dress in my Converses, t-shirts and jeans. I'm not a fem-bot and I refuse to have my goods just hanging out. The girls that he takes back from the concerts are thin rails. Blonde little bimbos with their tits and ass hanging out of their clothes.

"Hey Ivie, are you fucking listening to me?"

Shit, I spaced out on him again, he's going to be pissed. "Sorry," was all I manage to get out before he spins me around and slaps my ass.

He's pushed me into our bedroom and I know where this is leading. He likes to pick a fight and then fuck the ever living shit out of me. Normally I'm okay with that, but the last time he choked me until I almost passed out. It really kinda scared me. I'm pretty sure he's on something or roided out because paranoia and anger have taken over most of his life. At first I pushed it off as being a cop and always having to watch out. Now, I just try to get through the days.

As I expect, he shoves me on the bed. "Is this how you imagine those dumbasses taking you?"

"Just stop."

"No. You are mine, Ivie. Do you understand that?" Suddenly he has my hands over my head. He snaps handcuffs around them. I start to panic realizing that I'm cuffed to the bed.

"Chad, I'm not okay with this. Un-cuff me."

"No, it's time you learned some lessons. You do as I say, I let you live in my home." He rips my shirt open and cuts my bra off. He continues by snatching my shorts and panties down. He looks at my now naked body and laughs. "I shouldn't be worried, though. Those guys don't normally go for fatties like you." He runs his hand up my chest. "You know that, don't you? I'm the only one who could care for you like that. Those guys will never want you. They like pretty little girls, like trophies. I'm the only person who feels sorry enough for you that I'd be seen with you."

That remark hurts and I just stop arguing back, letting him do whatever he wants. Spacing out always helps me get through it.

Besides, he's right. I always say that I know I'm not fat, but the truth is I may not be obese, but compared to other girls, I'm fat. Not to mention what girl of your dreams plays bass in a band? That's my talent. I should've not let my father and aunt get in my head. I should've kept my ass at school, doing what I'd done my entire life, excelling, and I could be in medical school now.

Instead, here I am hand cuffed to a bed, letting some little prick bastard fuck me, like a drunk teen on Spring Break.

He pops the side of my face. "Pay attention, Ivie. Get into it or I swear I'll leave you here cuffed to this fucking bed for a day or two."

I guess he has trouble concentrating without me so I give it my best fake. I act like what his over-compensating ass is doing turns me on. "Good girl, now call out my name." He pinches one of my nipples. "I said scream my fucking name, Ivie." I do and he finally finishes. He leans down and kisses me. "Good girl." Then he stands up, throwing the condom in the garbage.

"Chad, aren't you forgetting something?" I jiggle my hands in the cuffs.

"Oh no. I'm coming back after I catch my breath. We are going several rounds today. When I let you go to your little band practice in the morning, I want you to be sore and thinking of me."

~*~*~

The alarm is going off. I try to reach and turn it off but my hands are still in the handcuffs. I kick Chad. "Wake up. I can't turn the alarm off. Get these damn cuffs off me, the joke is over."

He chuckles as he turns off the alarm. When he reaches to undo the cuffs, he looks at me. "This was no joke, baby. It was a reminder that you are mine. I can do whatever I want to you. I am the law."

A few minutes later, I'm standing in the shower and he was right. I'll be thinking about him all day. Thinking about how much I hate him, thinking about how to explain the bruising around my wrists. Thinking about how I'm fucking raw because of how much he fucked me.

Getting out, I make my way to the room and dress for practice.

Walking into Keeg's house, the guys stare at me. I stop and stare. "What?"

Stoney chuckles. "You look like shit, that's what." He flails his hands around, making fun of my bitchiness.

I walk over to get my bass out of the case. "Just had a long night."

I'm reaching for some notes I made about a song when Keeg grabs my arm. "What in the hell happened to your wrists?"

I look down to see that I do have bruises forming now. "It's nothing."

I try to play it off. I can't appear weak to these guys. I'm already the relationship fuck up, they can't see that I let someone chain me to a fucking bed all night against my will.

Stoney looks down at them. "Nothing?"

Gable steps over. "What do you mean nothing? Did someone hurt you?"

I can tell they aren't going to stop. "Look, I don't ask you guys about your kinky sex lives, I'd appreciate it if you didn't ask about mine."

That makes them go away finally. Nothing like the girl you consider your sister grossing you out with kinky sex. Gable just stares at me, almost as if he can see through me, but more than likely it's that he can't believe someone would want to have kinky sex with someone like me.

"Let's just get to work." I say.

Gable stops in the middle of the floor. "Hey guys, a woman for the company promoting Ransom's End's new tour called me yesterday. They would like for us to get in contact with them about being an opening act, possibly starting in about three weeks."

We all stop and stare. Keeg leans against the door frame. "Did you just say someone wants us to tour and open for Ransom's End starting in a few weeks?"

Gable smiles and nods. "Yep. Well, a guy came and saw our show. He likes us, but they'll give us an answer after they come to our show tomorrow night. They want a second look. We might make some money, too."

Stoney grins and grabs me around my waist, spinning me around.

Stoney stops. "What's up, Ivie girl? You don't seem happy. You don't want to go on tour with us or something?"

I smile my best fake smile and shake my head. "No, it's not that. I think I'm still in shock or something."

They all chuckle and Stoney smiles. "Good. I was beginning to worry."

Twenty-one Years Old

Yesterday, when Holly from the tour company called me, it was like a dream. I know I had to sound like I was half stoned or something the way I was stuttering around my words. I had to ask her to repeat what she said. I couldn't wait to surprise the guys today at practice.

I have to say though, Ivie's reaction was a little off. I hope she's not planning on leaving the band. That new douche nozzle she's been living with isn't very supportive of her being in the band. She never says anything but I can tell he doesn't. He never comes to our shows, when he's around he guards her like a freakin' hound, and he talks down to her. I don't think she realizes we know that, but Stoney overheard a phone call one night. So needless to say, we don't like him.

I think if we get this tour, it will be good for her. She's been beat down a lot in her life but she never cries about it. How her nasty whore mom took off and left her. How her dad was sent to prison or her aunt that treated her like a second class citizen when she was forced to live there.

Stoney found an old report card when she lived with him. She was a fucking honor student. I don't know what happened, but she got kicked out. She got her GED and has been on her own ever since.

How does one girl take up this much space in my head? It's not like I want her or anything either. I just worry about her. I'll admit, when we first met and I was a horny 17 year old boy, I would've fucked her and not thought twice about it. But she's one of us and I can't let that get messed up by my dick.

Once practice is over I glance over at her wrists again. If I find out that asshole has been hurting her, I'll make him wish he was never born. I don't care that he's a fucking cop.

I make my way down to Bay Street Blues, the bar we play at on Bay Street, to talk to Dottie, the bartender/manager of the place. I need to let her know about the show tomorrow night. She's probably going to cuss my ass out, but she'll be proud, too. She gave us a shot when none of the other bars liked our sound.

I walk through the tinted glass front door. "Hey Sexy, how's it going?"

She laughs. "Son, if I thought you were half serious and I weren't so *in love* with Frank, I'd take you in the back room and teach you all about sex."

"Hey, I haven't gotten any complaints."

"Yeah but have you gotten a standing 'O'?"

I shake my head, she never ceases to amaze me with what comes out of her mouth.

She leans up on the bar. "So what brings you by today?"

I sit down at the bar and she shoves a Blue Moon beer in front of me. "Well, a lady called me yesterday from a tour company. A guy from their group came in here and watched our show one night. They are interested in signing us up to open for Ransom's End in the fall, well technically in about three weeks. They are coming back tomorrow night with a couple more guys to watch us."

She yells. "Whoo hoo! My kids are gonna make it big time. I think you are an asshole for leaving me, but I think I'll get over it."

"I just wanted to let you know about them coming in tomorrow night and so that you knew you may need to start looking for a new band."

She walks around the bar and sits down by me. "Gable, I'm proud of you guys. Now, I'm pissed that I won't have you guys here, because you fill every damn barstool and chair in this place when you play. I do understand it, though."

I look up. "Thanks, Dottie. You've been our rock, you know."

"Yeah well, you just don't forget where you've come from, and make sure those boys behave themselves. Keep an eye on Ivie, she's more fragile than she lets off."

I nod. "Well don't say too much, I don't want to jinx it. Holly said they'd watch us tomorrow night and get back with us within a week. I guess all the guys who were scouting are together now and looking at all the talent they found."

"You just stay positive and play your ass off tomorrow night."

~*~*~

Well, it's been exactly two weeks since Holly called us the first time, and she called me today to tell us we were in. I called up the band and told them and everyone is thrilled. Ivie has still been a little distant, but maybe it's just nerves.

I'm on my way now to meet my sister Scarlet at the bar and tell her our big news. She's getting ready to start SCAD in the fall so this is big for both of us. She's done some amazing artwork for our band. Hopefully some of the bigger names will like it and get her some work.

I know she's going to be upset that I'm leaving. We have always been each other's backbone. Once our dad went to prison and our mom was like a lovesick hippie that goes on spiritual retreats, we've only really had each other. Which Scarlet and I are lucky our mom put roots down here. My grandparents move around like gypsies and they did that when mom was young, too. I can respect the fact that she has done this for us, but after we got old enough to stay by ourselves, she started going on her retreats. She's never dated, or even attempted to, after our dad left. I wish more than anything she'd just move on from him.

Walking into the bar, she's already there talking to Dottie. I haven't even brought any of this up to her until now, so it's going to be a shock.

We sit down and talk. I explain it all to her, and she's sad and scared. She is proud of me though, my sister would give up damn near anything for me, just like I would for her.

She's had a rough go of it lately. She found out her boyfriend was cheating on her with not just another girl, but a guy, too. She lost it and beat the shit out of his car with an ax handle and now she has community service.

Of course, our free love mom has not been that supportive of my sister's *violent streak* as she called it. When I told mom that I would've beat the hell out of him myself, she wasn't happy about that either.

So me leaving makes her feel like I'm abandoning her like our dad. She actually liked him when we were little, he treated her like a princess, but doesn't he treat any woman that way? Considering we know he was married to my mom and our brother, Cade's mom at the same time. We don't have a clue about him since he got out of prison, and I really don't care.

I really didn't even want to find Cade, but Scarlet begged for her birthday for us to go find him. I'm glad she did though, he's a cool guy and obviously a lot better man than our dad. He chose his family over an NFL career. His wife is amazing and their friends are cool. I also found out that

I have a very cool ass three year old niece, Madison, who is bossy and hilarious. They also have a little boy on the way.

~*~*~

This week has flown by. Scarlet and I have had a chance to talk more. I think she's into this guy, Ryder, from her Community Service. She supposedly hates him, but her eyes dance when she talks about him. I haven't watched them do that in a really long time. I really hope that she'll let her guard down and give him a shot.

I have Scarlet drive me over to Stoney's. I'm going to let her use my car while I'm gone. Once we're in the driveway, I see the tears coming out of her eyes. "Scar, I'll be back before you know it."

"I know, I just worry, and I know I'll miss you."

"Look, just take care of my car and don't get arrested anymore. Okay?'

She nods and falls into my chest. "Okay, I'm going to go. I need to go pick some stuff up for mom."

I kiss her on her forehead. "Okay kid, I love you. Take care."

I watch her get in the car and drive away.

Stoney steps out. "She gonna be okay, man?"

"I think so. Everybody ready to go?"

"Ivie's not here yet."

"What the fuck man?"

"Look, I've tried calling her, and Keeg has tried. Hopefully she'll be here soon."

I let my head fall back. "She fucking better be. Is something going on with her? Is she on something? Is she flaking out? She's missed practice this week, calling after to apologize. We need to have a serious talk with her. "

Stoney looks at the ground with his hands in his pockets. "I know man. I know."

IVIE

So to say that Chad wasn't happy when he found out about the tour last weekend would be a serious understatement. I've paid for it all week. I've had to avoid the guys. He's told me I'm not going and he'll never let me go.

I've gotta go though or he's gonna kill me if I stay here. He's seriously strung out. It's not like I can call the cops on him, he is a damn cop. He likes to remind me of that when he has me tied to something, roughing me up and fucking the hell out of me. When I told him about the tour, he hurt me so bad I could hardly walk for two days.

Today I have to throw my shit in a bag and leave. I've got to get to Stoney's before he comes back home from his shift.

I'm in the shower. I've spent the last hour cramming everything I can into my car. I have to leave it at Stoney's in the garage so I'll have anything left when I come back. I look out of the curtain at the clock and it's two, I'm supposed to meet the guys at three-thirty. Chad isn't due home until four so I'm good on time.

As I walk into the bedroom with my robe on, the room shifts. I'm snatched by my hair and slammed into the wall.

"Where in the fuck do you think you are going?"

I try to stand firm. "Let me go, Chad."

He presses me harder into the wall, running his hand up my robe. "No. I told you that you were not going off to follow those guys around like a bitch in heat. They don't want you!" He slams my head against the wall. "You are stupid and fat, no one besides me will ever want you." He throws me on the bed and starts unzipping his pants. I try to fight him off, I hit and kick at him. In turn, he slaps me and punches me. Finally, I get my hands on the bedside lamp. I grab it and smash him over the head with it and he falls off of me.

"You fucking bitch!"

I jump up and run out of the room, adjusting my robe that is still half hanging on. I have my keys in my hand in the kitchen when he comes staggering out the bedroom door.

"You are going to pay for this."

I look over and see a gallon of cooking oil so I open it up and dump it all over the floor as fast as I can. "You'll have to come get me mother fucker!" I take off running out the front door. I hear him cussing and falling all over the place but by the time he makes it to the door, I'm driving like a bat out of hell to Stoney's.

I look down at the clock, praying they haven't left me. I reach to grab my phone and realize it's back at the house. Not going back to get it.

I see the guys glaring at me when I come flying into the driveway. Thinking he might be behind me, I scream for them to open the garage.

Once I'm in the garage, I step out of the car. "Give me a second guys to grab some clothes. I was in a hurry. I didn't want you to leave me. I'm sorry." I don't even realize I'm crying until Stoney grabs my arm.

"Ivie. Stop. Look at me."

Suddenly I realize why he wants to look at me. My face is starting to hurt, well throb is actually more like it. "No." I keep looking down. "I'm fine, just let me go get dressed and I'll be ready to go." I dart past him and run to his bathroom, shutting the door.

I step in front of the mirror and I'm horrified at what I see. I guess my adrenalin was pumping so hard I didn't feel exactly how many hits he got in. I didn't bring my make-up or anything in here with me. I gently wash my face to get the dried blood off of it.

Looking down at my bruised and battered body, I realize that Chad was right. I'm fat, and looking at this face, no one will ever want me.

I dress and hear the guys arguing in the kitchen.

Keeg is yelling. "No, I'm going to kick his ass! He did that to her. He's not going to get away with this."

Stoney is trying to talk to him. "Keeg, man we have to calm down, he's a cop. We have to play this smart."

I step around the corner and the guys catch the first full on look at my face. Gable knocks a bunch of shit off the counter. I know he's frustrated that, once again, I've brought my drama to the band.

I put my hands up. "Look guys, let's just get out of here. I can explain all day long, but all you need to know is I got my fair share of licks in and he was hurting, too." I didn't say I got one good lick in with a lamp and he was hurting from falling trying to get to me.

Stoney knows me best. He walks in front of the guys. "Look. The sooner she gets to leave town, the farther she'll be away from him. He's a cop and he'll get believed before a group of music delinquents will."

I nod. "Stoney's right, let's go. I want as much distance between me and this place as possible."

We meet the tour bus picking us up over by Keeg's mom's house so he can leave his car there.

After the bus pulls off, I can tell they want answers. "Look guys, I'm going to take some ibuprofen and take a nap. We'll talk after I get up. I just can't do this right now."

With that, I walk down the hall and crawl in the bunk I decide to claim. I pray for a long sleep, but once I lie down, the events of today and the past week catch up with me. I begin to softly sob into my pillow until I finally do doze off.

After Ivie walks down the hall and crawls in a bunk, we sit on the small couches. Keeg looks over at us. "What are we going to do? You see what he did to her, he deserves to die."

Keeg has a big problem with men putting their hands violently on women. His mom took abuse for years that he had to watch.

Stoney looks across to me. "Man, you haven't said much during all of this. What do you think? If this had happened to Scar, what would you do?"

I shake my head. "Man. Look, Ivie is a private person. She's a rock. Scarlet depends on me, it's totally different." I say, trying to distance myself. Because when I saw her earlier, I was ready to go get that son of a bitch, drop him in a pen of hungry hogs, and let them devour him. I have a plan but I can't get hot headed about it.

Stoney slams his fist down on the table. He whispers hard to me. "You hear her back there, don't you? She's crying. She's hurting. Does that sound like someone who's a rock to you?"

"Look man, all I'm saying is Ivie doesn't want us to make a big deal out of this. She wants our support and she wants to move on. She wants to put as much distance between her and him as possible." I shrug.

Keeg glares at me. "Whatever, Gable. I just think he deserves to pay."

I look over at him seriously. "He will, trust me. But it will be my style, calculated and planned. Plus, Ivie will know nothing about it. Get me?"

They both have known me long enough to know that I don't make idle threats. They nod that they understand. Keeg leans in. "Do you think she'll ever tell us what all happened?"

I look down the vacant hallway. "When she's ready." I lean back and take a nap on our way to our first show.

~*~*~

Our first show is going to be in the Florida Panhandle at some Festival. I let Cade know it's close to Destin, where he and his wife have a beach house. They are going to be down anyway, so he's going to drive over for the show. Daria said she's too pregnant and too tired to come out, plus Madison is not really old enough.

I arrange for Cade to come to the bus before show time so he and I can talk.

When we met, he got a little drunk that night. He and I were sitting out back talking and he mentioned some stuff to me, some connections that Daria might have. I have to say I want him to see Ivie and see what happened to her. Then, I'm going to ask for his help. This dipshit Chad is a cop and he has to be dealt with carefully.

I look over at Keeg and Stoney when we pull into the parking lot. "When Cade gets on here I'll introduce you guys, then I want you to wake Ivie up so I can introduce her, then he and I are going to take a walk."

They shrug. "Okay."

An hour later someone knocks on the door. I let Cade on the bus and he gives me a back slapping hug. "Hey man, this is awesome, I'm proud of you."

I nod. "Thanks." I wave my hands around at the dated tour bus. "So this is it, home sweet home, for a few months, anyway."

He chuckles. "Well, you have to start somewhere, right?"

I laugh and nod. "So these are my two best friends and bandmates, Keeg and Stoney. We've been friends since we were kids. And coming down the hallway is our lovely Ivie."

I see Cade tense when he sees her face. I shake my head slightly. "Guys, Ivie, this is Cade, my brother."

They all mumble hellos. "Let's go for a walk. I have a feeling I'm going to be cramped up in this bus for long enough."

He laughs. "Sure."

We step off the bus and walk to a nearby tree. "Cade, I need a favor, like a big brother favor."

He nods. "Sure. If I can." He looks off into the distance. "Does it have anything to do with that poor girl's face that looks like someone used it for sparring practice?"

I nod. "She showed up like that this morning, right before we left. Her ex, or now ex-boyfriend, is a douche, but he's a douche that's a cop." I give him that look, saying he's untouchable to the normal guy.

His jaw tenses. "I see. So he thinks he's above the law and he can do shit like that to girls."

"I guess. She hasn't really talked to us about it, but something tells me it wasn't the first time. But Ivie has always been a private person. Look man, I know after you got drunk that night and said those things, I promised I'd never breathe a word of it to anyone, even Scarlet, and I haven't. But if you know someone who could effectively get the point across to this guy, I would appreciate it. I would go kick his ass myself, but then I'd go to jail and ruin the band. This band is really the only thing she has."

Cade looks across the fair grounds. "I never use Daria's connections, but I can tell this is important to you. Plus, the caveman in me wants to help her. Hell, if Daria saw that girl right now, pregnant or not, I'd have to stop her from driving there and putting that guy in the ground herself." He shakes his head. "Look, Daria does still have some protection and some friends. Give me everything you have on the guy and give me info on Ivie, too. Where did you say her family is?"

"Her dad went to prison years ago and her mom, last time we knew, was married to a loan shark in Biloxi."

He nods. "This might be easier than I thought. I'll talk to Daria, her parents may be able to help."

"Humph, I doubt it. They've never took care of her."

"Nope, but in my years with Daria I see things in a whole new light, and people like her parents owe someone favors, too."

He pulls me into his big arms. "Thanks, Cade. I've never known what it was like to have someone help me. I'm always the one helping. I've always tried to take care of Scar and my mom. I'm always the level headed one in the band. I was really afraid I'd do something stupid if I tried to take care of this myself, but I don't want Ivie to know anything about it."

He nods. "Hey man, no big deal. So you really care about this girl, huh?"

I shrug. "Yeah, I mean she's Ivie, she's been my bandmate and friend for like five years. She's had a rough life."

He shakes his head with a smirk. "No man, that's not the look I saw on your face when you were telling me about what happened to her. Trust me, I have my own inner caveman, as Daria calls it. I come out swinging my damn club every once in a while, flare my nostrils, scratch my balls and piss around my wife. Figuratively speaking, of course."

I chuckle. "Yeah, whatever, it's not like that for us."

"Dude, you care about that girl, don't fuck that up."

I start walking back toward the bus. "Yeah, I gotta go get ready. I hate that as soon as you got here, I had to ask you for a favor. That wasn't my intention."

He shakes his head. "No man, it's cool. I can't wait to hear your band play." He stops and grabs my arm. "Remember what I said about her though. One thing I do know, what happened to her with that other guy was wrong. But I know from Daria, with everything she's been through, she thinks she deserves it, she believes since her family doesn't care about her or want her, no one else does either."

Cade makes his way out to the area he'll watch the concert from and I head to the bus.

Once I'm inside, I walk down the hallway to the bathroom. I open the door and Ivie is just stepping out of the shower. "Sorry." I say as I back out of the bathroom. Her delicate sweet curved body is covered in bruises and whelps. I hope Cade makes sure that son of a bitch pays.

She tucks her head down as she walks out of the bathroom. "S-sorry. I thought all of you guys were gone." She shuts herself in the back room to dress.

I lean back against the wall. Cade was right, she really is fragile. Big question, why do I care? Ivie will get through this.

I'm so embarrassed. Gable just saw me completely naked. Not only did he see all the bruises, but he saw me. Chunky Ivie, naked. Great, now he actually saw my big ass and cottage cheese thighs.

I dressed quickly and made way out to the main part of the bus. Keeg and Stoney are sitting on the couch, they weren't here earlier. I raise my hand and wave slightly as I flop down in a chair. I really didn't say much when they woke me up earlier. They just wanted me to meet Gable's brother, so after they went for a walk, I went back to my bunk to make a list of things I needed to accomplish by the end of this tour. I was only going to depend on me when I was finished with this. I wouldn't need Stoney or any man to 'let' me live at his place. I would have my own.

Once they were all out of here, I went to shower and found myself naked in front of Gable. *Great!*

"So, what time do we have to be out there for sound check?" I ask.

Stoney looks up from the magazine he's reading. "Oh, she does still speak. See Keeg, I told you she hadn't lost her voice in all of this."

I roll my eyes. "Shut up, I have a headache."

Gable walks back in. "Well, since you've had the hell beat out of you, slept like twenty hours and haven't eaten anything since before we left town yesterday, I bet you do."

I shake my head and stand up. I walk over to the fridge and grab a bottle of water and some ibuprofen. "So what time is sound check?"

Keeg stuffs a cookie in his mouth. "At two. So you have a couple of hours to make yourself look pretty."

I knew he was just playing but it still hurt a little. I nod. "Yeah, I need to go get started." I walk down the hallway and I hear a low argument between the guys.

"Real smooth jackass, remind her she looks like hell right now with your fucking pretty comment. And you, Gable, why don't you remind her just a little more how much her life is sucking right now."

I didn't need to listen anymore, I just locked myself in the back bedroom to get ready. We'd put all of our clothes in here and agreed that this would be a dressing room, the only way someone would sleep in here is if they had someone with them, and it couldn't be some groupie trash. The guys really tried to give it to me since I'm the only girl, but I took a rack just like one of them.

I sat down and looked in the mirror and noticed the bruising on my face was becoming very obvious. I tried to work some magic with my concealer and some foundation. I normally never wore this much make-up on stage because I would just sweat it all off, but tonight I was going to need it. I don't want all the other bands to see what a fucked up mess I am.

A couple of hours later I'm behind the guys, making my way to the stage for sound check. We pass by a group of girls who obviously want the guy's attention. They are dressed like something you would find on a runway in a shit hole strip club or on a street corner.

I'm used to the sneering looks that are sent my way when I pass by with the guys. There is always a loud drunk girl in the group. She puts her hand out to stop me. "Hey, can you get the guys to turn around?" I shake my head no. Trying to work my way past them, she grabs my shirt. "Hey, I was talking to you. Can you give Gable my number? He's so fucking hot."

"No. Now if you'll excuse me, I need to get the stage."

I hear her talking as I walk on by. She turns back to her friends. "She's just wants me for herself, you know she's probably gay, and if she's not, she might as well be because those hot guys are never gonna want her big ass."

I shuffle on past the crowd and make my way to the stage. Gable looks up. "Where were you?' He looks pissed.

"I was battling the skanks off of me. The ones who stopped me to get your number or for me you give theirs. I thought I might have to get a shot for STD's once I got away from them."

The guys never cease to amaze me because they look straight past me to see the group of women. "Look guys, just go on out there, ask them back to the bus, whatever, but we need to sound check. I'll make myself scarce until the show. I'm dressed anyway."

Keeg and Stoney lit up like Christmas morning. "Thanks, Ivie. Are you sure?" Keeg says.

"Yeah I'm sure, I'm gonna go for a walk around the grounds."

Gable stops. "Ivie."

I put my hand up. "Stop, I'm in a band with guys. I understand that. You guys like to bang anything that walks." Besides me. "So who am I to stand in your way? You play better after you've nutted, anyway."

We do a great sound check. I stop when I see one of the event coordinators. "Hey, um I need a new cell phone. Is there a store near here that   I   can   walk   to   or   something?"

She smiles. "Yeah, it's right down the street, but let me get one of the crew to take you there. That way I know you'll get in and out of the gates okay."

I nod. "Thanks. I can't believe I left it."

She radios someone to come over where we are.

I seriously don't know why I'm worried. The only people who called me on it were Chad and the guys. Well, and Dottie on the rare occasion that Gable didn't answer.

A young guy, probably fresh out of high school, pulls up in an SUV.

The lady looks at me. "Ivie, this is Jacob, he'll run you down to the store."

I nod. "Thanks again."

I slide into the SUV and head to the store.

The half-naked girl sitting across me would normally be great for me, but all I can think about is Ivie. What is she doing? Where is she at?

The girl starts rubbing my dick through my jeans. "So, Chubby really told you guys about us, huh? I didn't figure she would. I figured she was a lesbian or that she was a jealous girl keeping you guys to herself."

I grab her hand. "What did you call her?"

The girl shrugs. "I thought she was a lesbian or that she was an insecure chubby girl who likes keeping you guys to herself."

I stand up and she falls on the floor. "Get out!"

She jumps up. "What in the hell?"

"I said get the fuck out."

"My friends are in here." She looks down the hall to where two of her friends are in the bunks with Keeg and Stoney.

"You can wait for them outside."

She slides the scrap of material she was calling a top back on. "Unfucking believable. What, do you have a hard on for chubby girls?"

"What the fuck makes you think she's chubby? Because she's got a gorgeous fucking rack and an ass to kill. And you are a scrawny bitch with enough fucking padding in that push-up bra for a queen size mattress." I know this is true about Ivie because I just saw them in the flesh a couple of hours ago and it is all I can think about.

She stomps to the bus door. "Fuck you and your fat girlfriend!"

I grab up my shit for the show and walk out the bus door, just in time to see Ivie getting out of the passenger side of a really nice SUV. She has a bag in her hand and she makes her way back stage.

Who in the fuck was she with? I make my way backstage and find her in the small area set aside for the bands in large tents. She's messing with a phone. I sit down beside her. "Hey. Where did you go?"

She shows me the phone. "I left my phone at Chad's yesterday. I needed a new one."

"Oh, well who took you? I saw you getting out of an SUV."

"It was one of the volunteers, he was a young kid. One of the event coordinators set it up for me. I was going to go myself and just walk, but she didn't want me to have trouble getting in and out of the gates. After I paid for it I realized I really don't need it. You guys and Chad are the only people who call me."

I put my elbows down on my knees. "So, do you want to talk about it?"

"Not really. But I guess I owe you guys an explanation. He didn't like me playing in the band. He thought I was trying to sleep with you guys. I told him I wasn't and that you guys didn't think of me that way, either. He said he knew you guys could never look at me that way, but that I lusted after all of you. I'm pretty sure he's on something. He's been getting paranoid about little shit. It just started to get out of hand."

"The other week, when you came in with the bruises on your arms?"

"He left me handcuffed to the bed for a day. Yesterday was by far the worst that ever happened. I was trying to sneak out and leave before he got off duty."

She drops her head in her hands. I touch her knee and she jumps. "Ivie, why didn't you tell us this sooner?"

"I was determined to make this relationship work, plus I was living with him. I really didn't have money for my own place."

I shoot her a look. "Seriously? Like you couldn't go back to Stoney's or anything."

"Look, I'm tired of being the group fuck-up. I'm tired of dating shithead guys, falling for their crap, and then having to go back to Stoney's and be the laughing stock of the group. This tour just happened to come along at a good time. Now, when I get back home, I should have enough money saved up to get my own apartment and maybe a dog. NO man. I'm not going to be poor Ivie who's homeless again."

"Ivie. You are not the laughing stock of the group."

She stands up. "Yeah, well it sure feels that way some times." Then she turns to grab a bottle of water and walks off.

I sit there waiting for her to come back but she doesn't. Does she really see herself as being that messed up? That asshole, Chad, really told her that none of us would ever go for her. Obviously he didn't meet the seventeen year old versions of us who made a pact not to mess with her. We knew that if one of us screwed her over it would fuck up the band, and she was too great to lose. Who the fuck does he think he is to treat her like that?

I run my hands back and forth over my head. He left her hand cuffed to a bed for a day, and there is no telling what he did to her while she was handcuffed. I saw so many bruises on her today.

I shake my head, she thinks we laughed at her. Cade is right, she really does have some self-worth issues.

Soon, I see Stoney and Keeg walking through the tent. "Hey man, why did you kick their friend out? Luckily we were finished before they found out you kicked her out."

"Get over here and sit down douche canoes, we gotta talk."

I start off telling them why I kicked bitchy girl out, which they were pissed that she said those things, too. Then I told them about my talk with Ivie.

Stoney looks up sadly. "Why would she think we were laughing at her? I'd never laugh at her life. I love her like my little sister, I want to protect her. I honestly don't think I would care if she lived with me for the rest of our lives."

About that time, Ivie walks up. Keeg stands up and hugs her. "Sweet girl, I want to kill that bastard."

She glares at me. "You told them. I didn't realize I was fucking talking to a blabber mouth. Look, fucking stay out of my business, all of you. I don't try to counsel you guys on the whores you fuck, don't worry about my pathetic life. I'm a big girl, I can handle it. Now let's go, we have a show to play." She storms toward the stage and we follow.

The guys are trying to catch up but I stop them. "Look, just give her space, I guess that's what she wants. I guess she needs time to process it or whatever. I know dealing with my sister can be a pain in the ass roller coaster ride of emotions sometimes, but she works through it."

The boys nod and we walk to the side stage and wait to go on. I'd be lying if I didn't say I had not butterflies, but fucking birds, flying around in my stomach right now. I'm so damn nervous.

Ladies and Gentlemen, please welcome to the stage Beautifully Tainted!

Six Months Ago...

My Life List:
1. *No more men*
2. *Save enough money to rent an apartment on my own*
3. *Get rid of the flab*
4. *Work out*
5. *Restrict my fat ass to 800 calories a day, if not less*
6. *Learn to survive on my own. I don't need to lean on the guys. They have their own lives and I don't need their pity.*

These past two months on tour have been long hours. I'm still a little embarrassed in front of the guys and it's hard to avoid them when you live on a bus together, but after my melt down at our first show, they don't ask any more questions. I steer clear of the bus right after the show, unless we are pulling right out, so that the guys can screw whoever they want to. The only thing I ask is that they have the girls gone within an hour and stay the hell away from my bunk. It's easier when we stay at hotels. I get my own room, which is good because sometimes I wake up from nightmares about Chad coming after me. Gable stares at me all the time like I'm going to go off the deep end or something. He's always trying to get me to go eat with them. They don't understand that I'm trying to eat healthy and they eat junk. During this tour I'm making some changes. I go jogging or running wherever our location is and if we stay in a hotel that has a gym, I use it. I have restricted myself to 800 calories a day. I only drink water, no alcohol, and I keep a food journal. I'm starting to see results in the mirror. My body is pretty much healed from the fight. Of course, I'm still wearing the same clothes so no one else notices. I've only picked up a few new pieces, though I might would get a whole new wardrobe if these fucking boobs would go away.

I'm still in my own thoughts when Gable slaps my curtain. "Hey, we do sound check in fifteen."

I put my list down and grab my shoes as I slide open my curtain. "Thanks, man."

"Hey, our show is over kinda early tonight, the guys and I want us all to go out for dinner. We will pick a place where you can get something *healthy*. We just want you to come with us."

I shrug. "Sure, how are we getting there?"

"I called and got us a car."

I realize that I really haven't talked to any of them much at all. I need to try and be better because they are the only family I have. "So, how have things been with Scar? I mean after that wreck she was in." A month or so ago Scarlet had been run off the road and it totaled Gable's car.

"She's been good. Cade sent her his old car, which was fine with me. She was working at some shithole bar, it was kinda a dangerous place. So he gave her the car and made her quit. She's dating the guy that called me, Ryder. She seems happy, like really happy, for the first time in a long time."

I nod as I slide my long necklace over my head. "That's good. She deserves it, you know."

He puts his hand on my shoulder. "Everyone deserves happiness, Ivie." With that, he turns and walks out the door.

~*~*~

"Man! That was an awesome fucking show!" Keeg yells as we walk to the bus.

I can't help but notice the groupie whores outside the bus when we get back there. I speak softly to the guys. "Just let me grab a change of clothes and I'll give you guys your time."

Gable stops me. "Hey, I thought you were going out to eat with us?"

"Well, I mean you guys have some hot ass waiting here at the bus, so I figured we would go after."

Keeg steps up. "The only hot ass we are interested in doing anything with tonight is you. So let's get on the bus, shower, and go fuckin' eat. I'm starving!"

Stoney puts his arm around my shoulder. "Nope, you are stuck with us tonight. I know you don't want to hang out with a bunch of stinky guys but too bad, we wanna hang out with you."

We dodge around the groupies and get on the bus. I get first shower and then take over the back room to get ready. I need to dress nice if I want to be seen at a restaurant with them. Not that they care, but other people will have shit to say.

I pull on a denim skirt I bought a few weeks ago with my hot pink skull and cross bones tank top, a black studded belt, and my biker boots. I spend a few minutes on my hair and make-up before I make my way out into the front part of the bus. The guys must have dressed in the hall because they are ready to go.

Stoney rubs his face. "Damn Ivie, you look like a rocker's wet dream."

Keeg chuckles as Gable runs his hand on the back of his neck, shaking his head. I know they are full of it and just picking at me for wearing a skirt.

"Are y'all ready?"

They nod and we walk out to the SUV waiting for us.

My pants instantly tighten when she walks in with that outfit on. I knew looking at her face over the past few months that she'd lost weight, but seeing her in clothes that fit, she's a skeleton version of herself. Her boobs are mostly the same, but the curves of her ass are definitely smaller and her collar bones are sticking out. We need to put some weight back on her.

But today when she got out of her bunk, her *list* fell out and I picked it up after she walked off. She really sees herself as fat. I can't help but wonder what that fucker Chad said to her to make her feel that way. Then it could be bitches like that damn girl I kicked out a few months ago. I will never understand where women get off tearing each other down. Don't they know men find that shit stupid? It upsets me that she seriously thought we'd back out on our plans with her for a piece of ass. I'm just glad Cade helped me out with the Chad situation. That motherfucker isn't a cop anymore. He was strung out on all kinds of shit and some of Daria's acquaintances suggested that he leave Ivie alone. Well, more like physically persuaded.

It hasn't gone completely unnoticed to us that she disappears after the shows are over. She's told us that as long as we stay away from her bunk and are done within' an hour, she doesn't care. I just hate that she feels that way, like she's a guest on our bus. I've talked to the guys about stopping that shit.

After that first girl, I just haven't wanted anyone. It feels wrong for some reason. I'm tired of endless skanks. So my moodiness may be the fact that the only release I've had is in the shower courtesy of myself, and as much as I don't want to admit this, visions of Ivie.

Once we arrive at the restaurant, I sit on the side with Ivie so I can try to get her to open up. "So what's up? You live on a bus with us and we hardly see you."

What? I've never been one for beating around the bush.

"You guys see me all the time." She tries to blow me off.

Keeg rolls his eyes. "You are full of shit. We see you during practices and performances. Otherwise, you are like a ghost. You're either running or sleeping. Then whatever you do right after we get finished with shows."

She looks at us like she could punch us. Stoney glares at her. "You act like you don't belong on that bus with us. Like we don't want you there or something. We do. I mean, yeah, it's nice to get the attention that some of the girls give us, but most of the time we are just killing time. I'd rather sit around after a show sometimes and play Xbox or some shit without having to deal with some over made up diva chick who is drunk and trying to piss her daddy off."

She shakes her head. "You guys are full of it. You like getting your brains screwed out by random chicks. If I'm on the bus right after a show, it cramps your style. Trust me, girls have a way of letting each other know. And most girls let me know that I don't belong with you guys."

I speak up. "See, that's where you are wrong. We don't care if they think, or anyone thinks, you don't belong with us, because you do."

She looks at me and is about to fire back when the waitress shows up. I speak up. "We'll have four shots of tequila and four bud lights."

Ivie glares at me. "I'm not drinking. That is wasted calories. Plus, I haven't had anything to drink in months."

Keeg chuckles. "Well good then, you'll be a cheap drunk."

The waitress is back soon to take our orders. She looks to Ivie first.

Ivie smiles. "I'll have a spinach salad with no cheese and no dressing."

Holy shit, no wonder she looks like a skeleton. I speak up. "And she'll have the 7oz sirloin, medium, with a side of broccoli."

Ivie glares at me. "No, I'm only eating the salad."

"Ivie, you are eating something other than fucking spinach leaves. Now, the sirloin is the healthiest steak and I got your fucking broccoli, so there, it's healthy. You need the protein."

I look back to the waitress. "I'll have the 16oz Ribeye, medium, with the loaded baked potato. Oh yeah, and can I get some of that crab soup to start with?"

She looks to the other guys for their orders while Ivie glares holes into my body. "I'm not drinking, and I'm not eating that damn food."

I look at her with the same glare and whisper sternly. "Yes, you are. Take today as a cheat day, or whatever the fuck you want to call it, but you will be a member of this band tonight other than just on the fucking stage."

I really feel like a jackass for talking like that, but I can only handle so much. *Right now I'd love to bend her over a table with that skirt up over her ass.* Whoa! Shit, I have to stop my brain from going there.

She actually does take her shot with us and drink her beer along with another round we order. I'm proud that she actually eats most of her food.

When she asks me to let her out to go to the bathroom, I can't help that my dick pure groans in agony when her ass brushes against him. Finally, after she's gone for a minute, I make my way to the guy's bathroom to throw some cold water on my face.

She walks out of the ladies room about the time I'm walking down the hall and runs straight into me.

She stumbles and laughs. "See, I told you I didn't need to be drinking." As she slumps back against me smiling. Seeing that smile I haven't seen in a very long time does it for me.

My dick is hard as a rock again. *Fuck, I'm in trouble.*

After our second round of drinks I know I'm in trouble. I ate most of my food hoping that they wouldn't catch up with me so fast. Screw that idea, I'm so drunk that when I slide out in front of Gable to go to the bathroom, I'm pretty sure I feel his dick get hard against me.

I look at myself in the mirror while I'm washing up. I look kinda skinny in this outfit, or else I'm drunk enough to believe that. I feel kinda bad that in my own pity party, I've excluded them from my life. They have always been there for me and here for the past two months, we've been traveling the Gulf Coast and I've ignored them. Made excuses and ignored them. Why? Because I got my ass kicked by some asshat with a little man complex?

Wow, these drinks must really be helping my self-esteem right now, because I seriously want to go kick Chad's ass. I laugh at myself in the mirror and walk out the door, running right into Gable.

I laugh. "See, I told you I didn't need to be drinking."

He runs his hands down my sides. "See, that smile you just gave me, I've been missing. It really is a beautiful smile."

I look up into his chocolate brown eyes. "You really like my smile that much, huh?"

I don't notice we've backed up until my ass hits the wall. "Yes, I love your smile. I always have. It's killed me these past couple of months to see you so down." His hands are on my ass now. "Plus, we have to put some of this ass back on, it was one of my favorite curves of yours."

I giggle. "Oh really, well I got all of this flab off and it isn't coming back, sorry to disappoint."

He looks at me sternly. "Who told you that you have flab?"

I shrug. "Everyone. Girls. Guys. Chad."

He glares when I say Chad's name. "Look, they are all fucking stupid. You were perfect the way you were. All of your curves were in the right places and Chad is too much of a needle dick to realize it."

I start laughing uncontrollably at the needle dick comment.

He brushes the side of my face, lifting it up for him to see. "See, that's what I like to hear and see."

Suddenly his lips are on mine and his hands somehow end up back down on my ass.

I break from the kiss breathless. "Gable, what are we doing?"

He groans, pressing the crotch of his jeans into my lower stomach without even trying, resting his forehead on mine. "Fuck, I don't know."

"We can't do this. It'll fuck everything up, Gable."

He steps back, running a hand through his hair. "Fuck I know, I know. I've did my best to stay away from you all these years."

I'm standing here in shock by his admission. "So let me get this straight, you've been trying to stay away from me? Did you not want to be seen with me or something? Was I really that horrible to look at?" I feel myself tearing up as my insecurities come tumbling out.

I turn to walk back into the bathroom before he sees the tears in my eyes. "Ivie. Fuck, that isn't how I meant it."

I throw my hand up with my back to him. "Save it." I step back in the ladies room as tears start falling uncontrollably from my eyes.

Its only seconds later when the door bursts open and in comes Gable. I glare at him with tears running down my face. "Get out, this is the women's bathroom!"

He reaches behind him and turns the bathroom lock. "No. You are going to fucking listen to me." He grunts out. He backs me against the counter. "I know you felt how hard my dick was out there, do you really believe all that shit you said to me?"

I start to feel a panic come over me, I feel trapped. I start to shake uncontrollably in fear that he may hurt me.

He brushes away my tears with his thumbs. "Ivie. I know I sound rough right now but I would never hurt you. Never. Please don't shake like this, it breaks my heart."

He wraps his arms around me. "What I meant earlier was I was trying to stay away from you for the good of the band. I didn't want to complicate things."

"Look, I'm just a little over sensitive right now. Having someone tell you how ugly you are for months, along with beating the ever living shit out of you every chance he got, makes me that way."

He pulls me into his chest. "When you got out of that car and I saw your face, I was ready to kill him. But I-."

About that time someone starts beating on the door.

I start to giggle now. Jeez, I'm losing my mind. "They are going to think we are in here having sex and get us kicked out." I whisper in a giggle.

He looks at me. "Just follow my lead. Don't dry those tears up just yet." He tucks me into his side stroking my hair.

As we walk out the door, two women are standing there staring at us. He coos. "It'll be okay, sweetie. We'll get you there as quick as we can." He glances at them. "She just got a bad phone call from her family."

Both of the women act in awe over him stroking my hair. I hear them as we walk off comment on how sweet he is.

I stop him. "I really have to clean my face up before we get to the table."

He grabs my hand and pulls me around the corner. "Here, I'll help." He wipes the tears from my face, cleaning up the mascara as he does. He fans my face to pull some of the redness away.

Fuck, between crying my fucking eyes out and being horny, I probably look like shit.

"It's okay, if the guys ask I'll say I got sick."

Once we get back to the table, the guys look up and Keeg says, "I was beginning to wonder about y'all. Have you been crying?"

I shrug it off. "No, I got sick in the bathroom. I told y'all I haven't drank in months."

They nod and Stoney laughs. "Well, come on then light weight, let's get you back to the bus."

I laugh. "Fine, I suppose it's time to go."

We pay our bill and make our way out to the SUV. I slide in the backseat next to Gable and he reaches over to take my hand. I can't help but feel the heat in my face from the blush creeping up on it. Thank God it's dark in here.

I know we'll spend most of the day on the bus tomorrow. We actually go down the Space Coast to do some local festivals around West Palm so we should get plenty of rest, but I'm still ready to crawl in my bunk and pass out.

The guys agree as we get back on the bus. It isn't long before all of us are snuggling in our bunks. I don't even realize I've dosed off until I feel a shift in my bunk. I'm startled until I hear him whisper. "Hey. We weren't finished talking."

GABLE

Lying here in my bunk listening to Keeg and Stoney snore, I can't help but think how if those ladies hadn't interrupted us, how different things would have went. I remember how soft her lips were, the small demanding thrusts of her tongue.

Once again, I can't think about her without my dick getting hard. I'm doing something about this right now. I slip out of my bunk, making sure Keeg and Stoney are still snoring.

I slide open her curtain and I can make out her lying there, sleeping like an angel. I slip into the bunk alongside of her and slide the curtain closed. She jumps. I whisper into her ear. "Hey, we weren't finished talking."

She whispers back. "I'm pretty sure we were."

I continue to speak in hushed tones. "I'm pretty sure you said we'll finish this conversation in my bunk on the bus."

She giggles. "Um no, I don't think that is what was said at all."

I lean in and kiss her lips. "I'm pretty sure it was."

"No-." Before she can say more I'm consuming her lips.

"Damn, Ivie. You drive me crazy and I think you make my dick permanently hard."

She brushes her hand down against my boxers. "Hmm, seems I do."

I push her over on her back, quickly realizing this bunk isn't very big. How have Keeg and Stoney been banging girls in these things?

"Shit Ivie, this is small. We can't do much in here."

She reaches inside my boxers and starts stroking my dick. "Well we'll just have to improvise." She says.

I slide my hand into the front of her sleep shorts and find her wet. I rub her clit with my thumb while gliding two fingers into her. She lets out a soft moan. I put my mouth back to hers to keep us from making too much noise, working my way down to take her tight nipples into my mouth.

Fuck, this is like high school. But there is something fun about it. The make out session is intense. Man I want to bury my cock balls deep. I feel her shudder against me and the walls inside her sweet slice of heaven clutch around my fingers. I feel my balls drawing up and I explode on her. We both look down and giggle.

I whisper. "Why do I feel like I'm in high school all over again, trying not to get caught?"

She smiles. "Because we can't fuck things up, that's why."

I nod, knowing that she is right. If the other two guys ever figure this out, we'll be screwed.

She kisses me gently. "You should probably slip back into your bunk. I need to go clean up."

"You're right. I just wish I could get cleaned up with you."

"Yeah, well then we wouldn't get much cleaning up done, would we?"

I laugh and make my way quietly back over to my bunk. I hear her tiptoe to the bathroom and a few minutes later come back to her bunk.

As I lie here thinking about her, I can't wait to get her alone and show her how much more I want to do to her.

~*~*~

Today our show is a music festival in West Palm. We sit around in the back listening to the other bands. Ransom's End will be going on soon and we go on right before them. Right now a young band called Mind's Eye is rocking the stage with some serious old school skills. I look over at Keeg. "Man, if we ever get to headline our own tour, let's get them to open."

He nods. "Shit yeah. They've got some serious skills."

Ivie nods. "Holy crap, that kid playing bass is fucking awesome." She is listening intensely. I've always been amazed by how she can concentrate on the music like that, but I know it's the reason that she can just about pick up any piece of music and play it.

I sit in my own daze, thinking about what she sounded like when she got off. Her soft gasps and moans. Ivie has always been so hard core, but she seems so gentle during those moments.

Damn it, thinking about it I'm getting hard again. I'm going to have to go to the bus and take care of my problem. I stand up. "Hey guys, that food is messing with my stomach, I'm going to the bus to the bathroom. Just a fair warning."

Stoney nods. "Thanks for the heads up, man. We'll give it time to air out."

I look over to Ivie. "Hey, if you'll walk with me, I'll introduce you to that other female bass player I met. She's on the way."

Ivie stands up, playing along. "Sure, let's go."

Keeg looks at me. "Dude, you better not be getting some stomach flu. The rest of us have to live on that bus and if we all get sick, we only have one bathroom."

"Dude, I really think it's just the food."

He nods as Ivie and I walk away. She laughs once we are out of hearing range. "So I'm guessing you wanted alone time on the bus."

I nod and chuckle. "Yes. I've been thinking about you all damn day. I can't get that sound of you coming out of my head."

She tilts her head down. She's blushing, actually blushing.

Once we are inside the bus, I grab her and pull her to me. "Fuck Ivie, you are killing my dick." I pull her down the hall to the back bedroom. It's still not a very big room, but it's bigger than a bunk. I spin around to face her and grabbing her ass, I hoist her up to put her legs around me.

Slamming our mouths against each other, we are both breathless. She reaches for the bottom of her shirt and pulls it over her head. I start tugging at her bra and she finishes getting it off. I take one of her nipples into my mouth before lowering us to the bed. She reaches up, trying to pull my shirt over my head as I'm trying to work her jeans down. As soon as I get her jeans and panties off, I drop my jeans and boxers.

I'm about to take her but she puts her hand up to stop me. "Condom?"

I nod and grab one out of my wallet. "Sorry, it's been a while and well, I'm not normally this worked up. I'm not in the habit of going without one. Ever."

After I roll the condom on and lower myself into her, those beautiful brown eyes of hers grow large. "Oh shit."

"Are you okay?"

She smiles. "Yeah, it's just, well, it's been a little while, and the last time wasn't with someone as blessed as you."

I lean down, attacking her neck with my mouth. "Oh Fuck Ivie, what you do to me is insane."

I've never, and I mean never, wanted someone like I've wanted Gable Johnson. Before, I wouldn't let myself admit it, but when we had sex a few hours ago, it was hot. I'm still not sure exactly what we are but I'm not going to push it. Hell, we both have needs and it would be nice to have someone help us out with those.

We played a hell of a set tonight. Now, it's dark and I'm just taking a walk around the buses thinking while the last shows finish up.

I just know that one day we are going to be headlining our own show. That is the reason I know we have to keep whatever this is quiet and not even let the rest of the band know. If Gable and I decide that we don't want to do this anymore, then I don't want it to mess up our band.

We have a few more shows to play this week, then a day or so after Thanksgiving we'll be in Hilton Head. That's the closest we've been to home yet. I think from the sounds of things that guy Scarlet is dating has set up a trip for her to come see Gable.

Scarlet is a sweet girl and she is a fool over her big brother. I always thought she was kinda whiney, that is until she beat the shit out of her ex's car with an ax handle. Now I'm pretty sure she's a bad ass under that layer of debutante. I'm glad she's found someone to make her happy, and it seems like this guy Ryder would hang the moon for her if she asked him to.

I feel arms wrap around my waist from behind and I smell him before I turn around. "Yes, Gable, can I help you?"

We are in between the buses so I know that no one can really see us.

"Yes ma'am, I think you can. See, I have this problem in my pants. There is this girl who my dick can't seem to not be hard around. When I'm near her, even on stage. Especially when she sings." He nuzzles into my neck.

"Oh really, and what do you want me to do, make the girl stay away?"

He shakes his head. "Oh no, she can't go away."

I spin around to face him and back him up against the bus. "Maybe I can help another way."

I drop to my knees in front of him, undoing his jeans and pulling out his thick cock. I lick the tip of it and then continue by sliding my mouth down over it as far as I can go, working what I can't fit in my mouth with my hand.

"Fuck, Ivie."

After a few minutes I can feel his balls tightening, then he snatches me up and pulls down my pants. I turn around and face the bus, bending over and bracing my arms against it. I feel him thrust into me and it doesn't take us long to both explode into an orgasm.

I smile as we are getting our clothes back on straight. "So, did that help with the girl problem?"

He chuckles. "Well for now, but I may be addicted to her."

~*~*~

We only have three more days until we play the show in Hilton Head and I'm glad we will get to spend a couple of days there. We have one more show after tonight until we get there and I'm glad, I can tell I need a rest. All of the extra cardio that Gable and I have been sneaking in is doing a number on me.

The guys are horsing around on the way back to the bus. Gable and I have devised a plan to get alone time.

I stop. "Shit guys, I left my phone back by the stage. I'll catch up with you guys." Step one complete. Now I just wait between the buses until he gets here.

I do not know how the guys haven't caught us yet. The other night a roadie for Ransom's End almost caught us behind one of the storage trailers.

I giggle, suddenly feeling an arm around my waist, until I feel it tighten and a hand go over my mouth. "So you weren't ever fucking him, huh? Then how come for the past three nights I've watched you guys sneaking around? Seems you've turned into quite the exhibitionist." He puts his mouth next to my ear, running his nose by it. "You know, it might turn me on, I might would take you up against this bus right now if you hadn't fucking pissed me off so bad."

My heart feels like it is about to pound out of my chest. Where in the fuck is Gable?

"So, you know you cost me my fucking job, I think I deserve some sort of repayment." He tries to nuzzle my neck and I start trying to get away. I finally bite his hand. "FUCK! You bitch!"

I manage to pull away but at the same time he throws me into the side of one of the buses. I fall to the ground. "Chad, I didn't do anything to make you lose your job."

"Oh yeah, then why did they drug test me you lying fucking cunt?" He kicks me in the side. "I got fired for that and my anger problems. Then a couple good ole' boys came and beat the shit out of me." He rests his boot on my hand. "So, why don't you start explaining before I break that fucking hand you play bass with?"

My voice quivers. "Chad, I'm serious, I don't know anything about any of this." He pushes his heel down further into my hand. "Chad, I'm sorry, but I really don't know anything. Please let me up."

I bury my face in the dirt and suddenly he's gone. I look up to see him and Gable rolling all over the ground fighting. I scream for security. Finally, a big ass guy from one of the other bands comes over and grabs Chad, slamming him into a bus hard enough that it shook. By that time security is there calling the local police and escorting him away. A couple of the officers take a statement from me before they leave.

Walking back to the bus, I realize I now have an audience. My band looks angry enough to kill Chad on the spot. I look around and Gable takes me under his arm. "Come on sweetie, let's get you on the bus. Is your hand okay?"

For the first time since Chad's boot was lifted off of it, I think about it. I flex it. "It feels okay, but it's going to be sore."

He kisses the top of my head. "Are you sure we don't need to have a doctor check it or anything?"

I stumble a little, feeling drained and dizzy. "No, it'll be fine."

Gable stops me and turns. "Are you sure you're okay?"

"I'm just a little dizzy, I think the adrenaline is hitting me."

The next thing I know he's scooping me up off the ground and I'm being carried to the bus. Keeg and Stoney have beat us there, they open the door for me and Gable walks straight through the bus to the back bedroom, kicking the door shut behind him.

He starts undressing me out of my sweaty show clothes and grabs a pair of my pajamas. "Here baby, put these on and lie down. I'm going to get you some water and something to eat."

I nod. "Thanks."

He steps out the door and I can hear the guys talking to him as he gathers up some stuff for me. Once he steps back in the room, he brushes my hair back from my face. "Babe, are you sure you're okay?" He sits some crackers, water, and pain medicine down for me.

"Yes, I'm fine, I just need some sleep. I know I'm going to be sore, but I've been through worse."

He nods. "I know, but don't remind me." He steps back. "Look, you're going to sleep in here tonight so you can stretch out. I'll check on you in a little bit, okay?"

I slide into the bed after eating my crackers and taking my pain medicine. I do my best to drift off into sleep.

Walking back out into the living area of the bus, I sit down to talk with Keeg and Stoney for a little while. They have a ton of questions, but I finally stop them. "Look, I'm sure Ivie will talk about it in the morning, right now she just needs to rest."

They both nod and we sit back, drinking a few beers, playing Xbox, and eating junk food. Stoney looks up at me after a few beers. "So, are you gonna tell us what's been going on between the two of you?"

I look at them like they are crazy, pausing the game. "What in the hell are you talking about?"

Keeg lets out a barking laugh. "Dude, it really hasn't been too hard to figure out." He smiles. "You went from looking like you *could* grudge fuck each other to death, to looking like you *have* grudge fucked each other to death." He takes a sip of his beer. "Then, the fact that you are now both going missing right after shows, and if that wasn't enough, one of the roadies told Stoney they saw you the other night."

I put my hand out. "Look-."

Stoney stops me. "Hey, we are okay with it, as long as you guys don't fuck it all up for the band. I mean hell, you've both been in a lot better mood, so I see it as a win-win."

I look at him confused. "A win-win?"

He laughs. "Yes, you guys are happy, not moping around anymore, and it means more pussy for Keeg and me."

I flop my head back and run my hands through my hair. "Look guys, we are both just figuring it out. We don't want to jeopardize the band either, so that is why we've been quiet about it. Okay?"

Stoney leans forward. "Hey man, it's cool, we aren't going to say anything."

Suddenly, we hear Ivie screaming from the back room. I jump up and run to the back. Bursting through the door, I see Ivie thrashing in the bed. I reach for her and she begins hitting me. "IVIE! Baby, it's me, wake up." I shake her a little. "Ivie, wake up."

Finally, her eyes pop open. She gulps a breath and I see the tears dried on her face.

Finally, I sit her up and start rubbing her back. "Are you okay?"

She shakes her head and covers her face with her hands. "Oh my God. It was just a dream. He was attacking me. It was crazy."

I shoo the guys away from the door. "I'll stay back here with her."

I stand up, strip down to my boxers, and slide into bed with her. I pull her back into me and stroke her hair. "Baby, just go back to sleep. I'll stay here with you."

"Gable. What about the guys?"

"I'll talk to you about it in the morning. Try to go back to sleep."

~*~*~

Morning comes way too quickly. The sun is shining in from the side windows of the bus and I feel the slow swaying motions of our movement. I look down at my chest that has Ivie's hair draped across it. This feels great, I wish I could wake up every day like this. *What in the hell am I saying?*

Sliding her off my chest, I slowly stand up to go take a piss. She stirs from her sleep and sits up, rubbing her face. "Hey."

"Hey, babe. I'll be right back."

She nods as I leave the room. Once I'm in the hallway, I can still hear Keeg and Stoney snoring from their bunks. I go into the bathroom and do my business, quickly returning to the bedroom.

As I enter the bedroom, she's looking at her arms and moves to feel the sides of her face. She looks up at me. "So, how did you explain sleeping in here all last night to the guys?"

I sit down on the side of the bed. "Well, right before you had your nightmare, the guys basically called me on the carpet about us. I guess we haven't been as discreet as we thought we were being."

She puts her hands over her mouth. "Oh my God! What did they say about it?"

I shrug. "They are cool with it, said we both seem happier and less bitchy. As long as it doesn't mess up the band, they are fine. Plus, they said it leaves more chicks for them."

She snorts a laugh. "They would add that in there."

I chuckle. "Yeah, they referred to it as a win-win. A minute or so after that, you started screaming. We ran in here and figured out you were having a nightmare. I decided to stay in here with you, so you weren't alone." I lean over and pull her in, nuzzling her neck. "But I have to say, waking up with you this morning was damn good. If I hadn't had to piss so damn bad, I might have tried out this bed with you."

She giggles. "Stop it, we are not doing that in here so that Beavis and Butthead out there can hear us."

I kiss her. "I'm just playing. I figure we'll be staying in hotels for the next couple of nights, and we can definitely take advantage of that." I kiss my way down to her collar bone.

"Stop before you start something neither of us will want to stop. Let's go eat some breakfast, and I promise tonight we'll stay in the same room." She stands and adjusts her clothes. "Come on, let's go eat."

We step out into the hallway where Keeg and Stoney are coming out of their bunks.

Keeg looks up. "Is somebody cooking, or are we gonna ask Tanker to stop the bus?"

I glance up at them. "No, let's just cook. Tanker is trying to get us into Birmingham as soon as he can. His son is in college there, he's coming to hang out and watch the show tonight."

They all nod, rubbing the sleep out of their eyes. Ivie makes her way through the group of us. "Come on, fucktards, I'll make some eggs and bacon."

Stoney laughs and pops her on the ass. "Get your ass in the kitchenette, little woman."

She spins around and nut checks him. "Just for that, I'm not making extra bacon for you."

He grabs her around the waist. "I'm just kidding. Please fix my extra bacon."

She shakes her head. "Get in there and sit down, guys. Play your damn Xbox or something and shut up."

They make their way into the sitting area while Ivie starts getting stuff out for breakfast. I step in the kitchenette area on my way and brush my hand on her ass. "Thanks."

IVIE

Okay, I'm too old to be feeling like the giddy school girl that has finally gotten the attention of her crush. Here I am, though, feeling like I'm alive for the first time in months. Even being sore and bruised from Chad attacking me last night, I still feel good. Gable makes me feel safe. I don't know what spurred Chad to attack me last night, other than being a horrible person, but the guys have assured me on this bus ride that he was arrested and is in jail.

Here we are, rolling into Birmingham. I walk back to the bedroom and gather my things to take to the hotel room. I feel hands slip around my waist. I texted ahead and let them know that our band would only need two rooms tonight.

"How are we going to explain that? They know we always get three rooms. Mine, yours, and those two."

He nuzzles into my neck. "I told them I was staying with some local friends tonight. If anyone asks later, I'll say that my plans fell through. Hell, we all stay on the same bus together, and we're adults. It's really none of their damn business." I lean my head further over to give him better access to my neck. I feel his crotch hardening against my ass.

"Alright you two. We're okay with this, but you can't fuck right in front of us."

Gable grunts at Stoney standing in the doorway. "We aren't fucking, man. Although, if you don't get the hell out of here, we may just put on a damn show for you."

Stoney storms out of the room, grumbling about us being *assholes*.

I pop Gable on his arm. "Don't say shit like that. I'm not putting on some sort of exhibition for anyone. Plus, just because they've given us the go ahead, I'm just not there yet. You know?"

He nods. "Yeah, I do. I was just bullshitting. If he hadn't walked in here and started trying to bust my balls, nothing else would've been said."

"I know, it's just still a little weird for me. Okay?"

He kisses me on the lips. "Yeah, babe. It's okay if you wanna keep me as your dirty little secret."

I punch him in the arm. "Asshole. Trust me, you aren't anywhere near the dirty secrets I have." With that said, I walk out of the room.

It's true, I really wonder if he knew all of the secrets I have, if he'd still be interested in me at all. I make my way to sit in front of the TV until we arrive at the hotel.

As soon as we enter the hotel room, Gable grabs me by my hips and I laugh. "You do know we have plenty of time, right?"

He strips my t-shirt over my head. "Yes, but I want to use all the time." He leans down, kissing my chest above my breast line. "Look, the guys know about us, and we aren't having to sneak around. I just feel like it's perfect and in my life, if it's perfect, it can be snatched away. I just don't want to waste any time."

I nod breathlessly. "Sure, I get it."

~*~*~

Standing under the stream of hot water pouring over me, I relax. I hear the bathroom door open and Gable speak. "Hey, you want company?"

I shake my head. That boy never ceases to amaze me. "If you get in here, we won't make it to the show. I'm almost done and then you can get in."

He sticks his head in the curtain. "I guess you have a point, because if I join you," he shakes his head. "I won't want to leave."

I turn off the water and step out. "Stop looking at me like that, you perv."

"Right now I want to lick all that water off of you."

I wrap my towel tighter. "Well, you're just goin' to have to wait." I laugh as he strips down and jumps in the shower.

I hear my phone ringing as I walk out in the room. Looking down, it's from an unknown number. "Hello."

It's a recording letting me know that I'm receiving a call from an inmate at a federal prison. Knowing it's my dad, I accept the charges.

"Ivie."

"Yes, Dad."

"How are you doing?'

"I'm doing fine. What's up?"

"I was calling to check on you."

"Why? You haven't called just to check on me in years. Normally you need money for your account."

"Well, not this time. I heard you were having some troubles."

I shake my head. "What are you talking about?"

"Well, that last boyfriend you had-"

I cut him off. "How did you know about Chad?"

"Look, there were some people asking about him. Then they put the word out that you weren't to be messed with. I heard that he didn't follow the rules."

"How did you hear all of this?"

"Don't worry about that. Look, I know I've been a shitty father, but just watch your back. He's a desperate man now."

"He's in jail, so I'm not worried." I hear the shower shut off. "Look, I appreciate the concern, but I have to get ready for a show."

"Yes, I heard your band was doing really well."

I shake my head, annoyed. "Really. Well, how is it that you know more about my life while you're in prison than when I was living under the same roof with you?"

"Ivie. Like I said, I know I've been a shitty parent. I'm sorry. Look, you get ready for your show. Take care."

"Yeah."

"Oh, and Ivie? I love you."

Complete shock is how I would describe the feeling. "A- yeah- you, too."

I hang up the phone, confused about many things. I'll wait until after the show and talk to Gable about it. I can't help but think about the fact that when we are in Hilton Head in a few days, we won't be far from where he's doing his time.

"Hey, babe." His kisses my neck. "Were you talking to someone?"

"Yeah. My dad called."

"What in the hell did he want?"

"We'll just talk about it after the show, I need to get ready. Plus, I'm not sure I'm ready to rehash it."

He nods, knowing that I'm done talking at the moment.

"Okay, well let's get ready."

I don't know what her dad said to her, but she's quiet. When Ivie is quiet, it gets scary. She withdraws from everyone and everything. Her dad calling and Chad showing back up doesn't feel like a coincidence. *Shit. Did I fuck up by bringing Cade into this?*

My mind is racing, even after the show. I can't wait to get her back to the room and talk to her. I know her dad is in prison just north of Hilton Head. Does he want her to come see him or something?

We bid our good nights to Keeg and Stoney as the driver drops us off at the hotel. I'm sure they are on their way out to hit up the clubs and find some ass.

"Do you wanna order a pizza or something?" I ask as we walk through the door.

"If you find a place that can bring me a salad."

"You just sweated off like a million calories, and I know I'll work some more off of you before the night is over. You need food, not garnishes."

"I can't keep eating like I am, I'll gain all of my weight back."

I step in front of her. "I'm going to tell you this one time. I don't care if you do gain it back. I was happy with you just the way you were."

She rolls her eyes. "Yeah, whatever."

"What the fuck does that mean?"

She walks over to the sofa and drops down. "Just that you say that, but you didn't seem to pay much attention to me before I lost the weight is all."

"That's bullshit. Just because I didn't make a move on you, doesn't mean I wasn't thinking about it." I flop down next to her. "Honestly. I've had a fucking hard on for you since I was seventeen. I'm just tired of ignoring it." I grab her hand as she's trying to not look me in the face. "Now, I'm going to order a fucking pizza and some beer. Then, you are going to tell me what the fuck is going on."

She goes to the bathroom and I order the pizza, some wings, beer and a little side salad for her. I'm fucking starving after a show, but maybe the salad will make her eat. She can eat some other food with it.

When she comes out of the bathroom, she's in her sleep shorts and tank.

"Hey, food is coming."

"Look, I'm tired and I want to sleep."

"Damn it. Ivie, if you don't tell me what's going on, I'm gonna spank your ass until you can't sit down."

"Fuck you!"

"Yeah, I'm kinda hoping that's going to happen. Until then, tell me what your dad said because this..." I point to the frown she has on her face. "Isn't working for me."

She sighs. "Fine."

She starts relaying her conversation with her dad, and I realize, yep, I have to come clean.

Once she stops talking, there is a knock at the door. I stand up and get our delivery. Setting it down between us, we start chowing down. As I suspected, she's hungrier than she tried to make me believe.

After I finish off the last beer of the six pack, I put my hand on hers. "Ivie, I need to talk to you about something."

She looks up at me, lost. "O-kay."

I take my time, carefully explaining my conversation with Cade.

"Gable, I- I just really don't know what to say. I don't know whether to be angry or to be somewhat relieved."

"Babe, I wanted to do whatever I could to keep you safe."

"I know this is going to sound strange, but I think when we get to Hilton Head tomorrow, I wanna go up and see my dad."

I nod. "Okay, I'll go with you. Well, if you want me to."

She nods. "Yeah, I think I'm going to need you."

I kiss her forehead. "Hey, baby I'm here for whatever you need."

"Oh shit. Isn't your sister coming in?"

"Yeah, but not tomorrow, it's Thanksgiving. Ryder is telling her tomorrow night and they'll come in on Friday."

"Okay. Can we just go to sleep tonight?"

"Baby, I want to be with you. Whether it's sleeping or fucking, I want to be with you."

She curls up on the bed and I slide in behind her, rolling her over so that she is curled into my side, with her head in my chest. I switch the lamp off. Tomorrow is going to be a long day.

"Gable?"

"Yeah?"

"Thanks for saying you'll go with me tomorrow. I'm really nervous about this."

"Babe, how long has it been since you've seen your dad?"

"The last time I actually visited him, I was fifteen, I think. He told me I needed to make better grades. The last time I talked to him was about six months ago, he needed money for his account and none of his *friends* would send it to him."

I'm angry. "He said you needed to make better grades? You were a fucking genius in school."

She tenses. "How did you know that?"

Shit, I forgot. "One of the times that we were moving you, your transcript fell out. We looked at it. Sorry."

"It's nothing, I shouldn't get upset about it. It was just after he told me that, I let my grades tank. It pissed me off because he was telling me to do better when I was doing the best. He didn't really know and he didn't really care."

I pull her in tight. "Well, he was an idiot, and it's his loss for not being a part of your life."

"I never understood what I did to them. Why they couldn't just love me."

"Baby, I understand, kinda. I mean, why did my dad have to be such a douche and have two, possibly more, wives now? Why did my mom have to be such a push over? I honestly worry that she would take him back if he showed up tomorrow."

"Our parents have really done a number on us, huh?"

"Yeah, babe. Let's get some sleep, you have a big day tomorrow if you still want to go."

"Yeah, I still want to go. I need to face him."

I sigh and pull her into me so we can sleep.

Waking up with my head resting on Gable's chest, I hear the slow beating of his heart. I feel the rhythm of his breathing and realize this is my favorite place to be. I kiss his chest.

He moves in the bed. "Good morning, babe."

I smile. "Good morning. I've decided you are my new favorite pillow."

He laughs. "Oh, am I now?" He quickly shifts, rolling me onto my back. He leans down, taking my nipple in his mouth through my shirt. "But you are so much softer than me."

"Mmm, but I like sleeping on something firm."

I feel the hardness of his cock pressing against my inner thigh and he starts kissing my neck. "Well maybe we can flip back and forth."

I smile. "Maybe we can." I run my hands down his chest.

He slowly slides my shirt over my head, then slides my shorts down my legs. Sitting back on his knees, he works his sleep pants down. He starts to slide into me, but I stop him. "Gable, condom."

"Shit." He jumps up and grabs one from his bag. Rolling it on, he leans down and slides into me. "I've never been this careless about condoms. I'm sorry."

"It's okay. I just know we've already pushed our luck one time, we just gotta be careful. I promise, while we are home at Christmas, I'll go back on the pill and we won't have to worry so much."

"Sounds like a plan." He slowly slides in and out of me, paying attention, moving like every move is going to be his last. This is the first time we've made love. We've had several rounds of hot, sweaty, body slapping sex, but this is a first. It's slow and meaningful.

An hour later, we shower and dress to go visit my dad. Gable knew I needed someone to show me how much he cares before we went to see my dad.

Walking out of our room, the tour company's SUV is waiting. He must've talked to someone while I was in the shower because it's just the two of us.

"I talked to Jana, you know, the lady who is over our cars and stuff. I told her you had a family matter you needed to take care of just north of here, but that you needed your privacy. So, she let me drive you up for the day."

I smile with tears in my eyes. "Gable, you are the sweetest guy I know. Thank you so much."

"Hey, don't go around saying that. I have a reputation to keep up after all." He winks at me.

"Ha ha so funny. So, how did you explain you driving me?"

He shrugs. "I told her you wanted one of us to go and that the others were busy. She really didn't pry. I mean, we are a pretty quiet group compared to some of the others. So I guess she feels like she doesn't have to babysit us like the other groups."

"That makes sense, I guess. I mean, Ransom's End is constantly having hotel security called on them. Hell, the only time security has even been called into our area was the other night."

"Right. So I guess she's counting her blessings with us being the good kids."

We both laugh. Truth is we aren't that band that likes to go out, tear up a town, trash hotel rooms and make a scene. We are all pretty laid back people, and we know that so many groups that act like it's Spring Break every day, crash and burn all too soon.

Pulling up in front of the prison, I get nauseous. I step out of the SUV and run to a trash can, emptying the food I ate late last night from my stomach.

Gable steps to my side, rubbing my back. "Babe, are you sure you want to do this?"

I nod. "Yes, I have to." I reach in my purse and grab some gum. "Okay, let's go. I looked and they are only visiting certain hours today because of the holiday."

Twenty minutes later, we've been searched, our belongings have been checked in and we've been patted down so many times I think I need a cigarette.

We sit down at a small table waiting for my dad to come out. I hold Gable's hand under the table. Once my dad enters the room, I realize how much he's changed in the past few years. He looks so much older and tired.

He sits across from us. "Ivie. I have to say, I'm surprised by this visit."

"Yeah well, I needed to know what all you know about the Chad situation."

"Is that the only reason for this visit?"

"No. I have a few other things to say, but I want to know the other first."

He nods to Gable. "Who is he?"

"Dad, this is Gable. He's in the band with me and one of my best friends." I feel Gable flinch, but I turn my attention back to my dad.

"Once people asked me about you, I found out what he'd done. Then I found out that some, let's just say, influential people had been made aware of the situation. He was informed to stay clear of you. He decided not to listen to that advice and attacked you. Yes, he is in jail now, but if he's ever released, watch out for yourself. He's desperate and won't think anything of taking you to hell with him. If he gets out again, they'll kill him. So please, just lookout for yourself."

I roll my eyes. "I always have. So anything else?"

He shakes his head. "Just I'm sorry."

"Look, I just want to say some things and then I'm going to go." He nods. "I think you and mom were really shitty to me. I walked around feeling like you guys hated me. Then, when you went to prison and told me to get better grades, it proved you never knew anything about me. I was at the top of my class, even though I never really had parents to guide me." I swipe a stray tear I didn't realize was falling until it hit my cheek. "Then, I had an aunt who treated me like a common whore. She said I was no better than my mother and she always made it painfully obvious that I was a bother to her. So, I quit caring, and once I got kicked out of school, she kicked me out." I shake my head. "I guess I'm just saying I'm pissed, and maybe you can't see past your own problems, but the shit you and mom did to me started a cycle. I know you said you are sorry for being a shitty father, but sometimes words don't cover it."

He nods and I swear I see tears in his eyes. "I'm sorry, I know that doesn't cover it. I didn't know your aunt was treating you that way. She always made it seem to me like you were a rough teen and that your grades were in the shitter."

"My grades started out great, but once I lived with her for a little while, she constantly reminded me that the only reason I was there was because of my check. That she hated my mother, even though she was her sister. I didn't care anymore and yes, my grades went to shit. As a sophomore, I already had colleges looking at me for their medical programs, but I lost all of that."

We make small talk for a few more minutes, in which he apologizes numerous times for how I was treated. I decide I'm ready to go knowing that I didn't want this visit to be very long. I wanted him to know how I felt and move on.

After retrieving our things from the check-in area, we make our way out to the parking lot. Once inside the SUV, I slump down in the seat and close my eyes.

The ride back to the hotel has been quiet to say the least. I feel the tenseness coming off of her body. I still feel a little twinge of anger that she referred to me as her bandmate and best friend. How in the fuck am I just that? As we pull into the parking lot, she looks over at me. "I better get my own room tonight." *What the fuck? Is she running now?*

I look at her like she's lost her mind. "Why?"

"Well, Scarlet is coming tomorrow. Aren't they going to stay with you?"

"No, she and Lover-boy already have a room for themselves. You are staying with me."

"What are you going to tell her about us?"

"It's none of her business, right? Besides, you said it yourself to your dad. We are *just friends*." I know she can hear the sarcasm dripping off my tongue.

"What's the problem with that?"

I roll my neck around to get it to pop. "So, we aren't any more than that? Just friends that fuck around."

She starts rubbing her temples. "How do I explain it to my dad, or anyone for that matter? What do I say, then? I'm not ready to label us. Hell, we are still keeping this a secret from everyone but the band."

"If it was up to me, we wouldn't be a secret from anyone. I want the world to know you're mine, Ivie. I'm nervous as fuck because I'm afraid I'm going to wake up one morning and you'll be gone. The only reason I haven't told you any of this is because I'm afraid you'll run." We've made our way into our room, slamming the door behind us.

"That's bullshit, Gable, and you know it. If it all goes wrong, I can't leave the band."

"Exactly, you don't want to leave the band."

She turns, grabbing her purse. "Fuck you, Gable. I'm going for a walk down by that lake we saw on the way in. Leave me alone, I'll be back when I get back."

With that, the hotel room door slams again. *Fuck, they are going to call security on us.* I sit around texting with Ryder about his and my sister's trip tomorrow. He said he's telling her tonight at Thanksgiving Dinner, so I'm sure I can expect a call from her just after they finish.

After an hour or so, I pull out my guitar, thinking about Ivie. I didn't mean to be such an ass, but it's as if she wants to just blow off what we have. I start fiddling with the strings and humming.

> *You unlock the door and climb inside-*
> *You don't need seat belts for this ride-*
> *You take my heart and hold it in your hands-*
> *Taking for granted where you stand-*
> *I've never been one to let go of control-*
> *But with you I seem to do that more-*

About that time, the door opens and Ivie comes back in. I look up. "Hey."

"Hey." She says softly.

I place my guitar on the floor and pull her by the hand to the sofa. "Sorry about losing my shit earlier. You've had a bad couple of days. You don't need me acting like some over possessive shitbag."

She shakes her head. "No, I can understand why you would be upset. It's just that right now, I need some time to figure all of this out."

I nod. "Okay. Look, I'm going to head down to the hotel restaurant and grab some food. Maybe a beer or two with the guys. You coming?"

"No, I think I just want to relax. We have a pretty big show tomorrow night and it could mean big things for us. I just need to rest and put my visit, and everything else, behind me."

I nod, grabbing my wallet and heading out the door.

Sitting at the hotel bar, my phone rings. "Hello."

"Hey big brother!"

"Hey there."

"So you and Ryder pulled one over on me, huh?"

"Yep. So I'll see you tomorrow?"

"Yes, I'm so excited!"

"I'm glad, kid. Look, they are bringing out my food so let me go. Text me when you guys get on the road tomorrow. Okay?"

"Yes. I can't wait to see you."

She hangs up and I stare at the food that's been sitting in front of me for ten minutes now. I hated lying to get her off the phone, but Scarlet and I have always been close and I would probably spill my guts to her.

I can't eat. I want to feel Ivie's soft body against mine. I motion for the check and ask for a take-out box. I'm going to need some food in a little bit, after I ravage her body.

I quietly open the door to the room, noticing the lights off. She's asleep in the other bed. NO fucking way, she sleeps with me. I put the food in the fridge, and strip out of my clothes. I pick her body up and place it on the bed below me.

She stirs, startled awake. I put my hand on her face. "Shh baby."

I slide her shirt up and pull her panties down her legs. Picking up her leg, I start kissing at her ankle and make my way up her thigh. Hearing her breath catch only makes my dick harder. I start on her other leg. Once I reach her center, I spread her wet folds with my fingers and work her throbbing nub with my tongue. I keep tantalizing and teasing it over and over.

"Gable." She sighs out.

I move and start making my way with my lips up her body. I kiss her stomach and breasts. I take her nipples in my mouth, one at time, and I lick and suck on them until she cries out.

She reaches for her shirt, sliding it over her head. I slide into her, and our bodies start moving together as one.

Our movements become faster and driven. We are both clawing and kissing our way over each other's bodies. As I slam into her repeatedly, I feel her tighten around me as she's going over the edge. She says my name as she comes. Moments later, I explode into her.

Rolling off of her, I cuddle her into my side. I pull the blankets over us and we both start to doze off quickly.

I wake up to the sound of Gable's phone going off. "Babe, your phone is going off."

He picks up his phone. "Scarlet is on her way," he says as he lays his phone back down, adjusting the blankets.

He rolls over facing me. "Baby, I'm sorry for coming in here last night and just taking you."

I start laughing. "I don't think I was complaining. If I remember correctly, I was thanking God."

He chuckles. "Well, glad you were happy about it. I was just sitting there trying to eat and I really wasn't hungry. I need you. Sitting there without you, I felt nothing." The more he says, the more serious he sounds.

I stand up, pulling on one of his t-shirts. "Gable, I know. For me, these past few months have been crazy. Right now, I need you, but I need time, too. So, can you handle that? I can't make us public yet. I can't put a label on us. Can you be patient with me?"

He stands up on the other side of the bed with a mixed facial expression. "So, what exactly are you saying? You say you can't put a label on us, does that mean we see other people or what? I'm confused."

Man, he just isn't getting it. "I'm not saying I want to see other people, I'm just saying I'm not ready to go public. I want you. I only want you. If I'm being honest, I've only wanted you since the day I met you as a young, stupid seventeen year old girl."

I can see the look of shock across his face. "You really have wanted me since we met?"

I nod. "Yeah, since you shook my hand."

"And after I told you basically the same thing the other night, you decide to share this now?"

"Yes, now. Really, you never said you only wanted me for that long. You said you had a hard-on for me since then. It's different. The way you used to go through girls, why should I take for granted that you've changed or that I would've been any different back then? Maybe I'm just convenience right now, maybe I'm not, but I need time to figure it out."

"Are you fucking kidding me? I haven't been with anyone else in months. Do you remember our first show on this tour? The fake girl with the fake hair and fake boobs? I kicked her off the bus. Before I realized that my feelings about you were true enough for me to pursue, I kicked her out. She said something bitchy about you and I kicked her fake ass out. Before we went on tour, it had been at least two months." He gets real close to my face. "So no, Ivie, you are not just some piece of ass to me. You've always been more, even when I was too dumb to realize it."

I feel the tears threatening in my eyes. I softly put my hand on his chest. "I'm sorry. I didn't mean for it to get this intense. I'm also sorry for judging you by your past. It's just that I've always felt like I jumped from relationship to relationship, lumping one shitty guy in with another. Gable, you aren't a shitty guy, and I don't want to lump you in with them. My feelings for you run deeper than anything I've ever known, I just need a little bit to work on myself before I go announcing to the world that we are together."

I look up in his eyes to see his heated stare. He pulls me into his chest. "Okay babe, I get this is all inner turmoil for you. So, as long as you and I are on the same page and we know that it's just the two of us, I'm not looking at anyone else and you aren't either."

I shake my head. "No. I don't want anyone else. I just don't want us to get ahead of ourselves and be public fuck-ups."

He puts his hands on my upper arms. "Okay then. No more running away, or trying to run away. We don't have to label this or explain it to anyone else. For all I care, they can go to hell, what we do is our business. Just please trust me, Ivie. I can honestly say I've never felt like this before, even if we don't know what this is."

I fall back into his chest. "Thank you for trying to understand me."

He kisses the top of my head, inhaling my scent. "Thank you for giving me a chance."

I look up into his eyes and I'm pretty sure I see unshed tears.

I step back. "I'm gonna order some breakfast. Do you want some?"

He sighs. "No, Scarlet will be here soon and we are going to lunch, I better jump in the shower."

I nod. "Okay. For now, can we tell her that the hotel was overbooked and neither of us will share a room with the other two? Which is a partial truth. I can't face your sister right now."

He chuckles and nods. "Yeah, babe." He turns to go in the bathroom.

~*~*~

A little while later, there is a knock at the door. I open the door to see Scarlet and her boyfriend, Ryder. She's looking at me like, *What in the hell are you doing in my brother's room dressed only in one of his shirts?* "Hey Scar, Gable is in the shower." I can tell she wants to know something. "The hotel was short on rooms last night so Gable bunked with me. Normally, he and I both get rooms to ourselves."

She has a flash of worry across her face. "Oh, okay."

She nods and thank God I hear the shower shut off, so I know Gable will be out here in a minute. As soon as he opens the bathroom door wrapped in only a towel, I really want to push his ass back in the bathroom. I start gathering my things up to take in the bathroom and mumble to Gable on the way by. "I'm getting a shower. See you later."

After stepping in the bathroom, I try to compose myself. I take a seat on the edge of the tub and my thoughts are racing. *What is Scarlet out there saying to Gable? What is he going to tell her? Why do I really care? Of course I care, it's his sister, the person he loves more than life.*

I almost jump out of my skin when there is a tap on the door, and I stand up and open it just a little. It's Gable. He steps in the bathroom and shuts the door.

Pressing me up against the counter, he slams his mouth into mine. He whispers. "Fuck, baby. I want you right now. I started thinking about you while I was in the shower and then the thought of you getting in now. Fuck, it's about to do me in."

"Babe, you gotta go with your sister, and I'd prefer that you walk out of this bathroom without a fucking huge ass hard-on."

"Well, then we need to fix the problem."

We are still whispering. "We cannot do that with your sister in the next room."

"What do you suppose I do then?"

"Think about something that turns you off, quickly."

He chuckles softly. "Like what?'

An idea pops in my head. "Do you remember the time Stoney was wasted bad and we caught the toothless Waffle House waitress blowing him?"

He slumps. "Yep, that did it. Thanks, babe. I'll probably just meet you guys at the venue. You call me if you need me though, okay?"

I smile. "Okay. Now go." We give each other one last kiss and he leaves the bathroom. *Now off to my own cold shower.*

GABLE

I knew my sister was going to try and get information out of me about Ivie and she damn sure did. Well, that is until I turned the table on her and Ryder to start answering questions. I really did have a great time catching up with her, though. She seems really happy, which I haven't witnessed in a very long time. It's like Ryder was made for her, and as long as he keeps her happy, I'm happy.

Now, I'm just ready for tonight's show. There is another record guy coming to watch us and he may invite us to go do our own gigs in Seattle until Christmas. That would be great for our careers, plus it would give us a break from Ransom's End. Those guys can be real shitbags.

The only bad thing about today is not getting to spend much time with Ivie. I've come to the realization that once I decided to get over my fears with her, I can't live without her. I have also come to the conclusion that I sound like a real pussy about her.

I've gotten my sister and Ryder to their seats. My girl should be here anytime now.

The side door to the dressing area opens and there she is. I want to take her right now, but there are too many people back here for me to even kiss her. I give her a smile and walk over to her. "Ivie, come with me. I've got some new lyrics for a song and I wanna go over them real quick somewhere quiet."

"Sure, okay." She grabs her bass and follows me.

Once we get to a small side room, I open the door and shut it behind us.

I take her bass and sit it down. I lift her so that her legs are tightly wrapped around my waist.

"Baby, fuck. I love my sister but today I have missed you like crazy." I slam my mouth into hers. Then, I trail down her neck nipping at her collar bone. "Fuck, I need to be inside you right now."

She unwraps her legs, kicks her boots off and slides her jeans and panties down in one movement. At the same time I unbuckle my jeans, sliding them and my boxer briefs down. Rolling a condom on quickly, I slam into her. Her legs go back around my waist.

"Fuck, babe. If it was up to me, we would be joined like this for the rest of our lives."

She giggles. "Well, I think it's medically impossible to stay hard that long, first of all. Second, people might look at us funny walking down the street."

"Shit, it wouldn't matter to me if they took pictures and sent them to National Geographic."

She's about to quip back at me when I thrust into her again. So now all I hear is a moan.

"Baby, this is going to be quick, but I promise to make it up to you later." She nods as I quickly pound into her. As soon as I feel her tightening around my cock, my pace quickens even more. I feel her letting go and I thrust again, doing the same.

I lean in and rest my forehead against hers. "Damn, babe, you wreck me."

She looks up at me, kissing me on the lips. "Ditto."

Suddenly, there is a knock at the door. "Hey, um, when you guys finish in there, we have a show to do." Stoney's voice rings through the door.

"Okay, just a sec." I respond back.

Once we are presentable again, we walk back out to our waiting area. Keeg looks up. "Nice of you two to come back and join us."

I mouth "*Fuck You.*"

We both fall into the overstuffed sofa next to Stoney.

"How much time do we have?" I ask Keeg.

"About ten minutes." I nod my head.

A few minutes go by when the stage hand comes to get us.

Alright Hilton Head, South Carolina. Get your asses out of your seats and welcome to the stage Beautifully Tainted!

~*~*~

We just finished our show for tonight and I have security bringing Scarlet and Ryder back to meet us.

Scar comes bouncing through the door and hugs me. "Oh my God! That was an awesome show big brother, I'm so proud of you guys."

"Thanks." I look over at Ryder. "Hope you enjoyed the show, man."

"Yeah man, you guys were great."

I see the record company guys coming in. Fuck, I hope that means good news.

Rex, one of the record company guys, steps forward. "Hey guys, great show. The other guys agree. We want to offer you guys the month long headline gig in Seattle. You'll still be back home for Christmas, but it may open some big doors for you guys right after the first of the year."

There is a lot of excitement. Rex walks back over to me. "You guys are on your way, Gable, I've watched groups with half of your talent get far. Have you started working on anymore original stuff?"

I think about the song I started working on the other night. "Yeah, I actually started on something recently."

He shakes my hand. "Okay, great. Keep working. I gotta get these other guys to their flight. I'll be in touch in the next few days."

"Okay, and Rex, this is unbelievable. Thanks again."

"Hey, you guys kick ass."

After they leave, Scarlet hugs me with a death grip.

"Oh my God! Congratulations you guys. Seattle is so damn far away, but from what that guy was saying, I'm thinking I better get used to it. It sounds like you guys are going to be doing worldwide tours before you know it."

I smile. "Thanks little sister." The other guys and Ivie give her hugs. Ryder shakes everyone's hand.

Ryder smiles at Scarlet. "So, how about y'all join us for dinner? Sounds like we have some celebrating to do. Do y'all have to stay until the other band finishes?"

I shake my head. "No, we don't, but you don't have to do that, Ryder."

"I want to, this is a big deal. It's important to Scarlet so it's important to me."

Everyone else is walking out ahead of us. I look over at him. "Ryder, man I just wanted say that you seem okay. My sister really seems to like you and really seems happy."

He looks back at me. "I hope she is, man. She's everything to me."

I understand that more than he knows. I slap my hand on his shoulder. "You're a good guy, man, I'm glad you and Scar found each other."

IVIE

We've been in Seattle for two weeks now. The weather here fucking sucks. I thought southern humidity was bad, this rain, snow, slush shit is for the birds.

Rolling over and looking out the hotel window, it looks the same as it has for the past two damn weeks. However, getting to stay in a hotel rather than a damn bus is great.

I look over at a still sleeping Gable, running my hand across his tattoos. God, he's beautiful. I run my hand further down his chest, rubbing his abs, and he startles me by grabbing my hand.

"Mmm. That's a nice way to wake up."

I get up and straddle him. He smiles. "But this is better."

I lean down, taking his mouth with mine. Suddenly his phone begins to ring.

I roll off of him. "Ugh!"

"Who in the hell is calling my phone this early?"

I laugh. "Hon, everyone else is on east coast time."

He picks up the phone. "Yeah." He sits straight up. "What? When? How long since anyone has fucking talked to her? I'll be there as soon as I can. I'm finding a way out of here." Jumping up, he throws the phone on the bed.

"Gable, what in the hell is going on?"

He's throwing shit in a bag. I reach over and grab his arm. "Gable, stop and tell me what is going on. You're scaring me."

"That was Cade, Scarlet is missing. Her car was left over night at the college. They called him before they towed it because his name is still second on the car title. She and Ryder had a fight, so he thought she was being stubborn and wouldn't answer her phone. Cade called him this morning, and then he found her phone on the ground." He stops and I can tell he's getting upset.

"Well, do they have anything else? Have they called the police?"

He sits down, putting his elbows on his knees and his face in his hands. "Yeah, but they can't really do anything because she's an adult and they don't have anything other than a dropped phone. I've gotta find a flight."

I put my hand on his. "Baby hold on, I'll call Jana and see what we can come up with."

It's been a few hours since Cade called this morning. Gable has been going crazy because we can't get him a flight out for the fog. He's trying to get a car and drive to another airport. I've got Keeg and Stoney helping me keep him under control.

I got a frantic call from Whisper a few minutes ago saying they found her, but they were on their way to the hospital. I didn't get much else before she said she had to go and she would call back as soon as she could.

I walk over to Gable and the guys. Looking into his eyes. "Okay, your mom says they have her. They are taking her to the hospital for something. Whisper said she would call as soon as she knew more."

He stands up. "The hospital, what the hell?"

Keeg grabs him by the shoulders. "Sit down, man. Your mom is going to call back soon. You gotta keep your shit together. Rex got them to reschedule the show for tonight. Just fucking keep it together. Scarlet has plenty of people there with her."

Just then his phone rings again. I grab it and see that it's Cade. "Hello."

"Hey, is this Gable's phone?"

"Yeah, this is Ivie."

"Did Ryder or one of them get ahold of you guys about Scarlet?"

"Yeah, do you know anymore?"

"Just that she's going to make it. I will be there in about an hour. How is Gable doing?"

"Well, he's going nuts because he can't get a flight out. We are trying to keep him from tearing the place apart."

He sighs. "Let me talk to him."

I step back over to Gable. "Baby, Cade is on the phone. He wants to talk to you."

He takes the phone. "Yeah." "So when will they know more?" "Okay I'll try to calm down. Call me the minute you get there and find out more. I fucking mean it." "Well, you weren't the one who was all the way across the fucking country from her." "Okay, I'll settle down, just call me."

He sighs, sitting down on the sofa. "Fuck, I'm going crazy just sitting here."

I sit down by him and put my hand on his. I look up to the guys. "Hey guys, just give us a little bit, okay? Go grab us some food or something." They nod and head out the door.

I look over at him and pull him into my lap, rubbing the side of his face. "Hey, she's gonna be okay. Scarlet is stronger than you give her credit for. It takes a badass to wreck someone's car with an ax handle."

He kinda chuckles. "Yeah, I guess so."

I kiss his cheek. "Hey, you've been a great big brother. Plus, she's at the hospital now and Cade is almost there."

We sit there for another hour. Stoney and Keeg brought us back some subs and I manage to get him to eat and take some headache medicine.

Finally they call us to say that she'll be fine, she has some broken and fractured bones. She was taken by an asshole that was friends with her ex. It was really a crazy story. If the cops don't take care of that guy, I'd hate to see him when Cade and Gable get ahold of him. From the sounds of things, Ryder did a pretty damn good job on him.

I think they've finally convinced Gable to stay put for a week until we go home for Christmas. I sent Keeg and Stoney back to their room. Gable talked to Scarlet on the phone, so he feels a little better now.

He moves toward the bathroom. "I'm going to take a shower, this has been a shit day."

I nod. After I hear the shower going, I slip out of my clothes and quietly go into the bathroom.

I open the shower door. He looks up and I smile. "I figured you could use some help washing your back. I know I've got some areas that I could use some help with."

"Oh, really. How nice of you."

I wrap my arms around him, putting my head on his chest. "You've had the day from hell babe, I figured you could use a little extra TLC."

"How did I end up so lucky? You held me together today. When I first got that call this morning and I couldn't get out of here, I thought was seriously going to lose my mind."

"Holding each other together is what we are supposed to do. Do you know how many times you guys have held me together? More times than I care to admit. It was my turn to be the strong one, and as long as I have you, I know I can do that."

He leans down take my mouth with his. "Babe, you have me as long as you want me. I told you before, it's you, it's always been you."

Going home for a week or so is definitely what I need. I've talked to Scarlet several times since she was hurt a little over a week ago. She's getting better, still nursing some bones, but I need to see my little sister in the flesh.

As we walk out of the security area, I see an older man holding a sign with my name on it. I'd arranged with Ryder for someone to come get all of us. I knew he was sending a guy named Nelson that works for them. I know Scarlet likes Nelson, she always talks about how sweet he is. I guess Ryder thinks of him like a second father. We all wanted to surprise our families by just showing up. Ryder had called me to tell me about his gift for Scarlet. He'd gotten her a promise ring and he wanted my whole family there for dinner at his house, so we were telling Scarlet that I'd been delayed and wouldn't get in until late Christmas Eve. She was not happy, so I can only imagine when she sees my face tomorrow.

I approach the man and he juts a hand out. "Hey, you must be Gable, I'm Nelson. How was the trip?" He asks as he's shaking my hand.

"It was good, not too many delays."

"Okay, well I drove the suburban from the farm so we should have plenty of room for everyone and their stuff."

We follow him out the door. I see a large white suburban with the Abbott Farms logo on the door. I stow mine and Ivie's bags in the rear.

I worry about her. This is the first time we've been home since that fucker beat her up so bad and since her attack while we were on the road. I've already told her she's staying with me at my house. Not only do I want her there, but I need her there. I need to know that she's safe, I need to feel her body against mine while I sleep.

I had Nelson drop Ivie and me off at Stoney's so we could grab her car.

Once we are in her car, she looks around at the mess she'd left in it a few months ago. There's a bloody towel she'd obviously wiped some of the blood with. I see her shake a little and I grab her hand. "Baby, it's okay, we are going to clean out this car and get your shit unpacked somewhere."

She nods. "O-okay."

I take a deep breath, I know I'm about to have an argument with her. "So, I want you to come with me to Ryder's tomorrow night for Christmas Eve."

"No, I've already told you I'm uncomfortable enough staying at your mom's house."

"Look, you were my family before and especially now, even if we don't put a label on it. Plus, Ryder told me to invite you."

She slumps back in the seat. "Fine."

Suddenly, my phone rings. "Hello."

"Hey man, it's Rex. Merry early Christmas. I wanted to call you guys personally and let you know that your time in Seattle paid off. You guys were selected to be on a USO tour after the first of the year, so you'll actually get a few extra days at home. If it's possible, we want you to play your old bar before you leave home. That way you can drum up some support for the USO stuff, your hometown will promote the hell out of you. But you guys did it, you're good to go. We've had the USO people contact to get your passports sped up, so you should be ready in a week or so."

"Holy Shit! Thanks Rex, man that is awesome. As soon as I hang up with you, I'm calling the guys to let them know."

"Good, I figured it'd be great to share with your families at Christmas, too. I know moms like to brag about their kids and all."

"Okay, good. You have a Merry Christmas Rex, and thanks again."

I whip into my driveway. As soon as I turn the car off, I'm out and pulling Ivie from her side. I'm slinging her around in the front yard like a mad man. "Gable, what the hell are you doing?"

I fall to the ground with her in my arms still. "We did it! WE fucking did it!"

"Okay, I know you were on the phone with Rex. What did he say?"

"We just got booked on a USO tour after the first."

She squeals, hugging me so hard we fall down. "Holy shit!"

I look up at her. "We gotta call the guys. You call Stoney, I'll call Keeg."

We both scramble to get our phones. I know with all the screaming and squealing, the neighbors are wondering what the hell is going on. Luckily my mom won't be home until in the morning. She doesn't know I'm here either.

Once we both hang up, I smile at her. She grabs me, shoving me back against the car. She's running her hands up and down my shirt, kissing my neck. Our bodies are grinding against each other. I maneuver around and pick her up. "Babe, we can't put on a show for the neighbors."

We make it just inside the front door before I slam the door and we start shredding clothes off. We devour each other with our mouths. I take her right up against the back of my mom's sofa. It was rough, raw, lust, pure passionate sex.

Her naked body slumps against me, the sweat on our bodies making us stick together. I adjust her so that her legs wrap around me and walk us back to my shower.

Neither of us have said a word to each other since we were in my front yard.

Once we are in the shower, she giggles against my chest. "Well, that's one way to christen your mom's house."

"Yeah, I guess it's a good thing she wasn't here, huh?"

"Um yeah, I'd have made a hell of an impression, that's for sure. *Hey mom, you remember Ivie? Yeah, last time you saw her I wasn't ramming my dick into her snatch. I'm sure she looks a little different this way.*"

Laughter rumbles through me. "Hey, it would have been worth it." I look down at her. "That was fucking intense."

"Tell me about it, I think I'm going to have fabric burn on my ass from the couch."

For the next few minutes we wash each other, taking our time teasing each other. We make small talk and laugh together.

Once we make our way to my bedroom I throw her one of my t-shirts and I slip on boxers. Normally we sleep mostly naked, but since I don't know what time my mom is coming in tomorrow morning, we don't need any surprises of that sort.

She snuggles into my side after we crawl in bed. I kiss the top of her head. "Babe, are you nervous about being back around here?"

She yawns and speaks sleepily. "Yeah, I guess. I mean, I know he probably won't come back around me. It's just thinking about it all, you know?"

"Yeah, I get it. Let's just get some sleep, don't worry about him."

She nods, her breathing is heavier. I hear her whisper. *I love you, Gable.*

I know I have a smile on my face so big right now, I look like a jackass eating briars.

Christmas isn't really my time of year, Mom left at Christmas, Dad got locked up around Christmas. So, imagine my surprise when my mother decides to call me this morning for Christmas Eve. Really, I mean did she want to reminisce that she's a shitty mother who left a small child? We had a short conversation in which I pretty much told her some of the same things I told my father. She called me ungrateful and said I'd had it made living with my Aunt. I promptly told her to *fuck off* and hung up the phone.

It always leaves me feeling empty and unwanted. I really don't want to go with Gable tonight, but I also don't feel like running off the only person who seems to care for me. I know Scarlet is going to question us again once we get there. I know she is really only looking out for her brother, and my past is more than questionable.

Gable reaches for my hand. "Hey, don't worry, okay? My mom was happy to see us together. Scarlet will be too, she just has to get used to the idea. I've never been serious about anyone before. I think she's as worried that I'll hurt you as much as she's worried you'll hurt me."

I nod. "I just really wish she hadn't called me this morning. My psyche would have been a hell of a lot better."

"Hey, don't think about her. She's not worth your damn time. No more thinking about her today, okay?"

He leans over and kisses me softly as we come to a stop in front of Ryder's house. This damn place looks like something out of *Gone With The Wind*. I guess it is only fitting for Scarlet to be here then.

I have to admit, I'm a little excited for Gable and Scarlet to see each other. I know the hell he went through when she was hurt. I can only imagine how scared she was, I know the day I left for the tour how scared I was.

From the sounds of things she was beaten pretty badly, so I hope it doesn't upset Gable too bad to see her.

Gable knocks on the front door and she squeals as soon as she sees him. She welcomes us in and Ryder speaks to us.

Ryder asks him to come out back and help with the steaks.

He looks over at Ryder. "Sure, man. Ivie, you wanna come out with me or do you want to hang out with Scarlet?"

I speak soft. "I'll go with Scarlet."

He smiles. "Okay, good."

Following Scarlet into the kitchen, there are two other women in there. An older lady turns around.

"Well, Scarlet, who is this pretty thing you've brought in here?"

Scarlet laughs, "Ivie, this is Nana and Ms. Naomi. Ladies, this is Ivie, she's in Gable's band, and even though my brother isn't admitting to anything, I'm pretty sure she's his girlfriend." My mouth drops open and she laughs. "Nana is Ryder's grandma and the coolest old lady I know. Ms. Naomi is Nelson's wife-."

"Oh, I met Nelson at the airport, he picked us up."

Scarlet puts her hands on her hips. "Oh, he did? That means that my love was wrapped up in this to his eyeballs."

She motioned for me to sit down across from her at the table, pouring me some sweet tea.

I laugh. "Yeah, everyone wanted to surprise their families." Taking a swallow of my tea. "Oh shit, I've missed this. Being in Seattle for almost a month and having to drink coke and stuff isn't the same as a good ole' glass of sweet tea."

Nana laughs, joining us at the table. "Yeah, honey, they don't know what they're missin' up there. So, now are you going to be visiting your family while you're home?"

I see Scarlet tense. She knows part of my story.

Come on, Ivie, you can handle this.

"Um well, Ms. Abbott-."

She stops me, "Call me Nana or Nana Pearl. Ms. Abbott was my mother in law and she was a catty old bitch."

We all laugh. "Okay Nana, my mom ran off when I was young and my dad went to prison when I was about fifteen."

"What in the hell is wrong with these people these days? Running off leaving their kids, doin' mess to get themselves locked up." You could tell this all hit a nerve with Nana. She's a feisty one, I like her.

"So Scar, how are you doing? I see the cast, but what about everything else?"

She shrugs. "A day at the time. Listen, thanks for keeping Gable under control that day. I know it was you, which is the reason I know there is more going on than friendship. I suspected it when we went to the show. After I found out how you took care of him and kept the phone line going between here and Seattle, I knew it."

I look back and forth at Nana and Naomi. Nana puts her hand on mine. "Honey, there ain't no secrets in this house. As a matter of fact, just this mornin' I told Scarlet and Ryder if they don't quit spending so much time naked in that bedroom up there, I'm gonna be a great-grandma."

Scarlet rolls her eyes as I bark out a laugh. "Okay, it's more than friendship. I'm just not ready to put a label on it yet. I've screwed up so many times in my life with men, and I couldn't bear the thought of messing up what I have with Gable. So, he's being patient with me."

"What is it with these kids and their 'no labels' stuff? I just don't get it, Naomi."

Naomi looks up. "Well, look at Ryder, that boy couldn't keep his pants on to save his life, until he met this beauty here. I guess it's all about finding the right person and until they do that, it's their no labels rule. That's like Judd. That boy, I know he was seeing a girl before he left, has he been forthcoming about any of it? No. He told me they were just *hanging out*. Whatever that means."

Scarlet stands up. "Come on, Ivie, I'll show you the house."

I stand up. "Okay, sure." What is she up to?

As soon as we are out of the kitchen, she looks at me. "Okay, I'll need your help tonight. Judd is Ryder's best friend. Well, you met my friend Annabelle, she's coming here later. She's the girl Judd was seeing before he left, but we don't need all the grown-ups knowing that. He'd kill me and Ryder. He's private, kinda like my brother."

"Scarlet, we are grown-ups."

"Not compared to them. I mean really, you saw how they questioned you for my brother, who they hardly know. Can you imagine Judd's mom or Nana with Annabelle?"

I laugh, "Good point. So diversion is the game, then."

She nods. "Yep."

"Got it."

"Ivie, I am glad you're here and I'm glad you and Gable are together."

Hearing Scarlet and Ivie laughing together when they came outside to get us was like music to my ears. They seem to have come to peace with things.

Sitting down at Ryder's massive dining room table, Ivie looks over at me and whispers. "Oh, the ladies know about us. Scarlet called me out and Nana beat it out of me." She laughs. "But they know we don't have a label."

Scarlet looks up as my mom walks in. "Oh, hey, Mom. Nana and Naomi, this is my big brother, Gable. You know, the one we talked about in the kitchen."

Naomi laughs and Nana looks at me. "Oh yeah, Ivie's friend with no labels."

Ryder almost spits his beer out. "Nana, chill out."

"I am chilled out."

He shakes his head and I laugh. "Yes ma'am, that's me. Although I want labels, someone is being cautious."

My mom looks like she's entered a television talk show audience the way she's watching us.

Nana looks at Dustin. "So, now Dustin, what is it like for the gay people these days?"

Ryder chokes and Dustin laughs. "It's getting better, Nana."

Greer, Ryder's dad, looks at Nana. "Momma, you are making everyone uncomfortable."

We all laugh when she swats his hand. "No, Ivie, I see that lovely artwork poking out of your shirt sleeve, what is it?"

Ivie pulls up her sleeve a little. "Oh, it's just a little music tattoo, nothing big. All the guys have way more than I do."

"I wanna get a tattoo."

Ryder laughs. "Nana, you're too old to be going and getting tattoos."

"I'm not too old for anything."

The rest of dinner is spent with Nana's quips and everyone's laughter. When we were eating dessert, Ryder gave Scarlet her promise ring, and she almost freaked out thinking he was going to purpose. Which he basically did. I'm not real sure about the promise ring thing, it was all kinda weird to me. He wants her to move in here, too.

Mom decides to tell us that she's moving to Augusta with a man she's been seeing. This makes all of us happy for her. Scar and I never really thought she'd ever move on from our dad, but I'm glad she is.

I decide to share my news and everyone is happy. I almost choke up when Naomi comes over to hug me. She looks at me with tears in her eyes. "You be careful over there. I know you guys are supposed to be safe, but just take care, your sister needs you back here. If you happen to run into my son, you tell him I said the same to him."

Later, on the way back to my mom's house, I look at Ivie. "So, I'm glad you and my sister seem to be getting closer."

"Yeah, she's lightened up since she's with Ryder. Maybe it's all that sex Nana was telling me they've been having."

I almost run the car off the road. "Shit, I don't want to hear that. His grandma knows about it?"

She laughs telling me about Nana calling them out this morning. Now I have to say that is funny. She's a tough old lady, I like her.

"Well, as long as he doesn't knock up my little sister, we'll be okay. Oh shit, speaking of that, you have your doctor's appointment set up for while we're home, right?"

"I didn't but Annabelle said she's pretty sure she can get me in with her doctor on the 28th. I guess she's a family friend. She said with me going out of the country, it'd probably be best if I went to someone besides the clinic. That way he can kinda check me over, to be on the safe side."

"Yeah, that's a good idea. I mean we should be careful, you know? We have a lot riding on this tour."

She laughs. "Well you're the one who gets so carried away."

I rub my forehead. "Yeah, I know." The 28th jogs my brain. "Hey, don't let me forget to call the bar about us doing a show there on the 28th."

She nods. "Yeah, sounds good."

Once we are back at my mom's house, she and I exchange gifts that neither one of us knew we'd picked up for each other. Sitting in the living room, I suggest we watch a movie. She smiles. "Okay, what did you have in mind?"

"How about something scary?"

"Really, on Christmas Eve, you want something scary?"

"No, really I just want you to snuggle with me."

She laughs, "Well all you had to do was ask."

She scoots closer to me and we start watching some cheesy Christmas movie.

After about an hour she's dozed off. Picking her up in my arms, I take her to my room. She smiles, "Hmm, I like this."

I lean over her. "Oh, you do? Do you want me to do more?"

She nods. "Oh yeah. Let's make it a Very Merry Christmas."

I laugh. "Sure thing." I start stripping my clothes off.

She puts her hand out to stop me. "No, I'm in charge tonight."

Damn that's a turn on. "Baby, you keep bossing me around and I may blow before we ever get started."

She stands up and pushes me back on the bed. While I'm naked, she still has her clothes on. "Hey, are you gonna lose the clothes?"

"Shh, I'm in charge." She slowly starts taking her clothes off.

After what feels like an eternity, she crawls on top of me, and if my dick gets any harder, it's going to explode.

She slowly slides her pussy down on my cock and it starts out slow, up and down. Up and down. She leans over me and starts riding me harder and harder.

She's slick with her own wetness and I feel like we are both about to explode. She's riding me faster and I grab her hips. Suddenly, she makes an erotic move with her hips and my dick slides out of her. The next thing I know pain shoots through my body.

"ARGH!"

She freezes. "Are you okay? Oh my god, I think I broke your dick."

I roll to the side, now holding my limp dick. In some roll with her hips, it felt like she bent my dick in half.

I look up at her with tears leaking from my eyes. "I think I blacked out and I think you may have broken him."

She looks scared and she's trying to touch me. "Do I need to call a doctor or something?"

"Babe, if you call the doctor, they are going to laugh us out of the ER."

"I'm so sorry, so sorry."

A few minutes later, after the pain has stopped throbbing through my junk, I start laughing. "Holy crap, we are like the Special Olympics of sex right now."

She can't help it, she starts laughing, too. "Are we insane? Are you sure you're okay?"

"Probably yes on both questions." I'm still laughing. "Okay, but if you ever tell the guys this happened, I'll spank your ass."

"Really? Do you think I want to tell the guys that I'm a dick breaker? Literally."

We both burst out laughing again.

She smiles. "Do I need to check on him?"

I instinctively put my hand over myself. "Um no. He's going to be out for the night."

We both keep laughing until we fall asleep.

I would really like to go back to Christmas Eve and start this week over. First, I thought I broke Gable's dick. He was in pain, I could see it. I was concerned and embarrassed. At least before it was over with, we could laugh about it. Then, my mother called again on Christmas Day and come to find out, she's running low on money because her latest money ticket kicked her out. She saw that I'm in a band that's on tour, actually she knew I played in Biloxi, but she just didn't have time to make my show. Yesterday, I got a phone call that Chad was out on some kind of house arrest until his trial. Now, the lovely doctor I'm seeing just came in here to tell me that I'm pregnant, she did an ultrasound to see how far along I am and I'm five weeks. So this must've happened the first time we forgot a condom. I just laid back and cried, my life is too much sometimes. She's giving me a few minutes and she'll be back in to talk. I hear the door rattle and I know my few minutes are up.

She sits down next to me and gently touches my hand. "Ivie, everything is going to be okay. I can tell you weren't expecting this."

I shake my head. "No. This is not a good time at all. I'm leaving in a week to go on a USO tour in the Middle East. They won't let me do that if I'm pregnant."

She rubs my arm. "Well, you have other options. I will say you should talk to the father about your decision, unless you don't have a relationship with him."

Oh my God, Gable. What am I going to tell him? This is all wrong. We can't do this. "I have a relationship with him. Thank you for being so kind."

"Well, if you decide to terminate, we don't perform that procedure in this practice, but I have a friend who is an OBGYN and I can give you his number. I don't personally have anything against it, that was just the policy set in place when I started working here."

I nod. "Yes, ma'am. Thank you again, but I really need to go, I have some things to think about."

She smiles. "Okay, well once you decide, let me know and I'll get you the number. I do know the earlier you decide, the easier it will be on you mentally and physically."

I nod as she leaves the room. *What in the hell am I going to say to Gable?* What if he hates me? What if he never wants to see me again? What do I really want to do about this? Do I want to keep this baby? That means giving up everything I've ever worked for. It will all be gone. I can't ask the band to wait for me, I can't ask them to give up this tour, this opportunity. Once again, I'm the fuck up of the group.

I sit in one of the Historic District's many squares until it's time for us to perform. I can't face the guys about this right now. I'll just get through tonight and then figure this out.

Before we go on stage, I can tell Gable wants to talk to me. He finally corners me about the time we are walking to the stage. "Hey, how did your appointment go today?"

I am about to cry, I know it. "Um, it went fine. Come on, we can't be late getting started."

We make it through our set. We stop at the bar to talk to Dottie and she offers us a round on the house. "I'll just have some water, I'm really thirsty."

Gable walks around to me. "Hey, is something wrong? Do you wanna talk?"

"I'm fine, just tired tonight. I think I'm going to head on out."

"Wait, where are you gonna go? Why don't you wait for me and I'll go with you."

"No, you should visit with Dottie. Between Mom calling and all of that crap, I just have a headache. I'll head back to your house, we can talk when you get there."

He nods. "Okay, well call my cell if you need me."

"Okay."

~*~*~

After getting to Gable's, I take a long shower. Well, I mostly sat in the shower and cried. I have to tell Gable and it's the hardest damn thing.

Walking into his room, I open my towel, looking at myself naked in the full length mirror. What will I look like pregnant? Will I gain a ton of weight?

"You look just as shitty as you looked when you left me."

That voice, "Ch-Chad, what are you doing here? You can't be near me." I close my towel, clutching it tight.

He walks to me grabbing my arm. "You are coming with me. Once I'm done with you, no one will recognize you to ID your body."

"Why can't you just leave me alone?"

"Because you fucked up my life."

I look around the room to see if there is anything I can use as a weapon. I see a bat by the door, there is a huge lamp on the night stand, and a jagged looking statue thing on his TV stand.

"Can I at least put some clothes on?"

"Yeah, put some fucking clothes on, I can't stand looking at your fat ass."

I reach for some clothes and I touch the icon with Gable's number. Hopefully Gable will try to figure out why I don't talk to him when he answers.

Pulling on some yoga pants and a t-shirt, I try to work my way over to the lamp or something. I'm worried that if I ever leave here with him, I will never make it back.

He moves closer to me. "Let's go"

I start walking towards the door and I reach over, grabbing the bat. "Back away from me, Chad. Just leave."

He laughs. "Do you really think that bat is going to scare me away?"

The next few minutes go by in slow motion and in warp speed all at one time, between the hitting, kicking, punching and being thrown across the room.

I feel my stomach cramping really bad and I feel a hot gush in between my legs. I have to protect this baby until Gable knows. I finally manage to grab the large lamp and knock him over the head with it. He stumbles but runs back towards me. I grab a large shard of the lamp and drive it straight into his chest.

I fall backward and darkness takes me over.

The next thing I know, I hear Gable far away. "Ivie, baby hang on. You're in the ambulance."

I hear the paramedics asking him questions, but I can't make any of them out.

Darkness takes me over again.

GABLE

On my way home from the bar, my phone started ringing. I look down to see Ivie's face on the screen.

"Hello, beauty."

She doesn't say anything, but I hear noise in the background. *"Back away from me, Chad. Just leave."*

"Do you really think that bat is going to scare me away?"

I automatically floor it as I hear screaming in the back ground along with stuff crashing around. Then the phone disconnects.

"SHIT!"

I call 911 and pray to God that she's at my house.

I skid into the driveway as the cops do. Running inside, I make it to my bedroom. There is busted shit everywhere. I see Ivie on the floor and there is blood all over the place. Looking at her, I can't tell which of it is hers and what of it is his.

Chad is lying on the floor and I see a large piece of glass jammed into his chest. He's gasping and gurgling. I hope the son-of-a-bitch dies. I run my hands over Ivie. I don't see that she's stabbed, but I still see blood coming from somewhere.

Everything is happening at once. The paramedics get here to load them up and I jump into the ambulance with Ivie. Once we're moving, I call my sister to meet us and let the guys know.

"Ivie, baby hang on. You're in the ambulance."

Her eyes flutter a little. The paramedics start asking me questions about allergies and medical conditions.

Finally, once we make it to the hospital, we are rushed in. I overhear the doctors saying that Chad coded on the way here and wasn't able to be brought back. I can't say it bothers me.

The doctor steps over to me. "Sir, are you with Ms. Butonelli?"

"Yes, I'm her only family. Is she okay? There was so much blood."

"Yes, we located the source of the bleeding and she is being moved up the fourth floor to take care of everything."

"Okay, can I go up?"

"Once she's in her room yes, but they have to do a small procedure before they can allow visitors."

"What kind of procedure?"

"I'm sorry sir, that's all I can say. The nurse will let you know when you can head up."

For the next hour I sit there on pins and needles, waiting for the nurse to come talk to me. My sister, Ryder, and the guys come in.

I look at Scar, "There was so much blood her pants were soaked, I don't know if he stabbed her or what. I'm scared."

Just then the nurse comes in to let me know that we can go up for a few minutes.

When the elevator doors open to the fourth floor, I storm out. Right before I reach her room, Scarlet grabs my arm.

She's looking around the halls. "Gable, you said Ivie's pants were soaked in blood, nothing else."

I just need to get in her room. "Yeah."

"Gable, look what floor we are on."

I look around, finally taking in the area. It's the Maternity floor. I burst into Ivie's room. She's sedated still looking at her face.

Scarlet grabs my hand and locks it in hers. "Gable, had she told you?"

"No, she had a doctor's appointment today with the doctor Annabelle told her about."

"She probably just found out today, then."

"She was acting strange all day today."

Keeg and Stoney step over to me and hug me. "Man, since we know she's okay and the nurse is giving us the evil eye, we are going to head out. Keep us posted and um... we're ah sorry, man."

"Big brother, do you want me to stay with you?"

"No, you and Ryder go ahead and go home. I know she's safe now. I'm gonna stay here. Will you let mom know about the house and after the cops are finished, I'll clean it up?"

She hugs me tight. "You would've been an amazing dad, big brother."

"Umm yeah." Cold is running through me. "You guys be careful going home. Thanks, Ryder, for bringing her up here."

He shakes my hand. "No problem, man, let us know how your girl is doing, okay?"

I nod and they leave the room.

So many emotions are surging through my body.

Why didn't she tell me? Why did she have to go home without me? Would I have even been a good father? Did she want to keep the baby? Was she just going to get rid of it and not tell me?

I feel like I'm angry and I'm not even sure who I'm angry with. Am I angry at her for not telling me or going home alone? Maybe I'm angry at that asshole, Chad, for taking something from me I'm not even sure I wanted. I'm glad that he's dead, the world will truly be a better place without him.

I sit by her bed holding her hand until I can't keep my eyes open anymore and sleep takes over.

Waking up in a hospital bed, feeling like a cement truck ran over your head and that same trucked turned around and drug you behind it for 20 miles isn't the greatest feeling in the world. To top that off, the greatest guy in the world is asleep holding my hand and I feel like the biggest asshole in the world because I'm pretty sure I lost his baby that he knew nothing about.

Gable starts waking up. "Hey."

He looks up at me. "Hey, are you feeling okay?"

"Not really, I feel like shit. I have a headache from hell and my body feels like it's one big bruise."

"Let me get you the nurse." He jumps up and darts out of the room.

An older lady in pink scrubs comes in. "Hey sweetie, I understand you need some pain medicine." I nod. "Okay, well the doctor will be by to talk to you soon. She will fill you in on everything we had to do last night."

"Um. Okay, thank you."

After she walks out I look at Gable. "What happened? What did they have to do?" I start to panic. What if he did more damage to me than I thought? What if I can NEVER have kids now?

Gable puts his hand on mine. "Ivie, it's okay. You're going to be fine. That piece of lamp you stabbed Chad with guaranteed he's never coming after you again. You have no broken bones or anything like that. They really wouldn't tell me anymore because we aren't married. I'm going to jump to the conclusion that you had a miscarriage since we are on the maternity floor and your pants were soaked in blood. Since I didn't know you were pregnant I couldn't tell them."

Ouch, that hurt worse than the bruising. "Gable, I'm sorry. I just found out yesterday and I wasn't sure what to do with that information yet.

I needed time to talk to you, but yesterday I needed some time for me to even figure out if I wanted to keep it."

"What are you saying? Are you saying you would have had an abortion? You would have killed my baby?"

"I don't know, Gable. We both know they would have never let me go on the tour with you guys to a war zone."

"You know-."

He's cut off by the doctor coming in. She's just as well put together as she was yesterday in her office. She sits down on my bedside. "Good morning, Ivie. Is it okay if we talk in front of the gentleman?" I nod. "Sweetheart, first off I want to say how sorry I am for this happening to you. I know yesterday was a shock to you and you really hadn't had a chance to wrap your head around it all yet. As I'm sure you've figured out, you did have a miscarriage last night. We had to go in and remove what was left of the fetus, but the man who attacked you didn't do permanent damage to you by any means that we can see right now. I would prefer that you wait at least a year, if you intend to try again, just due to the severity of how you lost this baby. I am going to put you on birth control because your hormone levels will be off the charts crazy for a little while. This will help regulate them. Now, I'm sending you home in a little bit, but I want you to take it easy."

"Okay. Will I be cleared to leave for an overseas USO tour next week?"

"Sure, as long as you don't have any complications between now and when you leave. I'm going to go get your paperwork in order to check out and you'll be ready to go. I'll grab you a set of scrubs to wear home, they said the clothes you came in were ruined. Now remember what I said about your hormones, they are going to be all over the place for a little while. Oh, and the police are outside, they do need to speak with you for a moment."

"Yes, ma'am. Thank you."

Gable looks at me. "Um, I haven't had a chance to go back to the house and clean it up." *And he probably doesn't want me there anyway.*

"It's fine, you can take me to Stoney's if you want. I'm not sure I could sleep there after everything with the attack. I know he can't get me, I'm taking from what you said that he's dead, but I'm afraid I'll still feel him there."

He nods. "Okay, I get it. Let me call Stoney and see about you staying there."

He steps out of the room to call Stoney.

Well Ivie, you've done it again. Royal Fuck Up. Gable hates you, he can't trust you anymore.

He steps back in the room after a few minutes. "Um, bad news, all the rain that they got while we were gone did a number on Stoney's roof and he has a bunch of water damage. You can't stay there and risk getting sick so you are going to stay with Scarlet at the Abbott's. She said you are more than welcome. Hell, you know it's a big ass house."

"No, I don't want to intrude. I can just stay at a hotel."

"No, the doctor wants someone looking after you."

Great, Ivie the Royal Fuck up strikes again. Scarlet probably hates me now. I killed her brother's baby that he didn't even know he had.

I'm not going to win this argument. "Okay. Just for a few days, I don't want to be a burden."

"She said you were no burden."

An hour later I've made my statement to the police, who said it clearly looks like self-defense, and given the history involved. They are sure me leaving for the USO tour won't be a problem.

Scarlet comes to pick us up and I sit quietly in the back seat. When we pull onto the street where Gable lives, my heart sinks to my feet. I see all the crime scene tape around their house. *I did this. I brought crazy to their front door.*

Scarlet stops in front of the house. Gable gets out and leans in the back window. "I'm gonna clean up in there some, I'll bring your bags and your car over in a little bit. Okay?"

I nod. "Yeah, I'm gonna take some more medicine and rest anyway."

He nods and walks away from the car without as much as a handshake.

We pull away from the curb and Scarlet speaks. "Ivie, I'm so glad you're okay. Gable was scared out of his mind last night. He loves you, you know?"

I pretend like I've dozed off with my head against the window. This hurts too much.

Once we arrive at the Abbott house, Scarlet leads me up to a guest room. "There is a bathroom through there if you'd like to take a shower. Here are some of my comfy clothes you can use until Gable brings you some." She hugs me again and I realize she has tears in her eyes. "I'm so glad you're okay. You went through a lot yesterday. I think it's going to take Gable a little while to wrap that big ass head of his around it all, but don't give up on him."

I look down at the ground. "Thanks, Scarlet. Hopefully I'll be out of your hair in a couple of days. I don't want to burden you guys."

"Ivie Butonelli, you are family, you are never a burden."

"Thanks, again. I think I'm gonna take that shower and then take a nap."

"Okay, well Nana is bringing some food over later and she'll expect you to eat something. Just a heads up."

I nod and actually laugh thinking about Nana.

GABLE

I'm an asshole, I know I am. I never even kissed her goodbye. For the first time since all of this started between us, I don't think I can handle it.

I was going to be someone's father. What if I was a complete piece of shit like my dad? Was that the reason she hadn't told me about the baby? Was she afraid that I would have several families and wives? Was she even planning on keeping the baby? Maybe she was just going to get rid of it and not tell me.

Walking through the crime scene tape at my house is agony. In my bedroom the furniture is all busted up and trashed. She fought like hell in here. I see the two large puddles of blood on the floor. *She almost died right there on that floor.* The doctors kept screaming about how much blood she lost last night.

I just don't know what I would've done if she hadn't made it. I can't handle this. Relationships like this are too much for me to handle. Maybe that's the reason my dad isn't good at them either. The gut wrenching feeling I was having last night in the pit of my stomach, I thought it was going to kill me.

I need some space. I've got to try and process all of this. I mean, Ivie should understand that, right? I keep giving her time and space. Hell, it's not like we even put a label on what we have.

I start putting stuff in the trash but I'm not going to be able to clean the carpet in here.

I pull out my phone and call Stoney.

"Hello?"

"Hey, man. Can you and Keeg come over here and help me get this shit out of my bedroom? I've gotta snatch this fucking carpet out."

"Yeah, man. I'll swing by and pick him up and we'll be there."

"Okay, thanks."

Yeah, I need to call Scarlet and let her know that I'm not going to make it out there tonight because I'll be busy with this shit. I call her as I'm grabbing a beer out of the fridge.

"Hey, big brother."

"Hey, I was just calling to let you know that I'm gonna be busy here for the night. Um, can she borrow some of your clothes and stuff?"

I hear Scarlet's aggravation in her breathing. "I already gave her some clothes and stuff. I really think you need to close up the house and come on out here tonight. She needs more than just damn clothes."

"What else does she need?"

"Well, she needs panties and pads and all of those lovely things, since she has a river flowing out of her vagina right now. But the biggest fucking thing she needs is someone here to support her."

"Look, I've got to snatch the damn carpet out of my room from all of the blood on it. Can't you run to the store and I'll pay you back?"

"Fine, Gable. I'll do this. You know, when you guys started doing whatever it is you're doing, I was worried she'd hurt you. Guess I was backwards on that one."

"What the fuck is that supposed to mean?"

"Gable, she needs you and you're finding excuses to pull away. You were such a dick to her today when you got out of the car. She's broken. Oh, but don't worry, I'll take care of her. I'll make sure she feels safe. I'll make sure she's healthy and ready to go on tour with the band."

"You don't have to be such a bitch, Scarlet. I'm coming over there tomorrow. I just can't look at this blood anymore tonight. The guys are coming over to help me move the furniture and shit so I can rip up the carpet."

"Yeah, and Dad was coming back after he got out of prison." I hear a well-known click.

Wow, that was a low blow. Scarlet even bringing up my dad is a big thing. I reach up in the liquor cabinet and take a few shots of whiskey before I sit on the couch, drinking beer until the guys get here.

An hour or so later, I hear a knock at the door and in walk Keeg and Stoney. "Hey, fuckers, thanks for coming."

Stoney looks at me. "So, how is your girl doing?"

I've had just enough to drink that I don't want them calling her *my girl*. I've got to put the distance between us again that worked for so many years. "Ivie is fine. She's recuperating at my sister's."

Keeg looks at me weird. "Why are you here and not there?"

"Look, I need to get this shit done. We have to leave next week and she's fine. Hell, I think my sister has fucking maids and butlers and shit in that big ass fucking house. Ivie is being looked after."

Stoney glares at me. "Dude, I know you've been through a lot of shit in the past 48 hours, but it's not near the shit she's been through."

"Fuck you, Stoney. I was going to be someone's dad and I didn't even know it. Now I'm not and I don't even know how the fuck I feel about it."

Keeg sits down by me. "Dude, if you pull away from her, you are going to kill her."

Looking over at me, Stoney glares. "I know you think she kept it from you, but she found out her life was getting turned upside down fucking like five minutes before she talked to you, and then her life got turned upside down even more. So give her a fucking break."

I stand up. "You know what guys, I'm kinda tired. I'll save ripping the shit out for another day. Thanks for coming over here but I'm going to bed."

Stoney tries to say something but Keeg stops him. "Just leave it man. Let's go."

I notice Stoney reaches down and grabs Ivie's bags I'd set by the door earlier and takes them with him.

Good, now I can stay here tomorrow and figure out what the fuck is going on in my head.

Gable never came last night. I don't even have my cell phone to see if he tried to call. If I'm really being honest with myself, I knew this is how it would end up. No one really sticks around in my life. I'm easy to cast aside. Hell, Chad was even right. Who would want to be with someone like me? Someone whose parent's didn't even want them.

Maybe that's what Gable and I would have been like if that baby had been born. We probably would've sucked as parents.

I hear a soft knock at the door. Scarlet sticks her head in. "Good morning. How are you feeling?"

I shift uncomfortably. "I'm fine, just still sore from the beating. You understand."

She nods. "Yeah, I do unfortunately." She says looking at the cast that is still on her arm. "Here are your bags, I figured you might want some of your own stuff. Plus, I picked up a couple of things I figured you might need from the store." She reaches in the bag smiling. "Now, I know these aren't Victoria's Secret or anything, but I'm sure they'll be comfy as hell." She pulls out a pack of what we like to call granny panties, or period panties.

Panties that have no sex appeal to them what so ever, just pure cotton comfort.

I giggle a little. "Well, I don't need to worry about anyone seeing them for a while, so it's not a big deal."

She laughs. "Yeah, I get what you mean. I got you some of the mattress thick pads, too. I figured the thin ones wouldn't do it."

I shake my head. "Nope." I have to ask, I have to. "Did Gable come by and drop my bags off?"

She shifts nervously. "No. Stoney did. Gable was still cleaning at the house. He had to take the carpet out."

"Oh, okay."

"Hey, Nana is on her way up with breakfast. She said stay up here and she'll bring it to you."

I shake my head. "I'm not really hungry."

"Ivie, you gotta eat. You need to get your strength up. Plus, I let you get away with not eating yesterday."

"Okay. I know Nana can *take me* anyway, so I'll do what she says."

She smirks. "Smart move."

A few minutes later, Nana Pearl comes in the room. "Oh, sweet girl. You and Scarlet have to stop scaring an old woman like me. I thought Ryder was gonna be the death of me, but you girls are too damn much."

I smile. "Sorry, Nana."

She sits down on the bed by me. "Well, I'm glad you're okay. I'm sorry about the baby, the Good Lord knows more about what he's doing than we do, that's for sure."

I nod. "Yes, ma'am."

"Now here, I brought you a little light breakfast. Just some eggs, grits, bacon, cathead biscuits and orange juice."

I laugh and wince at the pain from a good ol' belly laugh. "A little breakfast? Nana, that sounds like the entire buffet."

"Well, we need to kick your strength up so you can be a badass rocker chick on that tour."

I clutch my stomach laughing. "You are too funny old woman."

"Well, I'm just glad I could make you laugh. I could see in your eyes that you needed it."

I kinda frown. "Thanks. You are right, I did."

"I saw that boy looking at you at Christmas. He just needs some time. He almost lost you and he lost a child, he's scared."

"But doesn't he realize how scared I am, too?"

"Baby, men are dumb. They don't realize because they don't have hormones. How are you doing with that by the way?"

"The nurse told me before I left that they'd hit me. They haven't yet, but she said I'd probably cry for like a solid day or something."

"Honey, I think my late husband was about to commit me when we had a miscarriage because I cried for almost two solid days."

"You had a miscarriage?"

"We did, before we had Greer. I wasn't supposed to be able to have kids after it. They didn't know as much as they do now. So when we had Greer, we realized how blessed we'd been. He was the only child we were meant to have, but like I said, the good Lord knows better than we do."

"Yes, ma'am, I guess he does."

"Now, you eat that big breakfast and get your strength back up. Like I said, you have to be ready to go on that tour. We women rockers gotta stick together."

"Rocker women? You were a rocker?"

"Well, I knew how to strum a guitar back in my day. As good as any damned old boy, that's for damn sure."

I laugh. "Thanks for stopping by, Nana. You are a trip."

"Don't worry, he'll come around. Y'all will get a chance to talk about all of this before you leave, and if not, then it's his problem. You, my dear, are a catch. Don't let anyone tell you different."

I nod and start eating my breakfast as she leaves. I see why Scarlet got so attached to her. She's pretty badass herself.

After finishing my breakfast, I take a look at myself in the bathroom mirror seeing the battered body before me. I never have to worry about Chad again. He's gone. I take some more pain medicine and lay back down for another nap.

GABLE

My sister decided to have my band over for breakfast this morning before we leave for our tour. Ivie and I have only texted back and forth since she got out of the hospital a few days ago. I feel like a big piece of shit and well, as a matter of fact, my sister has called me that much. Even my mother, who is all *violence isn't the answer,* smacked me in the back of the head the other day.

I finally did get the house back in order. Some company is coming to lay new carpet next week since my mom is putting the house on the market when she moves to Augusta. I know the guys think I'm a huge assclown for staying away from Ivie but I couldn't face her. I'm not sure how I feel and I don't know what to say. I know I've hurt her more than I ever intended to.

I can't give her what she needs, she needs a guy who will stick around. Hell, at the first sign of trouble I dipped out.

As I drive down the long gravel road to Ryder's house, I feel like I'm about to throw up. I drove Ivie's car since I still don't have one and I never made it over here to drop hers off.

Getting out of the car, I see my sister walk out the front door. I hug her neck. "Hey, little sister."

"Hey. Um, will you give me Ivie's keys? I'm going to go ahead and pull the car into the barn."

"Why are you parking the car in the barn?"

"Well, that way it's taken care of and when she comes back, she's moving in here with me."

"Why?"

She snatches the keys from my hand. "Are you that fucking dense?"

"I guess I am."

She puts her finger in my chest. "She has no fucking body, Gable. You made promises to her and you didn't keep them. She doesn't want to depend on Stoney or Keeg to store her stuff, so I offered and I told her when she comes home, she's staying here until she can get on her feet."

"How did I become the villain in this? She's the one who was keeping secrets."

"We all have secrets, Gable, so get over yourself. She lost y'all's baby in a fight for her life. It had been less than twelve hours since she found out that she was pregnant. Her body was so racked with hormones that she didn't know how she felt. But I can tell you that Nana and I held her when she cried for two days straight a couple of days after she miscarried. I don't think this has a damn thing to do with secrets, I think you are a fucking coward."

With that said, my sister gets in the car and spins gravel all over me. She cried for two days... I remember the nurse saying something about a hormone crash or something like that. I head into the house and I see Ryder. I shake his hand. "Hey, man, thanks for inviting us for breakfast."

"Hey, that's all Scar and Nana."

"Well, thanks anyway."

I make my way into the kitchen where Keeg, Stoney and Nana are eating.

Nana looks up. "Well, look who crawled out from under the rock he's been stuck under."

"I managed to squeeze out."

"Well good, now pull your head out of your ass and get over here and eat some of this food."

I sit down and make my plate. We talk about our schedule a little and some of the upcoming events.

Scarlet and Ryder have joined us by now. I still catch the death glares from my sister. I notice Ivie still hasn't been down here to eat. I finally work up my nerve to ask. "Scar, where is Ivie? Is she still packing or something?"

She shakes her head. "No, she headed out last night. She's gonna meet you guys in country. She said she had some things to do before she left, and the record company sent her a day ahead so that she could talk with the tech guys and all."

"How did she get there to fly out? I had her car."

"Ryder rented her one, even though she fought him on it."

Great, she is avoiding me. How in the hell is this going to work out? We are in the same fucking band. We are about to be in a fucking country thousands of miles from home.

"What kind of things did she have to take care of? Why did they send her ahead?"

"I don't know, she said it was private and I didn't push. As far as the other, you'd know if you'd been by here."

With that, my sister stood up from the table and dumped her plate in the garbage. She is seriously fucking pissed with me.

How did I screw things up this bad? Oh yeah, I fucked my band mate.

Flying military transport with all of our equipment was extremely weird and totally different from flying commercial. I called Rex a couple of days ago and asked if I could help out in anyway. I also said if our instruments were going over early, I'd be willing to go with them and the tech guys to get our shit together. I knew that was always a big deal when we were on the road, so I wasn't surprised when he agreed.

I knew I couldn't handle being on a flight that long with Gable. Plus, I needed to stop by my old high school and get copies of my transcripts. I need to figure out if this is what I want to do for the rest of my life or if I want to go to college like I had originally planned. I've been floating around for enough years now. No one wants me, that's been made clear. Losing that baby was God's way of telling me that I'm not even supposed to have a child, so I'll just figure out what my career needs to be and that will be my life.

When I sat in the room at Scar's for two solid days and cried, I said no more men. I'll use B.O.B., as long as I give him fresh batteries, he never disappoints. He doesn't beat the shit out of me. He can't knock me up and he won't break my heart.

~*~*~

The guys finally got here to Kuwait a couple of days ago and we've been busy practicing. They have us at what they call a Camp, it's a pretty big base. Besides practice and meetings, I haven't had to run into Gable much. They have fast food restaurants, coffee shops, movie theatres and recreation places. We are going to be playing shows in Kuwait for a few weeks, then we'll do a couple in Afghanistan. They don't allow that many to be done there, but they want us to do a few shows at one of the bigger bases. The rest of our tour will be in places like Germany, Japan and Italy.

I love having coffee shops here. I need my caffeine fix daily, and having decent coffee just makes it better. Walking out of the coffee shop here on base, I run straight into a wall of muscle. It's a nice looking guy, I can see from his workout clothes that he's ripped and built like a fucking champ. "Excuse me, ma'am."

"Oh, excuse me. I need to watch where I'm going."

"You're with the band, right?"

"I sure am."

"Wow, okay. I'm Judd, Ryder's friend. You must be Ivie."

I smile. "Yes. Oh my God, I never thought we'd actually run into you over here. Scarlet and Naomi asked me to keep an eye out for you, but I never dreamed I'd actually run into you."

"Well hey, will you join me for some coffee? Catch me up on everyone at home?"

An hour later, we have laughed and talked about all of the people we both know from home.

He shakes his head. "Well, I'm glad to know Nana has still got her spunk."

"So at Christmas I had to help Scar keep your mom from finding out about Annabelle. What's the story there?"

He chuckles. "Wouldn't I like to know?"

I smile. "I think you do."

"She's confusing. She's this gorgeous little firecracker. You know, all full of piss and vinegar." He rolls his head around making his neck crack. "We met one night in a bar, when Ryder was doing anything he could to get Scarlet's attention. My job was to distract Annabelle and well, she distracted the hell out of me."

"So you guys hooked up for the night?"

"Well it was supposed to be for the night because I was leaving. But then some shit happened and she needed me, now we are friends. She didn't want anyone else to know, it's her story not mine. I know Ryder and Scar think it's more, but it's not."

"So how long have you been on this base?"

"Well, I'm here for a couple of weeks at the time, then I go to Afghanistan a month or so at the time and we run some missions."

"Oh, well are you going to catch our show tomorrow night?"

"Yeah, I plan on it."

"Okay great, the guys made friends with Ryder before we left so I'm sure they'd be thrilled to meet you." I reach in my backpack and grab some laminated passes they gave us and hand it to him. "Here, this will get you back where we are. Do you want one for a friend or anything?"

"No, thanks, this is awesome."

I look at my watch and realize the time. "Shit, we've got practice, I need to go. I'll catch you tomorrow."

He stands up, giving me a hug. "Thanks, again. It was great catching up with someone from home."

"No problem."

Walking out, I see Gable in line grabbing coffee and he gives me a *go to hell look*. I roll my eyes and keep walking.

He follows behind me to our practice area. "So who was that?"

"Who?"

"The guy at the coffee shop."

"None of your business."

He stops me. "None of my business?"

"Yep, he's a friend."

"Yeah, right."

"No, for real. But I'm glad you stopped me because I think we need to talk for a minute." He goes to speak but I put my hand up. "You lost the right to question me about who I hang out with. You lost a lot of rights in my life. You are only my band mate. That's it. This band is all we have together."

"So we can't even be friends now?"

I shake my head. "No. Friends don't abandon someone the way you abandoned me. You never even showed up. Do you think I wanted all of that to happen to me? I was trying to figure out a way to tell you and I was going to tell you when you got home. So, WE could decide what WE wanted to do. I can't help all hell broke loose before that could happen. I just never thought you'd treat me like you did."

"What the fuck? You took off and flew over here before any of us."

"I couldn't be on a flight that long with you. I've been disappointed my entire life, people that were supposed to be there for me weren't. You made this big fucking speech about how my dad treated me and you did the same thing. You left me when I needed you the most. You are a fucking hypocrite. Now, if it doesn't pertain to the band, we don't talk."

I turn my back to him, walking over to our area to get practice started.

She's right, I did abandon her. I am just like my dad. Seeing her having coffee with someone else, talking and laughing, almost killed me. I wanted to rip that guy's fucking head off, *well if he didn't look like damn Arnold Schwarzenegger did in the eighties.* Don't get me wrong, I know I'm pretty tough, but that guy could've killed me.

I know in my heart though that we can only be in this band together. I need to go back to my one night stands and blow jobs in the broom closet. I was a lot better person to her when I wasn't that close to her.

Once we finish the longest practice of my life, I can see the pain still in her eyes when she looks at me. Well, I'm not sure if it's pain or hate. I wouldn't blame her if she hates me.

Making my way back to my room, I bump into a chic. She's fucking hot and smiles at me with sex appeal dripping from her. I give her my signature cocky grin. "Sorry, I didn't see you there."

She smiles, "It's okay."

"So, are you in the military?"

"No, I'm a contractor. I work for MWR, and you are Gable Johnson with the band."

I nod. "Well, you've done your research on me and I feel at a loss because I don't even know your name."

"It's Celanie. Like Melanie but with a C."

"So Celanie, what do you do with MWR?"

"Well, I work over at the rec center. I help run the gym, organize social nights, and stuff like that."

"So you wanna go grab a bite to eat or some coffee? You can tell me more about you."

She grins. "Oh, you wanna know more about me?"

"Sure do."

She nods. "Okay, then. Let's go."

~*~*~

I wake up this morning thinking about how last night has to be one of the most fucking embarrassing nights of my entire life.

Celanie and I grabbed some food and coffee. She was fucking hot. My thoughts on the matter were the old saying, *"The best way to get over one woman is to get on top of another one."*

I turn on all of my sweet guy charms. It works, and a couple of hours later, we're in her room. She's all over me, standing up as she peels off her clothes. Damn, she has some nice fucking tits. She rakes her hands down my chest to my belt buckle, sliding my pants and boxers down, but as soon as she goes to put her mouth on me, I can't do it. I back away but she pulls me back to her and puts my dick in her mouth. Too many flashes of Ivie saying my name flash before me. I pull away again. "Stop. Sorry, I can't do this. I just can't."

She shakes her head and sits back on her feet. She smirks. "Damn, that's a shame."

I pull up my pants and button them. "Sorry, look, it really has nothing to do with you. I've got a bunch of shit going on in my head."

"Girl at home?"

"Something like that."

"Well, I'm gonna be here for a few more weeks if you change your mind."

I smile, she just wants a good time. "Come by the show tomorrow, I'll introduce you to Keeg and Stoney."

She pulls a long T-Shirt over her head. "Sounds like a plan."

I walked out of her room feeling like a big fucking piece of shit. What is it with me here lately? I can't be a normal person so I'm just going to fuck up everyone else's life along with it.

We have a few hours until the show. I grab my guitar and start fiddling with it again. Rex said we needed some original stuff when we come back stateside.

I start strumming the song I've already started writing.

You unlock the door and climb inside-
You don't need seat belts for this ride-
You take my heart and hold it in your hands-
Taking for granted where you stand-
I've never been one to let go of control-
But with you I seem to do that more-
I always seem to screw things up with you-
For some reason I always do-
You're the one I must confess-
You tilt my heart off its axis-
How do I repay you? I break yours in two-
I owe you more-

Someone beating on my door draws me out of my writing.

I open the door to a pissed off Keeg. "You are killing her, man. Now I didn't get in this all before when Stoney was ready to fucking kill you, but I may be ready now. Why in the fuck are you doing this to her? Hasn't she been through enough?"

"What do you mean?"

"She saw you last night."

Those words echo through my brain.

"That wasn't what it looked like. Plus, she was out with some guy yesterday. Afterward she told me to stay the fuck away from her and out of her business. That if it didn't pertain to the band, she had nothing to say to me."

"She was having coffee in a public place, not walking out of a guy's room adjusting her clothes. Dude, you know how many times that girl has had her fucking heart ripped out. She is putting those walls back up. She's separating herself again and we may not get her back this time. If you weren't going to take care of her, you should have just left her the fuck alone. She kept a secret from you for less than twelve hours, grow the fuck up, man."

"I'm backing away from her, giving her what she asked for. She wasn't even sure she was going to keep my baby, so how can I be sure she'd have told me about it?"

"Because it's fucking Ivie. You know, the girl who always has our back. The one who ran that fucking crazy chick out of Stoney's that decided to set up shop there. The one who made that bitch, Kara, admit that she wasn't really pregnant with my baby. She's always looked out for us and yes, we looked out for her, too. But man, you just became another statistic in her book. You are another person who made her feel like she's not worth anything. Congratulations. When we get home, we may be looking for a new bass player."

"She won't quit, she loves music too much."

"No, she loves you too much. She can't handle it, but I'll give her credit, she has lady balls enough to try. But I also saw college info and her transcripts. She's making other plans for her life. A life without us."

He walks out of my room slamming the door.

Fuck, I was just told off by Keeg. Not to mention the song I just wrote was completely for Ivie. I've got to get my shit together.

IVIE

Squalling my eyeballs out like a kid was not how I intended to spend the night before and hours before my first USO show.

I know I said all of that shit to him yesterday, but I guess the finality of our situation hit me last night when I saw him walking out of that blonde Barbie bitch's room.

All of those things he said to me about my body being perfect the way it was and me being all the sex appeal he ever needed were all lies. He dumps me and goes for the first breast implants and butt lift he sees.

Keeg came by a little bit ago to bring me some coffee and took one look at me and threatened to call Scarlet if I didn't start talking.

When I talked to him about college, he said he was happy for me and could understand why I would want to go, but couldn't I take classes online or something?

He left out of here damn near taking my door off the hinges.

I take out my bass and start popping out chords, trying to work up some new music.

I don't know if I'll ever trust you again-
You crushed me and left me-
I can't do this anymore-
Even though it's the hardest thing I'll go through-
I know I'll never get over you-
You abandoned me and it didn't take you long-
To find a new bed to keep you warm-
I should've know this was all too good to be true-

I happen to glance at the clock and realize I have one hour to get ready for our show.

I lay my bass on my cot and start getting my hair and make-up done. I rush a little faster knowing that Judd is supposed to be waiting on me so he can meet the guys. He was really nice when we talked yesterday. I can totally see why Annabelle is in love with him. She may not admit it but she is, and I can tell he feels that way about her, too.

Making my way to the stage, I see Judd standing by the security entrance. "Hey, I told you to go on back."

"Yeah, I decided I'd wait on you. That guy in the coffee shop yesterday looked like he wanted to tear me limb from fucking limb. Now, I know he can't do it, but I also don't want him to try." We both chuckle.

"Okay. Let's go."

Making our way backstage, I see Keeg, Stoney and Gable staring at me.

"Hey guys, this is Judd. He's Ryder's best friend from home. We ran into each other yesterday. He's only gonna be here for another day or so. I figured since he's a hometown boy, we'd give him the ultimate backstage experience."

I see Gable's facial expression soften but not much.

Judd puts his hand out and shakes theirs. "Nice to meet you guys." He looks at Gable. "Man, you've got an awesome sister. She's the greatest thing that ever happened to my buddy."

"Thanks, I appreciate it."

"You know, I always knew it'd only take Ryder finding that one girl to tear his walls down around his heart." Judd shakes his head while he's talking.

I bark out a laugh. Everyone looks at me and I shrug my shoulders. "Walls are good, and they are there for a reason, to keep people out." I turn and walk off before I say anymore.

~*~*~

I haven't been in touch with Judd since he left here. We only have a few more shows here before we go to Afghanistan. Playing for soldiers has been some of the greatest moments in my life. I'm still playing with the thoughts of leaving this life behind, but I can't make up my mind.

Being a part of this band is the only thing that has made me feel human for the past four years. These guys are my family.

True, Gable and I are still steering clear of each other, but maybe, just maybe, we can get past this. We can go back to acting like we've never been more than friends.

Who am I kidding? I curl into a ball with my pillow and doze off.

"Mmm. Oh shit, Gable, right there."

"Fuck baby, nothing feels like your pussy."

He thrusts into me harder and faster. "Fuck, Gable. Oh God! Harder!"

He grabs my hips, flipping me over on to my knees, and starts pounding into me from behind. He grabs a handful of my hair, slamming into me.

"Oh GOD! GABLE!"

"I love you, baby. I never stopped."

I hear the headboard pounding into the wall and someone talking.

I jump at the sound of someone pounding on my door. *Fuck a dream really?*

"Ivie! Open the door."

I stand up and open the door to a grinning Keeg. "I could hear you, you know. Damn, if Gable wasn't the reason I was coming here to see you, I would've sworn he was in there."

"Fuck you. What do you want? What's wrong with Gable? Crabs? The clap? They make shots and lice kits for that shit."

"No, his Dad has been in touch with Scarlet."

I can see by the look on Keeg's face this isn't good.

"Fuck." I say putting my shoes on to walk out the door.

I throw the soda I'm drinking across the room. "He's fucking dying and he chooses Scarlet to call!"

"Slow down, man. What did she say?"

"She said that he has some kind of stage four cancer and he's trying to make amends, with all of us."

"So did he call Cade?"

"No, he knew the best way to get his foot in the door with us was to talk to Scarlet first. He's a fucking professional con-artist. He knew she had the softest heart. Actually, he probably tried to call mom first but since she's moved, he couldn't get in touch with her."

Stoney grabs my arms. "Man, come over here and sit down before they call those damn MP's or some shit."

My door opens and Keeg and Scarlet walk in. They sit down across from me. Keeg motions to me. "Okay man, tell us what all exactly Scar said."

I sit down and tell them. "He has stage four cancer and he wants to meet with us to discuss his last wishes and will. He also wanted to try and have some sort of relationship with us. He found out from Scarlet that we met Cade and would like to get together with all three of us."

I notice that Ivie is shaking her head. She stands up, looking mad as hell. "Who in the fuck does he think he is? He thinks that just because he's dying that he can walk back into y'all's lives and make peace and go to heaven and shit. Fuck him!"

Keeg pulls her back down in the chair. "Ivie, settle down. Damn. I know this hits close to home for you but I brought you here to keep him calm."

She looks at him like he's lost his mind. She's right, who in the hell does that guy think he is? I stand up. "I'm gonna call Cade."

They all nod at me.

I finally get a call through to Cade and he's as pissed as I am. He's going to keep in touch with Scarlet, make sure the asshole doesn't just show up.

When I walk back in the room with the band, Stoney looks at me, trying to break the tension. "So man, did he happen to say if you had anymore siblings, like maybe another hot sister?"

"Fuck you man. I find out that my asshole dad is dying, wants a relationship with me, and you want to know if I have a spare sister you can nail."

Keeg laughs. "Come on, man, it's Stoney. He didn't mean anything by it, he's just trying to lighten the mood."

"I know, I know. Thanks for trying to help me."

Keeg pats my back. "It's okay man, we know. But... you know, if you do happen to have another sister or two." He shrugs his shoulders.

"Thanks, with friends like you I damn sure don't need enemies." I flop back on the bed and don't even realize that Ivie is sitting next to me.

She rests her hand on mine. "Don't forget both of them are brain damaged. The oxygen has been cut off to their brains too many times by sticking their faces in big fake breasts."

We start laughing. It feels good to laugh with her and the guys. She has a beautiful laugh.

With her hand on mine, I realize how much I've missed her touch, the softness of her skin, and then it hits me. I want to feel her lips on mine.

I shake my head and jump up. "Okay guys, enough of my fucking crazy family. Let's go practice."

Keeg and Stoney slap me on the back. Stoney smiles. "Alright man, let's go."

~*~*~

After practice, we sit around discussing the upcoming shows in Afghanistan and how we're excited and a little nervous about them. The guys leave to go meet up with a couple of the girls from the USO, one of them being Celanie.

I stop Ivie as she's walking out the door behind them. "Thanks for coming by today, Ivie. I'm glad that we could be this way with each other."

She nods, walking toward the door, but then she stops, still looking out the door. "I still can't put everything behind me, you know."

I walk to her, spinning her around. "I'm not a good person. I loved you with everything I had in me and I still fucking ran like a coward. You're right, I am like my dad."

"Gable, can't you see? You can change it. Get him out of your fucking head before he ruins the rest of your life. So you aren't calling kids that hate you on your death bed."

She walks out of the room, not saying anymore.

Sitting down, I work a little more on the song I've been working on.

I realize a few hours have passed and I'm still thinking about her. I need to talk to her. I know deep down I love her, but I have to let her go.

I make it to her door and I'm about to knock when I hear a loud thud inside like someone fell.

I shove the door open and see a very weak looking Ivie on the floor.

Falling to my knees beside her, I touch her face. It's clammy and sweaty. She's burning up. "Ivie, baby what's going on?"

All she can do is groan and shiver. She's clutching her stomach.

Oh my God, what if they didn't fix everything?

She begins throwing up on me. "HELP! SOMEBODY HELP ME!"

A couple of people rush in the room and start screaming for someone to get the medics in here.

"Ivie, keep listening to me. I love you, babe. I still love you. I'm sorry I'm such a fucking loser. Please don't leave me."

I realize I'm crying. Keeg and Stoney burst in the room, pulling me up off the floor so the medics can pick her up. I look at Stoney. "Something is really wrong with her, man."

Sitting in my room thinking about Gable isn't how I intended for tonight to end. He and I both have some real winners for parents. Well, I guess his mom Whisper is okay, but his dad is like mine, a real piece of shit.

Man, my stomach has been cramping all night. I'm really hoping this isn't how my periods are going to be from now on. I never had cramps this bad before and I thought birth control helped with that. Which a part of me wonders if this is that type of cramping because I'm starting to feel like shit.

Great, just my luck. I'm probably getting some kind of stomach flu or something. I'll just take some stomach medicine and lie down, maybe that will help.

Waking up soaking wet with sweat and shivering, I look over at the clock and see that I've been asleep for two hours. My stomach lurches and I need to throw up. I stand up and try walking to my bathroom but the world tilts, and the next thing I know, I'm on the floor.

Oh God, my stomach hurts! I'm gonna be sick. Someone is holding my head and talking to me.

"Ivie, baby, what's going on?" I know that voice, I love that voice.

I try unsuccessfully to say his name, but every time I open my mouth I vomit. I'm still shivering and I'm tired. I can't hold my eyes open anymore. I can still hear him a little, but it's foggy sounding.

"Ivie, keep listening to me. I love you, babe. I still love you. I'm sorry I'm such a fucking loser. Please don't leave me."

~*~*~

Waking up, I can see that I'm in some type of treatment room. I see the guys sitting in chairs and I lift my head. "Hey, guys." I croak out.

They jump, almost knocking the chairs over that they are sitting in.

Stoney grabs my hand. "Ivie, you have to stop scaring the fuck out of us."

"Sorry. What happened? I remember feeling sick part of the night and then falling in my room. It's all kind of jumbled."

Gable sits on the end of my bed. "Well, at first they thought you had some kind of thing called MERS, *Middle Eastern Respiratory Syndrome*, but it wasn't that. You and about a quarter of the base got E-Coli from the mess hall."

They hand me a cup of water and I drink some. "I was scared. I woke up sweating and shivering and trying to get to my bathroom. I felt like I was dying and drunk or something at the same time."

"Well, Gable found you. He thought you were dying. You gotta quit doing this shit to us. I swear I may be twenty-three, but you are shaving years off my heart. I think my heart is like fifty-three now." Keeg says laughing.

"Really? That many people got sick? What in the hell from?"

Gable looks over at me. "Well, Judd said that it's happened before. They hire nationals on contract to work in the kitchen and they don't wash their hands like they are supposed to. Not according to our standards, so people end up getting sick."

Keeg looks sick. "Yeah, meaning they don't wash their hands after they go to the shitter."

I look at them confused. "Judd?"

"Yeah, he was back on base for a day or two so he stopped by and saw us." Gable shrugs.

"Wait, how many days have I been in here?"

Keeg looks at me with big eyes. "Shit, you were really out of it. You've been in here four days. With a big part of the base being sick, plus part of the entertainment, they rescheduled the shows."

I shake my head. "Damn. I know in my room it felt like someone was ripping my stomach into shreds."

Gable looks at the ground. "Well, they said that your immune system still hadn't fully recovered from before we left home so it was very susceptible to infection. For the past few days they've pumped you full of liquids and antibiotics."

"Is Judd still on base?"

Keeg laughs. "No man, he moves in and out of here like the fucking wind. No wonder Ryder was bitching about never being able to talk to him. He just advised us to only eat packaged food or food we prepare ourselves from now on, no matter what base we're on."

Stoney smiles like a jackass. "He also said to tell you that he'd be in touch while we play the Afghanistan shows." Then he makes kissing noises like a five year old.

"Fuck you, Stone. He's just a friend. He's being nice to all of us because we are from the same hometown."

Keeg and Stoney grunt. Stoney glances up again. "Hey, Keeg and I are gonna grab some coffee and let the doc know you're up. If he says you can have some coffee, do you want some?"

I look at him like he's stupid. "How many years have you known me?"

"I'll take that as a yes." Keeg snorts.

I nod and they walk out of the room.

It's killing me, I have to know. "Gable, why did you come to my room that night?"

"I – ugh I just came to talk. You said the other night that I could still change.   I still love you-."

I put my hands out. "No, never mind. Stop. I can't do this. I can't talk about us right now."

"I was just going to say-."

"NO! I don't want to talk about it."

Man, this crap with my dad has really screwed with my head. As much as I hate the guy, I don't want him to die. My sister is upset and I'm far away from her. I know she has Cade and Ryder, but damn it, it's always been me and Scar against the world.

Needless to say, our mom is upset. I've Skyped with her, and with Scarlet and Cade. They all say the same thing. "That I need to concentrate on my job for right now."

On top of all of this shit, there is Ivie. I can't shake her out of my head. I love her more than anything, and finding her the other night felt like my world was being torn the shreds.

To top it off, she has guys asking her out all the time. Really? Those fucks have one thing on their mind asking her out here. Like you can really take a chic on a date. Where are you going to take her on this damn base? The coffee place, the gym, a shitty movie theatre or the mess hall. Hell, Ivie hasn't eaten in the mess hall since she got sick. Our schedule got changed up a little bit so we've been in Kuwait for an extra couple of weeks. Judd has stopped by a few times.

Everyone keeps telling me that he isn't anything but friends with Ivie, but I don't like it. Plus, it's creepy, he's in and out of here all the time. He's like a puff of smoke, a damn ghost.

I'm still working on my song but I can't seem to get any further. Keeg and Stoney heard a little of it by accident the other day and they like the sound.

There is a knock at my door and in walks Stoney. "Hey man, what's up?"

I shrug. "Just thinking."

"Ha, I thought there was smoke coming from this room." He sits down in a chair.

"Shut up, dick."

"So have you talked anymore to your sister?"

"Yeah, I got on Skype with her, mom and Cade. They all just want me to chill out and concentrate on work until I get back home."

"Sounds good. Plus you need to find your fucking head, which you've stuffed up your ass somewhere when it comes to Ivie."

"Man, I'm leaving her alone. Do you see the shit I'm dealing with right now? My fucking loser father-."

"Stop! Quit using that. Your dad may have jumped fucking ship, okay, but Whisper didn't. You know she was there too when you were conceived. Although sometimes I do think that you were hatched from a serpent egg, but that is neither here nor there."

"Have you met my mom?"

"Yes. I saw a woman who loved her kids enough to put everything she loved aside and raise them in her own fruitcake, peace loving, flower child sort of way."

"Mom was-."

"There. She was there. No, Whisper wasn't the kind of mom who did bake sales, or joined the PTA and shit, but she stuck it out in a town that wasn't her home. A town that knew her husband just got shipped off because he had more than one family. Hell, I'm surprised she didn't take you and Scar off in some kind of gypsy caravan, but she didn't. She didn't drag different jackasses in and out of your house. She took care of you. So how can you think that you are all Dan Johnson and not any of Whisper? I can tell you right now, if Whisper loved someone, she wouldn't give up on them."

"I know, but the evidence on my part shows to the contrary already. I fucking left her to deal with all of that herself. I bailed just like him."

"Yeah, well people make mistakes. You just need to have big enough balls to admit to them and apologize. She's lost without you, man."

I shake my head. "No, she deserves someone who won't bail on her when times get tough."

"The fact that you realize that shows more than you know. Plus, I saw you the other night, man. You were holding her screaming."

"It scared me, man."

"Yeah, you thought the love of your life was dying. I see you when those guys around here ask her out. You look like you're ready to fucking murder someone, and you're jealous as hell of Judd." He shakes his head. "For no reason, I might add. That boy is wrapped up in your sister's best friend so bad it's crazy."

I flop back on my bed. "So what, man? Even if I want this to work, she won't let me talk about it. She says I hurt her every time I talk about it, and she's right. She won't listen to me."

"So, make her listen. Look, I actually heard all of that song you were working on the other day. I know it's about her. Sing it to her."

I bark out a laugh. "Oh yeah, that'll work. *Hey baby, just listen to this song I've been writing for you but I can't finish.* Great pick up line, man."

"No, I mean tell her you want her to listen to what you've been working on. You wanna see how some bass lines lay down with it."

I let out a huge breath. "Do you think it would work?'

"Yeah man, I do." He stands up. "Now, remove your head from your ass and get to work." He walks out the door.

Yep, I'm fucked.

Standing in line at the coffee shop, someone bumps into me. "Excuse me, ma'am."

I turn around to see a very handsome soldier. I smile. "No problem."

"You're Ivie with the band, right?"

I smile. "Yep, the one and only."

"Would you like to grab coffee sometime?"

I hold my cup up. "I think I'm grabbing coffee right now."

He smirks. "Ah, you are. So how about we sit and drink it together?"

I shake my head. "Really, is that the best you've got?"

"Yes, so now you should feel sorry for me and have coffee with me."

I laugh and nod my head. "Sure, why not?"

An hour later, I feel like I'm chatting with an old friend. His name is Chris and this is his third tour. He's from Louisiana, has two sisters, and a dog named Buster.

He's telling me a story about his time in the Army. "So my buddy goes in the porta-potty and we lock it and roll him down the hill. He comes out at the bottom of the hill covered in that blue stuff they put in there, shit and piss."

I'm laughing hard. "That is funny, it sounds like something Keeg or Stoney would do."

"Yeah, it was pretty funny, but he never dumped ice water on us in the showers again."

"So, do you have a girl back home?"

He shakes his head. "No, I did, but she said she couldn't handle all of the stress from the deployments. So I guess it was at the first of my second tour she told me in an email that we were finished."

"That bitch!"

He laughs while several people turn and look at me.

I cringe. "Sorry."

He chuckles. "It's okay, I felt the same way."

"Yeah, but she should've picked a better time or something. It just seems really shitty that she waited until you were like 3000 miles from home to say *Oh, you know, hun? This isn't working out.* What a fucking coward."

He shakes his head. "Hey, I'm better off. It sucks, but unfortunately it's really common. Sometimes the people left at home just can't handle it."

"Yeah, well I think she's a selfish thunder-cunt. That's what I think."

"You are really funny. You know that?"

"No, I just hang out with guys who have the mentality of middle school boys way too much. I swear it's all farts, penis jokes and boobs."

He looks over at me. "So what about you? Anybody back at home?'

I shake my head looking down. "No, there was but not anymore. It's kinda recent."

He nods that he understands. "Yeah, I remember how that felt."

"I thought we were in love. He promised that he'd never let me down and he did."

"Damn, that sucks. I know how it feels. Lia was my best friend, one of the most important people in the world to me, and then it was just over."

I nod. "Yeah."

"So, did this guy try to make it up to you?"

"It's complicated."

He nods and we change the subject.

We finish our coffee and start walking back toward the area I've now deemed the trailer park. I laugh.

He looks over at me. "What are you laughing about now?"

"Well, I was just thinking you know, I've lived in some pretty bad areas, but I've never lived in a trailer park until now."

He starts laughing. "Yeah, that is pretty funny."

We reach my door, I look at him. "Thanks for this afternoon. You're a funny guy."

"Well, you are welcome. You, my dear, are a funny girl. We should do this again sometime."

I keep talking about moving on, I guess I need to. "Well, I'll be wrapped up with the show tomorrow, then we are pulling out for Afghanistan. What about you? Are you here or are you moving somewhere else?"

"Well, I'll be here for the next six months and then my tour is up."

"I think we are coming back through here in a month or so. We are supposed to be going home for a couple of weeks in March, I think. We are stopping on the way home."

He leans in towards my face. "Well then, it's a date."

I nod. "Okay, it's a date."

"Ivie, can I kiss you?"

"Umm, yeah."

It's a polite kiss, but there are no sparks. No need to explore further. I don't feel like I want to tear his clothes off and have him fuck me senseless.

We say our goodnights and I walk in my room, sliding down the door after I close it. Gable ruined me and there will never be anyone else.

My heart just shattered. It literally feels like one of those confetti cannons exploding in my chest. I just watched her kiss someone else.

That's it, I can't handle this. I know that I shouldn't feel this way and I told her to go, that we couldn't be anything, but I have to have her. She's mine. I can't see her kiss someone else. How would I ever handle it if she married someone else, or for fucksake, had a baby by someone else?

How in the hell do these guys make it around here without drinking? Because I really need a fucking drink right now. This girl is going to be the death of me, and these guys get shot at and are sober. What the fuck?

Breaking from my mental melt down after I see the guy walking off, I make my way to her door.

I knock on the door and she opens it a little. When she sees me, she has a confused look on her face. I push the door open and walk in. "Gable, what do you wa-."

I don't let her finish before my mouth is on hers and I'm slamming her door.

She shoves me in the chest. "What the fuck?"

I pull her back. "I can't- ah fuck it."

I pick her up and basically throw her on the bed, crawling up between her legs. She's panting. It's causing my dick to try and bust out of my pants. I'm not playing, he's probably going to have a permanent zipper print embedded in him.

When I grind my crotch into her, she groans.

I rub my hand down her chest as I work my lips from her mouth to her neck.

She lets out a gasp. "Gable?" She says with a questioning tone.

"Shh. No talking right now. I promise we'll talk, just not right now." I say as I kiss my way down her chest.

I lift her, pulling her shirt over her head, unclasping her bra and throwing it to the floor. I slide the shorts and panties she's wearing down her legs.

She starts tugging at my shirt for me to remove it. I snatch it off and make quick work of my pants and boxers.

Sinking into her, it's home. It's like breathing when you've been holding your breath forever.

This feels amazing. I love the feel of her body. It was made for mine.

I stop. "Shit, condom."

She looks up at me with hooded eyes. "I'm on the pill. Have you been with anyone else?"

I exhale and thrust back into her, devouring her neck with my mouth. "No. No one else."

She raises her hips to meet my thrusts.

Our movements are slow and synchronized. We are making love this time, I'm not just fucking her.

Looking down at her face, I realize that this is all I've ever wanted. I have to quit being so damn afraid and take the leap.

I feel her start to tighten around my cock, she's close. In moments, she's falling over the edge, moaning and rambling incoherent words.

I quicken my pace and slam my last thrust into her, spilling my seed into her.

She tries to sit up and I stop her. "Let's just lie here and rest. We'll talk after a nap."

"Okay." She says lightly and snuggles into my side.

I lie here awake, rubbing her arms. I have to get her to forgive me. I need her in my life, in my bed. She is everything to me.

I'm going to be the man she needs or kill myself trying. She's right, I need to change. I can't be my dad, I'm not my dad.

I slide out of her bed to take a piss. I bump into the small desk in her room when I come back out of the bathroom.

I see some papers fall on the floor. Reaching down, I pick them up.

She's been working on music, too. Once I start reading the lyrics, my heart breaks. I really almost killed her, emotionally.

Once I read over them several times it hits me. This is what I need for my song. We could do this together.

I jump up. Holy shit, I've gotta go get my guitar. She needs to hear this when she wakes up.

I quietly leave her room and make my way over to mine. Grabbing my guitar and the music I've been working on, I head back over to her room.

I walk in as she's sitting up on the bed, looking confused. Her long dark hair is hanging down and covering her breasts.

"I thought you left."

"I just ran to my room to grab this." Holding up my guitar and my music book.

She nods. "Oh."

"Okay, I've been working on this song for a while now and I can't seem to finish it. But I think I have a plan now, I just need your help."

"Okay."

She sits back and I start to play, I see unshed tears in her eyes.

Pulling a shirt over my head after Gable comes back in with his guitar, I'm really beginning to question my sanity because I'm waking up alone, when I'm pretty sure I had mind blowing sex with Gable. Until he walked back in here, though, I wasn't positive.

I shouldn't have done that but my hormones are still all over the place. I mean my damn dreams here lately would give any sixteen year old boy a run for his money.

He's started playing a song and it's beautiful. Once he finishes, he grabs another piece of paper and I realize is mine.

"Hey, what are you doing with my song?"

"I'm sorry but I accidentally knocked it off the desk when I went to take a piss."

"So, you just felt the need to read it."

He shrugs. "Well, yeah, kinda. Just give me a second to explain." I nod. "Grab your bass and play these lines with me. When I finish my verse, you sing what you have."

> *You unlock the door and climb inside-*
> *You don't need seat belts for this ride-*
> *You take my heart and hold it in your hands-*
> *Taking for granted where you stand-*
> *I've never been one to let go of control-*

But with you I seem to do that more-
I always seem to screw things up with you-
For some reason I always do-
You're the one I must confess-
You tilt my heart off its axis-
How do I repay you? I break yours in two-
I owe you more-

*

I don't know if I'll ever trust you again-
You crushed me and left me-
I can't do this anymore-
Even though it's the hardest thing I'll go through-
I know I'll never get over you-
You abandoned me and it didn't take you long-
To find a new bed to keep you warm-
I should've known this was all too good to be true-

He stops playing and looks over at me. "See how they flow together? I figure we could go into a verse that we play together."

"Yeah, that really works. I see a couple of other spots for us to work on. We need to work on a chorus in between our parts, I think."

"Yeah, I think so, too."

I look over at him. "So, are we gonna talk now?"

He nods. "Yeah, we are."

"Those lyrics, is that how you really feel about me?"

He smiles. "Yeah, I mean you're it for me. I don't know how else to explain it. I don't know what we both really want. I know we both have our demons we're fighting. We've both got shit to get through, but I can't be without you."

"Why this all of a sudden?"

"My brain has been going crazy for days. The guys were right, because you scared the shit out of me the other night. I-."

We are interrupted by a knock at the door. I open my door to see our tour manager, Kevin.

"Hey you guys, wheels up in two hours."

"What, I thought we had a show tonight? We aren't supposed to leave until tomorrow."

"Huge sand storm coming in, we need to get you guys out today or you won't be getting out for another week."

I look over at Gable. He looks at Kevin. "So what all do we need to do?"

He looks at Gable. "Pack your shit and meet us at the van in an hour. We'll head to the airfield from there."

We both nod and he walks away.

I turn and start throwing items into my bags. He grabs my hand. "We will continue this conversation later." He kisses my temple and walks out the door.

Sitting down on the edge of my bed, I'm getting lost in my own thoughts. Is he bi-polar? He is so back and forth. He wants me then he doesn't want me. He tells me he'll love me forever, then he bails on me when things get tough.

I want to trust him, I want him to love me, but most of all I want him to be with me for the rest of my life. I love Gable Rhett Johnson with all of my heart, but I'm not sure I can hand it to him again.

I know I have my own faults in what happened, but him ignoring me for almost two weeks was almost too much for me to bear.

I'm afraid if I give him my heart this time and he breaks it, I'll never come back from it.

I finish throwing my stuff into my duffle bags and head out to meet the band.

GABLE

Man, they weren't kidding about fucking sand storms. We missed most of it but what I did see, I wouldn't want to deal with on a daily basis.

Judd stopped by to see us today. He said he won't be able to make the show because he's got some mission to go on in the mountains. I'm becoming accustom to him, only because everyone is pretty sure he's in love with my sister's best friend, Annabelle.

I was telling him that we were going home for some time around March or April *from the looks of our ever changing schedule,* and that I think Ryder is planning on asking my sister to marry him on her Spring Break from SCAD. We're hoping it works out so that I'm home and we can all go to Cade's beach house in Destin. My mom may even try to be there.

No one but Cade, Ryder and Judd know I'm hoping to be home during that time though, just in case it doesn't work out. That's one thing Judd has taught me. He said. "Anything that has to do with the military is *subject to change.*"

I still haven't had a chance to talk to Ivie like I want to. She and I have both been so busy with getting ready for the show tonight, and restrictions on this base are tighter on us because we are in an actual conflict zone, so we don't have as much time to hang out.

Looking at my watch, I realize it's time to get to the concert area for rehearsal.

I start walking that way and realize how they were right and another sandstorm is moving in. Judd warned me that if it moves in while we are here, they may put us on lockdown since we aren't soldiers.

That makes sense though, we don't need to be in their way while they're trying to protect us.

I really do need to talk to Ivie, but her hormones are still all over the place and I don't want to hurt her. I know I need to be positive without fear before I talk to her. She deserves that, she deserves the world. I'm just trying to figure out if I'm the guy to give it to her.

I finally reach our area. Shaking out my scarf, I look over at the guys and Ivie. "Man, this sand is for the fucking birds."

They all nod in agreement and Ivie laughs. "Yeah, well you should try having long hair in it."

We all laugh and start rehearsing. After a couple of hours, Keeg and Stoney tell me they've got some shit to take care of before the show in a few hours. Which means they found a couple of chicks to hook up with.

When it's finally just Ivie and me, I touch her arm, pulling her to sit by me. "We need to finish our talk from the other day."

She looks at me. "Gable, I don't know if I can handle it right now. It kills me that you have this power over me. You have the power to ruin me. This time I don't know that I'd recover."

I touch the side of her face. "Look, I know we have so many things to work through. I just want you to know that you're it for me. When I saw that guy kissing you the other night, I was ready to rip his head off."

She looks at me like I am Satan and I just set her on fire. "You saw me the other night? So that's why you came to my room and fucked me. You don't want me, but you don't want anyone else to have me, either!"

She spins around to leave and I try to grab her arm. "Ivie, it's not like that."

She makes it to the door when the horns go off. We were told that means we have to stay where we are. She kicks the door. "FUCK!"

Good, this means we are stuck here together and she'll have to listen to me.

"Don't you come near me!" She screams at me with tears in her eyes. She slides down by the wall. "Why do you do this to me? You know, at least when Chad beat the shit out of me it was just physical. I can't handle all of your mind games. Emotionally you are killing me." Tears are freely rolling out of her eyes.

I sit down on the floor across from her and she draws her feet up, bringing her knees to her chest.

"Ivie, I don't deserve it, but please just listen to me."

"What choice do I have? We're locked in here, right?"

"I wish that wasn't the only reason you were listening to me."

About that time, we hear an explosion. It shakes the walls around us. A set of stage lights fall over and shatter.

Another explosion, this time more shit around us starts falling. I look over at her and she is shaking with pure fear.

Grabbing her hand, I pull her to me, picking her up and throwing her over my shoulder fireman style. I run over to the stage area and let her down. "Get up under the stage, baby, and cover your head."

She crawls quickly up under there and I go in after her.

Pulling her to me, I wrap my arms around her and kiss the top of her head. "I love you, Ivie, I really do."

Hiding up under a stage shaking in fear isn't my idea of a good time. Especially being that I just had this melt down with Gable and now he's holding me. I want to be angry with him, I want to tell him to get the hell away from me. I can't though, I need him.

He strokes the side of my face. "Shh baby, it's okay."

"D-don't c-call me ba-baby."

"Just rest. Just rest. We'll talk later."

I must have dosed off because the next thing I know, I'm being put on the stage on my side.

I open my eyes and Gable smiles. "The firing has stopped but the sandstorm still has us on lockdown."

I sit up, hanging my feet off the stage. He sits down by me. "Ivie, I'm gonna talk and you're just gonna listen. I've got some things to say and I'm going to try and make them come out like they are supposed to, but I can't promise anything."

I nod and shrug. "I'm kinda trapped so what else am I going to do?" This annoys me.

He throws his hands up in frustration. "I'm a fuck up. The other night, I was on my way to tell you all of these things in my head. I stopped when I saw that guy kissing you. I was going to just go back to my room and keep it to myself."

He touches my hand and looks into my eyes. "But I couldn't. I thought about the fact that I couldn't stand to see you with someone else, you're supposed to be with me. The thought of you kissing someone else, having sex with someone else, marrying someone else, having kids with someone else, I can't do it. You have always been mine. Hell, whether or not either of us were willing to admit it."

He looks at me as if he's expecting me to say something.

I motion to him. "Can I speak now?" He nods his head. "How can I believe you, Gable? The whole pregnancy thing brought so many things to the front burner. So many things that we'd been avoiding. Then, how you treated me after I lost the baby." I shake my head, trying to avoid the tears that are ready to spill. "I cried for two solid days. You made me feel like I was nothing but a mistake to you. I was freaked out and I guess I should've called you the minute I found out, but I was scared. How was I to know that before I could tell you, some psycho would take all of it away from me? He took my spirit, my drive, a baby I didn't even know that I wanted, but most of all, he took you."

He scares me by grabbing my face and pulling it to his. "Baby, he did not take me from you."

"Yes, he did, you left me. Had it not been for Scarlet, I don't know what I would have done. I thought I was losing my mind, and besides a few generic texts, I never heard from you."

He looks up at me with tears in his eyes. "I planned on coming out to Scarlet's like I said, but when I went back in the house..."

He stops and I see him trying to swallow, he continues. "I saw my room and how hard you fought. Then, I walked around the bed and the carpet was saturated with blood. One spot was his, but there was a good sized spot that was yours. I lost it. I knew that you could've died right there, along with my baby. I began to wonder if maybe that was one of the reasons my dad never came back after he went to prison. Was it because he was afraid to lose it all when someone walked away from him?"

I go to say something and he stops me. "I know that's not true, my dad was a coward and a jackass. I acted like one, too, but I learned I was trying to distance myself so it didn't hurt so fucking bad. What it did show me, though, was how it would feel to not have you in my life, in my bed as my partner. That's not a life I want, Ivie, not even close. I want you with me for the rest of my life. I love you."

"Gable." I wipe the tears from my face. "I can't promise I'll go right back to how we were before. I can't promise to go straight back to being in your bed every night. I can promise you that I love you and I want to be with you. It's just, trust is going to be an issue for me right now. I lost a lot. So, at the risk of sounding like a broken record, I'm not putting a label on this. I don't want to be with anyone else, but I can't give you myself completely yet. If I do and this doesn't work, it'll kill me this time."

He slams his mouth to mine. "I love you and I'm going to spend the rest of my life proving it to you every day."

All of the emotions and adrenaline pumping through my body seem to go straight to my core while he's kissing me. I run my hands down his chest to his crotch and I feel his hardening cock though his jeans.

He runs one of his hands over my hardening nipples. Lowering his head, he bites at the nipple through my shirt. Pulling my shirt over my head and taking my bra off, he pushes me back on the stage. He starts unbuttoning my jeans to slide them down and he looks up at me, with hooded eyes. "Baby, I have to taste you."

Kissing my inner thighs and working his way to my core, the first flick of his tongue on my clit makes my back arch up and I practically start bucking off the stage.

He whispers to me. "Hold on baby, we are going to do this right."

After a few minutes of exhilarating pleasure, he climbs up my body. Looking down, I see at some point in all of my bliss he's stripped his clothes off, too.

I can't help but chuckle and he smiles at me. "Babe, that does nothing for my confidence."

"No, it's just I didn't realize you'd taken your clothes off, too. I guess I was too busy eating up all the pleasure you were giving me." I glance back down at his amazing cock. "And nothing should ruin your confidence."

He grins. "Oh, well by all means, I'll continue."

A few moments later he's thrusting into me. We both at first enjoy the slow tantalizing way we are enjoying each other's bodies, but after a few minutes our need for each other wins. We are both grinding and moving faster and faster. Nipping and biting at each other, my legs are over his shoulders while he's slamming into me. We are both sweating when we finally both come. I scream his name as I feel a warm jet shoot inside of me.

Looking at each other, we smile. As he kisses my temple, I look into his eyes. "I know I'm on birth control now, but should we be using condoms anyway. Nothing is 100%."

He smiles. "Baby, I want nothing between us, and if we are that 2% that gets pregnant with birth control, then that's what happens. We will deal with it. I'm proving to you that this," he motions between us, "Is the real deal."

"I love you, Gable."

About that time the door bursts open with Keeg and Stoney.

Stoney screams. "WHAT THE FUCK! OH MY EYES, MY DAMN EYES. I CAN'T UNSEE THIS SHIT!"

Keeg laughs. "Well it's about fucking time. If I had to walk up on her in mid sex dream again, I was seriously gonna lose my shit."

We are finally home for a couple of weeks. I surprised my sister, which was awesome considering I knew the huge surprise she was getting a day later.

Ryder and I had been working on the plan for weeks. He was surprising her with a Spring Break trip to Destin, where Cade's wife has a house on the beach. Ivie and I showed up the day after they did. The next day, my Mom even snuck in. Ryder walked her out to the beach and asked her to marry him.

I've never seen my sister so happy. I'm so glad she's found her happiness because I know I've found mine.

The record company liked the demo that Ivie and I made of our lyrics combined. We worked on a chorus and a couple of more verses to go with it.

The song finally came off as *stupid guy hurts girl he loves, she can't get over him but he broke her heart. They finally talk to each other and work things out and figure out there could never be anyone else.*

Sound familiar? They say the test market on the song is off the charts, that people like the "couple" singing to each other. After we finish the last leg of the USO tour, we are heading in to the recording studio.

They even got us a place in Atlanta so we don't have to be so far from home.

But today is a big day. Today, I'm going to see my father for the first time in years. Actually, Scarlet, Cade, myself and our mothers are all meeting with him.

Our mothers met at the beach house and hit it off. Who knew you could bond with a lady that was married to your shitbag dying ex-husband at the same time you were?

He is meeting us here at Ryder's house. I had mom sell her place while I was gone, so now when I'm home, I guess Ivie and I are staying with Scar and Ryder.

Of course when I got here, I got a very long and scary lecture from Nana, which I deserved. She gave me hell for acting like child and running from my responsibilities. Then, she told me if I ever treated a sweet girl like Ivie that way again, she'd do something involving a baby calf thinking my dick was his mom's tit.

Needless to say, I promised her it would never happen again.

"Gable, he's here." I hear mom call from outside the room I've been hiding in.

I meet everyone in the living room, and I see a very sick, weak old man.

Cade and I take seats on each side of Scarlet with our mothers on our sides.

He looks up from his chair. "I know you guys are thinking this is Karma. You're right."

My mother looks at him. "Dan, are you throwing that in for my benefit, since you know I believe in karma?"

He shakes his head. "No, I just wanted to come here and apologize for it all. I'm glad you kids found each other. I'm not much of a man, I know that. God has a funny way of teaching me lessons."

Finally, I break out of my reserved status. "So, I'm glad you're happy we found each other, but should we be looking for other siblings around the United States? Or are we just the lucky bastards that ended up with you as a father?"

"You three are my only children. I had wives after prison, but I made sure I'd never have any more children."

Scarlet looks up at him. "Good thing to know. I wouldn't want anyone else to feel the heartache, disappointment and hate we have for you. We were just kids and you caught us up in the middle of your fucked up head games."

He puts his hands out. "I know y'all will never forgive me and I deserve that. I came here to let you know that when I pass, all of my assets will be divided amongst the five of you in this room. I know it will never make up for anything, but I want you to have it. Now, please know that I'm sorry. I was young, I fell in love with two totally different, beautiful women, and then had three beautiful children. The only part of my life I regret is not getting to spend more time with you. I'll be going now. All of my arrangements have been made, after I pass you'll each be contacted by my attorney."

With that, he leaves. I'm shocked, very shocked.

We walk into the kitchen where, Ryder, Nana, Annabelle and Ivie are waiting. We go over what he said and in talking to everyone else, we decide that none of us will keep his money. We will all vote on one charity when the time comes.

Ivie and I go upstairs to lie down after mom, Cade and his mom leave. Not long after dozing off, I hear a blood curdling scream from down stairs.

Ivie and I fly down the stairs to find Nana sobbing, Ryder beating the shit out of a wall, Scarlet trying to stop him, Annabelle in shock crying, and Judd's parents holding each other.

I look between all of them. "What's going on?"

Nelson has finally went over to help Scarlet with Ryder and Scarlet looks at me. "It's Judd, he was injured and medevacked out to Germany. They aren't sure...they aren't sure how...if he's..." She breaks completely down.

Ivie is crying and she rushes over to be with Annabelle, who we know is more than just his friend.

I hold Scarlet and hug Nana.

Nana, being a true strong Southern woman, stands up and gathers us around. "Alright children, we are gonna pray. We are gonna pray that they bring that boy home to his family. Now, join hands." We all join hands and Nana prays. She breaks up a few times trying to get through it, but once she finishes, we all go in the kitchen and Nana puts us to work.

"Ryder, call your daddy and have him get his butt to the house. Nelson, Naomi, go home and get packed for Germany. If the military isn't sending you there to be with your boy, Abbott Cotton is. Scarlet, you call my friend Ms. Parker and tell her what's happened and to fire up those old ladies on the prayer chains. Ivie, Gable, you guys field the phone calls at this house and run up to Tom's Deli and tell Mrs. Phanie we are gonna need some food. She knows what we normally get." Annabelle looks at her, lost. "Annabelle, baby you come sit on this couch with Nana. I know he's more to you than you're letting on. I know this because he told me you're more to him before he deployed."

Annabelle collapses on her lap and sobs. Everyone else starts doing as they were told.

One Year Later...

"Gable, come on! We are gonna be late for the press interview." We have an interview for winning a rising star award.

He runs in, kissing me on the lips. "I'm coming, babe. Sorry, I ran late working out. I know you don't want my body going to hell."

I laugh. "Babe, I've always loved your body, even when you were a seventeen year old who still had some baby fat."

He slaps me on the ass. "Hey, I never had baby fat."

I giggle. "Okay, I'll agree to make you happy."

He runs to the bedroom to put clothes on. "This conversation isn't over. Tonight, you will be punished for saying lies about me."

Once we make it downstairs to the press room and meet up with Keeg and Stoney, it's not long before the reporters start firing off questions.

"So is it true, Gabe, that you and Ivie have been together for years?"

"Is it true that you said you'll never marry her?"

"Ivie, do you see other men?"

I finally put my hand up. "Okay, I'll address all of those questions and then I want all questions directed to the award we are here to talk about."

"Gable and I have been in a relationship for almost two years. We don't really discuss marriage, and I will never see other men."

After fielding some questions about our new album coming out and PR stuff, they start back on Gable and me.

"So Gable, we've heard you guys say you don't have labels on your relationship."

"That's right, labels are for other people, not the people in the relationship. Ivie knows that she's the only person for me and that's all that matters. I'm her only and she's my only."

"We've heard that your first original song was about your love. Is that true?"

I look up and smile. "The truth is we have secrets in all of our lyrics. Any song that has ever been written was someone's story."

Gable looks at them. "Now, thank you all for your time, but we have a show to get ready for."

We have a show at a Military Hospital tonight for wounded soldiers. After Gable's dad passed away, they decided that due to what happened with Judd, they would donate all the money to programs for wounded soldiers and their families.

Making our way back up to our room, Gable pins me to the wall in the elevator and kisses my neck. "You did good in there, babe. You really took charge, it was kinda hot."

"Ha ha. They were reaming the shit out of us."

He looks over at me. "Did you find out from Scar what time they'll all be here?"

"Yeah, their plane is due in at three this afternoon."

He nuzzles into my neck more. "Good, so we have the suite for a few hours to ourselves."

"Mmm, sounds good."

"Oh, don't think you aren't paying for your baby fat joke this morning."

"Oh, Mr. Johnson, are you going to spank me?"

He tugs at my ear with his mouth. "Oh, Mrs. Johnson, you'd like that, wouldn't you?"

I laugh. "Those reporters would shit if they knew we were already married."

He smiles. "Yeah, good thing we ran off to Vegas before we got super famous. Do you regret us not having a big wedding?"

"No. Do you regret us never telling anyone but our families that we're married?"

"Nope, I told you a long time ago, Ivie. You are all that matters, the rest of the world can fuck off."

"So sexy, this is the kind of stuff awesome songs are made from."

The elevator doors open and I think about the pregnancy test sitting on the bathroom counter in our room waiting for Gable to find it.

We walk in our suite and Gable heads to the bathroom as I sit on the couch with my bass.

When he walks out with the stick in his hands, I look up and start to sing.

I'm having his baby.

I'm having his baby.

I don't even get to finish the lyrics I made up when he picks me up over his shoulder, slinging me around.

"You just gave me the best song on Earth." He sits me down on my feet. "So, you really are gonna have my baby?"

I nod with tears in my eyes. "Yeah, I really am."

"I can't wait to hear our lyrics that come out of this experience."

I smile and kiss him. "Me, either."

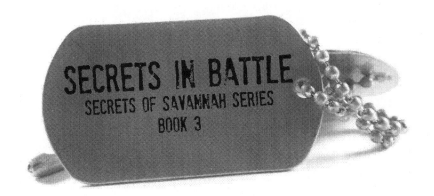

BY:
S.M. DONALDSON

DEDICATION

FOR MY MILITARY FAMILY. WE HAVE A BOND THAT MOST WILL NEVER BE FORTUNATE ENOUGH TO UNDERSTAND. YOU WILL ALWAYS HAVE MY LOVE.

"The Silent Ranks"

I wear no uniforms, no blues or army greens
But I am in the Army in the ranks rarely seen
I have no rank upon my shoulders - salutes I do not give
But the military world is the place where I live
I'm not in the chain of command, orders I do not get
But my husband is the one who does, this I cannot forget
I'm not the one who fires the weapon, who puts my life on the line
But my job is just as tough. I'm the one that's left behind
My husband is a patriot, a brave and prideful man
And the call to serve his country not all can understand
Behind the lines I see the things needed to keep this country free
My husband makes the sacrifice, but so do our kids and me
I love the man I married, Soldiering is his life
But I stand among the silent ranks known as the Army Wife
Author: Unknown

Secrets In Battle

Editing by Chelly Peeler

INTRODUCTION

- Due to mature subject matter this book is for readers 17+.
- This book is written in a true southern dialect, from a true southern person. Therefore, it is NOT going to have proper grammar.

A LITTLE NOTE FROM S.M. DONALDSON

Let me start by saying that as a military spouse, PTSD is something that is very near and dear to my heart. My husband and I were only 21years old when he was sent on his first deployment. A deployment that was supposed to just be a support mission in Kuwait. That support mission turned into a combat mission on March 20, 2003, when he and his unit were among some of the first soldiers to invade Iraq. This was a thirteen month long deployment with no R&R for him.

I can still remember watching the news on pins and needles, waiting for every phone call and driving home from work every day at lunch to check the mail just in case there was a letter in there. I probably spent over $10,000 between food, snacks, hygiene products and postage to send care packages. At this time, there weren't PX/BX's set up for the soldiers to buy items. All of them were sent from home. I also made some of my best and closest friends throughout this deployment with soldiers and spouses.

I was so excited for him to return home, all put together and in one piece. The only thing is, no matter how much they prepare you in the Return and Reunion Briefings for the battles that may still be occurring in their minds, you and your soldier are never completely prepared.

Dealing with PTSD is an ongoing battle for a soldier. It isn't a wound that can be seen from the outside. I was lucky that my husband's process of working through the biggest issues only took 9 months. He still has moments of anxiety and fear. I've learned how to help him and draw attention away from the problem, whatever it may be.

Some soldiers can't manage to get through it and turn to vices to help. Some feel as if they'll never be able to deal with it and take their own lives. I've watched all the different scenarios play out.

It's not just the soldiers dealing with the issues, it's the family, too. The stress from being a sounding board or a caregiver can be a lot on a loved one. I'm a firm advocate for Family Readiness Groups in the military and counseling for everyone involved.

This story was personal and sometimes hard for me write. I felt a little too close to it. There were parts of this story that were hard for me to write and even harder to relive in my mind. When it was complete though, I was glad that I slaved through it. I hope you have enjoyed Judd and the rest of the Savannah characters as much as I have enjoyed bringing them to you.

XOXO

S.M. Donaldson

If you know a solider or a soldier's family who is having trouble, please share these websites with them.

http://www.militaryonesource.mil
http://www.woundedwarriorproject.org
http://www.ptsd.va.gov
http://veteranscrisisline.net

PROLOGUE

A YEAR AGO...

Going out with Ryder tonight was what I'd been looking forward to this week. I have an upcoming deployment and it's my first one at my new job, this is going to be my last mission with my old squad. Going into Special Forces has always been my goal, but it's still nerve racking to actually be doing this.

Ryder has been going on and on about the chick he's doing community service with. When he sees her friend's car in the parking lot, he practically jumps out of his jeep.

We make our way inside and he scans the room. We grab a beer from the bartender and he looks at me. "Judd, I may need you to keep that little raven-haired beauty on the dance floor busy tonight." He says, pointing to the blonde girl's friend.

Fuck me, she is a raven-haired beauty. Holy shit, she's hot. I will definitely take one for the team on this. "Damn bro, I don't think that'll be a problem for me."

She's sexy, and way too classy for the shithole we are in. I see her walk over to the bar to grab another drink and George Strait's *The Chair* pipes through the speakers. The ultimate *get a hot chick in a bar* song.

I walk up to her. "Hey beautiful, would you join me on the dance floor?"

She looks up at me with her big green eyes. "Wow, a gentleman. I sure will." Sitting her drink down with her friend, she takes my hand.

We make our way on to the dance floor. "I'm Judd. What's your name?"

She grins. "Annabelle."

"So, what do you do, beautiful?"

"I'm in nursing school and I'm a princess." She says with a cute drunken smirk.

I burst out laughing. "Well, what kingdom are you the princess over?"

"I'm the princess in my family. My parents are loaded, my mom is Queen Bitch and I have four older brothers who are the court jesters. So I'm the princess, I've been in training since I was in princess panties." She shrugs, being a smartass. "What do you do, besides being completely mouthwatering hot?"

Damn. I grin. "I'm in the Army, right now I'm stationed just over at Ft. Stewart. I grew up around here, though. My best friend is Ryder Abbott, we grew up together. My dad has always worked for his family and we have been friends since we were both in diapers."

She points her cute little finger into my chest. "Oh, so you are using me as a distraction. I know Ryder. He's been sniffing around my girl Scarlet."

"Well, I hate to tell your friend, but if Ryder wants a girl he normally gets her. For the night at least."

She smirks. "Ha, well I hate to tell Sir Douche Bag, but Scarlet's not easy."

"Oh, I'm sure that will wound him. He seems a little caught up on this one. Can't say I've ever seen him this way."

She smiles drunkenly at me. "Well, the last guy that pissed her off ended up with an ax handle taken to his car. So best of luck to Ryder." She lays her head on my chest, rubbing over it and making my dick strain in my pants.

Normally I would say drunk girls are off limits, but with her, I can't. I want her and I need this distraction before I go. I nibble her ear. "So Princess, you wanna get out of here and show me those panties?"

She looks up at me with those beautiful green eyes and whispers. "Yes."

I knew what I was doing tonight was stupid, so stupid, but for a little while I just wanted to not feel. I shouldn't have went to that bar alone. Ever since I met Judd a little over a week ago, I can't get him out of my freaking head. I know he's leaving and we agreed to be friends after our wild night/morning of passion, but there is something about him. Something about how I screamed his damn name so loud the hotel called and asked us to quiet down.

When I think about all of the times he made me scream out like that, my panties are flooded. I figured maybe if I went out tonight and met someone it would get my mind off of things. Scarlet's at work and I don't have anyone else I wanted to go out with me, so my stupid ass went alone.

Now, I've escaped a possible rape situation and I can't fucking drive. That little preppy college prick seemed so nice. I knew I should've stuck to buying my own drinks.

A loud knock at my window scares me. "OH SHIT!"

"Princess, open the fucking door."

I open the door and Judd pulls me out. I start crying into his chest. After a few minutes he pulls back from me. "Are you okay? Let me see you."

He looks down at my torn dress, the bruise forming on my face and my split lip. "Do you know the guys who did this to you? Because I'm going to kill them."

I shake my head. "No, they just bought me drinks in the bar. I know I was stupid taking them. I'm sorry I had to call you but Scar is at work and I can't hardly see, much less drive."

He brushes the hair from my face. "Hey, it's not a problem. But promise me you'll never go out by yourself again. I'm about to leave and I need you here when I get back."

I nod my head. "I know, this scared the shit out of me. I'm just glad that I never finished the drink. When I started feeling woozy I left, but they tried to stop me, that's where the tear in the dress came from and I fell into a door. Then I ran to my car and hauled ass. When the road started getting fuzzy, I pulled over and called you." I wipe my eyes. "I was scared they would come after me."

He pulls me back into his massive chest and strokes my hair. "Shh. Shh. It's okay, I will never let anything happen to you."

I look up and get lost in his blue eyes. "Take me to your place."

"Princess, normally I would never turn you down, and yes, I'll take you to my place to get you sober and cleaned up, but we can't have sex tonight."

I start kissing at his chest. "Why?"

"Because you are doped up and I'm not that kinda guy. Now tomorrow, when you are sober, I'm gonna fuck you so that you remember me until I come home."

He puts me in the passenger side of my car and drives to his house on post. I can feel him carrying me inside and putting me to bed. *Hmm, he'll fuck me so I can remember him until he comes home.* I look up as he lies down beside me. "Please come back home."

"I promise, Princess."

CHAPTER 1

Staring at the walls of this hospital room for the past few months has been hell. I'm ready to get the hell out of here and go home. Well, to Ryder's house anyway. I can't stay with my family yet, my mom would smother me. Along with rehabilitation, both mentally and physically, I have to get used to the fact that the career I chose is over.

My door swings open. "You ready to go home, man?"

I look up at my best friend Ryder. "Yeah, I'm ready to get out of this fucking place." I grab up my crutches and start toward the door.

He shakes his head. "Whoa. Slow down. Don't worry man, I have the downstairs set up for you and your physical therapist. Nana is all ready to have you home to feed and take care of."

"Please tell me they didn't plan some kind of welcome home shit. I'm tired and I really don't feel like seeing people." I love my family and friends, but I don't want to deal with everyone else.

He shakes his head. "No, man. Not today, but I can't promise about another day this week."

"I just really want to be alone."

"Okay, man. I'll do what I can."

"Look, I know everyone means well, but I just can't handle crowds right now."

He puts his hand on my shoulder. "Alright, we'll just take it one day at a time. Okay?"

"Yeah. Thanks for letting me stay with you. I don't think I could handle my mom 24/7 right now."

He walks out with me to his jeep. "I know, man."

After we get everything loaded and ready to go, we hit the road for the long drive home. I look over at him. "Thanks again, man, for everything. Getting my parents to Germany so quick, coming to get me. Just everything."

"Hey, you're like my brother. I'd do anything for you. So, have you talked to Annabelle?"

I shake my head. "Nah. I really haven't wanted to talk to anyone while I was here. I just wanted to concentrate on getting well enough to go home."

Ryder turns up the radio a little bit trying to break the tension. It's weird, he's my best friend, practically my brother. The person who knows me better than anyone else, and I'm nervous and scared to be around him. I guess because I know he'll see through the facade, see all the things I've done. I don't know why I'm so uncomfortable in my own skin right now. I just keep staring out the window, watching small towns and mile markers go by.

After a few hours, Ryder looks over at me. "Hey man, I'm gonna swing in here to refuel and take a piss, you want anything?"

"Yeah, grab me a water. I need to take my meds."

He nods and goes in the store.

Once he's back in the jeep, I take my pain meds and lie back in the seat.

Finally, he looks over at me a little bit later, trying to break through the invisible wall in the vehicle. "So, I heard you got to spend some time with Ivie, Gable and the guys overseas."

Whew, something generally easy for me to talk about. "Yeah, they were all pretty cool. They're an awesome band. Ivie is great and she's one of a kind, that's for sure. I'm guessing she and Gable have worked things out."

"Oh yeah, more than anyone knows." I look over at him with a questioning look on my face and he smiles. "Don't tell anyone but since you're family, you can know. Well, once we get home Nana would tell you anyway. Right after I proposed to Scar, they slipped off to Vegas and had a quiet wedding. They don't want the media getting ahold of it yet. They have this whole thing about labels, blah, blah. I don't really get it, but I can understand how they wouldn't want people all up in their personal lives."

I shake my head. "Wow, that's some crazy shit. Oh yeah, so how is engaged life?"

He takes a deep breath and exhales. "It's great. I never thought I could love someone at all. Never thought I deserved someone like her. She and Annabelle have been working on wedding plans, we both want something small at the farm." He shrugs. "Waking up next to her everyday just feels right."

I smile. "Sounds good." I shake my head. "Damn, I never thought I'd see the day that Ryder Abbott settled for one woman. Son, hearts are breaking all over Dixie right now. I'm happy for you though, man. Scarlet is good for you. Let's face it, she passed the Nana test, that says enough right there."

He chuckles. "Tell me about it. Nana likes having all these girls around now. Between Scar, Annabelle and Ivie, she has a house full of them."

"I feel like I've missed so much."

"You have but we'll catch you up. So, what have they said about your enlistment?"

I prop my elbow on the window and rest my head in my hand. "They are probably going to medical discharge me. With all the shit with my leg and back, I'll never pass a med review board."

"What are you thinking about doing?"

"Shit, I don't know. I thought maybe about going to college and taking some classes." I shrug. "I have a little time to make up my mind and I have quite a bit in savings. It's just, I never thought I'd need a backup plan."

"Hey man, you can stay with me as long as you want. You know how big and empty that damn house is. Dad is spending more and more time in Atlanta, I honestly think he's seeing someone there, but he hasn't said anything to me. Ivie and Gable stay with us every once in a while when they're in town, but other than that it's just Scar and me."

I need to change the subject. "So you think Greer has a woman?"

He shrugs. "Well, like I said, he's been spending more and more time up there. I've also noticed him texting more. He's never been into texting before and he's all secretive about it."

"Whoa! Do you think your dad is sexting someone?" I chuckle.

Ryder's face contorts into this look of sickness. "Dude. What the fuck? I don't even wanna think about that. Don't ever say something like that again."

I laugh, holding my ribs. "Why? I'm sure Nana has already said something like that."

"No, she's much more colorful about it."

"Gotta love Pearl."

"Ain't that the damn truth?"

"I bet Nana is wanting you to have her some great-grans, though."

"No, actually she wants us to take time for ourselves, get to know each other and not rush into the whole kid thing."

I shake my head. "You know she sent me homemade wine while I was overseas at Christmas?"

He rolls his eyes. "Who do you think helped her package it so it didn't look like wine?"

For the next few hours, it feels good to laugh and carry on with my best friend. Not worrying about physical therapy, nightmares, anxiety or my future, just laughing. This is the exact reason I needed Ryder to be the one to pick me up.

CHAPTER 2

What is that fucking ringing sound? Would someone please shut it off?

Finally realizing that it is my phone, I fumble with it to answer it, seeing Scarlet's face on the screen.

"Hello."

"Hey, what time are you gonna be over today?"

"Huh?"

"Today. You know, our little cookout for Judd? Ringing any bells?"

"Shit, I forgot."

"You forgot?"

"Yes, I had a damn twelve hour shift last night with my ER Clinical rotation for school. I had a freakin' meth head go nuts trying to tear in to a locked cabinet, and we had a big car wreck. So I'm still a little out of it."

"Shit. I'm sorry. It's just I was hoping you being here would bring Judd out of his shell a little. He's been kinda withdrawn since he's been home."

"Scar, don't get caught up on that. He's been through a lot. He's not going to be himself right off the bat."

"Yeah, I know. We sat through the reunion briefings with his parents, but he's really withdrawn."

"I'll be there around noon. Is that okay?"

"Yeah, that's great. I'll see you then."

Hanging up the phone, I glance over at the clock and see that it's already after ten. I groan, get up out of bed and make my way to the bathroom to jump in the shower.

Is it weird that I'm nervous to go see him? I mean I haven't went out of my way in the past week that he's been home to go see him, but he hasn't really invited me over, either.

He promised me that he'd come back home to me and he almost didn't. My mind drifts back to the hotel room in Richmond Hill.

We barely make it in the hotel room door before I'm reaching down to unbuckle his belt and jeans. He's shoving the straps of my dress down. Realizing that I don't have a bra on with this dress, his mouth goes directly to my nipple. Lifting me under the ass, I wrap my legs around his waist. I feel his erection against my panties.

As he's kissing across my breasts, I groan. "Judd, I need...I need you."

He spins around, throwing me on the bed and snatching my panties down. He whips his shirt off, shoving his pants and boxers down.

He drops to his knees, planting his face in my pussy. This boy must have taken extra credit classes in Oral Communications because Holy Shit. I know he's saying something to me but I'm not sure what the hell he's saying. I'm screaming something incoherent, I'm sure, as I come on his face.

Climbing up my body, I see him roll a condom on and he bites my nipple as he thrusts inside of me. Fuck, that is awesome.

As the water starts to turn cold, I'm brought out of my sex daydream to the present. I rush through my shower to finish before the water is ice cold.

I slip on a cute sundress and flip flops, throwing my hair up haphazardly in a bun on top of my head.

I've gotten to the point that I'm actually more comfortable with everyone that will be there than my own family. I'm not so worried about how I dress around them. Funny thing is, until I started my clinicals I would have still worried, now I'm too tired to care.

My parents would prefer that I find some nice, wealthy young man to take care of me for the rest of my life. I refuse to be like my mother, though. I'll never know what my father saw in her, much less saw in her enough to have five kids with her. I guess he saw her as weak, and he likes to dominate his world and everyone in it. My goal is to pretty much avoid him. He's always been a little abusive to all of us, even the boys. A slap here and there, telling us we'd amount to nothing without him.

No one really knows about our life, not even Scarlet. Who would believe it anyway?

That's the reason it's so important that I get through nursing school. I need something to support myself. I need to get out of this house and put distance between us.

I look in the mirror again. *The secret life of rich people, what a fucking joke.*

I throw a swimsuit and a change of clothes in a bag. Then I make my way downstairs to the kitchen to make a cup of coffee.

Great, my mother is in here, another person I try to avoid.

"Annabelle, please tell me you aren't leaving the house dressed like that?"

"Yes, I'm going to a cookout. Most people dress very casual for a cookout."

She looks like she just drank sour grapefruit juice or something. "What people? Hobos and white trash?"

"I'm going to the Abbott's house."

She shakes her head. "Oh, too bad you let Scarlet snatch up Ryder, he'd be a heck of a catch."

"Mom, a year ago you said he was nothing but an embarrassing male whore."

"Well, he's grown up."

"Yes, because of Scarlet. He loves her. Besides, I could never be with Ryder." I laugh.

"You have dark circles under your eyes."

"Yes, it comes with lack of sleep. I worked a twelve hour shift last night." My God, is this coffee ever going to brew?

"Like I've said before, if you'd find a nice young man to take care of you, working wouldn't be something you'd have to worry about."

"Mom, as I've said to you before, I don't want a man to take care of me. That's not the kind of relationship I want. I want to be an equal partner, not a dependent."

"Oh, so you think I'm dependent on your father?"

"Yes. What would you do if you didn't have dad? What kind of job would you do?"

As I'm finally pouring coffee in my cup, she throws her hands up and storms out of the kitchen.

I make my way out to my car and leave for Scarlet's. Ten minutes later, I'm pulling up in front of the house. I hear the noise from out back so I know everyone is already here. I let myself in the front door.

I hear what sounds like weights moving in the den area. I walk through the doors to see Judd on a rowing machine.

I give a small wave. "Hey."

He nods and exhales. "Hey."

"It sounds like everyone is out back. What are you doing in here?"

Wiping his chest with a towel, he looks up. "Just getting a little exercise in before I go out there."

I nod, feeling uncomfortable. "Oh, okay. Well I'll just leave you to it then. I'll go on out back." I point as I'm walking toward the door.

"Hey, Princess?"

I turn around. "Yeah?"

"It's great seeing you."

I give him a half smile. "Yeah, you, too." I say as I walk through the house to go out back.

CHAPTER 3

Damn, seeing my Princess for the first time since coming home makes me a little nervous. I promised that girl I'd come back to her and I almost didn't. She hasn't been over here since I've been home. Then again, I didn't call her or let her visit while I was still at the VA Hospital recovering, either.

I take a quick shower, get dressed, and make my way outside for the cookout. I know my Mom and Nana have been fussing over it for the past few days. Ryder has been great this past week. He's tried to give me my space, but also make sure I'm never alone.

"There he is!" Greer shouts from the other side of the pool.

I throw my hand up to wave and carefully make my way down the back steps. I'm doing pretty well with my walking, the doc cleared me to ditch the crutches. I just tire out pretty quickly. My mom comes up and gives me a kiss on the cheek.

"You okay, honey? Do you need to sit down?"

I shake my head. "No Momma, I'm fine."

I walk over where my Dad and Ryder are standing by the grill. Ryder reaches in the cooler and hands me a beer. I nod, taking it from him. "Thanks, man."

"No problem." He nods his head toward my Princess in a very tiny bikini lounging on a chair next to Nana.

I have to keep my dick under control, this is a family event. No one wants to see the huge ass boner I have for this girl.

I walk over to the chairs and sit down next to Nana. "So, how are two of my favorite ladies doing today?"

Nana laughs. "Well, I'd be doing better if I looked like Annabelle here in a swimsuit and if you'd refill this fruity drink that Ryder fixed for me."

I laugh, taking her glass and motioning to Annabelle. "What about you, Princess?"

She smiles. "I'm good, thanks."

Damn, that smile. I'm tempted to snatch her up and take her inside and fuck the hell out of her. I keep reminding myself everyone is here to see me. This is a family event.

I go over and refill Nana's glass from the pitcher on the table. As I hand it back to her, she laughs. "You're a mighty cute cabana boy, Judd."

"Thanks, Nana, maybe that'll be my new profession. I'll try to go get a job down at the country club."

She laughs. "Nope, can't let those damn jaguars get ahold of you."

Annabelle and I both look at her confused. Scarlet walks over confused, too, but then starts to laugh. "Nana, do you mean cougars?"

"What the hell ever. I don't want them rich ass old house wives making googly eyes at my boy."

That gets a laugh out of everyone.

Greer sits down in the chair beside me. "So, have you thought any about what you wanna do now?"

Ugh, the questions, this is the part I don't like. I know people are just trying to make conversation but I'm just wrapping my head around everything.

"Greer, hush. The boy just got home, give him time to breathe." Nana says over her drink.

I chuckle, thanking God for Nana. She's the one person, besides Ryder, that I trust with my every thought. Well, I feel like Princess knows me too, without me even having to tell her anything. It's like she can read me.

Greer looks at her. "Momma, I'm sorry, I was just trying to talk to the boy."

"Well, mind your own business."

I put my hands up to stop them. "Whoa. It's okay. Greer, I think I'm going to take a few classes in the fall. Not sure of much else yet."

"Well, you are welcome to stay here as long as you want."

"Thanks, Greer. I appreciate it."

A little later, it's just Nana and I left sitting here talking, making general chit chat.

She looks over at me. "So, I've gotten to know little Miss Annabelle and she seems quite nice. She works hard with school and her intern stuff."

"Yeah, she's a sweet girl. I don't know about us, though."

She pats me on the hand. "Just give it time. You don't need to be rushing into anything. When my sweetie came back from Korea, he had some rough times. Grayton was a tough man, but he still had his moments of weakness."

"Thanks, Nana."

"I'm glad that I've gotten to know Annabelle a little bit, she's quite different from her damn momma. Her momma, Kelsie Grace, is one of those little debutantes, never gotten her hands dirty a day in her life."

I have to laugh at Nana, she's always spoke straight from her heart. "Thanks. I don't really know what's going on with us."

"Like I said, you have time."

Ryder steps out the back door. "Hey, you two old ladies quit gossiping about everyone and get your asses in here and eat."

Nana stands up and points her finger. "Who in the hell are you calling old, Ryder Grayton Abbott? I'll take a switch to your ass so fast you won't know what hit ya!"

Ryder quickly moves back inside. She smiles over at me. "Come on, let's go eat."

~*~*~

Walking through the living room later, after I think everyone's left, I head to the den where I've been staying. When I walk through the door, she's sitting on the sofa and staring off into space.

"Hey."

She's a little startled. "Oh, hey. Sorry, I hope you don't mind. I just came in here for a little bit. I'm kinda tired. I worked a long shift last night."

I shake my head. "No. It's no big deal. So you're doing you're rotations now with the nursing stuff?"

"Yeah, last night was rough. I worked twelve hours in the ER. We had a meth head go crazy and try to break into a locked cabinet thinking it had drugs in it, and then a really bad accident came in. It was intense."

"How is everyone at your house dealing with the Princess working?"

"My dad is actually okay with it, I guess. I don't really talk to him about it. He says that he worries about me being out so late, coming in and out of the hospitals. My brothers are like whatever. The only person who takes real issue with it vocally is my mother."

"What's her problem?"

"She thinks I should find some nice young man with a fat bank account and get married. Let him *keep me* and care for me. Well, they all think that, she's just more forth coming."

I laugh. "So basically she wants you to be her?"

"Yes. I told her I'm not interested in being a dependent to someone, I want to be an equal partner. Then she got all pissy and stormed out of the kitchen."

I shake my head. "Well, you know most princesses aren't supposed to work."

"I know, I'm a big failure to my kingdom." She rolls her eyes.

It feels good to laugh with her. "Look, I'm sorry I never asked you to come up to the-."

She stops me. "No, Judd, it's okay. You needed time. Everything was kind of thrust at you all at once." She puts her hand on mine. "It's okay."

"Thanks."

CHAPTER 4

Sitting on the couch just chatting with Judd is great. I feel more relaxed than I have in a long time. It's like he sees right through me, he gets me.

"So at the risk of sounding like every other nosy asshole around the world, have you thought about what you want to do now?"

He laughs. "It does get old with people asking, but I don't mind you asking. I am planning to take some classes, but I really don't know. I didn't think I'd be planning for a new career until I retired, and certainly not at twenty-two years old. Does that make any sense?"

I smile. "Yeah. You've always been very dedicated to your job, now you have to figure out life. It's not fun, trust me."

He brushes his hand down the side of my face. "I'd like to figure a little more out about you."

"Maybe that's possible." Our faces are only inches from each other now.

He grabs the back of my head and kisses me. Our kiss becomes needy and fevered for each other.

It's powerful. Here is a man that for a few days I wasn't sure I'd ever get to see again, much less kiss again. I need him, I want him. Oh God, I want him to touch me! The emotions become too much and I start crying.

He stops and pulls me into his chest. "Princess, what's wrong? Did I hurt you?"

I shake my head and start wiping my face. "No, it's just." I clear my throat. "It's just I was scared I'd never see you again. The day your parents came to tell us, I fell apart. If it hadn't been for Nana I would've really lost my mind."

He smiles a little. "Nana. She's always saving people." He tilts my chin up to his face. "I promised you I'd come back, didn't I?"

I nod. "Yeah, but there was a couple of days that it wasn't looking too promising."

He pulls me back down to his chest and brushes my hair with his hands. "I know, baby. I know. You were one of the things flashing through my mind."

"Judd, we left things so up in the air when you left. I know that we both saw other people-."

He puts his finger to my lips. "Princess. That girl I was seeing over there, she was just someone to fill the void."

"I know. I tried to go out with a couple of guys, I just didn't find them appealing. I had sex with one of them and it was nothing to write about. In fact, I faked it."

He laughs. "Oh, so are you saying that I've spoiled you?"

"Yes. You've ruined it for all other men, I think."

"Well, I'll say I slept with that girl twice, but she's nothing compared to you, and like I said, I was trying to fill a void. The void left by you."

I laugh. "So let me get this straight. You only had sex with her twice and I've only had sex once in the past year almost. We are pathetic."

"No, we just didn't feel like we needed to have sex with other people. We found perfection and nothing compared, so why even try?"

I laugh and look at my watch. "Shit. It's getting late, I should really go."

"Why don't you stay with me?"

"Do you think it's a good idea?" *Please say yes. I want to be wrapped up in your arms all night.*

"Yeah. This is the most relaxed I've felt in months. I like sitting here with you, holding you."

Thank God. "Okay then." He stands up and shuts the doors to the den. Leading me over to the area they've set up for him as a bedroom, he reaches in a drawer and hands me a t-shirt.

He strips down to his boxers and climbs in the small double bed. I put on the t-shirt, leaving only my panties on underneath it. I slide into the bed beside him and our legs automatically intertwine.

My eyes grow very heavy as he strokes my hair and before I know it, I've drifted off to sleep.

~*~*~

I'm startled awake by someone sweating and shaking. I pull away a little from Judd. He's still asleep, and I know from some of my classes that it can be very dangerous to wake soldiers from their nightmares.

Then I hear his soft sobs. I have to do something so I stroke his hair. "Shh Judd, baby, it's me. You're okay. You're at home. Please baby, wake up." I keep stroking and suddenly he jumps up.

I reach over and turn on the bedside lamp. He wipes his face quickly and starts to pace the room.

"Judd."

He won't look at me.

"Judd. Look at me."

He keeps pacing the room.

"Judd!"

Finally, he looks at me. "Judd, it's okay. You were having a bad dream."

His side of the bed is saturated with sweat and his body is coated. He still hasn't said anything.

"Judd, why don't you go shower off and I'll find some clean sheets, okay?"

He nods and walks toward the downstairs bathroom. I walk to the linen closet and find some sheets. I lay him out a clean pair of boxers and I grab a clean shirt for myself. His sweat has part of this shirt soaked.

About thirty minutes later, he returns to the room wrapped in a towel. He looks at me and seems defeated.

"I'm sorry if I scared you, Princess."

"No, it's fine. You didn't scare me." Well, he did a little, but I'm not telling him that.

He sits down on the sofa with his head in his hands. "I thought maybe I was ready to have someone stay with me, but I guess I'm not. Sometimes the dreams wake me up, sometimes they don't."

"Hey, this is okay. You've been through a lot, you're allowed to have some emotions."

"I know, but I thought maybe since everything felt so right with you that I would sleep, but I guess it's not meant to happen."

I sit down by him. "Look, I changed your sheets, go try to rest. I'm gonna go on home."

"No. I don't want you driving this late. Please go sleep in the bed, I'm gonna sit here for a little while and watch TV. I seem to sleep better sometimes while I'm watching it and sitting up."

I nod. I don't want him to worry about anything else, he has enough on his plate. "Okay. Here, I grabbed you a pair of boxers." I hand them to him.

He kisses my forehead. "Thanks, Princess."

CHAPTER 5

I wake up sitting on the couch with some random movie playing on the TV. Glancing over to the bed, I see my princess curled up sleeping. Last night comes back to me. No one has been around me when I had the nightmares. I definitely haven't let anyone take care of me like she did.

I have to go talk to my counselor. I need to see if I'll ever be safe to sleep with someone again or if this is the way it's going to be.

Walking to the kitchen, I fix myself a small drink to calm my nerves.

I'm going to have to tell her I'm not ready for this, and it's going to hurt like hell because I want nothing more than to be with her. I've got to get all of this figured out with myself, though.

I really need to look at getting my own place. Ryder has been great to me, but some of this I have to work out on my own. Movement startles me out of the corner of my eye.

Annabelle walks in the kitchen. "Hey, how are you feeling this morning?"

"Tired. Look, I'm sorry about last night. You know, if I freaked you out."

She shakes her head. "No. It's completely understandable. Have you thought about talking to someone about it?"

"Yes." I bark out.

She jumps noticeably. "I'm sorry. I was just asking."

Shit, I scared her. "Sorry. Yes, I'm talking to a counselor about everything. Look, I really want to explore what this is between us, but I think maybe I need a little more readjustment time."

She rubs her hand on my arm. "Maybe you're right. I just want you to know I'm here for you. I'm gonna go shower real quick and then head home. I've got some studying to do today."

"Okay." I rub my hand through her hair. "Thanks."

She leaves me sitting here in the kitchen with my 7am mixed drink.

~*~*~

I've been living in the apartment in one of the barns for a few weeks now. I feel better about being out here, less dependent. I help Ryder and my dad out around the farm. Ryder wants to pay me but I won't let him because I'm living here for free and he's done so much for me.

I haven't saw much of Annabelle, I guess she stays pretty busy with her nursing stuff. The counselor had me put on some kind of sleep medicine to help with the nightmares but I don't see that it works too well, I still have to take several shots before bed so I don't wake up. I don't really feel like it's doing me any good talking to that guy anyway. Once my mandatory sessions are up in a couple of weeks, I'll probably quit seeing him.

A knock at the door pulls me from my thoughts. Looking through the window, I see it's Ryder. I open the door.

"Hey, man."

He smiles back. "Hey, I was gonna see if you could ride into town with me? I gotta pick up a few things for the farm and Nelson is at a doctor's appointment today."

I look at him strange. "What's dad at a doctor's appointment for?"

He shrugs. "I think it's just a usual physical or something. He didn't say."

I grab my cap. "Yeah, I'll go." I make a note to ask my parents what the doctor's appointment was about.

"So, are you enjoying having your own space out here?"

"Yeah." I say climbing in to the front seat of the work truck. "It's nice. It's not like we ever got in each other's way in the house, but smaller is better for me. " I chuckle. "Plus, I don't run the risk of seeing you and Scarlet having sex God only knows where."

"Hey, that was one time that we got carried away in the kitchen."

I laugh. "Um no, that's the only time that you guys know I saw. I almost walked up on you guys in the pool one night. One night I heard a noise in your dad's study and went to go check it out only to glimpse the two of you playing some fucked up version of CEO and secretary. Then I about walked in the barn mudroom the other day until I heard *Scarlet, you are so fuckin' tight.* Nana's right, you guys are gonna be shooting kids out soon."

He starts laughing. "Dude, I'm so sorry. We are just a very romantic couple. What can I say? I'm in love with her and no, no kids anytime soon."

"Yeah, yeah. I get it. I'm happy for you."

He smiles. "Thanks. You could still come up to the house more often though. Hell, today's the first time I've laid eyes on you in almost a week."

I can't tell him that I like being alone. That I feel more secure this way. "Yeah, I've been catching up on some reading."

I see something lying in the road. "Ryder, slow down!"

He starts slowing down. "What?"

"Go around that!" I point to what looks like a deer maybe.

He looks at me confused. "Okay." He slowly goes around it. "We okay to speed back up now?"

I shake my head. "Yeah. Sorry. It's just sometimes dead animals are used to hide IED's in. I have to remember I'm still getting used to not having to worry about that anymore."

"Hey, it's okay, man. It's gonna take you a little while to get used to everything around here again."

We pretty much ride in silence the rest of the way into town. I feel like my family and friends keep looking at me like any moment I'm going to lose my shit. If I'm honest, there are days that I feel like I will.

CHAPTER 6

This ER rotation gets more insane by the day. Last night we had three car wrecks, one attempted suicide, a couple of heart attacks and two meth addicts tearing the damn place up.

I haven't had much time to do anything other than study and go to work the past couple of weeks. I've texted Judd a couple of times but not much else. I'd love for us to pick up where we left off before he deployed, but I have a feeling that's never going to happen.

I felt so bad for him the morning after his welcome home cookout. He looked so defeated. I know Scarlet said he's moved into the apartment in the barn.

The funny part is, even with all of the problems he has, I still feel safer with him than anyone else in this world.

My mother is constantly bitching about how late I come in from work. My dad has his own snide remarks, but he tries to mask them with sugar coated shit basically.

I'm supposed to go with my family to the cookout at their country club for the fourth of July in a few hours. I really don't want to, I'd rather go to Scarlet's. I'll never hear the end of it, though, if I don't go with them for at least a little while.

"Annabelle, are you almost ready to go?"

I wish my mother would just go away. "I thought we didn't have to be there for like three more hours?"

"Yes, but I've arranged to have tea with the Wilsons in an hour."

"Why do I need to be there for that?"

She opens my door without knocking. "Jesus, Annabelle, you aren't even close to ready. We are having tea with the Wilsons and their son Patrick."

Fuck, I know what this is. I snatch a light blue dress with a bright red belt out of my closet and a pair of bright red heels. "I'm dressing now, mother. Why do I have to have tea with them?"

"Well, it would be nice for you to meet some young men of our, well, our caliber in society."

I look at her like she's lost her mind. "Mother, really, that is complete bullshit."

"Really, Annabelle, do you have to talk like a sailor? He is a nice young man and he's already lined up for a position at his father's firm. He's an active member at the club and your father really likes him. They play golf together quite regularly."

Arguing with her at this point is not going to work. "Whatever, I'll be ready in a few minutes, but I'm driving myself. I'm going to Scarlet's later for their cookout."

She rolls her eyes. "Please make sure you do something with your hair and makeup." She spins around, stomping out of my room.

"Yes, mother." I call out after her.

~*~*~

Sitting across the table from Patrick Wilson, his parents, and my parents is actually quite painful. I think I would rather go for my annual pap smear. He is completely boring and is stuck so far up my father's ass I can't tell where my father ends and Patrick begins. He keeps staring at me. It's fucking creepy, like some sort of perverted stalker.

"So, Annabelle, what do you do?" His father asks.

"I'm in nursing school and I'm doing my clinical rotations right now."

"Well, that is a noble profession, I guess." He comments.

The distain for my *noble profession* drips off of his tongue. I want to slap the shit out of him. "If you'll excuse me, I need to use the ladies' room." I stand, placing my napkin on the table.

Once I'm in the ladies' room, I sit on the small sofa. These people drive me insane, they are so hung up on their money that they can't see anything else. My phone pings, alerting me to a text message.

Judd: R U coming to the farm

2day?
Me: Yes as soon as I can blow off
my parents.
Judd: Good haven't saw u in a while. Oh and Scar said to
bring your ass on.

Me: Tell her to keep her damn hair on. Trust me I'll be
there ASAP. The longer I stay here the more likely I am
to end up with a drinking problem and a prescription
habit. LOL

Judd: Good to know C U Soon.

Me: :)

I need to figure out some way to blow this hot dog stand early. I
don't know how much longer I can sit with the Hob Snob family and mine.

My brothers Gregory, Shane, Victor and Christian are due here
soon and it's only going to get worse. Vic and Chris are okay, they're still
intimidated by my dad, but Greg and Shane are his cronies. They are my
dad's little Dudley Do-Rights. Vic and I are the only ones who branched
out from my father's firm. Vic is in medical school and Chris wanted to go
to med school, but he couldn't bring himself to do it. He did, however, go
to work for a different firm.

Walking back out to my parents' table, I realize that I'm too late,
two of my brothers are already here. Gregory and Shane give me a made
for TV hug as I walk up. I smile. I wish it were Vic and Chris, they at least
have some normal tendencies. We all look like we've been carved out of
cream cheese or something.

Finally, I'm released to mingle around. Thank God, because if I
have to listen to the Wilson's and my family talk anymore about bottom
lines and mergers, I'm going to puke. I see the youngest of my brothers,
Chris, standing by the bar. I walk over to him. "Hey, brother. Didn't see
you come in."

"Are mom and dad really making you sit with Patrick Wilson? You
know he's a prick, right?"

I cringe at the thought of him. I let a big breath out, take the drink
from my brother's hand and start drinking it. "Yeah. He's kinda creepy and
I'm about to go crazy. I'm ready to leave here. Is Vic coming?"

He looks over at me slyly. "He's here somewhere. I think he's
seeing one of the cart girls and they are currently busy." He smiles.

My mouth opens and closes. "So, is he really dating this girl or is
he just getting his rocks off?"

He shrugs as he takes a sip of his new drink. "I think he really likes her. Just, you know how mom and dad are. I don't think he's ready for their scrutiny yet."

"Ah. I see. What about you? Any nice young ladies in your sights? We never get a chance to talk without everyone around."

"Yes. I'm seeing a girl from my office, Angie. I definitely wasn't bringing her here though, but I'm going to see her in a little bit."

"You know dad is still acting like a freaking wounded bird about you deciding to work for someone else?"

"What the fuck does he expect? I'd have to wait behind his two clones, Greg and Shane. Those two would make my life a living hell."

"You should have went to med school like Vic."

"Yeah. You know, I've thought about going back. I have all of my pre-reqs."

"Wow, really? You should do it. I mean, Mr. Wilson would tell you that is 'noble' profession."

He looks at me confused. "What?"

I roll my eyes. "That's what he told me about nursing."

"Did you tell him to go suck a dick?"

I shake my head. "No. But can you see our mother's face if I would have?"

He laughs. "She probably would've choked on the olive in her martini. She's probably on what, number six by now?" He sits his drink down. "Let's get out of here. You want to?"

I put my finger on my chin. "Um, let me think...yes. You text mom some shit to get us out of here. Tell them you need my help, then go grab your girl. Meet me at the Abbott's, Scarlet and Ryder are having a cookout for the fourth."

He grins. "Sounds good. Do we need to grab anything?"

"Just whatever you want to drink."

He nods, heading out the door. I run out to my car, making sure I threw my bag with a change of clothes in the backseat. As I'm about to get in, I feel a hand on my arm.

I spin around to see Patrick Wilson. "You aren't leaving, are you?"

"Um yeah, I'm going to help my brother Chris with something. I may be back in a little bit." A bald-faced lie, but maybe it'll make him go away.

"I was hoping we could go have an unchaperoned drink together."

I try to smile, even though I want to throw up. "Maybe later, after I help Chris."

He touches my arm again. "Really? I think your parent's wanted you to stay."

I pull my arm away. "Well really, I think I'll be going."

About that time, Vic steps up. "Is there a problem here?"

I look up at Vic. "Well, I was just trying to leave. I have to go meet Chris somewhere."

Patrick looks at Vic. "I don't think your parent's wanted her to go."

Vic looks at him and cocks a grin. "Well, it seems to me she's a grown woman. I'd suggest you let her go, Chris will be expecting her."

Patrick nods and walks away.

Vic looks at me. "Where are you really going?"

"To Scarlet's for a cookout. Grab your mystery girl and come on over."

He chuckles. "Chris told you."

"Yeah. He's gone to go get his girl now. They're going to meet me at Scarlet's."

"Well, Kari doesn't get off until six. Think it'll be okay if we come after that?"

"Yeah, that'll be fine. It's only a couple of more hours." I jump in my car, wave to my brother, and head off to Scarlet's.

CHAPTER 7

I really wish Ryder hadn't invited all of these people. I know he always does a big party for the fourth, but I'd just like something a little lower key.

I'm ready for my Princess to get here, that way maybe we could escape for a little while.

"Hey, buddy." A guy I knew growing up named Josh says. He's already well into a case of beer.

"Hey, man. How's it going?" I shake his hand.

"Good, man. Welcome home."

"Thanks."

Princess walks up to me and smiles. I look down at her. She's gorgeous wearing a dress with a pair of awesome fuck me red heels. "Hey, I was wondering when you were going to get here, beautiful."

"I got here as quick as I could."

"Josh, this is my friend Annabelle. Annabelle, this is Josh, he grew up just down the road."

Princess smiles. "Hey."

"Damn Judd, you got you one of those high class girls."

I try to ignore him and so does Princess. Then he looks at me. "So, how many of those rag head mother fuckers did you get to kill while you were over yonder?"

Before I can say a word, Princess slaps the shit out of him across the face.

He looks at her. "What the fuck, bitch?"

Everyone at the party starts looking, and Ryder and Scarlet make their way over to us.

Ryder looks around. "What's going on?"

Princess looks up at Ryder. "Well, this boy needs to learn some manners." She looks at Josh. "That was rude, you son of a bitch."

After all of the story gets hashed out, Ryder asks Josh's brother to take him home.

Princess smiles at me. "Hey, let's go take a walk. You can show me what you did to the apartment."

"Yeah. I need a break from the crowd."

As we walk across the yard, she asks. "So, do people ask you stupid shit like that often?"

I shrug. "Yeah, unfortunately. I mean, people act like it's really something I should be bragging about or something. I don't get it. It's not something I wanted to do, it was something I had to do."

She shrugs. "Yeah. Sorry if I stepped on your toes back there."

"No. You were awesome. A cute little spit fire. I'm afraid if I would've hit him, I wouldn't have stopped."

She smiles. "The way I'm feeling today, I'm not sure I would've stopped you."

"So how did things go at the Country Club?"

"Well, besides my parents trying to set up with a creepy perv? Not bad, a couple of my brothers are coming in a bit with their girlfriends. They aren't like my oldest two brothers, Chris and Vic are pretty cool. Greg and Shane are dickheads."

"Wow, tell me how you really feel about your family."

"Ha. Then I might scare you off."

I think about the mouth full she just said. "Wait a minute, your parent's were trying to set you up with a creepy perv?"

She laughs. "Well, I don't know if they know that about him. Chris says that Patrick is a prick. Anyway, the guy gave me the creeps. I think he's more in love with my dad or my dad's money."

We make it to the door of my apartment. I open the door and she walks in. "So, here is my home sweet home."

She sits down on the small futon in the corner. "Nice. Sometimes I'd love to live in a little place like this. At least then I'd know it was mine. My parents have this way of still trying to run my life since I still live with them."

I smile at her. "Well, you are welcome to crash here anytime." I say before thinking about my nightmares. Shit.

She gives me a sly smile. "So, how are things going? You know, with the dreams and stuff."

I nod. "Better. They have me on some medicine to help me sleep. That coupled with some shots of Jack help."

"You know you shouldn't be mixing the two, right?"

"Yeah. I know."

We sit there quietly for a few minutes when she starts laughing.

I look at her. "What are you laughing about?"

"Us. We are so nervous around each other." She stands up and walks over to me, then straddles my lap. "You know, once upon a time we knew each other quite well."

"Hmm. Yes we did."

She starts kissing my neck. "Well we should get to know each other again."

I stand up, grabbing her under the ass as she wraps her legs around my waist. I tilt my head down, taking her nipple in my mouth with her teeth, through her dress.

I walk over to the bed and lay her down, then pull my shirt over my head. She goes to take off her shoes and I shake my head. "No, you leave those on." I reach up under her dress, pulling her panties off.

She sits up and unbuttons my shorts. Then she starts pushing them and my underwear down. "My my, some things don't change."

I reach over and grab a condom out of my nightstand. She takes it from me as I feel her warm, wet mouth on my cock. After sucking and humming on my dick, she leans back, smiling as she rolls the condom on. I lean over and start kissing her neck. I snatch down the top of her dress, revealing her great breasts.

"Fuck. I've missed you, Princess."

I crawl over her on the bed. She smiles up at me through hooded eyes. "Well, let me welcome you home, soldier."

I thrust into her. "Fuck, baby. I wondered if I'd ever get to do this again."

"Oh fuck, Judd."

I start moving faster. "Baby, I'm embarrassed to say this probably isn't going to last long. It's been awhile."

She's panting and moaning. "It's okay, it has been for me- ah, too." Her eyes widen. "Oh shit, Judd, harder!"

I start pounding into her warm center faster and harder. I feel her start to tighten around my cock as she starts to scream. I thrust into her hard and find my release. "Oh shit, baby. You feel like home."

She wraps her arms around me. "Oh handsome, you, too."

CHAPTER 8

I didn't realize Judd and I had dozed off until I heard my phone chirping. Fumbling around, I finally find it on the futon.

Scarlet: Hey your brothers are here. Where are you?

Me: Fuck I'll be there in a minute. Stall for me.

Scarlet: LOL don't guess I should ask where Judd is then huh?

Me: Shut it.

He slaps me on the ass as I'm bent over digging around looking for my panties. "Hey, where you goin'?"

"My brothers are here. I gotta get out there."

He jumps up from the bed. "Shit." He starts snatching his clothes back on.

I look in the mirror, trying to tame my *just fucked* hair, then straighten my dress and put my heels back on.

Finally feeling put together enough to go back out, we both laugh and he looks at me. "Hope your brothers don't want to kick my ass."

I laugh. "I doubt it. Vic was banging his girlfriend, the cart girl, before I left the club."

"Come, let's go, you little harlot."

We walk out to the party. My brothers are standing there talking to Ryder and Scarlet. "Hey, guys."

"Hey, Prissy Pants. Where have you been?" Vic asks.

"I don't know. Where were you right before we left the club?"

He laughs and puts a hand up in defense. "Annabelle, this is Kari, Kari this is my little sister, Prissy Pants."

I pop him on the arm. "Hey Kari, nice to meet you."

Chris steps forward. "Guys, this is Angie."

We all wave and greet her. I smile looking at Judd. "Vic, Chris, this is Judd. Judd, these two jackasses are my brothers."

About that time, Gable and Ivie come in. I've missed them. There are times when I'm closer to Gable than my own brothers, even though he's Scarlet's brother.

Ryder laughs and throws his hands up to his mouth like a teenage girl screaming for Elvis back in the day. "Oh shit, the stars just got here."

Angie and Kari gawk momentarily at Gable and Ivie.

Ivie hugs me. "Hey girl, long time no see."

I laugh. "Shit, I've been crazy busy at the hospital and with classes."

I turn to Angie and Kari. "Ladies, this is Gable Johnson and Ivie Butonelli." Not letting on that Ivie is actually Gable's wife. "Gable, Ivie, these are Vic and Chris's girlfriends, Kari and Angie." I say as I point out everyone.

Gable hugs me. "Hey ya, sexy. You look good."

I laugh. "Well you look like shit. Is Ivie not taking care of you?" I pat his arm, like I'm fawning over him.

He laughs. "Oh, she knows how to take care of me alright."

Ivie's mouth drops open and Scarlet looks like she may get sick. "You guys, we have guests."

Ryder pulls all the guys to go grab drinks for everyone. I try to spend some time getting to know the girls my brothers are dating.

Angie is very smart, probably too smart for my family. Kari is a sweet country girl who is very intimidated by my parents. Hell, I can't say as I blame her.

~*~*~

After a few hours, it's gotten dark and we are enjoying the pool and drinks are flowing.

Judd and I are taking a walk when suddenly the fireworks start.

I'm thrown to the ground with Judd on top of me.

"Shit, Judd. What the hell?"

He rolls off of me. "Fuck, I'm sorry, Princess."

More fireworks start going off and Judd grabs me and just holds me tight.

He's shaking. "Judd, let me go tell Ryder to stop them."

"No. It's okay."

"NO, it's not."

I try to get up and he grabs me. "Stop. Don't go. I don't want to look like the freak."

I put my hand on his face. "Baby, you're not a freak. Don't you ever say that about yourself."

"What do you call it then? Hell, I'm scared to sleep in the same bed with you because I might hurt you. I can't hear some simple fireworks go off without damn near crying."

"Baby, you have been through more than most any of us could imagine. Give yourself some credit."

He nods. "Sorry if I scared you."

"Hey, it's okay. Did Ryder tell you that he was going to do fireworks?"

He shakes his head. "No."

I sit up. "I'm gonna kick his ass."

"No. Don't say anything, okay? Please. I just want to get past it."

I nod as we both stand up. "What do you want to do?"

"Can you walk me back to my apartment?"

"Yeah, I'll even stay the night. Well, if you want me to."

He holds my hand tight. "I want you to, but I'm scared."

I put my arms around him. "Don't be scared, you have me. I promise."

"You're wonderful, Princess."

I smile, taking his hand as we walk back to his apartment. I have a feeling he's going to need me tonight.

CHAPTER 9

Looking out the windows of the Humvee, I'm a little excited and nervous. This is my first time out as team leader/truck commander. I just got my promotion to Sergeant and I've never been so pumped. I'm actually kind of young to have gotten promoted so soon, but it's all part of my plan to go Special Forces. I can't tell my guys, only my commander and first sergeant know I've already been doing a little work with them. I've picked up on the local language really well and they needed my help.

I hear the radio with our lieutenant talking. "Johnson, turn that down. It's distracting. Smith, keep looking at that ridge over there. Russell, you okay back there? Is Mack's truck still okay behind us?"

I hear Russell's deep voice. "Roger, Sarge. They're good."

Russell doesn't ever say much but he's going to be a good soldier. The squawking of the radio is still driving me crazy. This fucking butter bar lieutenant is going to drive me insane.

Johnson laughs. "Sounds like the LT is giving out his fucking grocery list on there. I'm waiting for him to ask us to pick him up some ice cream, Midol and tampons."

I chuckle. "You know, those college boys are book smart but they lack a lot of common sense."

I still hear the rambling of the radio from the lieutenant. "Shit! I'm going to talk to First Sergeant when we get back. He's gotta talk to the Commander, that fucking LT needs to learn how to talk on the radio and how to shut the hell up. This is fucked up. We couldn't get through if we really needed to."

Smith laughs. "Thank God. I swear, I don't understand a fucking thing he's saying, so it's not like it's doing us any good. He sounds like Charlie Brown's fucking teacher."

Looking ahead, I see some garbage on the side of the road. I motion to the pile for Johnson to see and avoid. He does a good job of steering around it without slowing down. You never know if it's just a trash pile or an IED. Dead animals and trash are normally the places they hide them.

"Good job, Johnson. So, I hear you are getting out after this tour. We hate to lose you, man." In our unit we try to do a lot of retention. It's always good to keep a team that has trained together, together.

He shrugs slightly. "Yeah, my wife is tired of living alone. She wants to have kids. She sees how crazy some of the moms are on post when they're left for a year to raise a kid by themselves. She told me she's not doing it. I have an uncle that runs a security firm in L.A. for some big name clients and he wants me to come work for him. It'll be some great money."

"Hey man, I understand. Family is the most important thing."

Smith leans up. "So what about you, brand new Sergeant? What are your plans after this tour?"

I shake my head. "I plan to retire with the military. That's always been my plan. I'm looking into going SF after this though." Even though I know I already am, probably before the end of this tour.

Smith barks. "Come on, Sarge, we know you gotta have a girl. We saw you talking smack to that singer chick from the USO group."

I laugh, thinking about Ivie. "She's just a friend of the family."

Smith damn near gets in the front seat with us. "Damn, if she's just a family friend, I want to meet her. I thought she was your girl, Sarge, so I was staying away. Shit, I'd have tried to hit that."

I put my hand up. "No way, man. That big ass guitar player is her guy. I know you could probably kick his ass, but you'd know he'd been there, trust me. He loves her enough to kill for her."

Johnson laughs at Smith. "So no girl for you, huh?"

I laugh. "You two are as nosy as Nana Pearl. There is kind of a girl, but we are friends right now. That's all I'm saying."

Smith stops laughing. "Wait, are you calling us old? Like an old lady old? That's fucked up, Sarge."

"Trust me, Nana may be old, but she'd still kick your ass, take your money at poker, out smoke you and drink you under the table. She's a badass old lady."

I sit up in a jolt and look at Annabelle curled on her side. It was a good memory, not my normal nightmare, but I still have to wipe sweat from my forehead. She rouses a little. "Hey, you okay?"

I sit there for a minute. "Yeah, I think so. I just had a dream about my first mission as a team leader."

She sits up. "Was it bad?"

I pull her to my side and breathe a sigh of relief. "No, it wasn't. That day was a good day."

She smiles. "Well I'm glad you have some good memories, too."

"Oh, I have a lot of good memories. When you are in the military you are truly a band of brothers. As bad as some of the memories are, trust me, there are so many more good ones."

We lie back on the bed and she rubs my chest. "Tell me a good story. A funny story."

I chuckle. "Okay, let me think." I think for a minute. "Okay, we had this guy in our unit from Texas. He was a big son of a bitch. Most new guys that came to the unit were a little intimidated by him. I had known him since basic training, we'd bonded when we were assigned as battle buddies. His last name was McAllister but we called him Mack, like a Mack Truck. Anyway, one night I came in to our tent with some of the younger guys. Mack had gotten into some of the wine that Nana sent me and there he was, dancing around in nothing but a towel that was a little too small for him to some damn *Katy Perry* song. The guys and I gave him shit about that for weeks."

She laughs against my chest. "Well yes, I imagine that was a sight to see."

"So tell me something funny that happened here while I was gone."

She puts her finger to her chin like she's thinking. "Okay, let's see. Oh, okay. This happened to me so you can't laugh too hard." I nod and she continues. "So I had to do a rotation at one of the bigger hospitals for school first. I was so nervous and well, really scared. Anyway, I'm bustling through all of the rooms doing what I'm supposed to be doing. The nurse in charge of us at this hospital was a real bitch, so when she came to get me to help her with a patient, I was terrified." She stops. "Is this boring you? I take a few minutes to tell a story."

I laugh. "No, keep going."

She nods. "Okay. Well anyway, we had this guy from the psych ward in. He thought he was a fire truck, he was running around the room with no clothes on, roaring like a siren. Anyway, we are trying to get him to calm down to keep him from hurting himself. Well, we have to try to wrap him up so the doctor can sedate him. When the nurse and I try to wrap him up, I get shoved into the corner of one of the cabinets. It catches the thin material of my scrubs and tears the seat of them, but I'm too busy wrangling this patient to worry. After we finally get him settled down, the nurse looks at me and says, *"Annabelle, honey, if you're done showing your ass for the night, I've got some extra scrubs you can borrow."* I was so embarrassed. When my scrubs ripped, they ripped right across my ass cheek and since I was wearing a thong, my whole ass was practically showing."

I'm laughing so hard by the time she finishes because I can just picture her cute little ass jiggling while she wrestles with a crazy guy.

She pops me on the arm. "Stop laughing at me, asshole."

"I'm laughing with you, really." I try to calm my laughter. "Okay, so did you get into trouble with the nurse lady?"

She smiles. "No, actually she's become a really great mentor, even with me moving to a different hospital. I still call her. She said she liked the fact that I was too busy trying to do my job to worry about my own embarrassment."

I chuckle. "Or BareAssment."

She shoves me. "Stop it, you jerk. Here I was trying to make a good impression and I literally made an ass out myself."

"Hey, I'm rather fond of your ass." I pull her to me, looking over at the clock and seeing it's a little after three. "Let's go back to sleep for a bit. Okay?"

She nods. "Sounds good." She mumbles into my chest.

I stroke her back up and down until I feel my eyes getting heavy again and doze off.

CHAPTER 10

Waking up curled into Judd's chest reminds me of the weekend we met. Before life had to go and complicate things.

It was nice sharing funny stories with him in the wee hours of the morning. It makes me wonder if this is the kind of thing couples do.

I stroke his chest, playing with the dog tags he still wears. I get a little startled when I see the sheet lift up below his waist.

His chuckle echoes through his chest. "What? You can't expect him not to respond when the most beautiful girl in the world is touching me."

I let out a small giggle. "Oh, really?"

He rolls me on to my back. "Yes, and he also thinks you should be punished for giggling. It's not good for his self-esteem."

"He's a person now?"

He grabs a condom from the nightstand. "He's always been a person. You trying to say you don't like him? Well, he and I both know that's a lie. Hell, the people at that Days Inn in Richmond Hill know that's a lie."

I act like I'm blowing him off. "Whatever, you were just trying to distract me so that your friend could seduce my friend."

He rolls the condom on and thrusts into me. "Oh yeah, well I was very willing to take one for the team that night. I'm so fucking glad I did."

I look at him through hooded eyes. "Oh, so you were taking one for the team, huh?"

He starts picking up pace and I start clawing at his back. "Oh yeah, I'd say I went above and beyond that night."

All I can do is nod and let out a moan. "Judd."

"Fuck, Princess. I've missed your sweet pussy so much, it's like my own personal glove."

"Oh shit, oh shit." That's all I can manage to say until he starts pounding harder. "OH FUCK! I'M COMING!" He slams into me twice more before blowing his load in the condom.

He collapses on me, still inside of me. "Shit, Princess. I need to start working out in the morning like that more often."

I laugh. "Um, I can't breathe, you're squishing me."

He rolls off of me, pulling the condom off and throwing it in the trash can by the bed. "Sorry, Princess. I really could wake up with you like this every morning, you know?"

I curl back into his side. "You seemed to sleep okay last night."

He nods and strokes my back. "Yeah. I have to say, though, I was really scared about you staying here."

"Hey, it all turned out okay."

"Yeah, but I'd hate myself if I accidentally hurt you or something during one of my dreams."

I grab his chin, turning him to face me. "Hey, what happens in your dreams?" I shake my head. "Not your fault. Besides, last night you had a good dream. So your memories aren't going to always be bad ones."

He nods. "I guess you're right."

I wink. "I'm always right."

He smacks me on the ass. "Sassy in the morning. You hungry?"

As if on cue, my stomach growls. "Yeah, I guess so."

He jumps up from the bed. "How about I cook something? Then we can laze around until you have to go home and get ready for your shift."

I look up at the naked, fine male specimen in front of me. "Only if you cook naked and I get to watch."

He leans down to kiss me. "That can be arranged, but what if grease pops me and I get burned?"

I flop back on the bed as if I'm exhausted. "Well, I guess you have a point. You may wear boxer shorts, but no shirt. I like looking at your chest."

"I'm not just a piece of meat, you know. I have feelings, too."

I laugh. "You're right, you feel pretty good to me most of the time."

He spins around, jumping on top of me in the bed. "I feel violated and used."

I reach and grab his ass with both hands. "Oh you know you like it." I wink and smack his ass.

~*~*~

Unfortunately, I have to break from my holiday bliss of lying in bed with Judd and go home.

I start working third shift tonight. I have to be at work at ten, so I'm going home to wash my scrubs, study and catch a nap before work.

I dread going home because I know I'm going to catch hell for leaving the club early.

Hopefully I can just sneak in the house without having to see them. They'll be in for the night by the time I leave for the hospital.

That hope is crushed when I pull my Camaro into the garage. My father is getting into his Audi to leave for work. *Great!*

"Annabelle."

"Dad."

"Well, your little scene at the club didn't go unnoticed yesterday."

"I suppose not. I left with my brothers."

"Yes. I know this. Your assignment was to stay and have dinner with Patrick."

I scoff. "My assignment. I thought it was a date that was set up unwillingly for me."

"Look, young lady. I know you, Vic and Chris have this rose colored view of the world. You think hopes and dreams make things happen for you, but they don't. Money makes things happen for you. You children have never had to worry about that since I've made sure you've had everything you've ever wanted. Your older brothers realize this, you and the younger two boys are ungrateful little shits sometimes."

My blood is about to boil over. He's right, we haven't had to struggle, but I would have traded everything to be treated like a human being rather than a possession.

"I have to get ready for work."

"Yes, because after the way you treated Patrick yesterday, I doubt he'll have anything else to do with you. Hopefully you can find some schmuck doctor to fall for you." He sits in his car and slams the door.

I make my way into the house preparing to do battle with my mother now.

I don't even make it through the kitchen before a wine glass is being hurled at my head. "Annabelle, you are such an ungrateful little bitch!"

Luckily, I duck in time and it shatters on the wall. If this were the first time this had happened I might be upset, but I'm used to it. Hell, the fact that it's ten in the morning and my mom seems already half lit doesn't even faze me. I try to ignore her. I know this means she's paying me back for how pissed my father was about yesterday.

"Are you just going to ignore me?"

I get to the bottom of the stairs. "I was really hoping to." I make my way up the stairs as she breaks shit and cusses me from downstairs.

After I reach my room, I look around. This is my life. I really need to get my own place. How though? I don't have any money of my own and I'll be damned if I'll ever use the trust account they have set up for me.

My school is paid for through scholarships that I earned. That's really the only thing though, my car and lifestyle belong to them. It's the only thing I've ever known.

I need a job that pays money, but with my hours for clinicals, it's hard. I just don't know if I can live here for another year.

Ugh! Fuck My Life!

CHAPTER 11

My phone pings letting me know I have a text.

Princess: Wish I was back in our bubble already.

**Me: Well come back when you feel
like it.**
**Princess: I wish it were that easy. Thanks for a great
night. Gotta get some rest for my shift.**

Me: Sweet dreams Princess.

I make my way down to the main house to see if Ryder is going to need my help today with anything. Walking in through the kitchen, I see a blonde lady sitting at the breakfast bar.

She smiles. "You must be Judd. I'm Sarah."

I'm confused. "Um. Hey."

About that time, Ryder walks in. "Hey, man. You meet Sarah?"

I nod. "Yeah." With a *What the Fuck?* Look on my face.

Ryder laughs. "Shit, I forgot you dipped out early last night. She's dad's girlfriend."

I chuckle, finally getting it. "Oh, okay. I was lost for a minute. Sorry, Sarah, I didn't mean to act strange. I'm just not used to walking in here and finding new people sitting at the breakfast bar."

She laughs. "It's okay. I'm sure it was a little bit of a shock to you to find some weird woman you weren't expecting. I've heard wonderful things about you."

I nod. "Thanks. It's nice to meet you." I turn to Ryder. "I came to see what we had planned for today." I see Sarah slip out of the kitchen.

"I need to run into town and grab some feed and shots for the Waycross farm for tomorrow. Can you go check the back forty? I noticed the fence over there the other day had a couple of broken boards. Can you take care of that?"

"Sure, I'll get right on it."

"No rush. I just don't know if I'll have time today and Nelson has a doctor's appointment."

"Again?" I look at Ryder. "What in the hell is going on? I've never known that man to have this many doctors' appointments."

Ryder rolls his shoulders. "I don't know. I'm getting curious myself. He said it's just some normal checkup stuff."

"Well I'm going to get to the bottom of this shit. I don't like being kept in the dark by my own damn dad."

"I hear you, man."

I motion to his dad's study. "So what do you think of Sarah?"

"She seems nice. Dad's happy, that's what really matters."

I nod. "Okay. What did Nana say?"

He shrugs. "Nana seems to like her. Will she ever love her as much as she loved my mom? No, probably not, but Nana practically raised my mom, so it's just different. I think she's glad to see my dad happy again."

"Hell, I'm happy about that, too. Greer deserves to be happy. Hell, he deserves a commendation medal for putting up with your ass for all those years and surviving."

He punches me in the shoulder. "Asshole. I'm pretty sure for most of that I wasn't alone."

I laugh. "Yeah, I guess not."

"Oh and family dinner tonight at six, per Nana Pearl."

"Okay. What's going on?"

He shrugs. "Don't know. I'm sure it has something to do with my dad and Sarah. She asked if Annabelle could come, too."

"Annabelle has to work tonight, she goes in at ten. I'll text her, she may be sleeping."

He nods. "Okay, well just let her know."

We head out the back door. Ryder looks over at me. "Speaking of Miss Annabelle, where did you and she disappear off to last night?"

I shake my head. "I swear, you gossip as bad as Nana."

He laughs. "Yeah, I figured. Her brothers were looking for her, you know?"

"Great. Well, if you must know, I made a little bit of an ass out of myself."

"How did you do that?"

I sigh. "The crowd made me a little nervous so we decided to take a walk. Then when the fireworks started...well, they caught me off guard and I threw her down to the ground. I freaked out a little bit, started shaking."

Ryder's eyes are huge. "Oh shit, man. I'm so sorry, I didn't even think to warn you about the fireworks. I just, shit man, I'm so sorry."

I put my hand on his shoulder. "Hey, man. It's okay. You can't help that normal everyday shit has the capability of sending me on the short train to crazy town."

"Yeah, but common sense should have told me better." He looks defeated and sad.

I shake my head and punch him in the arm. "Hey, no one ever accused you of having a lot of common sense."

He shoves me. "Thanks, asshole, I really feel bad. I wanted you to enjoy last night."

I laugh, trying to lighten his mood. "Hey, trust me, I did. I enjoyed this morning, too."

"So she stayed the night? How did that go?" Ryder is the only person, aside from my counselor and Annabelle, who knows about the dreams.

I nod. "It was okay. I had a dream, but it was actually a good one. She wanted to stay with me because of the fireworks. Just in case I had a bad dream." I shake my head. "Why would she want to put herself in that situation? I don't know, but I wanted her to stay so bad because I'm selfish like that."

"She stayed because she cares about you. Just like the rest of us. Plus, trust me, she must be hanging out for something she likes." He motions to my crotch.

"Oh, so it's not my personality she's after?"

"Yeah, damn sure not your personality. It's that monster in your pants. Snuffleupagus."

"Yeah, well at least I can go through the airport without my junk getting groped by an over friendly TSA agent because my dick can't go through the metal detector."

"Hey, Scarlet gives no complaints, asshole. And for the record, when I go to the airport I put a plastic ring in so I don't give the old ladies working too much of a thrill."

"Trust me, I lived in the house with you for a bit. I know Scarlet gives you no complaints. I know more than I want to know."

He shoves me. "I'm going to get that feed, you go fix the damn fence." He calls back over his shoulder. "Don't forget to call Annabelle about supper."

"Yeah, yeah, asshole."

I grab my phone while walking out to the barn.

Me: Nana Pearl has called a family dinner at 6. She said you'd better be here.

Princess: Okay well I'd better go ahead and take my nap.

Me: Bring your stuff for work so you don't have to leave early.

Princess: Sure thing. What do you think is going on?

Me: IDK I met Greer's lady friend this morning. That may be what it's about.

Princess: Holy Shit! Okay I'll see you a little before 6 going to lay down now.

Me: Sweet Dreams. I'm going to fix a fence.

Princess: XOXO

CHAPTER 12

It's weird that I feel so much more comfortable about going to a family dinner at the Abbott's than I do at my own home.

I think it's because they just accept me for me. Nana once told me that class isn't about money or where you stand in the community, it's about the person. She's right, my parents have no class. They are a couple of self-righteous assholes.

I quietly try to make my way out of the house and avoid my parents. They'll wonder why I'm leaving so early and why I have my bag.

As I get to the bottom of the stairs, I hear my father's voice raised.

"Christopher, I'm not putting up with this bullshit! Are you, your sister and Victor trying to kill me? Trying to go into bullshit careers. I'm not paying for you to go to med school."

"Dad, you didn't pay for me to go to school in the first damn place! Grandpa's money paid and scholarships. Plus, I'm a big boy, I can afford to put myself through school now. Those two dipshits, Shane and Greg, are the ones you had to pay for schooling. Fuck, I bet you still pay their bills."

I hear glass breaking against the wall and my mom scream. I run in the den. "What's going on?"

My father glares at me. "None of your fucking business! Where are you going, young lady?"

I square my shoulders. "I'm going to Scarlet's for dinner and then to work." I step over to Chris.

My father throws his hands up. "You two are some of the biggest disappointments in my life, along with Vic."

Chris tenses up. "Hey, don't talk to her that way."

He grabs Chris by the collar. "I'll talk to my daughter any damn way I please."

I try to get him to let go. "Dad, stop. Calm down."

I taste the blood on my tongue from the slap before I even realize it happened. Chris in turn shoves dad over the back of the couch.

My mom screams. "Get the hell out of here! Both of you!"

Chris looks at me. "Prissy, go grab some more stuff. You are not coming back here for a few days. We are going to figure something out, you can't live in this shit anymore."

Chris and I run up to my room, grabbing my school stuff, my scrubs, some other essential clothes and my box of mementos, and run down to my car. I stop at the door and realize this is their car. I look over at Chris. "Can you give me a ride to Scarlet's?"

He nods. "Yeah, jump in." Once we are seated in the car he looks over at me. "I just came to tell him that I planned to go back to school and he went ape shit."

"I know, I heard most of it before I ran in. Sorry. He and I had it out in the garage when I got home this morning about me leaving the club yesterday. Then I went inside and had words with Mom, so I probably primed the pump for your argument."

"Hey, it's not your fault. If they were fucking normal people we wouldn't have to worry about it."

I shake my head. "Tell me about it."

"So, how are you going to get to work in a little bit? You need me to come pick you up or something?"

"No, I'll get Scarlet to take me or let me borrow her car or something. I'm going to ask her if I can crash in her spare room for a few days, until I figure some shit out. You are right, the stress from them is killing me."

He nods. "Yeah, I understand. Look, I know my apartment isn't big, but if you want to crash with me you are more than welcome, little sis."

"I know, thanks. Scarlet has a lot of room though, and you need your space with Angie."

"So what's up with you and that guy Judd?"

"He's a friend of Ryder's. He and I met last year before his last deployment. He got injured a few months ago, we're friends."

He laughs. "Friends, huh?"

"Okay, a little more than friends, but we are taking it slow. He needs to because he's still having some adjustment issues. He's is a great guy, though. He's just been through so much."

"Is he going back or can he?"

I shake my head. "No, he was medically discharged. It was a pretty bad injury."

He nods as we pull down the gravel drive to the Abbott House. "Okay, well call me if you need anything."

"I will. Thanks, Chris."

Grabbing my bags, I make my way in the house. Scarlet gives me a funny look as I enter and she makes her way to me. "Hey, what's going on?"

"Just a little argument at the house. Can I crash here for a few days?"

"Yeah, use the room upstairs that you normally stay in."

She grabs one of my bags and follows me up the stairs. After we get in the room, I turn to her. "Thanks. Dad is kinda pissed with me and Chris right now. Chris dropped me off here."

"Is that why your lip is split?"

"Yeah. I tried to stop him and Chris from fighting. Oh, I left my car there, can I use yours to go to work tonight?"

She nods. "Sure, but you probably need to clean your lip up before supper or Judd will go beat the shit out of your dad." She turns to walk out. "And I wouldn't stop him. We will talk about all of this more tomorrow."

I go in the bathroom and clean up my face. I'm sick and tired of this shit and it's time for a change.

I make my way back down to the dining room, taking the seat in between Judd and Scarlet. Judd eyes me suspiciously. "Hey, are you okay?"

I nod. "I'm good, I'm happy to see you."

He smiles. "I'm happy to see you, too."

We settle in to start supper. I'm introduced to Sarah and she seems very nice. She works in an accounting firm in Atlanta. Her husband died ten years ago and she has two children that are in college.

Ryder looks up to Nana. "So what is this meeting about, Nana?"

She looks at him. "Ryder, we are eating first and then we'll talk."

He nods. "Yes, ma'am."

I have to say I'm kind of curious myself. I love Nana, but I don't know why she wants me here.

I've really bonded with her over the past year. She knows how I feel about Judd, my family, everything really. She hates my mother, I know that. She's the only person besides Scar that knows how my family can really be.

I love Nana, she's the coolest old lady I know.

CHAPTER 13

After we finish the banana pudding my momma made for dessert, we go in the den and sit down. I'm really worried. Nana never calls meetings like this that often. I also noticed my dad didn't eat much tonight.

Nana draws our attention. "Alright y'all, sit down. You look like I'm gonna shoot ya or something."

Ryder glares at Nana. "Well, Nana, you kinda have us all worried."

"Good, you know I mean business."

We all sit down. She takes out a cigarette and lights it. "Alright boys, some things are going to change around here. I'm still the major shareholder in this farm and I've decided to make some changes."

We all look at Nana confused. Greer looks at her. "Momma, what are you talking about? Also, what did I tell you about smoking in the house?"

She stabs her cigarette out in the ashtray. "Fine, Debbie downer. First off, Greer, I know you want to move to Atlanta, why don't you let Ryder take over things here full time? He's doing a good job as it is and I don't like having you running up and down the road so much. It would give you and Sarah more time to spend together."

"Momma, how did you know that I wanted to move?"

She brushes him off. "I'm your momma, I know everything. Plus, you cramp my style with all of your rules."

She looks over toward Ryder and me. "Now Ryder, you are going to need some more help around here and I'm going to say you need to hire Judd to be your right hand. You need someone you can trust like your daddy has trusted Nelson all these years."

"Why can't I just keep Nelson? Not that I don't want Judd, but he may not want to be my right hand. We can't just assume that he wants to do this."

Nana glares at Nelson. "Well Nelson, do you want to talk about why Judd needs to take over or do I need to try and share that, too?"

My dad looks at me and Ryder. "My doctor says I'm diabetic and I've got some blood pressure issues. I need to start taking it a little slower. I was going to talk to all of you soon enough about me retiring. How did you know, Nana?"

"I didn't know exactly what was going on. Naomi has been worried, I can tell. Plus, these two boys aren't dumb. You've been to the doctor more in the past couple of months than in your whole life."

My dad shakes his head. "I should've known better than to try and keep secrets. I just wanted to find out what I was dealing with myself first."

She turns to look at me. "So Judd, how would you feel about working on the farm with Ryder? He'd make sure you could still go to school, if you want to."

I shrug. "I think I'd like working here. It's all I've ever known except the military. I do want to do my classes, but I know I'll need a job."

Nana huffs. "Now that I have all of you boys using your words and communicating, maybe people will start working around here again."

As she starts to walk out of the room, she looks back. "Scarlet and Annabelle, come help me with something, please."

The both jump up and follow her out. Ryder, Greer and Sarah go to his dad's study and close the door.

I look over at my mom and dad. "So when were you guys planning to tell me? Nana is right, I was getting suspicious. I'm kinda pissed. My imagination was running wild, you know."

My momma pats my leg. "Sorry, honey. We just thought that you had enough on your plate right now. We didn't want you to worry. I guess it worked in reverse, though. I'm sorry, we really didn't want you to worry."

My dad looks at me. "I have a lot of changes coming my way, like the banana pudding I couldn't have tonight. I don't want you to feel like you have to work on this farm like I have. I know it's no dream job."

I put my hands up to stop him. "Dad, I love the idea of working here. Ryder and I have always done things together. Going in the military is the only thing we didn't do that way. But my plan was always to come home, it was just earlier than I'd thought about."

He nods. "Okay, as long as you're sure."

"Hey, we've always had a nice life with you working for this company. How many other employers would have thrown you two on a plane to Germany so you could get to me as soon as possible? Not many, I can tell you that."

My dad nods his head. "It's good that you see those things, son, and can appreciate them."

I see tears in my mom's eyes. I look at both of them. "When you see the places and things I've seen, you learn to appreciate everything."

I stand up, walking into the kitchen to find Nana, Scarlet and Princess in a heated discussion. I can see Princess has been crying.

"Hey ladies, what's going on?"

Nana glares at me. "Well, I may need bail money. I'm going over to Annabelle's house to kick her daddy's worthless ass."

I put my hands on Annabelle's shoulders. "Whoa, what's going on? Wait, what happened to your lip?"

Annabelle shakes her head. "A little heated discussion before I left home. I'm staying here for a little while."

Nana is still raising hell with Scarlet on the other side of the kitchen. "Winston Garrett isn't above the law, I don't care if he thinks he is or not!"

I look at them. "Nana, calm down, please. Scar, why don't you take Nana on home?"

Scarlet nods and Nana looks at me. "Judd Hughes, you make sure this doesn't happen to her again. I'm a good mind to take a bull whip over there and whip his ass with it." She turns around to look at Annabelle. "Sweetie, you think about what I said. If you want it, the job is yours."

With that said, Scarlet walks Nana out to the ranger to take her home.

"Princess, what in the hell is going on? Why did I just notice your lip?"

"Please just calm down. I hope Nana's calmed down. I don't need her going over to my parents' house."

I chuckle. "Well you are safe from Nana right now. She's not allowed to drive after dark. Now, let's go to my place and you can catch me up to speed."

I lead her out the back door to walk over to my apartment.

CHAPTER 14

Once we get to Judd's apartment, he turns to me. "So, now I want to know about the lip."

I sit on the futon. "My dad and Chris were arguing and I got in between them. This isn't really anything new. I'm taking steps to change my life right now." He sits down beside me.

He nods, trying to stay calm even though I can see a storm behind his eyes. "What are you doing to change things?"

"Well, I brought some things and I'm staying with Scarlet for a little bit. I have money, I could go get my own place right now, but it's really their money. I don't want it. I even left my car there. I need to start making my own way in life."

"Sounds like a good plan. What did you mean by this isn't anything new?"

I shrug. "We may have money, but that doesn't mean that our house didn't look like some of the episodes on cops when I was growing up. We just lived in a two story colonial in a gated community versus a trashed apartment complex with a shitty security gate. It was all kept hush hush and we never went to the hospital to get checked out. If anything ever got out of control, my dad had a friend that was a doctor that came to check on us."

He shakes his head and looks off somewhere else. "How bad did it get, Annabelle?"

I shrug. "The boys took the most of it. Greg and Shane pretty much always did what Dad said so they avoided most conflict and kinda became his thugs. Vic, Chris and I all wanted something different in life, so we were kind of targets. Vic and Chris were bigger targets because they didn't want to follow in my father's footsteps. I could sort of hide the fact that I didn't want to follow in my mother's. Don't get me wrong, I'm still a huge disappointment to them."

"Is that what your text this morning was about?"

"Yeah, as soon as I got home, I was in an argument with my parents about leaving the club. So by the time Chris got there tonight to tell he planned on going back to med-school, they were ready to pounce."

"So let me get this straight. Your brother is a disappointment for wanting to be a doctor?"

I chuckle at how ridiculous it sounds. "Yeah. In my parent's world, it's money or nothing. Doctors are considered blue collar to them. Like the Abbott's would just be simple farmers to them, except Greer has money invested in other places so that makes them "worthy". Seriously, they are horrible people."

"So I'm guessing your nursing isn't something they appreciate."

I bark out a laugh. "As creepy Patrick's dad said, it's a 'noble profession'. I might as well have said I was shoveling shit out here in the barns for Ryder."

He looks up at me with an eerie calmness in his eyes. "A nurse is who saved my life. Your father is a piece of shit. I'm almost on board with driving Nana over there."

"Look, I've dealt with it most of my life. Thank God I met Scarlet or I might be like one of them. I just want to find a new path and Nana has given me some options to do that."

He relaxes a little. "I heard Nana saying something about a job."

I nod. "She wants me to come help her with her memoirs. She started them years ago, she just needs to organize them. She wants to add the last few years, but other than that, she's pretty much done the work and it's something I can do in my spare time around school and clinicals. That way I can make some money and I can stay with Scarlet and Ryder as long as I want to."

He laughs. "You might want to be careful around there at night. They are somewhat exhibitionists about sex. That's one of the reasons I moved out here."

I laugh. "Oh, so what do you suggest then?"

He runs his hand down my shoulder. "Well, you could stay with me some." He looks panicked for a minute. "Not like move in. I know we aren't there yet and hell, I'm not even sure I'm safe to sleep in the same bed with. I'd like to experiment some with you, though. If you want to."

I nod as I lean up to nibble his neck. "I like experimentation." I straddle his lap. "I'm always up for it."

He dips his head down to my neck. "Sounds like a plan." He starts kissing my neck. I tug his shirt off over his head, running my hands down his chest muscles. He has some scars on his chest from his wounds and the US Army insignia over his heart.

He kisses down my collar bone as he tugs my tank top down under my bra, running his tongue along the swell of my breasts.

Suddenly, there is a beating at the door startling us both. He jumps up and I fall to the ground. I can't help but start laughing, tugging my tank back up. I lean back, holding my ass.

He grabs the door, swinging it open. "Fuck, Ryder, what do you want? You scared the shit out of us."

Ryder laughs, motioning to the obviously uncomfortable state Judd's crotch is in. "Oh okay, so Annabelle is here. We were just wondering. Scarlet was worried when she got back from Nana's."

I stand up and walk over to the door. "Hey, we were just talking for a few minutes before I take a nap. Tell her I said to stop being a mother hen."

He nods. "Okay, well, Scar was worried. I'll let her know. You gonna take your nap here or are you coming back to the house to get ready? I know that'll be her next question."

"I'm gonna come back there to take a nap." I look over at Judd. "I doubt I'd get a nap here. Plus, I need to get her car."

Ryder laughs and turns around. "Okay, I'll see you in a few."

We shut the door to Judd's apartment and start laughing. "I'm not sure if Ryder was asking me about coming to the house because he was curious or if he wanted to know so they could have crazy sex or something. Thanks for putting those thoughts in my head, asshat."

He flops back on the futon. "Hey, I was just warning you. I wish someone had warned me."

I lean over and kiss him. "I'm gonna go take that nap. I'll see you tomorrow?"

He nods. "Yep. Why don't you come here and sleep in the morning when you get off? I'll be out all day so it'll be quiet."

I nod. "I just might take you up on that."

I walk back over to the door and blow him a kiss before I leave.

CHAPTER 15

"Hey Hughes, you see that?"

"Where?"

"Over a just a bit."

"The kid. He can't be more than thirteen."

"Yeah. Doesn't he seem a little strange?"

I shake my head. "Yeah. Fuck." I grab my radio. "Walton, there is a kid at the door of the market."

"Roger."

"Check him out. It's a little sketchy, looks a little nervous..."

"Roger."

Watching him make his way to the kid up the side street, everything happens in slow motion. The kid opens his vest. "ALLAH!!"

I fumble with the radio. "Pull back! Get the fuck back!"

The explosion, the screams, the smell.

I sit up in the bed with a jolt, sweating and panting. The smell, it's in my nose. I can't get rid of it.

Running to the bathroom, I empty the contents of my stomach in the toilet. I try to rinse my nose out with salt water to get the smell out but it's still there.

I rip open the shower curtain and step in. Turning the water on scalding hot and scrubbing my body with soap, I try to wash the inside of my nose so I can't smell it anymore. Burning hair and flesh, I can't forget it.

I heave again in the shower. Finally, I sit down, shaking, and cry. I let the scalding water run over me, hoping it washes away my sins.

That kid was fourteen, he was a suicide bomber. Walton was a twenty-two year old soldier from Ohio, with a wife and a six month old baby. There were countless people in that market. What was it all for?

Finally, after the water runs cold, I get out of the shower and wrap myself in a towel. Walking over to my kitchen, I grab my bottle of Jack and sit on the futon.

Taking the cap off, I turn up the bottle.

~*~*~

"What the fuck?"

"Shut up, Ryder, my head is killing me damn it."

"Judd, get up. You are naked in a pile of puke in the god damn barn."

I slowly sit up and look around. "I don't remember coming out here."

He helps me up off the ground. "What do you remember?"

I shake my head slightly. "I don't know."

Ryder shakes his head. "Fuck. Go over to the mudroom and get a shower. I'm sure there is something in there of mine you can put on."

I try to walk, but it's hard for me to stand. Ryder takes my hand and walks me over to the mudroom that's in the barn. He sits me down in a chair and turns on the water. He pulls me up and takes me to the shower.

"Man, try to sober up a little. You smell like a damn distillery. If Nana or your momma see you, we are in deep shit."

"Fuck, man. I think I had a bad dream, but I'm not sure."

I see him through the clear shower curtain grabbing some stuff out of the cabinet. "Here's some shit to put on. I'll wait for you outside."

I shake my head while I'm washing up. I really fucked up this time. Shit, Princess is going to come to my apartment this morning. I have no clue what kind of shape I left it in. Damn it.

I jump out of the shower, throwing on some clothes and running out the door.

"Fuck, Ryder, I need to get back to the apartment. Annabelle is supposed to be coming there this morning, she can't see it like that."

He hangs his head a little. "Too late. It's almost ten. She came in saw the place ransacked, then she ran up to the main house to get me. She didn't say anything to anyone else. We both figured it was something like this. I didn't exactly expect to find you butt ass naked in my barn, but drunk, yes."

I punch the barn door. "Fuck!"

"Sorry, man. She's up there cleaning right now."

I run to my apartment and once I'm inside, I see exactly how bad it got last night.

My lamp is shattered, my furniture is turned over and upside down, and I see broken liquor bottles on the floor. Sadly, I don't know how much of that I actually drank and how much I busted. Considering I don't remember shit, I'm guessing I drank a good bit.

I'm startled when Princess comes out of the bathroom from cleaning. She runs to me and hugs me. "You scared me. I thought something happened to you."

I stroke her hair. "It's okay, Princess. Go on up to the main house and sleep. You don't need to clean this up. I'll get it."

She looks up at me and I can tell she's dead on her feet. "Why don't you come lay down with me and we'll tackle this after we get up?"

I shake my head. "No, you go get some rest. I can't sleep, and you just got off. I'll be here when you get up. I promise."

She nods. "Okay."

She slips out the door, making her way over to the main house.

I probably just all kinds of fucked that up.

Ryder knocks on the door as he comes in. "Man, you fucked this place up. Let me help you clean it up."

"No! Just go, I can handle it."

"Man, I'm just trying to help."

"I didn't need help tearing the shit up, I don't need help cleaning it up."

"Hey, are you still talking to that counselor guy?"

"What the fuck about 'I don't need your help' didn't you understand, Ryder? I can handle this."

"Look man, I'm just trying to say I care. Pull your head out of your ass."

"Fuck you, Ryder. You don't get it and I hope to God you never have to." I say as I shove him out my door and slam it shut.

"FUCK!"

CHAPTER 16

I toss and turn in the bed at Scarlet's.

After a night of meth heads and gunshot wounds, I thought I'd be able to relax when I got home. All I could think about was snuggling in Judd's sheets, smelling him as I went to sleep.

I came home to find his apartment door standing wide open and everything trashed, and it scared me. Then when I couldn't find him, I started calling his name. I ran out in the yard and over to the main house. I saw Ryder in the kitchen and ran in panting. I didn't realize I was crying until he grabbed me.

"Annabelle. What's wrong?"

I shake. "I can't find him. His apartment is busted up and he's gone."

Ryder took off out the back door and I went to clean up his apartment.

Then he was so off and short when he came back.

I was worried his dreams weren't under control. God, I hope he didn't drink all of that whiskey that was busted on the floor.

I wonder what set him off and I hope he's still seeing his counselor.

Can I bring that up to him? Will it hurt him, insult him?

Finally, all of my thoughts wear me down and I feel my eyes getting too heavy to hold open.

~*~*~

I wake up seeing it's three in the afternoon. I get dressed in some lounge clothes and make my way over to Judd's apartment.

I knock on the door and he doesn't answer. I walk over to the barn and find Ryder.

"Hey, Ryder."

"Hey, Annabelle. He went to town for a little bit."

I kick a little dirt on the ground. "Was he okay?"

He shrugs. "I don't know. A little embarrassed, I think, more than anything. He didn't want you to know that happened. The fact that you're the one who found the apartment that way upset him."

"Do you think that he'll ever be able to get through this? Ever be able to get a decent night's sleep?"

He shakes his head. "I don't know. He doesn't talk about much. He doesn't want to talk about what the counselor says."

"What can I do? I feel so helpless."

He sits down on a bucket. "I know. I do, too. You know, Judd has always been there for me."

"I know, he always tried to keep you from getting locked up." I laugh.

He shakes his head. "I'm going to tell you something I haven't ever really talked about."

I nod. "Okay."

"You and I grew up together in school, but Judd was my best friend. He's a couple of years older than me, but he's been my best friend since diapers. Not many people I went to school with knew about my life. I didn't trust many people." He looks away and then back to me. "When my mom passed away, I quit talking. Judd spoke for me. A little while later, my dad started dating a woman. I wanted my dad to be happy because he'd been so sad. She had a thing for young boys like me. Judd kept wondering what was wrong with me. Finally, I broke down and told him. I really didn't understand what was going on, but I knew it was wrong. Once I talked to Judd, he told Nelson. My point is, Judd and I have trusted each other our entire lives. I know the helpless feelings, though, because I feel like I'm letting him down. He's never failed me, but I feel like I'm failing him."

I wipe a tear from my face. "I'm sorry. I know this is rough for everyone. How much do his parents know?"

"He doesn't want them to know. I think his dad suspects but they won't talk about it. My biggest concern is the pills he takes to sleep mixed with the alcohol."

"Does Nana know?"

He shakes his head. "Not from me. I'm sure she does, though. Nana knows everything."

I laugh. "Okay, well I need to go over and work with her for a while. Let him know I'm okay and I want to see him."

He nods. "Okay."

I take one of the Rangers over to Nana's. As I pull up, she's sitting on her porch smoking.

"Nana, those things are gonna kill ya."

"Yeah. These, moonshine, wild sex and any food I eat. I figure I might as well go out with a bang."

I shake my head. "Nana, you have such a way of putting things."

"So what's wrong with you? You look like someone just kicked your puppy."

I sit down and shake my head. "Nothing, just tired form work."

"Child, don't lie to me. I don't tolerate lyin', I'll take you over my knee."

"When Mr. Abbott came home from war, did he have some hard times?"

She rocks back and forth a little faster. "Yes, sweetie. They all do."

"Can I help him?" I ask as my voice quivers.

She shakes her head. "Every man is different. They are still fighting a battle in their head. Sometimes it's guilt, sometimes it's fear. They have so much more information on it now than they did back with my Grayton. Just be there for him, that's the biggest thing you can do for him. Let him talk when he wants to talk and don't push him when he doesn't want to."

I nod. "I'm trying."

She pats my hand. "I know, baby. I know. It's not going to be easy. I'm guessing he hasn't talked about any of this with his momma and daddy?"

I shake my head. "No, ma'am, I think just me and Ryder."

She shakes her head. "Of course Ryder knows. Those two have a bond like brothers. It's the reason I knew they'd need each other when Nelson retired and Greer moved."

I nod. "I think you're right. I just hope I'm enough for him. I think I'm falling in love with him."

She shakes her head. "Baby, you think, therefore you are. Trust me, you're enough or I wouldn't have you here." She stands up to go inside. "Come on. I'll fix us some sweet tea and we'll get to work."

I nod. "Okay and Nana, Thanks."

"No problem, baby. In any matter, he's in love with you, too, he just hasn't realized it yet with all that other mess clouding his brain."

That stuns me a little as I make my way to Nana's computer and sit down.

He loves me. Wow. I love him. Wow.

Shit, this is hard.

CHAPTER 17

Sitting in my counselor, Luca's office isn't the way I wanted to spend the morning.

"So, what brings you in today, Judd?"

"I had another nightmare. I thought I was over this. I had a good dream about my friends the other night after the fireworks. I figured I'd have a bad night because I had some reactions to the fireworks, but I didn't."

Luca sits forward a little bit. "Judd, you are never going to be 'over this' as you say, but you can learn to deal with it. So, tell me about the last nightmare."

"I remember bits and pieces, but that's not what concerns me as much as what happened."

"Okay, start at the beginning of what you remember and walk back if you have to."

I tell him about this morning's events and what I remember about the dream.

He nods. "So, it was about Kabul this time?"

I nod. "Yeah. I should've noticed that kid sooner. I let Walton down, I let those people in that market down. I do know when I woke up I could still smell it. It made me sick."

"Now, you've mentioned Ryder and Annabelle quite a bit in the last few sessions. I know you and Ryder go back to childhood. What is Annabelle to you?"

I look up from the floor I was staring at. "Everything. I think."

"Judd, our time is almost up, but I want to bring up a couple of things. Please, once again I'm going to ask that you don't drink and take your meds. If you want to have a couple of drinks early in the evening, fine. Just not at night with the meds. You could have put yourself in a coma or choked on your own vomit. If Annabelle really means this much to you then you need to get yourself figured out. Quit shouldering so much blame on yourself. There were things that you had no control over. Also, have you thought about getting a pet?"

"Luca, I live on a farm. We have a ton of animals."

"No, a pet, like a dog or a cat."

I shake my head. "No, I really haven't."

"They have done a lot of research with dogs especially and PTSD. They can be supportive and comforting. Soldiers find it nice that they don't feel like they have to talk to them, but yet they can."

I stand up. "I'll think about it." I sigh. "Like a puppy or something?"

He shrugs. "Actually, some have said they like the idea of a puppy, where some like to adopt older dogs. Everyone is different."

I nod. "Okay. I will think about it, I promise."

"And Judd, don't be scared to make her your everything, but try to get yourself squared away a little first."

I nod. "Yes, sir."

"Look, you are going to have unprovoked dreams, it'll happen. It's how you deal with them that matters."

I shake his hand and schedule my next appointment.

On the way home, I see the sign out for animal adoptions today. Thinking about what Luca said, I pull into the shelter.

Walking in the doors, I hear dogs barking and growling. A young guy walks out. "Hey, what can I help you with?"

"Well, I'm just looking around. I think I might want to adopt a dog."

He nods and takes me down the aisle telling me about the dogs. He stops and turns around. "How long have you been home?" I nod. He looks prior service to me and we always seem to recognize each other.

"Well, back in the states almost six months, back home not very long. I was at one of the VA hospitals for a little while."

He nods. "I think I know what you're looking for, let me introduce you to Beau." I follow him and stop in front of a kennel with an older hound. He opens the gate so I can pet him. "Beau's owner had to move into a retirement facility. His kids felt it was unfair for them to take the dog into the city. A dog like him needs room to run or just be lazy in the sunshine. Beau is three years old. He's a full blooded blood hound. He's house broken and very gentle."

I smile and nod. "I think he'll do great. I live on a huge farm and even though I'd like for him to be inside with me some, I want him to like the outside."

He smiles and nods. We walk back to the office and I fill out the paperwork.

Beau wags his tail when we open back up the kennel for me to take him. As soon as we get in the truck, he flops his big head on the console for me to rub it.

"Beau, I hope you like your new home. I know you need a new friend and I could use one, too."

When I pull up to the farm, Ryder is walking out of the barn. He meets me when I park my truck. "Hey, how was your appointment?"

I shrug. "Fine. He suggested I get a pet. I told him we had a farm full of animals, but he suggested a dog. He said they've done a lot of research with dogs and people with PTSD." I open the passenger door. "So this is Beau. His owner had to be put in a retirement facility and he needs a new home." It hits me that I never talked to Ryder about bringing an animal here. "I hope it's okay. I should've asked you, but when I saw his face, I just knew."

Ryder shakes his head and smiles. He pulls me in and hugs me, slapping my back. "Man, it's fine. Whatever you need so that I don't find you like I did this morning is okay. This will always be your home, too."

"Thanks, man. I'm sorry for being such an asshole."

"Hey, you are dealing with shit none of us understand. Don't put yourself down. Annabelle understands, too."

"I'm scared I'm going to hurt her. She's been through enough hurt in her life, she doesn't need my shit, too."

"Hey, you let her decide that. Annabelle is a big girl."

"Luca told me I should probably work on myself for a little while."

He nods. "She'll understand. I promise."

I slap his shoulder. "Thanks, man." I tug Beau's leash to follow me to my apartment.

CHAPTER 18

I've been at Nana's for the past four hours working. Her stories crack me up. I'm typing as she's telling and I have to get her stop every now and then when I'm laughing.

She starts up again. *"Let's see, it was a couple of years ago. It was May of 2011. Yes, 2011. Anyhow, Merle Parker, Glenda Jones, Phanie Syfrett and myself went to Biloxi gambling for the weekend. We were gonna ride those little scooters from casino to casino. Now, Merle doesn't get out much. We decided to go through one of those drive-thru eatin' places on the way there. So we are sitting at the window waitin' for our food when I hear Merle catch her breath. She says 'Well I never, they should be ashamed of themselves! Drive on, Pearl, we'll eat somewhere else, not where they hand them things out at the window. That's disgusting.' So, of course, we're trying to figure out what she's talking about. I ask her. 'Merle, what in the land of Dixie are you babbling about, you old bat?' She scoffs. 'I'm not a crazy bat, I don't want to eat at a place that has a sign in the window that says 'Condiments upon request.' What kinda joint is this?' I can't control my laughter. I look at her and say, 'Merle, they are saying if you want ketchup, let them know. Not damn rubbers, you old bat.'"* Nana sits back in her chair laughing.

At this point, I'm laughing so hard I can barely type. "That's hysterical that she thought they were talking about condoms."

Nana shakes her head. "No, what's hysterical is she acts like them things are so nasty. Lord only knows how many times she'd have been knocked up in high school if it wasn't for them."

I put my hand over my mouth. "Nana Pearl."

"What, honey? We had sex before marriage back in the day and we even had condoms. We were just way more secretive about it. It wasn't as accepted." She throws her hands up. "Shoot, once me and Grayton were parking-.."

I stop her right there. "Whoa! Nana, what did I tell you about those parts? Write them down and I'll type them, but please don't tell me."

She laughs. "Hey, I read them Grey books with my quilting girls. We're waiting for the movie. We're gonna go watch it."

I laugh hysterically. "Oh. My. God. Nana, I'm so going with y'all."

She laughs. "Shoot, we'll load up Scarlet, too. Heck, if Ivie's in town, we'll grab her. We'll make it a girl's night on the town. Maybe go to a strip club or a drag show afterwards."

I laugh. "Nana, you guys might be a little too hard core for us."

She pats my leg. "You'll learn, don't worry."

I sit back and laugh. "Thanks, Nana, you definitely took a lot off my mind today."

She shakes her head. "Hey, baby, I know it's hard. He may need some time. He's gonna be more upset that you saw how out of control he could get than anything else. I know you wanna be there for him but don't worry, Ryder will keep an eye out."

"I know, it's just I don't want him to think I've given up."

She looks at me hard. "He'll know you haven't."

I smile and stand. "Thanks, Nana. I better go get ready for my shift."

She stands up. "Alright. You make sure you eat good before you go in tonight. We don't need you gettin' sick."

I nod. "Yes, ma'am."

I make my way out to the Ranger and drive back up to the main house. When I pull under the shelter, a big blood hound runs up and jumps on me.

I laugh. "Well, hey there. Who are you?"

Judd steps into the light. "His name is Beau. He must like you."

I rub Beau's head. "Well the feeling is mutual, Beau."

Judd smiles. "Beau, come here." Beau makes his way over to Judd and rubs his head on Judd's leg.

Judd looks at me. "He's part of my new therapy."

I nod and smile. "I've read about that."

He nods. "Listen, Princess. I'm really sorry about what you found this morning. I'm sorry I didn't come up to the house like I said I would, but I'm having some issues."

I nod. "It's okay, I know you probably need some time. We kinda jumped into this."

He shrugs. "Luca, my therapist, thinks I need to spend some more time on myself before I really get involved with someone else. I mean he didn't say it was a bad idea, just that I had some work to do on myself first."

I look at him. "I understand, Judd, and it's okay. I'm here. I'm not going anywhere." I walk over to him and touch his arm. "If Beau can help you, then it's great. He seems like he'll be a great friend. I really need to be working on getting loose from my parents completely and focusing on school."

He kisses my forehead. "Sounds like we both have some things to accomplish."

I look up at his eyes and smile. "Yes, but when we're done, let's go right back where we left off."

He pulls me to his chest. "Most definitely. I don't mean we have to avoid each other or anything. Just, I guess no sleep overs or heavy make out sessions for a little while."

"Yeah, I want you to take care of yourself."

He kisses the top of my head and speaks into my hair. "You got it."

I pull back. "I better get inside and get ready for work."

He smiles. "Yeah, go save some lives."

I shake my head. "Oh yeah, that's me."

He and Beau walk off and I make my way into the house. Ryder and Scarlet are at the bar eating pizza. Scarlet looks up. "Hey, how was your time with Nana?"

I chuckle. "Enlightening."

Ryder smiles and looks up with food in his mouth. "Did she talk about how cute I was as a baby? How smart I was?"

I grab a bite of the pizza. "No, but she did tell me a funny story about one of her friends getting confused about condoms and condiments. Then she told me about reading the Grey books." Ryder chokes. "She also invited me, Scarlet and Ivie to go watch the movie with her and the quilting group. Oh, and they may want to check out a strip club or drag show on the way home from it."

I continue chewing my piece of pizza. Ryder is coughing and Scarlet is laughing. She pulls her hand from covering her laugh. "Did you tell her we're on?"

I start walking out of the kitchen as I'm finishing off my slice. "I told her I didn't know if we could keep up with them." I shake my head. "Grandmas and BDSM, I don't know if we can handle it."

I make my way to the stairs and I hear Ryder freaking out about his grandma reading BDSM books. Scarlet is laughing so hard I'm sure she's trying to breathe. I'd love to stay and laugh but I have to get ready for work.

CHAPTER 19

Beau has been with me for about a week now. It took us a couple of days to get used to each other, but he's been great. He sleeps by my bed at night. I've had a couple of bad dreams, but when I woke up from them sweating and gasping for air, he jumped up on the bed and put his head in my lap. Petting him seemed to calm me down.

I've been doing some of the mental exercises that Luca had been telling me about. They seem to be helping also, and I'm glad. I don't like feeling like some sort of sideshow freak who can't be in control of his own emotions.

I'm working in the barn when Ryder walks in. "Hey, man, so we have set a date for the wedding."

I chuckle. "Really? So you helped set the date. It sounds more like Scarlet, Princess and Nana set a date." No one even asks who I'm talking about anymore when I say Princess, they all know that's my name for Annabelle.

He kicks some hay. "Well, yeah, they did. But I agreed to it."

I laugh. "So what are you in for?"

"Well, since we have to take into account that Scar or me neither one have large families, and also that Ivie and Gable need security, we are having it here on the farm. Just something small. I came to ask you if you'd stand up with me?"

I smile. "Man, you don't even have to ask. You have been a thorn in my side my entire life. I'd love to give you to someone else."

He laughs. "Thanks, asshat, but you're not giving me away."

"Nah, man, really. I'd be honored."

He nods. "Okay, well it's just going to be you and Annabelle. Cade is going walk her down the aisle. Gable and Ivie are going to sing."

"Sounds good. So when is this wonderful event taking place?"

He sighs. "Weekend after next."

"What? Why so quick? Did you get her pregnant?"

He chuckles. "There you go sounding like Nana again. *No, Nana Pearl,* I didn't get her pregnant. Even though if I did, I'd be happy. There is just no point in waiting any longer, plus Ivie and Gable have a lot coming up. This will make it easier on them, too."

I slap his back. "So what are we doing for the bachelor party?"

He shakes his head. "Nothing big. Dad got us tickets to a Braves' game."

"Who all is going? Where are we sitting?"

"Well, you, me, Nelson and my dad. Cade is gonna meet us there. Gable won't be in yet."

I motion my hand for him to keep going. "Seats?" He's holding out on me for a reason.

He grins. "We're in the Hank Aaron section."

"HOLY SHIT!" I fist pump. Actually fist pump into the air.

"Yeah, tell me about it. If I could've kissed dad through the phone when he told me, I would have."

I shake my head. We've been to games before. Growing up in Georgia, that's something you do, but sitting behind home plate is going to be awesome. "Well, damn. Tell Greer if I need to help with anything, let me know." I laugh a little. "Oh. What day this week? I need to talk to my boss about getting time off."

He laughs. "I'm sure your time off can be arranged. We're going to stay with dad Thursday night since his place is not too far from the stadium. The game is on Friday, come back on Saturday."

"Sounds like a plan to me." I start laughing. "What are the girls doing?"

He shakes his head. "I have no clue and I'm not sure I want to. Nana has taken over the party plans. There could be strippers or God only knows what else. Hell, she's already invited the girls to go watch that damn Grey sex movie with her and her quilting group when it comes out."

I burst out laughing. "You mean *Fifty Shades of Grey,* dude. Did Nana read those books? You know there's like BDSM in there and stuff."

He looks up at the ceiling. "Shit, I guess so, she told Annabelle she did. The quilting group read them together." He throws his hands up and then stops. "Wait. How do you know the name of those books and what's in them?"

"I was bored during one of my tours. Plus, the first rule in battle is always know your enemy. Thanks to those books, Christian Grey is now every man's enemy. Well, that and you can get some tips from those damn things." I point to him. "Remember that commercial they used to do on Saturday mornings, *The More You Know*? Just saying."

He shakes his head looking at the ground. "Holy shit. Damn." He turns to walk out of the barn and stops without looking back. "Do you still have those books?"

I chuckle. "Yep. I'll get them to you later."

He nods and goes out the door. "Thanks."

I have to sit on one of the buckets and laugh. Nana Pearl is always full of surprises. I need to talk to Annabelle and see if she can watch Beau while I'm gone. He seemed to like her and I don't want him to feel abandoned with me being gone two days.

Me: Hey I guess the bachelor party is a Braves game. Can you stay at my apartment with Beau some while I'm gone? Just look out for him so he doesn't feel alone.

Princess: Sure! We are supposed to hit up some bars with Nana, but I should be home at night. It worked out that I'm off the next two weekends.

Me: Great. Thank you so much. I just figure he'll be more comfortable in my apartment, since he's still learning it. He can go out during the day though.

Princess: Okay. I'll get up with you before you leave.

Me: Thanks again.

Looking at my watch, I see it's time for my appointment with Luca. I make my way out of the barn, catching a glimpse of Princess and Scarlet out at the pool.

Just seeing her makes me smile.

CHAPTER 20

Nana looks over at me while we're sitting at her dining room table sorting through her old journals.

"So, you called all those places I asked you to, right?"

"Yes, ma'am. This Friday night we have a table at Club One for Lady Chablis' early show. Then we come back here and everything for the Grey themed party should be set up in the living room. We have a couple of nice looking guys to be our wait staff. X-rated pastries will be served, along with drinks. A lady named Wendy from Pleasure Palace is coming to do a show and tell with *toys*. I can't believe we've pulled all of this off. I was even more surprised we got the table at Club One and that they would do an early show."

She pats my leg. "Well, when your family goes back in this town as far as ours does, and has as much money invested in this town as ours does, it opens doors. The Abbotts are what you call *old money*. This family goes back in Savannah's history as far as people standing on the walk ways yelling *high cotton*. Grayton was always proud of this family's roots in this town." I see the soft smile curve her lips thinking about Grayton. He's still and will always be the greatest love in her life.

Getting back on track. "Is Whisper coming in for the festivities?"

"No, she couldn't get away two weekends in a row. However, she sent me money for Scarlet to spend on gifts from the Pleasure Palace."

I smile and laugh. "I'm still surprised you wanted Wendy to come show sex toys and lingerie."

She waves her hand. "Ah, we'll have fun."

I laugh. "Well what about Ms. Parker? She might get offended."

"If anybody is too uptight to enjoy the fun then they can take their ass home." She scoffs.

I can't help but laugh at her. I hope one day I'm like her. I can just tell the world to kiss my ass. My phone pings telling me I have a message.

Dad: We would like for you to join us and your brothers for lunch at the house this Saturday.

Nana looks at me. "What's wrong?"

"It's dad, he wants me to join them for lunch at their house with my brothers this Saturday."

She sighs. "If your brothers are going to be there then you should go. I don't like that man and I damn sure don't like your mother, but keeping in touch with your brothers is important."

I nod. "Well, hopefully I'll be too hung-over to care what they have to say."

She barks out a laugh. "Now that's one way of thinking."

I grab my phone so I can respond.

Me: Okay. What time?

Dad: Noon. I'll have a car pick you up at 11:30.

Me: No, I can drive myself.

Dad: We'd like for you to take your car to drive at the end of lunch.

Me: Okay. Don't send a driver. I'll have Chris or Vic pick me up.

Dad: Fine. See you Saturday.

Nana looks at me. "So what did the old Scrooge have to say?"

"Not much." I sigh and tell Nana about our conversation.

"You know that car may come with some strings attached to it." She says, lighting up a Pall Mall.

I rest my head in my hands. "Yes. That is the reason I said no to the driver. If I tell of my brothers I'm ready to go, then they'll take me."

She puts her hands on the table. "Okay, good. Now, where were we? Oh yes, here. I found a couple more journals last night. Here you go, sweetie."

"Did you always keep a journal, Nana?"

She nods. "Yes. You have to remember that back then your closest neighbor may live a few miles away, and phones weren't in everyone's house. So besides school, you didn't see much of your friends. I kept journals to feel like I was talking to someone, I was an only child so I got kinda lonesome. I didn't have a sister to share all my thoughts with, but I had my notebook."

I smile. "Nana, you're awesome."

She laughs. "Well you're pretty awesome, too, baby."

"Okay, so give me a story to type in for today and then I'm gonna call one of my brothers about Saturday."

She nods. "Ah, here's a good one. So my daddy made some of the best moonshine this county had ever seen. One afternoon, he and my crazy Uncle Jesup had been fishing. They'd drank probably a quart jar full together. Well, they got into an argument over something dumb, I'm sure. Uncle Jesup decided he was gonna leave my daddy at the fishing hole. He threw his boat in the back of the truck and hauled buggy. Well, Daddy jumped in his truck chasing him."

She shakes her head, snickering. "What sense it makes for two grown drunk men to chase each other, I don't have the slightest, but they did. Well, when they got to the old courthouse square, Uncle Jesup slung that truck around the corner and his boat flew out of the back. It took out the hot dog cart and damn near got the owner, Mr. Smith. Jesup's drunk ass hadn't tied the boat in, and the Sheriff got called. I thought my momma and my Aunt Kitty were gonna skin them two men alive."

"Sounds like you grew up with some real characters, Nana."

She stands up walking over to the sink. "I did, honey. They were some rounders', that for sure."

I stand up. "Well, I'm gonna go call Chris about Saturday."

She nods. "See you tomorrow."

On my way out to the Ranger, I call Chris.

"Hey, Prissy Pants."

"Will you ever get tired of calling me Prissy Pants?"

"Nope. You'll always be Prissy."

I laugh. "Fine. Just not in public."

"Deal, I guess. So. What's up?"

"Did dad get up with you about Saturday?"

"Yeah, he did. I'm going I guess."

"Can you swing by and pick me up? They want me to take my car."

I can hear him exhale. "Yeah. Are you sure about the car, though?"

"Well, he wanted to send a driver for me, but I'd rather have you as my backup in case I leave the damn car there."

"Good plan."

"Did he tell you it was no dates?"

Weird. "No. But I wasn't bringing anyone anyway."

"Well, that's what he said to me."

"They probably just don't want witnesses to their explosive tendencies."

He chuckles. "Probably. I'll pick you up on Saturday at 11-11:15."

"Okay. Thanks, Chris."

"Bye, Prissy Pants."

I shake my head. "Bye."

CHAPTER 21

I pat Beau on the head. "You be a good boy for Princess. Keep her safe." He nuzzles against my hand. "It's okay, boy. I'll be fine." He whines. "I'll be back, I promise."

Princess walks out Ryder's back door. "Hey, sweet boy."

I smile. "Hey, sweet girl."

She shakes her head. "I was talking to Beau." She runs her hand around his head, rubbing his ears. "'Cause he's the only sweet boy I know."

I throw my hand over my heart as if I'm offended. "Well, thanks."

She gives me her wicked smile. That smile I dream about. "Just call them like I see them."

Beau nuzzles his head into her hand. "So what does Nana *really* have up her sleeve for you girls tomorrow night?"

She shakes her head grinning. "Nope. Not telling. She made me swear to secrecy."

I laugh. "Something tells me y'all are in for an exciting night."

She giggles. "If you only knew."

"Okay, well his food is in the bottom of the pantry."

"Any rules for him?"

I'm confused. "What kind of rules? Bedtime is eight o'clock or something?"

"No. Like is he allowed on the furniture? Where does he sleep? Those kind of things."

I lean back against the porch railing. "Oh. Yeah, he's allowed on the futon and sometimes he does sleep with me. If you get nervous while you're staying there, he'll probably crawl up in bed with you."

She looks at me sweetly. "So he's really been good for you, huh?"

I nod thoughtfully. "Yeah. He really has. He has this sense about him. You know?"

She kneels down in front of Beau and hugs him. "I've always heard animals have much keener senses than humans. I'm so glad you're taking such good care of him, Beau. How about let's go get a treat?" Beau lets out a bark. She smiles. "Oh you like that word, huh? Treat."

She stands and Beau stands up wagging his tail. I shake my head smiling. "Looks like you've got this under control." I kiss her cheek and pat Beau's head. "See you guys Saturday?"

She nods. "Well, my brother Chris is picking me up around 11, we have a family lunch. I'll see you after that, though."

This surprises me. "You sure you're okay with going over there?"

She looks down, shaking her head. "No, but I need to."

I lift her chin with my finger, making her look me in the eyes. "You listen to me. If your dad so much as lays a finger on you, I'll-."

She stops me by putting her hand up. "I'm not going to let him hurt me, Judd. It's just lunch. Plus, all of my brothers will be there."

"Yeah. That did so much to help you last time. I'm telling you right now, Princess. If your dad hurts you, I'll hurt him."

"Judd, just leave it, okay? I'll be fine."

I hold her shoulders. "I can't. I won't let someone hurt you."

She touches the side of my face. "Thank you. Really, this is something I need to do."

"I'm going to let it go for now. Just please be careful Saturday and I'll see you when you get back. You can leave Beau outside while you're gone."

She smiles. "I think Beau and I will be just fine."

I shake my head. "Alright. Well, I'm gonna go get my bags loaded in the truck for us to leave." I really wanna kiss her, but I think I still need some more time. If I kiss her right now, I'll take her back to my apartment and we won't leave until we are forced to.

A few hours later, Ryder, dad and I are getting close to Atlanta. I look over at dad as I drive. "So Dad, is Mom going out with the girls tomorrow night?"

He laughs. "Oh yeah, Nana didn't let her get away with not going."

Ryder shakes his head in defeat. "I can only imagine what my grandmother has set up for them."

Dad and I laugh. I look back at Ryder. "We probably don't want to know. I tried to get something out of Princess earlier, but she said Nana swore her to secrecy."

Ryder laughs. "That sounds about right. Scarlet knows nothing. They are keeping it all a surprise from her."

My dad laughs. "Probably a good thing. She might chicken out on them."

We all laugh but as we get closer to down town Atlanta, the traffic gets thick. I try breathing.

I don't like getting boxed in. Getting boxed in can result in being ambushed or stopped. I can't do it.

I feel my body start to shake from the loss of control over the situation. *Breathe, Judd. Damn it, just breathe. This is not a hostile area, you can drive like a normal person. Calm down, deep breath, count like Luca said. You've been coming to this city for as long as you can remember. Stop freaking out.*

Ryder speaks up. "Judd, you okay?"

I shake my head and get off on the closest exit. "I need you to drive, Ryder. The traffic is too much for me."

He nods. "Okay, man. No big deal."

We get back in the truck with me in the back seat. Ryder looks back at me. "Just take your breaths, man."

Dad looks back at me. "Let's talk about something to keep us occupied for a few minutes."

I nod. "Yes. Please." I say as I'm working on my breathing.

Dad looks at Ryder. "So, do you think you and Scarlet will start a family soon?"

Ryder shrugs. "Not on purpose. I mean if it happens, it happens. She's on birth control, so we aren't planning anything for right now. She'd like to get finished with school."

Dad nods. "Sounds smart." He glances back at me. "So how are things going for you and Annabelle?"

I nod, still working on my breathing and trying not to notice all the traffic. "We slowed things down a little. I'm working on my issues with Luca, and Beau is helping me a lot."

"He seems like a good dog. I had a blood hound when I was a kid. He lived until I'd just married your momma. She loved that dog, I think she likes having Beau around."

Finally catching my breath a little and being more successful at blocking out the traffic, I motion to dad. "So how's all the stuff going with your new diet?"

He flops his head back on the seat. "No sweet tea is for the damn birds and I tell you, none of that artificial sweetener shit is worth a damn."

"Don't use that shit, Nelson, they say it gives you cancer and *most importantly* leads to impotency or something like that." Ryder practically screams.

Dad and I both die laughing at Ryder's worries. I pat his shoulder. "Ryder, I think it's safe from giving you limp dick. I'm pretty sure the men on this planet would have rioted by now if it did. It's not salt peter, for God's sakes."

My dad and I continue to laugh while Ryder grumbles.

My big fear is I just hope I do okay at the game tomorrow. I know there'll be a big crowd. A crowd I can't control. I need to do this for myself as much as Ryder.

CHAPTER 22

"Oh my God! That was awesome, Nana. Thank you." Scarlet screams as she practically falls into the stretch Hummer Nana rented for us.

I shake my head and laugh. "I know, I can't believe Lady Chablis got us up on stage to do a shot of pussy juice with her." Pussy juice is her very own brand of shot.

Nana waves us off. "Honey, I remember when that show first got started here. It hasn't changed a bit and still funny as hell for a drag show. She's a hell of a comedian."

I look around the Hummer. We are a mixture of old ladies and people our age. We are a motley crew, that's for sure.

Scarlet jumps up and down in her seat like a kid. "Where are we going now?"

I laugh because this is the girl who was so depressed when Ryder left yesterday that she wanted to call tonight off.

Nana looks at her seriously. "We're going home."

Scarlet frowns a little. "Okay."

She doesn't know about the party at home. We made sure to tell everyone to park out by the barn so she won't see the cars.

Once we are back at the farm and walk in, Scarlet screams. "Oh my God!"

There is red chiffon hanging down the walls. A variety of the toys from the red room in the books is around the room. I can't believe Nana found a planner to put this on.

Wendy is set up over in the corner with her products. When the waiters walk out, I think Scar is going to flip. They are shirtless and shoeless with faded ripped jeans on.

She grabs my arm. "Holy balls. They are hot. Not as hot as my man, but they are hot."

Nana walks over and hands her a card. "Here, this is from your momma. She wanted to be here but she couldn't get here two weekends in a row."

Scarlet opens it and it's a gift certificate for two hundred dollars to the Pleasure Palace.

"Nana, did you and Annabelle set all of this up?" Scarlet asks.

We both nod. She smiles. "Y'all are crazy. Thank you so much for this whole night. It's been just crazy wonderful."

Nana hugs her. "I'm happy you're happy, baby. Now, go take that gift certificate and buy some goodies to surprise that boy with."

Scarlet turns red. "Nana, God. You could act a little bit shy about it."

Nana looks over rolling her eyes. "Child, when have you ever known me to shy?"

We all laugh. I grab us a couple of glasses of wine. "Scarlet, let's go shopping."

She laughs. "Hell, I'm kinda afraid Ryder will want to start using this stuff. I don't know what's going on with him, but he's been locking himself up in the bathroom reading. I found a copy of the Grey books in there the other day."

I grin. "Damn, lucky girl. Maybe he's studying."

With that we make our way over to Wendy's table.

The rest of the night has gone by in a blur with old ladies looking at vibrators, hand cuffs and other items that would make their church choirs blush with shame.

Finally, I make my way over to Judd's apartment with Beau following me inside. "Come on, boy. Let's go to bed."

He whines and hops up on the bed with me. He snuggles into my side and I rub his ears. "Beau, you better not tell Judd I let you sleep with me every night."

He huffs and my eyes get too heavy to hold open.

~*~*~

Waking up with a slight hang over isn't too bad, considering the amount of alcohol I consumed last night. I stand in Judd's shower thinking about his hands on me. I run my hands over my body, imagining they are his.

I stop myself, shaking my head. I can't get lost in thought, I have to go help clean up in the main house before the guys get home, as well as get myself ready to deal with my family.

As I walk out of the bathroom with nothing but a towel wrapped around my hair, the door swings open. I scream and Beau barks. Judd steps in. "Sorry to startle y'all. We got back early."

My heart is still racing in my chest. "Fuck. You scared the shit out of me, Judd."

He laughs. "It's not like I haven't seen you naked before."

"I know that. I had the door locked, I wasn't expecting someone to come barging in here."

He shakes his head. "Sorry."

I grab my clothes, sliding them on. "Shit, I gotta go help clean up in the main house."

"Why?" He looks at me confused.

I sigh. "From the party last night." I snatch the towel off my head and run my fingers through my hair.

He laughs. "Oh, I'm coming over to see this."

He follows me out the door and across the yard.

As soon as we go in the back door I can hear Ryder freaking out. I stop Judd so we can listen from the kitchen. We both laugh, listening.

"What in the hell happened here last night? Why is every food shaped like a dick? Hand cuffs. A dildo. Nana, what the hell?"

I peek around the corner. She looks at him. "We were coming to clean this mess up, you just got home early. Now you leave Scarlet out of this, she had nothing to do with it. She's up there sleeping the night off right now. Plus, she got some neat gifts for you and her to try out."

"Holy shit, Nana! Don't say things like that to me."

Judd and I make our way into the living room. Judd is laughing so hard he can't talk when he sees the left over mess from the party.

I smile at Ryder and he looks back at me. "I can't believe my grandmother threw a sex toy party in my house."

CHAPTER 23

Once we finish getting the house back in order, I get Ryder to go out back and have a beer with me. He's still a little freaked out.

Princess left to go to her parents. I'm still not thrilled about that. I don't trust her parents.

Scarlet finally made her way downstairs. We have figured out that Nana took them to a show at Club One and then had a Grey themed party here. Old ladies and sex toys, not something I want to picture.

I wonder if Princess got anything. I may need to ask her when she gets back.

I look over at Scarlet. "So Scar, you want something to drink? A little hair of the dog that bit you?"

She shakes her head. "No. I need bread, lots of bread. Ryder, can you please get me some toast and a Coke?"

He nods. As he walks in the house, I hear him grumbling about never leaving her in the care of his Nana again.

She looks over at me. "So did you guys have a good time at the game?"

I nod. "Yeah. It was a little intense for me, but I worked through it. There were just a lot of people in one place. Ryder kept me in check, though."

She smiles. "Good. I'm glad. I'm also happy that you have Beau. He's such a sweetie. I told Ryder that I want to get a girl blood hound to be his girlfriend."

"You already have Button, your pet cow, Scar." Ryder says as he comes out on the pool patio.

She looks at him sharply. "Are you saying that I can only have one pet?"

"No, I'm not. I'm just saying you're busy and-."

She cuts him off. "I'm going to find a girl dog and I'm going to name her Dixie."

Ryder rolls his eyes. "How original."

"Asshole." Scarlet says as she goes to get up.

He grabs her around the waist. "Sorry, baby. You can have whatever you want and you can name it whatever you want."

I shake my head. "You two are so damn cute it makes me a little queasy."

They laugh. Scarlet smiles. "I'm gonna go back in for a minute."

I look at my watch and Ryder shakes his head. "Man, she's been gone less than an hour. She'll call one of us if she needs us. Okay? Don't stress."

"It's driving me crazy. If she comes home with a busted lip again I may go to jail."

He nods knowingly. "Trust me, if that happens, you may be there right beside Nana."

I stare out across the back forty. "I'm sorry that you had to kind of babysit me at the game yesterday. I really wanted it to be fun for you."

He shakes his head. "Hey man, I had a great time. So what, you had to do some breathing exercises and take a break every now and then. You did better after you had a couple of beers. You're doing great. You realized while we were driving that you were going to have an episode so you stopped and gave it over to me. You admitted that you needed help. That is a big step."

I nod. "Thanks, man. I really am happy for you."

He looks over at me and pretends to wipe his eyes. "Are you gonna loan me some tampons now? We really sound like pussies."

I laugh. "Sorry, maybe should've had Nana throw you a bachelor party."

"Fuck, I'm like Annabelle. I don't know that we could hang."

I slap his arm. "So did Scar say if she got anything good last night?"

"From what I've been able to piece together, her mom gave her a gift certificate and Nana gave her some money to spend. I know there are bags of shit in our room."

"She know you're reading the books?"

"I think she found them in the bathroom. She hasn't asked me about them, though. I guess I'll find out more when I see what all is in those damn bags."

"I wonder if Princess got anything."

"What's the status with you guys? I mean Scarlet and I haven't really wanted to ask."

"We are taking things slow. No more sleep overs for a little while. No serious make out sessions. Just trying to get my head on straight and she's trying to get through some personal stuff."

He nods. "Sounds good. Her family, they aren't good people. You guys are right to try and get your personal shit straight first. She loves you, man. That day we got the call, she fucking fell apart."

I sigh. "I know. I love her, too."

Nana steps out the back door. "Y'all come on in. I fixed us some tomato sandwiches for lunch. The tomatoes are fresh, I just picked them. Y'all come on."

I look down at my watch again. He grabs my hand. "It's only been an hour and a half now. Chill out."

I sigh. "Okay. I'm going to try. I just worry."

CHAPTER 24

Sitting between Chris and Vic at my parents' table, I'm listening to my father talk about family. How our family has grown apart and how we should be sticking together.

I pick at my summer salad. Really, Heaven forbid my mother actually cook a meal. I zone out thinking about the food I'd be eating if I were at Nana's. If we were doing a family lunch, we'd have fried chicken, some fried okra, squash, butter beans, maybe some greens and fried corn bread.

"Annabelle, are you paying attention?" My father grabs my attention.

I look up. "I'm sorry."

"Ugh. Why must I be surrounded by idiots? We are concerned that you are working too hard. These long hours at the hospital seem to be taking a toll on you from the looks of things. You should really find someone who'll provide for you, take care of you."

Okay, it's my turn I guess for the insults. He, Greg, Shane and Mom have went over Chris and Vic's faults. Now on to me.

Greg looks up. "Yes, those dark circles under your eyes are just horrible."

My mother looks up. "Yes dear, how do expect to find someone suitable to marry if you don't take better care of yourself?"

Shane looks at me. "Have you gained weight? Probably, living in that hospital like you do, eating garbage from the vending machines."

I stand up. "Really? Okay, I look like shit because I'm hung-over. I went out last night for Scarlet's bachelorette party. Nana took us to Club One and then we had a sex toy party at the house. Guess what? It was a blast. Now, I'm not eating this summer salad because I really need some carbs to calm my stomach and this dressing tastes like shit."

My father stands up. "Young lady, don't you talk like that at my dinner table."

Vic stands up. "Why? Because you prefer her weak and defenseless?"

My father throws his glass against the wall. "Where did I fucking fail as a parent? I had two wonderful children and then somehow I ended up with three fuck ups. Well, I know how Vic ended up a fuck up, he's not even mine."

That stops everyone in their tracks. I grab Vic's hand. My mother is looking at my dad like she could murder him. Shane and Greg look like the freaking Cheshire Cat.

Vic sits down beside me. "What are you talking about?"

Dad looks down at him. "Your mother had a bit of a problem back then. She couldn't seem to keep her legs closed when it came to my business partner. You are not my son."

I stand back up. "This is bullshit. You are all crazy."

Vic starts laughing hysterically. I think he's finally losing it. I slide back down in my chair, trying to figure out if Vic's about to lose his shit. He stands up. "You know what? This is the best fucking news I've had in my entire life. Thank God I'm not related to you. I'm out of school, you have nothing to hold over my head, Winston. Just pray to God you never get brought into my ER because I'm not sure I can abide my oath with you."

Okay, shit officially lost. Vic walks out. Chris and I sit there stunned. Chris looks up. "What about us?"

My mother rolls her eyes. "You are both his. My God, what do you think of me?"

I look around. "I think this family is fucked up beyond belief, that's what I think."

My mother stands up. "Annabelle, quit acting like those hillbilly rednecks you've been living with!"

I walk over to my mother, who I stand a good five inches taller than, and look down at her. "Those hillbilly rednecks, as you say, are more my family than this shit storm will ever be, and they have more money than you've ever dreamed of. You are so damn jealous of them you can't see straight. So go screw yourself, Mother." I turn to walk away. "Wait, maybe you can get another one of dad's business partners to do it for you."

My father shouts as I'm walking from the room. "Annabelle, you get your ass back in here." I'm about to walk past the keys to my Camaro. "Don't think about taking that car young lady!"

I laugh grabbing up the keys. I run out to the garage and fire up the car. They want hillbilly rednecks, I'll give the lying, cheating bastards one. I squeal tires backing out of the garage. I see my brothers and parents run outside. I see my parents perfectly manicured lawn, complete with a bird bath that probably cost more than this car. They spend over ten thousand dollars a year on this lawn.

I slam the car into gear and drive across their lawn, spinning grass and making doughnuts all across it. Then I floor it, heading for the all mighty, expensive ass bird bath. I slam into it. Of course airbags deploy and everything else.

I get out laughing. Shane comes running over, grabbing me by my shoulders. "What the fuck is your problem?"

Vic shoves him away. I take the keys, walk calmly over to my dad and hand them to him. "Keep the fucking car. Park it up your ass for all I care, or maybe in mom's vagina. It would probably fit."

He attempts to slap me but Chris grabs his hand. "Old man, don't do it. I'll spill your business all over town." My dad looks at him oddly, like he's hiding more. "Yeah, I fucking know, that's right." Chris turns to me. "Annabelle, care to know why they wanted you to marry creepy Patrick? It was a business arrangement. Dad's company needs money and the Wilson's were his means to do it. You were just a pawn, he just needed you to play the part of a stepford wife.

I've stopped laughing. I glare at my parents and then turn to Chris. "I'm ready to go home." I start walking across the lawn to Chris's car, Vic is walking behind us. I turn around, looking at my oldest two brothers and my parents. "Oh and you guys can go to hell." I look at my mother. "See ya in the welfare line since Dad's business deal isn't working out for ya."

I flip them the bird and climb into Chris's car, saying goodbye to the vultures I'm leaving behind.

Once I'm inside the car, I look at Chris. "Okay, tell me what you know."

CHAPTER 25

Sitting on the swing with Beau, I see the car I've now come to realize is Chris's. Princess gets out and speaks to him, then she waves goodbye.

She walks my direction. I smile when she reaches me and sits down with us on the swing.

She pets Beau. Without looking up she starts to speak. "It was a disaster. Luckily, I won't have to deal with them ever again. What kind of father basically tries to make his daughter a business deal?"

I put my hand up. "Wait. What?"

"His company needs money, so I was supposed to marry Patrick Wilson." She puts up her hand. "Wait, let's go inside. I only want to explain this one time. Today was so fucking crazy they should do a Jerry Springer episode on it."

I laugh and follow her into the main house. Nana, Ryder and Scarlet are sitting in the kitchen.

Scarlet jumps off the stool she's sitting on. "How did today go?"

I shake my head, signaling for them to wait a minute. "She's gonna explain."

Nana stands up. "Did Winston put his hands on you again? I swear before everything that's holy that I will go over there and that man will know pain."

She shakes her head. "Nana, I'm going to explain." She makes the motion for her to sit down.

I take a seat next to Ryder.

Princess looks around. "Well, let's see, lunch started out with my father telling us how we were failures to him. Then he got pissed and announced that Vic isn't his son and that mom screwed around with his partner. Shane called me fat. They all said I looked like shit. Well, except Vic and Chris. We had to eat summer salad that tasted like shit. All I could think about was the lunch Nana would have fixed. They said I was turning into the hillbilly rednecks I was living with because I told them how fucked up our family was."

She was pacing the floor and speaking very fast. "Then when I got up to leave, my dad said I couldn't take the car, which I wasn't going to until he said that. I grabbed the keys and tore out of the garage. I tore up my mother's neatly manicured lawn and crashed that damn car into the bird bath. Probably totaled the car. My dad went to slap me but Vic stopped him. Chris ratted out the fact that my dad wanted me to marry Patrick Wilson so that the companies could merge. I was part of a fucking business deal. My dad is going broke and they needed money so he was basically willing to sell me to the highest bidder. They accused me of acting like a hillbilly redneck, so I acted like one. I flipped them off and told them to fuck off. I also told my mom I'd see her in the welfare line since Dad's business deal didn't work out."

She collapses in a chair and lets out a huge sigh. "Holy shit! That was a lot."

Nana laughs. "So we are hillbilly rednecks, huh?"

She laughs hugging Nana. "I told them they were jealous of y'all because you have more money than God."

We all burst out into hysterical laughter. "Shit, Princess, you really know how to tell a story."

Ryder looks over at her. "I guess you'll be staying a little while longer?"

Princess gets a serious look. "I'm sorry, Ryder. I can...I can find a place if I need to."

He laughs. "I'm just playing with you." He puts his hand on her shoulder. "You're family. You stay as long as you need to."

I laugh. "You just may not want to. Especially after y'all's toy party last night."

Scarlet turns red. "You're an ass, Judd."

Nana shakes her head and gets up. "Damn crazy people." She kisses Princess on the head. "I gotta go, baby. I'm sorry your family is such a bunch of assholes. You're always welcome to stay here as long as you can deal with those two." She points to Ryder and Scarlet. "With all of their damn exhibitionism." She walks out the back door.

Scarlet speaks up, yelling to her. "We're not that bad."

Ryder looks at me. "It's his fault. He loaned me those damn books you women have been raving about."

Princess smiles at me. "You've read the books? Hmm. That explains a lot."

I smiled. "Hey, gotta get the advantage where I can."

Scarlet smiles and kisses my cheek. "Well, thanks." Then she turns to Princess. "We'll try to keep the exhibitionism to a minimum."

I shake my head and grab Princess' hand. "Come on, let's go take Beau for a walk. Scarlet is planning on getting him a girlfriend so he needs to get in shape."

Princess squeals to Scarlet. "Are you getting a puppy?"

Scarlet jumps up and down. "Yes! I'm gonna name her Dixie!"

Ryder rolls his eyes. "Jesus. Scarlet, I'm going to dig in those bags from last night."

Scarlet takes off running upstairs with Ryder on her heels. Then we hear a bunch of giggling.

"We'd better go." I tug on her hand to go out the back door before we see some shit we don't want to.

After we step outside, Beau comes running up to us and lets out a bark. I rub his head. "Hey, boy. Yep, Princess is here."

She reaches down, rubbing his head. "You're a sweet boy. I heard you're getting a girlfriend. Let's go for a walk, we need you to get in shape."

I laugh and we start walking. "So lunch was a bust, huh?"

She snorts. "You could say that. I'm done."

"I'm sorry it was so shitty. I'm sorry your family is a bunch of fuckheads."

She smiles. "Yeah, me, too."

"So Vic is only your half-brother?"

"I guess so. We asked if Chris and I were his. My mother looked at us like we were accusing her of something. Like she wasn't just admitting to having an affair that led to a child." She starts laughing. "I know I sound like a crazy person this afternoon. I'm laughing at my family. All of the secrets, all of the lies. They are all certifiably crazy and they were making me crazy. All of their demands, trying to make me marry someone because of money, keeping my mom's affair a secret. Hell, Vic stood up and basically told them this was the happiest day of his life to find out he wasn't Winston Garrett's son. I know this just doesn't happen in regular families. The general population cannot be this damn nuts."

I pull her into my chest. "Hey, it's okay. No, not every family is this way. We'll get through this part."

She looks up at me and smiles. "You just said that we would get through this. Did you mean it?'

"Yes Princess, I sure did." I did and I meant every word of it.

CHAPTER 26

Scarlet motions to me. "Annabelle, do you have my something blue?"

I run over to my dresser. "Yep, here you go." I place the sapphire comb in her hair. "You look so pretty."

She smiles. "Thank you." She looks at us both in the mirror. "You do, too."

I smile. "Thank you for not making me wear some hideous dress." I look down at the yellow chiffon strapless, knee length dress and smile.

Her mom comes in. "Awe, Scarlet, you look just beautiful. Have your brothers and Ivie seen you yet?"

We both shake our heads and Scarlet speaks up. "No, ma'am." She walks to her mom's side. "Mom, are you still okay with Cade walking me down the aisle? I really just want you to be seated so you get to see everything."

Whisper, her mother, smiles. "Yes, sweetie. I want to see everything. I want the total mother experience. Especially since your brother ran off to Vegas to get married."

She hugs her mom. "Thanks, Mom. Now, will you go get them so they can see me? I need Cade here anyway."

Her mom leaves to go gather the people she wants to see. I sit down on the edge of the bed. "Scarlet, how crazy is all of this? A year ago, if you'd told me that you'd be marrying Ryder Abbott, I would have thought you'd been hit over the head."

"I know, right? Especially since I hated him. I think during our first five minutes of conversation I called him a blue-blooded, conceited, spoiled rotten, selfish bastard." She starts giggling. "Then he called me sugar tits."

I laugh. "After that, you had that boy by the balls. You know he set Judd up with me that night in the bar so that I'd be distracted from you?"

She nods and laughs. "Yes. I had my suspicions that night. He confirmed it later, though"

There is a knock at the door and I open it to see Ivie, Gable, Cade, his wife Daria and their two kids.

I smile. "Hey, guys. You ready to see her?"

Madison, Cade's little girl, runs through first and stops in front of Scarlet. "You look like a princess, Aunt Scarlet. I saw Uncle Ryder, he looks like a prince." She jumps up and down clapping.

Scarlet smiles down at her. "Well you look like a princess, too. Mr. Judd calls Miss Annabelle princess all the time."

Everyone giggles.

They walk in closer and Gable takes her up in his arms. "You look gorgeous, Scar."

She smiles. "Don't make me cry."

Ivie hugs her. "Damn, you are hot. If I went that way I'd try to stop this wedding."

She giggles. "Thanks, you guys." She winks at Ivie. "If I went that way, Ivie, I'd probably take you up on that offer."

They both laugh. Scarlet smiles, "So are you guys ready to sing your hearts out for me?"

Ivie nods happily. "Yes. I'm so honored you'd let us do this."

Scarlet laughs. "You're honored. Hell, I'm the one who should be honored that I have celebrities singing at my wedding."

Cade steps up. "Okay, my turn. I might have been later coming into your life, but I'm so happy to be here for you."

Daria smiles and hugs her. "You look great. I'm so happy for you and Ryder both. Now, I'm going to take Madison and her brother out to have a seat before you end up with little hand prints all over your dress."

We all laugh as she leaves with the kids in tow. Gable and Ivie excuse themselves a few minutes later to get ready for their song.

I hold Scarlet's hand. "You ready?'

She smiles. "I'm excited, I'm nervous, I'm ready to get it over with and go on my honeymoon."

I shake my head. "Like you two need any more time or places to have sex."

"Argh. My ears. Please don't say things like that in front of me." Cade says covering his ears.

We both laugh. There is a soft knock at the door. Nana walks in. "Oh baby girl, you look just precious. Ryder is going to lose his mind when you walk out there."

She hugs Nana. "Thank you."

Nana takes Scarlet's hand. "I hope that you and Ryder will be as happy as Grayton and I were. You two have an amazing life ahead of you. Take everything God gives you head on and face it together. Remember all you've been through to get you to this point in life. Now, this was my wedding ring from my Grayton. I'd love for you to wear it as your something old and borrowed."

Scarlet starts to cry. "Thank you, Nana. I love it. Yes, of course I'll wear it. I was going to say my bra was old, but I like this, too."

We all giggle. "Okay, well I'm gonna go see if Daria will let me hold that handsome nephew of yours." Nana stops and pats Cade's face. "He's as handsome as his daddy." Then she makes her way out the door.

I turn to Cade and laugh. "I think Nana's got a little crush on you."

He laughs. "All the ladies have a crush on me."

There is a knock on the door. I poke my head out and Mrs. Parker tells us it's time.

I look at Scarlet. "You ready to become Mrs. Abbott?"

Cade smiles at her. "If you're not, I've got a car gassed up and ready to go. We'll blow off this guy, the plantation, all of this. We'll burn rubber getting out of here."

She laughs. "No. I'm good. I'm ready to go."

I pick up our flowers as Cade takes her hand. "Let's go, little sister."

I grab the train of her dress as we make our way to the back doors. One of the ushers open the French doors that lead to the patio.

I look to Scarlet. "Alright. I'll see you in a minute."

I start down the aisle, making eye contact with Judd the entire way. The guys are wearing light weight suits with open collared shirts.

CHAPTER 27

"So man, you ready for this?"

Ryder nods. "More than anything."

The music starts and I see Princess coming out the French doors. She takes my breath away every time I see her. I can only hope and imagine what it would be like for her to be in a wedding dress walking down this aisle to be my wife.

She makes eye contact with me and smiles that angelic smile. I smile back, then the music picks up. Cade and Scarlet come through the back doors.

I look over and I'm jealous of my best friend. Ryder has always had a privileged life and I've never been the least bit jealous, but to watch him seeing the love of his life walk to him so they can be joined as husband and wife, I want to be him.

I know I sound like a big fat pussy. The thing is, when you've watched how short life can be, you know how important these moments are. Unfortunately, I've watched my share of loss up close and personal.

Standing here watching my best friend since diapers say his vows is amazing. I look over at Princess and think back to the day before I left for my last deployment.

"Hey, Princess, I've done this a few times now. I'm good, I promise. I'll be back before you know it."

She looks over at me through her tears. "I know, it's just I've never felt like I really had anything to lose. My life is all smoke and mirrors. Now I feel like I'm losing one of the only real things I've ever had."

"I promise I'm coming back. You are not losing me."

"I thought we said that we weren't going put a label on what we have? But you're promising me that you are coming back to me."

I pull her naked body on top of mine and kiss her. "Okay, I understand what you're saying. We haven't known each other that long so how about we put a pin in this? We are open to other people during this deployment. When I come back, we'll reassess and decide where we stand. If I have anything to do with it, though, we'll be right here in each other's arms."

"Ladies and gentlemen, I'd like to introduce Mr. and Mrs. Ryder Abbott." The preacher says breaking me from my daydream.

As I take Princess's arm, we follow our best friends down the aisle.

~*~*~

Nana is dancing with me. "Judd, you are smooth on your feet, boy. A regular Fred Astaire."

I laugh. "I try, ma'am."

"So how are things going?"

"Better. It was hot. I'm glad to be out of that jacket."

She looks at me crossly. "Judd. You know what I'm asking."

I nod. "I'm learning some signs of the attacks and how to control them. Beau helps with my nightmares. I'm a little scared, I still haven't had a sleepover with Princess. I still haven't explained it all."

She smiles. "You are doing so well. It takes a big man to take all these steps. You'll be better for it and you two will be stronger for it. You'll tell her when it's time."

"You think so? Why would she willingly stick around for this craziness?"

She looks at me like I'm crazy. "You heard her talk about her family the other day. You really think you're that crazy? At least you have a reason." We both laugh a little and she kisses my cheek. "Now, it's time for you young people to drink and for old bitties like me to take our asses to bed."

I laugh. "Do you need a ride back to your house?"

"Nah. Mr. Fitzgerald is going to drop me off. We're going to have a nightcap."

I shake my head. Walking over to the bar, I meet up with my dad and Ryder's dad. "So Greer, how's it going in Atlanta?"

He sighs. "I miss my farm, but I'm happy living with Sarah. It's great to have someone in my life again."

I nod. "I'm happy for you."

We make small talk for a little while. I look around and see all the happy couples on the dance floor.

I can't help but wonder where she is. I make my way into the house and check her room. I stop Ivie. "Have you seen Princess?"

She shakes her head. "No. Here, take this shot. Gable's trying to get me drunk so he can get me pregnant. He thinks he's being sneaky."

I laugh and down the shot. "Happy to help. So why does Gable think he needs to get you drunk to get you pregnant?"

"Because, I don't know, it's still not something we've really talked about. He's been making hints."

I laugh. "Only freakin' Gable would try to trick his own wife." I shake my head. "Well if you see her, tell her I'm looking for her, please."

I ask random people and no one seems to know where she went off to.

I'm offered a couple more drinks as I'm walking around. I shake my head, this is a typical southern wedding. Free flowing booze and an endless supply of food. Oh, and don't forget the cocktail sausages. It's not a wedding in the south without them.

I see one of the lights on in the main barn. Making my way to the ajar door, I see Princess rubbing Beau's head and talking to him.

I enter. "Hey. Between the two of us, he's going to start charging by the hour like my counselor."

She looks up and smiles. "Hey. There was just a lot of people out there. I needed a breather."

"That's supposed to be my line." Beau senses that his job is done and makes his way out of the barn.

She laughs and I can tell she's been crying. I sit down by her and pull her into my lap. "Hey baby, why are you crying?"

"I ran into one of the men from my dad's club out there. He said he was sorry to hear that things didn't work out for Patrick and me. Maybe I would find someone soon."

I'm confused. "What?"

"Taking in most of his conversation, my father had been telling them that I was engaged to Patrick Wilson. After everything that happened, he said that Patrick and I had split up. The man is insane."

I shake my head. "I'm so sorry. What else did the man say?"

"He said that he's sorry that many of the investors are leaving my dad's firm. He's worried that my father will lose it all. I feel like this is somehow my fault. I know that's crazy, I shouldn't care."

I rub her hair. "Hey, that's not your fault. Don't think about it. I know that's hard for you because somehow, even with those people as parents, you have a heart, but you can't let this all bring you down. They failed you, remember that."

I'd love to kick her dad's ass for putting all of these thoughts in her pretty little head.

I pull her tighter to my chest. "You're perfect. Don't let anyone ever tell you different."

CHAPTER 28

How did I end up with someone like Judd caring about me? Sitting here in his lap on the hay bales, I look up at him. "No, you're perfect."

He snorts. "I'm far from perfect. Hell, I can't even go to a Braves game without losing my shit."

"Hey, don't talk about yourself that way."

He nods. "Well, you don't talk bad about yourself, either."

"You know, you look kinda sexy in this suit. I was thinking all kinds of naughty things while we were standing up front."

I see his Adam's apple move. He dips his head into my neck. "Well, I was thinking how beautiful you were." He licks my neck. "And how I'd love nothing more than to rip this beautiful dress off you."

"Oh, well I'm glad you didn't. You know, since there was a preacher there and all."

He rolls us so that I'm lying back on the hay and he's on top of me. He's gently holding my hands above my head. He runs his hand up my thigh. "You are so damn sexy." He leans down taking my mouth with his. "God, I've missed you."

I try to touch his face. He shakes his head. "Nope, keep your hands up here." He holds my hands above my head.

I giggle. "Oh, so you did read the books."

He takes one hand and pulls down my top, revealing my breasts. Putting his mouth on my breast, he talks as he's licking. "Did you ever doubt me?"

I shake my head. "No." Looking into his eyes, I ask. "Are you sure we're ready?"

He nods. "Yes."

He lets go of my hands and reaches under my dress, grabbing my panties and tearing them off. He bites my nipple a little roughly. "Oh!"

I reach for his shirt, ripping the buttons open. He removes his hands just long enough to shrug out of his shirt and quickly undo his pants. He shoves his pants and briefs down, settling back in between my legs.

Pulling my nipple back into his mouth roughly, I cry out again. My senses are on overload. I hear someone's laughter outside. I stop. "Judd, someone could walk in."

He looks down at me through a lust filled haze and nips at my collar bone. "I don't care." He thrusts into me without warning. "God, I've missed you. I've missed us."

All thoughts of the person on the outside of the barn are gone. I'm so wrapped up in the passion of this moment. "Me, too." That's all I can manage to say.

He reaches back up, placing my hands back above my head. "Tonight I'm in control. Leave your hands above your head." He takes his hands away, grabbing at my hips.

He thrusts hard back into me.

"Oh, fuck. Judd, please. I need to come."

He licks at my nipples as he thrusts into me. "You will, just be patient."

"I can't. I can't."

He looks down at me with total control. "Oh, you can and you will. Don't come until I say."

He starts pounding into me harder. As always, he has me stretched to what I feel is my limit. I feel his cock pulsating and I know he's getting close.

With rapid movements he sits back on his heels, pulling me with him. He makes quick hard thrusts and from this angle it feels as if he may break me.

Suddenly, I'm down on my back again. "Now, Princess."

As I come he pumps a final thrust into me, coming himself. "I love you, Princess."

I nod. "I love you, too."

~*~*~

Waking up in Judd's bed this morning was just as fun filled as passing out in it last night was.

After having wild passionate sex in the barn, we made our way back to his apartment for a few more rounds. This morning, I woke up with his head between my legs. After screaming his name, I smile at him. "You are very good at that."

He smiles. "I can say the same thing about several of the things you do."

I giggle. "Hmm. Thank you." I roll over and he smacks me on the ass. "Ouch."

He laughs. "We better get up and go see the newlyweds before they leave for their honeymoon."

I laugh. "Yeah, Nana said she's doing a big family breakfast for their send off."

About that time my phone pings.

Scarlet: Get your skinny ass over here I leave soon and breakfast is ready.

Me: Wow I thought you should be bridezilla before the wedding not after.

Scarlet: Well this bride has a hangover. She is also ready to go start her honeymoon with all of the new toys she's been keeping her new husband from breaking out this week.

Me: Alright keep your panties on we'll be there in a second.

"We'd better get going. That was Scarlet, she's ready to hit the road."

He laughs as we get dressed. He pulls me in for a kiss. "Yeah, I kinda worked up an appetite anyway."

"Mmm. Me, too."

CHAPTER 29

Ryder and Scarlet have been on their honeymoon in the Keys for almost a week. Originally they were only supposed to be gone a week, but they've decided to stay an extra few days.

Annabelle and I have been spending a lot of time together. I've stayed with her in the main house most of the time. Her bed is bigger. What can I say? We needed room to play.

I think she's stolen my dog, though. Beau cuddles with her all the time. He still helps me, though, if I have a dream that wakes me up.

We have a few cows that are about to have calves so I've been riding the fields each day checking on them. There are a couple that I need to get moved back closer to the main barn. I'm headed back there now to get what I need and see if Dad can help me. It's really a two man job.

As I pull up to the barn, I see an odd vehicle. I walk up to the doors of the barn and see a ghost from my past.

Princess sees me come in and smiles. "Hey, Judd. Mack here says he's been trying to get in touch with you for months. I told him I had no idea that you'd forgotten how to return phone calls."

Mack looks over at me and grins. "I told her to give you a break. Phones can be complicated things for a guy like you."

I shake my head. "Yeah, yeah. Whatever, smartass."

Princess smiles. "Okay, well you guys have some catching up to do. I'm going to go in and study for a little bit."

I kiss her on the lips. "See you in a bit. Oh, can you call my dad and ask him if he can help me gather a few pregnant cows this afternoon?"

She nods and heads back up to the main house.

I look at Mack. "You want a beer?" I say reaching into the barn fridge.

"Yeah, man. That'd be good."

I hand him a beer and he looks at me. "So, Hughes. What gives?"

I shrug. "What do you mean?"

Suddenly he rolls his wheelchair my way. "I mean why in the hell are you avoiding me?"

I shake my head. "I'm sorry, man. I really didn't mean to. I've been having a rough time. I've been having some attacks and some dreams. I'm seeing a counselor and using a dog for PTSD."

He nods. "I've done the same. I wanted to come and talk to you. My therapist asked me something one day and I had to come talk to you." He looks down. "He asked me if I held ill feelings toward you. He pushed. He asked if I blamed you for what happened since you were in NCOIC." He shakes his head and I stop him.

"Mack, it's okay. I am to blame, I made that call that day. I live with it every night. I hear all of your screams. I smell the smell."

He throws his beer to the ground. "Damn it, Hughes! This is why I'm here. I came here to tell you, YOU ARE NOT TO BLAME! None of us were. We made the best decisions we could on the information and training we had. When you wouldn't call me back, I knew you were blaming yourself because that's the kind of guy you are. Judd, damn it, don't blame yourself."

"How can you not blame me? I made those calls."

He shakes his head. "You never made those calls alone and you know that."

I just stand there for a few minutes letting his words sink in, until a relief washes over me. Once we pass over that hurdle, we talk and catch up on our lives.

After Mack leaves, my dad comes to help me with the cows. I realize while I'm out working that Nana was right. She told me I'd know when it was time to tell Princess, and it's time.

Once we finish up with the cows, I make my way into the main house to talk to her. She smiles when I come in. She has supper fixed and it smells wonderful. I kiss her cheek. "Hey, Princess. What did you fix?"

"Oh, just some spaghetti. That way I can take left overs in tomorrow. I'm so glad to be on day shift for a little while."

"Oh, yeah." I pull her tight against me. "Well I am, too."

She nervously looks back at the pot and starts to stir the bubbling sauce. "So how was your friend Mack?"

I nod. "He was great. He came to talk to me about some issues." I place my hands on her shoulders. "I want to tell you what happened. But after we eat, I'm starving."

She turns to me with tears in her eyes. "I'm so glad."

We finish supper and make our way into the den to talk. Once we sit, I lean forward, placing my elbows on my knees. "I've never told anyone but Luca this story." She nods.

I think back to that day.

"We had orders to go out on a patrol. It was to a nearby town. We were supposed to pick up a high profile Afghan official. He was going to do some informing, but we were supposed to make it look like a government snatch and grab, so his people were clued in. I was the NCOIC. Sorry. I was the Non-Commissioned officer in charge. Basically, the sergeant in charge. We pulled off the grab with preciseness. The route we were to take back out of the town had a wreck that was blocking traffic. I made the call not to investigate the normal route, for us to take the alternate route. Once we headed down the alternate route, a large truck pulled out in front of us blocking the street. Before we could back up, we were ambushed. Guns, grenades, you name it, they lobbed it at us. The official we'd been sent in for died. A few of my men died. Mack and two other guys lost limbs. A few of us were ate up with shrapnel. By the time help got there, I lost a couple of the shrapnel victims. I was hit in my lower back and legs. The doctors in Germany said a few more inches and I would have joined Mack with a wheelchair or bled to death."

I stop and look at her. She's crying and up until this moment, I didn't realize I was, too. "There are nights I dream about it. I'm still trying to help them. I can smell the burning flesh and gun powder when I wake up. I hear their screams. My heart aches and races like I'm still trying to tie off Mack's legs to keep him from bleeding to death. I've blamed myself for a while. I made the call to take the alternate route. Today, Mack came to find me and make sure I wasn't blaming myself and to let me know that he doesn't blame me, either. I've avoided him the entire time I've been home because I was scared. I was scared that he hated me. Here I am, walking around and living a normal life. All the while, he's in a wheelchair with his legs amputated from the knees down. I felt so guilty for so long. Seeing him today helped me let go of some of that. I'm praying this helps me move on just a little bit. Some days, I wake up and I see a stranger in the mirror. I've never had this pent up stress and all of these emotions before in my life. I was always in control and now I'm like a fucking ball of nerves. I just need you to understand what you're getting yourself into."

She smiles. "Thank you for telling me. I'm not going to push you. I just want you to know that whenever you need to get something off of your chest, I'm here. I love you, just like you are, and I hope I never come that close to losing you again."

I pull her into my lap and wrap her up in a hug. I kiss her hard. "I love you, too."

CHAPTER 30

Since the night Judd told me about the mission that led to his injury, we have been inseparable. Well, whenever we aren't working, that is. Which here lately we've both been working a lot. He's been crazy busy with calves being born, and I've been wrapped up at the hospital and working with Nana.

With Ryder and Scarlet getting back a few days ago, we've been staying in the apartment more. It's like I have to have him to sleep and he's the same. It feels kinda weird since I'm a house guest there to have someone staying with me. Plus, no one, and I mean no one, wants to accidently witness those two.

The stories Scar shared with me from her honeymoon make me blush. It's funny to think about the fact that just over a year ago, my friend was a virgin. She met Ryder and went coo coo crazy for him. I went to school with Ryder and in the past year I've learned more about him than in our entire past. Like he's pierced, I could have gone my entire life without knowing that. Scarlet tells me about the amazing orgasms it brings on. To be honest, though, I'm glad Judd isn't. He's so damn big that if he added anything metal, it may puncture my womb.

I'm on my way to Nana's now for one of our sessions. Her stories always crack me up, but today I need to talk with her about Judd. I need to tell someone that he's told me everything.

I don't want to tell Scarlet and Ryder because that feels like gossiping. With Nana it doesn't feel like gossip, it feels like asking for wisdom.

Pulling up to her house on the ranger, she's sitting on the back porch smoking those damn Pall Malls.

"Hey, old lady, you ready to get started for today?"

She laughs. "I might be old but it's better than the alternative."

I laugh and nod. "True. True."

She gets up and we go in the house. She hands me a couple of stacks of journals. "These are the latest ones I've been through. I ear marked some pages."

I flip through the books. "Thanks, this makes it super easy."

She sits down in her recliner. "So, baby, what's on your mind? You have that scrunched up look on your face that says you have something on that brain of yours."

I sit down on the couch across from her. I start wringing my hands together. "Judd's friend, Mack, stopped by the other day. They spent some time together for the afternoon. Mack is in a wheelchair, he was with Judd the day he was injured."

Nana's face frowns and I know she's thinking about the day that we got that call. "So, was his friend okay?"

I nod and sigh. "Yes, ma'am. It actually did Judd some good to see him. I didn't realize that he'd been avoiding those guys. He told me what happened that day. It's hard to explain, but it's like a weight hast been lifted between us."

She looks around the room, trying to not get upset. "I'm so glad he finally talked to you. I knew he'd tell you when he was ready. I was beginning to worry if he'd ever be ready." She reaches over and squeezes my hand. "You're good for him."

I smile. "Thanks."

She lets her hand fall in her lap. "Alright, let's get to work."

I laugh and pull out my laptop. I get the file open I've been working in and look to Nana for her to start.

She laughs and starts her story.

"You know Ryder gets his personality from his grandfather. Grayton was always that 'bad boy with a heart of gold'. I remember the day he came to school on a motorcycle for the first time. I had just turned 15 earlier that month. It was April of 1949. Just watching him pull into school on that motorcycle did all kinds of things to my girl parts that, at the time, I didn't understand. He was a couple of years older than me and even though we'd know each other my entire life, I was pretty sure he thought I was just a pain in the ass."

She stops and smiles, shaking her head in a memory. "But that day he asked me if I wanted a ride home."

She looks back at me seriously. "Now, I wanted to say yes. I felt dumber than dirt for not saying yes, but if my daddy would've found out I was riding on his motorcycle, he'd have tanned my hide. Plus, if I'd have pulled up in the yard with my dress clad legs wrapped around him on a motorcycle, my momma would have fainted."

She smiles again. "Don't get me wrong, he wasn't all sweet and innocent. Like I said, everyone liked Grayton, but he had a little rebel side to him. He could be a cocky bastard, though. He had every girl in the damn school chasing his cute Levi covered ass, but I just wanted him to be mine one day. I could see Grayton growing up to be like Humphrey Bogart, all classy, but with Southern Sweetness."

Looking over at Nana, she's lost in her thoughts. "Nana, I'm gonna go grab a glass of sweet tea, you want some?"

"I made some fresh lemonade. I'd like a glass of that."

I grab our glasses and come back to the living room with her. "Here you go. So how did you and Grayton finally hook up?"

She laughs. "Well, I wouldn't call it hooking up."

She sits her glass of lemonade down and starts back talking.

"Well, that same year, summer had just started. I had went with Momma and Daddy to Atlanta for some cattle conference. I had saved up all my money from odd chores and babysitting. I took that money and snuck off to buy my first bikini. Now, it would be considered nothing by today's standards, but back in them days..." She shakes her head. "My daddy would have never let me leave the house again. So I waited until we got back home. I was shy about going in front of my friends in it. I was ballsy, but I wasn't that ballsy. So I snuck off to the spring behind our house one day. Our property joined this property behind there. There I was, swimming and having a good old time by myself in my bikini, when someone dove in the water with me. I screamed. It scared me more than a holiness preacher layin' hands at a tent revival. A sandy blonde head popped up out of the water. It was Grayton. He swam over to me and said, 'Did I scare you, Pearlie Mae?' I looked at him and called him an ass. He smirked and swam closer to me. With the water being crystal clear, I knew he could see the blue striped bikini I was wearing. He grinned. 'Nice swimsuit. Your Daddy know you got that on?' I smirked back at him. 'No, you gonna tell 'em?' He laughed and said. 'No, I like the way it looks too much to do that.' He gave me a wicked grin and pulled me in for a kiss. That was my first kiss."

"After that day, we snuck off to that spring every chance we got." Her eyes glaze over thinking of the fond memories. *"Eventually we had to tell my daddy that we were courting. To start with he wasn't happy, but Grayton, as stubborn as he was, never gave him the chance to think it could go any other way. Daddy finally came along, he said he always knew Grayton would take care of me until the day he died. Now all of the property is one big place. That spring is on the west forty. I ain't been back there since Grayton passed away."*

My phone starts ringing and I see it's Naomi.

"Hello."

"Annabelle." She sounds out of breath. "Can you come up to the main house? Nelson's passed out."

I jump up from my chair. "I'll be right there." She hangs up and I shove my phone in my pocket.

Nana jumps up. "What's wrong?"

"Nelson passed out."

She puts her hand on her chest. "Oh Lord. Let's go."

We both make our way out her back door and take off on the Ranger.

CHAPTER 31

I look up and see the Ranger, with Princess driving and Nana in the passenger side, flying up to the main house. She jumps out of the UTV and comes up on the porch where we have dad sitting.

She pulls her hair up in a loose bun. "Nelson, what's going on?"

The sweat beading off his forehead and the paleness of his lips is scary. He won't answer her. He's just shaking.

She tries for his attention again, getting closer in his face. "Nelson!" She looks to my mom. "Get me his testing kit. I think his sugar is out of balance. Ryder, grab me some orange juice out of the house."

Dad finally looks up at her and shivers a little. "I- I j-just g-got a lil' light headed. T-that's all."

She shakes her head. "Nelson, this is more than a little lightheaded." Mom comes back and hands her the kit. She pricks dad's finger. "Your sugar is very low. Have you eaten today?"

Dad looks at her. "I h-had s-something s-small th-this m-morning."

She hands him the glass of juice that Ryder brought out. "Drink some of this." She looks at him pointed. "You know you need to eat balanced. Have you been working out here all morning?"

He nods. "Yeah."

"You need to make sure you snack when you're out here working. You have to pay attention to your body." Dad finally starts to get some color back to him and stops shaking.

She looks at mom. "Naomi, I think he needs to go home for the rest of the afternoon."

Mom nods and hugs her tightly. "Thank you so much, Annabelle. He scared me to death."

She smiles. "No big deal. He's just got to remember his limits. I know it's a learning curve for him, he's not used to having to stop, but he's gotta learn."

Mom and Dad leave to go home. Ryder hugs Annabelle. "Thanks for coming."

She and I sit beside each other on the swing. "I knew dad wasn't feeling well this morning when he came out here to help Ryder and me. He knew we really needed to get this tagging done, so he was determined to stay. Finally, Mom came down here to make us stop for lunch."

"Y'all are gonna have to watch him a little until he figures all of this out. Diabetes is an entire new way of life. Not everyone has the same signs and symptoms. Just little things like making sure he stays hydrated and having some things for him to snack on are important."

I nod. "Yeah, he did a good job of scaring the crap out of us today. I'm sure Ryder and I will be on our toes from now on."

She smiles at me. "Hey, do you think you can take me somewhere on the Ranger?"

"Yeah, where do you wanna go?" We start walking toward the ranger.

"There is a spring on the west forty. Do you know what I'm talking about?"

I nod. "Yeah. Come on."

We head out through the pastures. Coming up on the spring, I turn down the little trail that leads to it. Once we get to it, I smile. "I haven't been down here since Ryder and I were little kids. How did you even know it was here?"

"Nana told me about it today. She and Grayton used to sneak down here and go swimming. This is where she got her first kiss from Grayton. Well, her first kiss period."

"Wow. I never knew that. You know this used to be her family's property?"

"Yeah, she told me that. You know she hasn't been here since he passed away."

I kick some rocks. "Yeah, they were who took Ryder and me down here. Pa would pick us up and throw us off that rock over there. It was fun."

She laughs. "I bet. From the sounds of it, the two of them did more than just kiss and swim down here."

I put my hands on my ears. "Oh, don't say shit like that. Those people are like my grandparents."

She winks. "Just sayin'. You know it really is a warm day." She tugs the shirt off that she's wearing. "Maybe we should go for a swim."

I try to act coy. "I didn't bring a pair of swim trunks."

She winks. "I was thinking we could just skinny dip."

I tug my shirt off. "Sounds like a plan to me."

We both strip out of our clothes quickly and jump in the spring. She screeches when she comes up out of the water. "Holy shit, that's cold!" Her teeth are chattering.

I swim over to her and pull her into my arms. "What did you think, we had a hot spring back here? There are a few in Georgia, but it's not this one."

She swats at me and I pull her up to me. "No, smart ass. I just really wasn't thinking it would be this cold."

I kiss her neck and nibble at her ear. "I think I know something that might warm you up."

She giggles. "I'm sure you do." Wrapping her legs around my waist, I reach down and take one of her nipples in my mouth.

They were already hard and sensitive from the cold water. I nibble on them she screams out. "Oh god, Judd!"

"Oh, I'm just getting started."

I doesn't take long before we are both calling out with an orgasm.

I wrap her tighter in my arms. "God, I love you."

She buries her head in my neck. "I love you, too. You're my everything."

CHAPTER 32

Judd and I have both been so busy that we haven't spent any time together since we were at the spring almost a week ago. I've been on day shift, but by the time I get in and go help Nana for a little while, I'm beat. He and Ryder have been being OBGYN's for cows this past week. It seems every night they have a new critter being born.

I try to wait up for him most nights in his apartment, but this week I've passed out before he gets there. When he woke me up with his tongue this morning, I was so excited. It didn't last long, though, before Ryder was knocking on the door.

I groan and he sits up. "Shit!" Making his way over to the door, I hear him and Ryder talking.

He walks back over to me and shakes his head. "Damn it. My dick is so hard right now it may blow apart soon from the pressure. But if we don't go help this cow now, she may die. I promise I'll make it up to you, Princess."

I groan. "Fine, but right now I guess I'm going to take care of this myself. You aren't the only one in pain here."

If we didn't have sex soon, I was going to scream. I don't know what's come over me these past few weeks, but I can't seem to get enough of him.

Here I am, hours later, entering damn chart info at the nurse's station and all I can think about is Judd entering me. Pounding into me, bending me over, and smacking my ass. Shit, I've got to fucking stop. My panties are drenched and I'm at work. This is embarrassing. He has to fuck me tonight, I don't care how tired we are. We have to.

I hear my phone ping that I have a text.

Scarlet: Hey Ryder wanted me to make sure you don't have to work tonight.

Me: No why?

Scarlet: He knows they've been crazy swamped and he wants us all to go out for dinner. He's buying. Maybe the steakhouse or something.

Me: So no birthing tonight?

Scarlet: Nope. I think the last cow is giving birth now. I told him if we don't have sex soon I'm going to kill someone.

I smile thinking about the uninterrupted sex I'm having tonight.

Me: I understand completely. I'm about ready to break something.

Scarlet: I feel your pain. So dinner is good for you then? I'm sure it'll be an early night. ;)

Me: Sure! Sounds great. I'm out at 3 today.

Scarlet: Okay. Plan to leave around 6?
Me: K- Sounds good. :)

I feel like today has been the longest day ever. First of all, I'm so damn tired. This schedule I'm keeping right now is insane. Nana and I almost have everything together like she wants it, though. I can't wait to get the final product together for her. We are going to work solid on it this Friday since I'm off. She wants us to get it all together in time for Christmas. I'm going to load it to one of the self-publishing websites and get printed copies for the family.

I climb in the shower to start getting ready for our night out. I feel the water pounding over me as I scrub my body. Wishing it were Judd's hands all over me gets me hot.

After I'm finished making sure every part of me is scrubbed, buffed, shaved and moisturized, I stand in front of my closet. I have been in tennis shoes and scrubs all week. I want to dress like a girl tonight.

I grab a turquoise cotton dress and my brown, silver and turquoise cowgirl boots. Throwing them on with some silver jewelry, I take one last look at my hair and makeup and head downstairs.

I smile when I see Judd. He lets out a low whistle since it's just us. "Well, Princess, you look super sexy."

I grin. "Thanks, that's what I was going for."

"I vote we stay in and I get to have my way with you over and over again."

I chuckle. "As much as I would love that, Ryder feels bad about you two pulling such long hours. Trust me, Scarlet is just as bent on us getting back home. We've all been missing out on our alone time."

He laughs. "Well, let's get going."

Scarlet and Ryder left a few minutes before us. They had to stop by for him to sign some papers at the lawyer's office for his dad.

We all meet at the bar and grill the guys decided on a little after six. This place has a live band going on tonight so it's pretty packed. Scarlet and Ryder go out for a dance after we order our drinks and food.

Judd leans over and brushes his hand up my leg to the apex of my thighs. He whispers closely in my ear as he brushes over my clit. "You aren't wearing panties. You are such a bad girl. Follow me."

He stands up and pulls me behind him. I can barely breathe. Between not having sex with him for days, him rubbing my clit at the table in a crowded place and his vibrating voice in my ear, I almost came at the table.

Once we reach the door to a small storage closet, we look around and step inside. He pushes me up against the shelving. "Damn baby, you are sexy. I can't wait to get home and make love to you all night to make up for the past week. Right now, though, I'm going to fuck you hard and fast, otherwise I won't make it through supper."

I reach down and unfasten his jeans, pushing them and his boxers down. He puts his hands under my ass, lifting me, and I wrap my legs around his waist.

He slams into my wet pussy. "Fuck, baby."

"Oh God, Judd."

He pumps harder and faster. I hold on to the shelving, trying not to scream loud enough that people hear us.

"Fuck, Princess, I'm about to come."

I nod, letting him know I'm there, too. He slams into me three more times, emptying himself inside me.

He slowly lets me down and reaches over on the shelf, grabbing some paper towels for us to clean ourselves up with.

"That was a great appetizer, I can't wait for the main course later." He rumbles in my ear as we are walking back down the hall.

Once we make our way back down the hall into the bar, I see a guy watching me. I don't think I know him, but maybe I went to school with him or something.

I shrug it off and sit down at the table about the time our food comes out.

Scarlet looks at me and smirks. "So what were the two of you doing?"

As soon as I cut into my steak, I look up and see that guy watching me again. I get a strange nauseous feeling. I stand up. "Excuse me."

I jump up and run to the restroom. After emptying my stomach, Scarlet comes in the bathroom while I'm washing my face and hands.

"Hey, are you okay?"

"Yeah, I guess my stomach got a little nervous from what we just did." I giggle. "Plus, there is this guy I keep seeing watch me in there, it's giving me the creeps."

"Should we tell the guys? Did he say anything to you?"

I shake my head. "No, but I feel like I should know him or something."

We make our way back out and when we come to the end of the hall, I see Patrick Wilson standing with the guy. "That's Patrick with him."

Then something about the way the light hits his face, it all floods back.

I don't even hear what Scarlet is saying.

"Scarlet, that is the guy who slipped me drugs."

CHAPTER 33

I'm just about to go check on Princess when they come back to the table. I can tell by her facial expression that something is very wrong.

"Are you okay?"

Scarlet looks at me. "Judd, we'll get everything boxed up and bring it home. You get her out of here."

Ryder looks up from his plate. "What's going on?"

Princess still won't speak.

Finally, Scarlet looks at me. "Patrick Wilson is here and he's talking to the guy that she's pretty sure slipped drugs in her drink that night."

I see red. Ryder knows me all too well. He puts his hand on my shoulder. "Get her home. This is upsetting her, and as much as I want to go beat that fuckers face in, she needs to go home."

I nod and take her hand, trying to make it through the bar. We make it just outside the door before we come face to face with some preppy ass douche bag.

"So Annabelle, this is what you are doing now? Your father's business is going into the toilet and you are fucking farm boys in storage closets in bars."

She finds her voice. "Shut up, Patrick! Get out of my way."

He shakes his head. "You're a real gem, aren't you? Glad I didn't end up with you. You know, the company you keep and everything." He motions to me.

She glares up at him. "Oh, so you'd rather hang out with people who puts drugs into women's drinks? That fucker you were talking to in there is a rapist. He put drugs in my drink one night."

"Like you wouldn't have fucked him anyway. He doesn't do that to girls who aren't already asking for it." She hauls off and slaps him.

"You're a stupid cunt, Annabelle." He turns and storms off just as I'm about to knock the shit out of him.

My heart is about to pound out of my chest when the door opens. The guy in question walks out.

He looks at Princess. "Nice to see you again, Annabelle." She shivers beside me.

His smirk sets me off. "You son of a bitch. You are a piece of shit." I charge toward him. I hear Princess telling me to stop but I just can't. I punch the guy repeatedly in the face until I feel hands trying to pull me back. I turn around and swing, almost hitting my princess in the face.

Ryder tackles me to the ground. He looks over at the guy. "You better get the fuck out of here before I let him up to finish the job. Don't show your face around here again. I know people who can make your sorry ass disappear."

The guy jumps up and runs to his car, tearing out of the parking lot. Ryder looks down at me. "Judd, get ahold of yourself. You could've killed that guy and you almost hit Annabelle."

I try to sit up. "Oh my God. Princess, are you okay?" She steps back a little and I feel like shit.

She nods a little. "Scarlet is going to take me home."

I stand up. "Wait. Princess."

Ryder puts his hand on my shoulder, stopping me as I'm trying to walk after her. He starts walking me in the direction of my truck and motions for me to give him the keys. "Man, give her a little bit. All of this scared this shit out of her. She just saw you try to kill the guy who was going to rape her a few months ago. She couldn't get your attention and about the time I was walking out was when she put her hands on you to stop you. I know not to do that but she didn't. You almost hurt her. She needs some time. Don't be stupid, give it to her. In the morning, go talk to Luca. You lost it there."

As we climb in the truck, I nod. "Ryder, I can't lose her."

"You won't but you lost it back there, man. You only saw red and while I understand wanting to kill that bastard, trust me, I do after what happened to Scar, you can't do it."

I nod and lean my head back against the seat. "Yeah, I know. I'll go talk to Luca in the morning."

~*~*~

I feel lost. In the past three days she's pulled away from me. She says it's just work and that she's always tired, but I know it has to do with the other night. Ryder says she's been sleeping a lot and helping Nana. She hasn't really texted me, she hasn't waited for me in my apartment. My bed is empty without her.

I talked to Nana about it, she says I just need to give her time. That she has a lot going on and we are strong enough to get through anything that comes our way.

I told Luca what happened. We tried to work through some of the issues, but he told me most of it will be up to me to learn to control the rage.

Ryder and I are working on residing one of the small barns today.

Ryder's phone starts ringing. He answers it.

"Hello." "Annabelle slow down." He's shaking. "What's going on, Annabelle?" He drops his tools. "I'm coming."

I look at Ryder. "Man, what's going on?"

He takes off running to his truck. After we jump in, I see the tears pouring out of his eyes. "Ryder! Talk to me."

"It's Nana."

He tears out of the yard headed for Nana's.

"Ryder, what do you mean?"

He's wiping his face as we sling the truck up in Nana's drive. "Annabelle found her." He's out the door before the truck stops.

I look up to see emergency vehicles flying down the private drive.

I bury my head in my hands and let out a sob. Ryder runs in the house with me on his heels.

As we enter the house, Princess runs over to us. "Ryder, I'm so sorry. When I found her it was too late."

Scarlet comes flying through the door a minute later and into Ryder's chest and sobs.

I pull Princess to my chest as she sobs.

A deputy comes in, he has to get a report from her. I walk her over to sit down on the couch.

"Ma'am, I know this is hard. I just need to know what happened so we can put it in a report." He gives her a kind smile and puts his hand on hers. "I'm sorry we have to do this now."

She nods. "My name is Annabelle. I've been helping Nana with her memoirs. I came down because we were supposed to work on them today. She didn't come to the door like she normally does, but I just let myself in. When she didn't answer, I started looking for her. I found her in bed. I screamed, I shook her. I tried to calm down. I'm in the last part of my nursing degree so I checked her pulse. She was already cold. I'm guessing whatever happened, it was last night. I called 911, then I called Ryder and Scarlet."

He pats her hand. "Annabelle, you handled this all very well considering the circumstances. Thank you. This should be all I need for now."

My mom and dad come barreling through the doors. My mom grabs Ryder, pulling him into her chest. I pull Princess in mine. "I'm sorry you had to find this."

"I'm just glad it wasn't Ryder." She cries into my chest.

My dad steps up and hugs her. "Sweetheart, you handled yourself very well. Nana would be proud."

She looks up. "Has anyone called Greer?"

Dad nods. "Yes, Sarah is driving him in."

CHAPTER 34

Standing at the podium at the community center, I begin to speak.

"Pearl Mae Cartwright Abbott was born at her parents' home April 3, 1934. She came into this world raising hell and I'm pretty sure that's how she went out. She married the love of her life, Grayton Abbott, at the age of seventeen, right before he left for the Korean War. While he was overseas, she finished high school and worked as a nurse at Ft. Stewart, then called Camp Stewart. After Grayton returned, they had one son, Greer Abbott, and made a very successful life for themselves continuing the traditions of Abbott Cotton."

I clear my throat. "Greer later married Lillian Conrad and produced Nana's biggest pride and joy, her grandson, Ryder. She would tell you the smartest thing Ryder ever did was convince Scarlet Johnson to go out with him and in turn, marry him.

"Now, I've told you all about her blood family, but if she were standing here today she would tell you that she considers Nelson Hughes her son and Naomi her daughter-in-law. She told everyone that Judd was her grandson just like Ryder and she was so proud of him. She liked to brag about her famous grandkids, Scarlet's brother, Gable, and his w-girlfriend, Ivie, along with their band for following their dreams in music and becoming famous." Whoops, I almost slipped up and said wife. They've got to tell everyone.

I wipe a stray tear. "Nana could sense when someone felt lost, like they had no one. She took in lost hearts like mine. She loved me for who I was, not what she thought she could mold me into."

"I was lucky enough to spend the past few months working with her on her memoirs. She certainly had some colorful, entertaining stories.

I feel like I got to meet the teenaged Pearl and Grayton with the stories she told me. Trust me when I say Nana was just as vivid in her stories as she was in real life. I, for one, am going to feel lost without her in my life every day, but I also know she'll be with me in spirit. She was proud to be from this town and loved the people in it. Most of you know just about everyone in this town calls her Nana. Look around, we had to have this at the community center because there wasn't a church big enough to hold all of you. With that being said, the family would like to welcome anyone who has a story they'd like to share to come up and speak."

I sit beside Scarlet and watch people of all ages stand up to tell stories about Nana.

Gable steps up to the podium. "As Annabelle said, Nana took us all in and loved us. Before we turn this back over to the pastor, she left us a list of songs she wanted sung. Just like Nana, some are traditional and some not so much. Please join us in granting Nana's request." He starts playing and we sing quite a few songs. *I'll Fly Away, Rainy Night in Georgia, Seven Spanish Angels, Angel Flying too Close to the Ground, Silver Wings, Who's Gonna Fill Their Shoes* and *I've Always Been Crazy.*

The preacher chuckles when he takes his place at the podium. "Well, as usual, Pearl had her way of saying what she wanted to say. She's even done it today, through Ms. Garrett speaking and through those beautiful musicians a few minutes ago. She wanted everyone to celebrate life every day and there isn't a doubt in my mind that's why she picked those songs. If you didn't want the raw honest truth, you didn't ask Nana Pearl. She always did whatever she felt was necessary to get the job done. If we needed to raise money for something, she'd get out there and beat the streets. If we were cooking or doing repairs, whatever it was, she was there. I'm pretty sure Nana went in her sleep because that is the only way the Good Lord could sneak in there and get her. I'm proud to say that I knew Nana Pearl and considered her a mentor and a friend. Please keep the family in your prayers as their matriarch has gone to a better place. Now, please join me in a closing prayer."

We make our way home after the funeral. There's more food than anyone could even attempt to eat here, but Ivie calls to order some pizzas for the band to go pick up. There's only so much fried chicken and ham you can eat before you start clucking or snorting. The men have all went out to the barn to drink, with the exception of Nelson. He can't drink anymore.

Scarlet laughs, taking a sip of her beer when Ivie's band mates make it back with the pizzas. "Southern funerals are just like southern weddings. Lots of food and free flowing booze."

I shake my head and laugh. Sarah looks at us. "Well, Nana would be proud, I'm pretty sure those men have gotten into her *shine* tonight. They were in rare form when I walked out there to check on them."

I'm so tired, this entire event has really taken its toll on me, along with my work. Naomi looks at me. "Sweetheart, are you feeling okay? You look a little pale."

I nod. "I'm fine. It's just been a stressful few days. With all of this going on, I haven't had much of an appetite and my stomach has been a little upset. I'm going on up to rest, I haven't had much in the past few days."

She nods and hugs me. "Do you want me to send Judd up in a little bit?"

I shake my head. "No, he should rest with Beau. Plus, he'll probably be too drunk to make it up the stairs."

She nods and makes her way back into the kitchen.

With everything going on, I still haven't had a lot of time to deal with his rage the other night. I'm still a little timid and I've been staying in my room. He wanted me to stay with him after I found Nana the other day, but I said I had to work late. It's not that I don't want him, it's just the rage I saw the other night freaked me out. I know it was an accident and he would never mean to hit me, but he almost did. He would've killed that guy if we hadn't stopped him. It was all a little too intense.

A few minutes after lying down, there's a knock at my door. "Annabelle, it's me." It's Scarlet.

"Yeah, come in."

She sits down by me on the bed. "Hey, I just wanted to say you did an awesome job today."

I nod. "Thanks."

She turns to me. "We are all supposed to meet with Nana's attorney tomorrow for the reading. You need to be there."

I nod. "Okay, I don't know why I would need to be there but okay."

She looks at me. "So when are you going to tell me?"

"Tell you what?" I try to play dumb.

"Annabelle, I know you too well for you to think you can keep secrets from me. I've been watching you. You, my dear best friend, are pregnant."

I sigh and start to cry. "Yeah."

"When did you find out? I'm guessing you haven't told Judd yet."

"No, I haven't. I found out right before I went to Nana's the other morning. I was going to talk to her about it. I needed advice."

She pulls me in. "Oh my god. I'm so sorry. Here everything has been so damn crazy." She starts crying, too. "She'd be so proud."

I shake my head. "She knew. She was the one who told me to get a test. She'd been watching me, how tired I was, my sense of smell was in over drive and I was emotional. She said, 'Baby, you are pregnant just as sure as I'm sitting in this chair. You better go get you one of them tests.' So I did and I am."

Scarlet shakes her head and flops back on the bed. "Holy crap. That woman knew everything."

I laugh. "Yep, she sure did."

"When are you gonna tell him?"

I sigh. "Soon. I'm just still a little freaked out myself, plus the stuff the other night. It's just a lot to deal with."

She grabs my hand. "I get it. I'm here for you."

I smile. "Thanks."

CHAPTER 35

I feel like hammered shit. I was trying to be a friend, Nana was always about living life to the fullest, so Ryder and I decided that meant drinking a bunch of her moonshine last night. Now, I'm pretty certain that a semi ran over my head several times.

To top all of that off, Princess still isn't really speaking to me. I don't know what to do. I don't have Nana to talk to any more but she told me to be patient. Well, I'm running out of patience.

She went to bed last night without even one word to me. When my mom told me she'd went upstairs, I asked her if she wanted me to go up and she said that Annabelle said I needed time with Beau.

Really? My fucking dog. She thinks I need time with him more than her. Don't get me wrong, Beau has been getting me through this, but I'd rather it be her.

Something is going on. More than just the fight with that douche bag the other night. She's pale and she's lost weight.

I walk in the attorney's office for the reading of Nana's will. I'm not really sure why I'm here, but I guess Nana left me something. Probably that old rifle I always liked.

Everyone is in the lobby when I walk in. "Hey, am I the last one?"

Ryder looks up. "No, we are waiting on Annabelle." She walks through the door about that time. "Well, I guess we are all here now." He says, motioning to the attorney.

Mr. Roberts looks around the room. "Alright. If y'all will join me in the conference room?"

We follow him in and take seats around the table. I sit next to Princess.

"First off, let me say I'm deeply saddened by this. Pearl actually came in not too long ago to update all of this. She was a wonderful woman. Now. She wrote a letter I'm to read and then settle the estate."

Dear Family,

If this is being read to you, well then I'm shit out of luck. Not really, I guess. I'm with Grayton now and my beautiful Lillian.

I want every one of you to live life to its fullest potential, don't be scared. Look at me, I've drank, smoked, talked bad and ate whatever in the hell I wanted to. I don't know how old I am when you're reading this but I know I'm over eighty now. So live it up and laugh. Laugh even when people think you're crazy.

Greer, you are the most important thing that ever happened to me and your daddy. Take care and remember, 'I love you this much'.

Ryder, I'm glad you've settled down. I don't have to go to Heaven with rumors that my grandson is moonlighting as a stripper, a porn star or just an overall asshole. I'm sure I'd be answering to your momma. Scarlet is the best thing that has happened to you. Take care of her, cherish her and give her a wonderful life.

Scarlet, take care of him, too. They say God protects fools and babies, I'm not sure if he still falls under those categories.

Nelson and Judd, take care of my two boys and each other. Watch out for Naomi and Annabelle, two wonderful strong women. I feel blessed that you've all been brought into my life.

Now, on to business. I have everything set up the way I want it. Don't argue about it or try to give back what I give you or I'll be pissed. I'll come haunt you, I'm serious.

I've been blessed with this great family and all the extras that came along with it.

Love,

Nana Pearl

At this point, there isn't a dry eye in the room. Mr. Roberts clears his throat. "Are you guys ready?"

We all nod.

465 | P a g e

"In the matter of Abbott Cotton and Farms INC., the 51% that Pearl still owned will be divided as such.

Greer Abbott will be given 15%, bringing his shares to 55% and now controlling shareholder.

Ryder Abbott will be given 16%, bringing his shares to 25%.

Nelson Hughes will be given 10%.

Judd Hughes will be given 10%.

This is only the business, it doesn't include the property it sits on. Ryder will retain Greer's shares in the event of his death. Judd will retain Nelson's shares in the event of his death."

"Judd will inherit her house and three acres with most of the furniture, any items not included will be listed here.

Scarlet Johnson (Abbott) will inherit her jewelry and the 1954 Corvette in storage.

Annabelle Garrett will inherit her memoirs and any profits from them.

The monies in her personal accounts are to be divided amongst the charities she was a member of, the most important being the Senior's Center and The Combat Veterans Charities."

He hands Greer a piece of paper. "This is a list of the possessions in the house she has allotted for people and who they are for."

He looks up at us. "Any questions?"

Ryder looks up. "What Corvette is she talking about and where is it in storage?" Greer shrugs. I guess everyone but the attorney is clueless.

Annabelle speaks. "Grayton bought it for her when he returned from Korea. Brand new off the show room in 1954, it's red with white accents. He paid less than three thousand dollars for it. She told me about it, showed me a picture even, but she never told me she'd kept it in storage somewhere."

Mr. Roberts hands Scarlet some paper with some keys. "This is the address to the climate controlled storage facility it's been in, along with the keys and title."

Once we are outside, everyone looks around at each other. Greer speaks up. "Let's all meet at Nana's and get things in order so Judd can get ready to move in. I think that's what she would've wanted."

On my way back to the farm, I can't help but think about the fact that I own a house and part of Abbott Cotton. *Holy Shit!*

CHAPTER 36

To say the reading of the will was a little shocking was an understatement. I expected some little trinket or something, definitely not her legacy. I was still going to finish her memoirs, but I just figured the profits would go to Ryder and Greer. I want to make sure they are finished in time for the holidays just like she wanted.

Everyone else headed straight there, but I needed a detour. I had some thinking to do. I know I need to tell Judd about this baby, but I have to make sure he's mentally ready. With his rage the other night and now losing Nana, I need to make sure of where he's at in his head. Is he the guy that I can talk to rationally or is he the guy that's going to wake up in the middle of the night choking me?

Pulling up to her house and knowing she's not coming out on the front porch to greet me is strange. I loved that woman, probably more than my own family. What I said was the truth, she accepted me for me.

I can't seem to get out of the car at the moment. I really need to look into getting my own, I've been driving Scarlet's now for a while. She drives any of the vehicles here, but I need to be able to stand on my own two feet for this baby's sake.

My phone rings. Looking, I see it's my brother Vic.

"Hey, brother."

"Hey, Prissy Pants. I was just calling to check on you. I heard about Miss Pearl Abbott passing away. I know you were close to her. I also wanted to check on Scarlet and Ryder. I know I've never gotten to spend much time with them to get to know them, but they seemed really nice and close to her at the cook out I went to. I can see why you love that family, they are the opposite of our family. They all have a welcoming demeanor."

"Yes, that is why I love them all so much. I'm doing okay. It's just an adjustment, you know I'd been working with her every day. I was the one who found her, Vic. It hurts but I'm working through it."

I see Scarlet walking out on the porch. "Hey, Vic, I need to go help Scar with some things. Can I call you this week for lunch?"

"Sure, Prissy Pants, but you call me before if you need to."

"Thanks. Bye."

"Bye."

I step out of the car. "Hey, Scar. I was coming in, I was just talking to Vic on the phone. He was calling to check on me and you guys."

"Oh, okay. Well we've got all the stuff from the lists. She mostly sorted out the guns and a few other pieces that people had given her. Judd wanted us to take whatever we wanted, but we just went by the list for now. We left all of the journals and memoir stuff where you guys were working on it."

I suddenly feel tired and weak. "Okay."

She looks at me curious. "Are you okay? You look a little pale."

"Yeah, I just need to eat a little something. It's kinda been an emotional day. You know?"

She nods thoughtfully. "Yeah. Tell me about it. I just inherited a classic car that is going to have both of my brothers blowing a load in their pants."

I laugh, "Wow, such a way with words, ma'am."

"So are you going to talk to him after we leave?"

"Yeah, I'm going to try. It's just really hard coming up with the words. You know, I don't know if we're really at a place where I can just say 'Hey, guess what? I'm knocked up with your kid.' You know?"

She nods and chuckles. "I think it'll all be fine. Plus, we have Nana watching our backs now."

I walk up on the porch with her and we go inside. "I know, but he has so much on his plate already."

"This little bit on his plate may give him something to fight for." She says as she grabs the screen door to go inside.

As we go in, Ryder, Nelson, Greer and Judd are loading some boxes out back in the Ranger. I guess there really wasn't much at all.

I take a small cardboard box and start clearing the desk that all the journals are on. A few minutes later, they breeze back through the room heading out.

"You could leave all of that here if you wanted to." I hear Judd behind me.

I sigh a little. "It's okay, I'll use my laptop to work on it. It will probably be a little more convenient anyway."

He grunts. "Princess, what did I do? You won't look at me or talk to me. Everyone keeps telling me to be patient. I'm not sure if I can any more since I don't really know what I've done. You let me hold you while you were in shock the other day, but you haven't looked my way since."

I spin around and put my hand up. "You don't know what you've done? You almost killed a guy the other night and you almost hit me. Forgive me for being a little freaked out."

He steps closer to me and I shiver a little. "I would never hit you."

I try to step past him. "You almost did!"

"Well, I'm sorry that I beat the shit out of a guy who drugged you, and probably countless other girls to rape them! Fuck, Annabelle!"

He called me Annabelle. I don't know if he's ever called me by my actual name.

He looks defeated. "I've talked to my counselor about the rage that unleashed the other night. He told me it's ultimately up to me to control my rage problem. He gave me some exercises to do when I find myself in a situation like that. I believe I can do it. I would really hope that you could believe in me, too."

I'm trying to be strong and not cry. "It's not just about believing in you. There is more to it than that."

He brushes his hand down the side of my face. "What more is there? What, you don't believe in us? I was pretty sure you would always believe in us. I guess I was wrong."

I start crying. I slam the box of journals down and try again to walk past him. "If you really believe that I don't care, then you're wrong."

He won't let me past. "What is the problem then? Explain it to me. What's wrong with us?"

I'm getting pissed off that he won't let me past him.

"DAMN IT! Judd, this is bigger than us. It's bigger than both of us. It's not just the two of us I worry about anymore! I'm pregnant, damn it!" I shove him in the chest and stalk past him. He stands there in shock.

CHAPTER 37

Surprised. Shocked. Bewildered. Dumbfounded. Stupefied. Those are all words that can be used to describe how I'm feeling right now. I shake from the thoughts racing through my mind. "Wait! Princess, stop."

She spins around and puts her hands on her hips. "What, now I'm Princess?"

"You are always my Princess. I was upset a few minutes ago."

She wipes a tear from her face. "You see, Judd, that's just it. I have to wonder what you are going to do every time you get angry or upset. Are you gonna get mad and shut down? Are you going to drink yourself into a stupor? Are you going to burst into a rage like the Hulk? What are you going to do? We have a baby coming, I have to protect this baby."

"You think you have to protect my child from me?" I'm starting to get pissed, but I'm trying my hardest to keep it in control.

"I don't know, Judd. The other night you were completely out of control, you scared me. I was never worried before because I could help you. The other night you never heard me begging you to stop. Then when I touched you..."

I put my hands on her shoulders and she starts shaking. "Hey, please don't be scared of me. The biggest difference is the other night I was hurting someone that hurt you. I will never let anyone hurt you or this baby, and if I thought I could do it myself, I'd back away."

She nods and sits on the couch. "I'm just scared of everything right now. This is so much at one time."

I squat down in front of her, taking her hands in mine. "We are going to get through this together. I love you."

She lunges at me sobbing, wrapping herself around me on the floor. "I'm sorry for how I've been acting."

I brush her hair with my hand. "So when did you find out?"

"Well, not so funny story. Nana kept telling me *she was sure that I was pregnant. That I needed to go get one of them test things.* I got one and well, you know the answer. I came down to talk to her and tell her that morning I found her."

I hug her. "You've been dealing with this alone, with everything going on after Nana."

"Scarlet guessed last night. She's been worried because I've been so tired and all."

Holding her tight with her ear close to my mouth, I whisper. "So that's the reason you didn't want me to come up to your room last night?"

She nods. "Yeah, everything was finally slowing down. I just needed time to process it all."

"I'm sorry you've been going through this on your own, but not anymore." I pull her in tight. "Do you know anything else?"

She giggles. "No. It's not like as soon as you know you're pregnant, they download a book into your brain."

"I was just wondering. You are a nurse, you know."

She laughs. "I'm a student."

"Can we get up off this floor? My lower back is bothering me."

She nods and stands up. I notice she weaves a little. "Are you okay?"

She nods slowly. "Yeah, I'm just gonna grab something to drink."

"Let me get it for you."

She's already walking. "No, I got it."

I hear her fall in the kitchen. "Princess!" I run to her and she moans a little. "Are you okay?"

"Yeah, I'm just a little woozy. I got a little light headed."

I pick her up. "Come on, let's get you to the doctor."

"We don't have to go to the doctor, Judd. I'll be fine."

I shake my head. "No, we are getting you and this baby checked out."

She sighs and her head flops back. "Okay, will you at least put me down?"

I sit her on her feet and help her to my truck. We make small talk on the way to the hospital.

After waiting for what seems like forever, they call us back. The doctor goes over everything with her. She tells him about her sickness and being tired, and about Nana passing away.

He looks at her. "Well, Ms. Garrett, I'm going to run some labs on the blood we've drawn. The urine you gave us shows you are most definitely pregnant. While we are waiting, I'll have the tech grab the ultrasound machine and wheel it in here so we can have a look at the little one."

She smiles a hundred watt smile as Nana used to say. "That would be awesome."

A few minutes later, a young girl wheels a big machine in the door. She smiles at us. "Sir, could you hit that light switch? The pictures show up clearer when the lights are dim. Ms. Garrett, if you would, step behind the partition and remove your clothes from the waist down. You can wrap up in this sheet."

A couple of minutes later, Princess sits up on the exam table.

The tech looks at Princess. "How far along are they estimating you are?"

"According to my last period, probably around five or six weeks. I just took the at home test a few days ago."

The tech smiles. "Well, in that case we'll use the transvaginal ultrasound. Slide down the table just like you do for your annual exam, put your feet in the stirrups." She pulls out a wand that looks frightening and rolls a condom over it. "Okay, I'm going to insert this, you are going to feel some pressure and we'll have a look around."

Princess looks at me. "You okay, Judd? You look a little worried."

I chuckle. "I'm not gonna lie, that thing she just put in you looks scary as hell."

They both laugh. Suddenly, I hear a whooshing sound. The tech smiles and then gives us a weird look. Princess senses it, too. She looks at her. "Is e-everything okay?"

The tech nods. "Yes, everything appears fine with everything. You're five weeks and four days." She turns the monitor so we can see. She points to the screen. "Do you see that little sack right there?" We both nod. "That's a baby."

We both smile and Princess looks back at the screen. "Wait. Is that two sacks?"

The tech nods her head. "Yes, ma'am. Congratulations, you guys are having twins."

I look hard at the monitor and sure enough, I see two little sacks fluttering.

I swallow hard. "Is everything okay with both of them?"

She nods. "Everything looks good here. I'm going to let the doctor come back in and talk with you some more."

She leaves the room and I look at Princess. "Holy shit, baby."

"I promise, I didn't mean to surprise you this much. I'm just now getting settled with the idea of one baby. Now there are two. What are we going to do?"

I look at her. "Love them, and love each other."

CHAPTER 38

The doctor breezes in the room. "Well, Ms. Garrett, I hear congratulations are in order."

I acknowledge him. "Yes, I guess so. I'm still reeling from it all."

Judd speaks up. "How did her blood work and all come back? Is everything okay there?"

The doctor smiles. "Yes, you are doing fine. You're a little dehydrated, that's the reason for the dizzy spell. You need to take it easy for a few days and drink. I know you may not feel like eating but drink plenty, especially if you've been vomiting. The little ones are going to take the wind out of you."

Judd looks up at the doctor. "So what else do we need to do? What about her school, is she okay to do her clinicals? What about being on her feet?"

The doctor holds up his hands. "Slow down, son. You're going to have a stroke. Good thing we're at the emergency room, huh?" The doctor laughs in my direction. "I think you may have to keep him calm."

I laugh. "Tell me about it."

The doctor looks back at me. "How much longer do you have before your nursing program is complete?"

"I'll finish in the Spring."

"Okay, so you'll finish up a couple of months before the babies are due. You'll need to drink lots of water since you're going to be up so much. Be careful what you come into contact with and be prepared, twins sometimes come early. Other than that, I suggest making an appointment soon with your regular OBGYN."

I smile and nod. "Yes, sir. I had planned to do that soon."

He reaches out to shake our hands. "It was nice meeting you, Ms. Garret, Mr. Hughes. Best wishes and good luck. The nurse will be in here momentarily to help you get checked out."

After the doctor walks out of the room, we look at each other. I'm the first one to speak. "Wow."

"Yeah. Wow."

"There is no way I was expecting that."

"Twins must run somewhere in your family. It comes from the mom's side." Judd shrugs.

"Yeah, must be, but I'm not asking my family. I do need to talk to Vic and Chris, though."

The nurse comes in and gives me my release papers.

On the way back to the farm, he looks over at me. We are trying to decide how to tell everyone and how his parents are going to react. He grins and looks over at me. "Okay, why don't we plan a dinner at our house? We could invite your brothers, their girlfriends, along with the rest of our family. I think Nana would be thrilled that we chose to share the news that way."

It hits me he said our house. "Judd, as great as that sounds, are you sure about all of this? I mean, I'm caught off guard by it, but that's your house. Nana left it to you."

He pulls off to the side of the road and turns to me. "Baby, that house became ours the minute they said Nana left it to me. I was going to ask you to move in anyway, these babies just make it harder for you to tell me no."

"Hey, I mean it sounds great, but I'm just scared I guess. This is a huge step for anyone, but add two babies on top of that and it's a little crazy."

He kisses my hands. "I know. Just think about it, though, we've never been a normal couple. We had mind blowing sex within two hours of meeting each other. My point is we don't do normal." He pulls back on the road. "Plus, Nana always said that normal was for uptight assholes."

I burst out laughing. "Okay, we'll plan the dinner, but let's tell everyone it's a housewarming dinner. Okay?"

He nods. "Sounds good."

"Oh, don't tell Scar you took me to the hospital, she'll be pissed I didn't call her. Plus, I want to keep the twin thing a surprise."

He smirks. "Got it."

Once we start down the gravel drive, he looks at me. "Do you want to go ahead and pack up some of your things and bring them over?"

"I'll just grab a few clothes and girl stuff. We need to get the house like you want it and get your stuff in there before we start moving stuff in."

"I guess we could stay in the apartment for a few days until Ryder and I take care of the things I wanted to."

I nod. "That sounds good. Let's stop by the house and make some plans."

We pull up to the house and go inside. I sigh. "Tell me it isn't always going to be like this, that we won't always feel this void when we walk in the door here?"

"It may, but when the babies come it will bring a whole new light to this place and Nana would be thrilled."

I laugh. "Yeah, she would. She'd rub it in my face that she was right. That she knew I was pregnant before I did."

He laughs. "Yeah, she would. It amazed me that she always knew everything, even with no one telling her."

I chuckle. "I know, right? She'd always tell me she didn't get that old by being stupid."

Judd sits on the couch. "I miss her."

I sit down beside him. "Me, too. I spent so much time with her these past few months, it's hard, you know? I have to finish her memoirs without her."

He claps his hands together. "Alright. Let's not get down, let's look around and see what you want to do."

I laugh. "What WE want to do."

We stand up and walk around, talking about paint colors, the furniture we want to keep, and which room we want to use for the nursery. Luckily, Nana was pretty on top of staying with the current styles in life. Judd said she also had all of the windows, doors, electrical and plumbing updated a few years ago.

After making our list and seeing how much of it is actually baby related, I look up at him. "So I guess we should probably plan dinner for this week so we can spill the beans. I mean, you can go ahead and tell Ryder if you want to since Scarlet knows, but don't say a word about it being twins. I want to surprise her, too."

He grins. "Sounds like a plan. Yeah, I need to go ahead and tell him so he'll know why I'm doing some of the things on this list."

I nod my head. "Exactly."

He pulls me close to him. "I love you, Princess. Please don't ever be scared of me again."

I shake my head. "I'll try not to, but you have to do your best to use your control like your counselor said."

He leans down kissing my neck. "You've got it."

Suddenly my hormones go into overdrive and I feel my panties getting wet. I start kissing him back and he works his way down my neck. "Oh, Judd."

He hoists me up and walks me over to the dining room table, laying me back. He pulls my pants and panties down, working my shirt off. I snatch my bra off and he palms my breasts. "I think these are already bigger."

I pant as he puts his mouth on my breasts. "It's probably just the hormones." I feel a zing run straight to my clit. "Oh God, Judd. I need you to fuck me right now."

He stands up and snatches his shirt off. Shoving his pants and underwear down, his cock springs free. Grabbing my legs under the knee, he pulls me to the edge of the table. He leans down, licking and sucking on the throbbing nub between my legs. I cry out as he thrusts into me.

He grunts out. "Fuck." He leans down over me. "I've missed all of this, Princess."

I look into his eyes. "Me, too."

He stands back up and starts thrusting into me faster. Within minutes we are both crying out in ecstasy. He picks me up off the table and we slide onto the floor together, still wrapped up in each other.

"I can't lose you, Princess. Ever."

CHAPTER 39

Standing here in what is now my backyard and manning a grill seems strange. The past couple of weeks have given me more ups and downs than all of my deployments rolled into one. Losing my shit at the bar, losing Nana, fighting with Princess, finding out I'm going to be a dad, not once, but twice.

"Hey, man. This place is coming together great. Nana would be proud."

I take the beer Ryder hands to me. "Thanks, man. That means a lot coming from you."

"So, when are you going to tell your parents?"

"Tonight at dinner. She wants to tell them and her brothers at the same time."

He nods and shrugs with his hands in his pockets. "Sounds good."

"Man, hearing the heartbeat was the coolest sound ever."

He puts his hand up. "Wait, when did you hear the heartbeat? Scarlet said that Annabelle's first doctor's appointment is this week."

"Well, she had a little dizzy spell the other day after she told me. I made her go to the ER and get checked out."

"Let me guess, you didn't tell Scar."

I shake my head. "She didn't want anyone to worry."

"Oh boy, when Scar figures this out you two are in for it."

A little while later, Ryder and I have finished grilling, and Scarlet and Princess are putting everything else on the table.

Once everything is set, we sit down. I look up at everyone sitting around the table. "Thank y'all for coming tonight." I reach and grab Princess's hand. "We hope this is the start of many dinners together."

Princess smiles and looks around the table. "We had another reason for bringing everyone here tonight. We have a little announcement to make."

Vic and Chris look up. Vic asks. "Are you guys getting married or something? Because you didn't have to feed us steak to tell us that."

Princess laughs. "No. I'm pregnant."

My mom screams and jumps up, running around the table and hugging us at the same time.

"Oh my God! I'm so happy."

I put my hand on my mom's shoulder. "Just hang on, we aren't through." I laugh when she looks at me strange. "We decided to double the fun. We're having twins."

This time it's Scarlet's turn to jump up and knock a chair backwards trying to get to us. She and my mom have us wrapped up very tight. My dad and all of the rest of the men in the room slap me on the back, while Kari and Angie hug Princess.

"Ladies, do you mind giving us a little breathing room?"

They laugh and break free from us. Princess laughs. "Now, let's eat."

Scarlet looks up, glaring at us from the plate she just sat back down to. "Wait a minute. How do you know you're having twins?"

Princess laughs. "Well, the other day when I told Judd, I got a little dizzy and kind of passed out. He made me go to the ER and they did an ultrasound. Trust me, we were both very shocked."

"You didn't tell me you went to the hospital. Oh missy, you are in big damn trouble." Scarlet points with her fork.

My mom looks concerned. "What did the doctor say? Is everything okay with the babies?"

I nod. "Yes, ma'am. It was just a little scare. She was a little dehydrated and stressed from everything that had been going on."

Chris looks up. "Well, Prissy Pants, I'm happy for you."

Vic raises his glass. "Me, too. I propose a toast. Here's to the new parents."

"Here, here. To the new parents." Everyone says.

My mom looks at Princess. "So how far along are you, sweetie?"

"I'm only six weeks today. We wanted to go ahead and tell y'all because we wanted our family to know what's going on. We just want to wait a little longer before telling everyone else."

I agree, nodding. "Yes, the doctor said everything looked great, but we just want to be careful. We have our first appointment with her regular OBGYN next week."

Everyone nods. My dad winks at me. "Son, you did good."

Ryder shoots up from his chair. "Wait, that means you got pregnant sometime around our wedding." He sits back down and shakes his head.

There's no way I'm telling him that we are pretty sure it happened in the barn during his reception.

All of the women are talking to Princess about her doctor's appointment next week.

Ryder Laughs. "I don't know why you guys want to go all fancy and get a doctor. Me, Judd and Nelson delivered a lot of babies just a few weeks ago. Even a set of twins. We could do it."

My mom motions to him. "Not my grandbabies, Ryder Grayton Abbott."

Scarlet pops him on the arm as my mom smacks my dad for laughing. Scarlet glares. "That's not funny, those were cows."

Ryder laughs. "Yeah, cows worth a lot of money. I say we can do it."

After Ryder gets scolded a few minutes later, he finally shuts up.

A little bit later, after my parents, Scar and Ryder have left, I'm out back talking with Vic and Chris. Chris looks up from his beer. "So, does she plan on telling our parents?"

"Maybe later. I don't want her to get stressed out this early. Plus, when she tells them, I'll be with her. Because if your father even goes near her, I'll hurt him."

Vic nods. "We completely understand. That's actually what we were going to suggest. If Winston hurt her or those babies, I'd kill him."

I motion back to him with my beer bottle. "So you are really okay finding out that your dad isn't really your dad?"

"When your father is Winston Garrett, you are praying you aren't his kid. Trust me."

"Have you tried to find said business partner?"

He shakes his head. "No. I know who it is and that's really no better. I'll talk to him when I get ready. I'm just trying to finish up my residency and go to work."

Chris sits forward. "You make her happier than we've ever seen her."

"Coming from you guys, that means a lot. I don't want you to think I'm never going to marry your sister or anything like that. We've just kinda had a lot thrown at us at one time. I actually planned to do it soon, she just kinda threw me for a planning loop when this happened."

Vic nods. "Hey, we understand, and putting a ring on someone's finger isn't the overall commitment. Look how we grew up. I'm fucking twenty-eight years old. I just found out that the man who belittled me, who called me a failure for going to medical school instead of being like him, a blood sucking vulture, isn't my father. Actually, I couldn't be happier to know I'm not blood related to that man."

Chris smiles at me. "My brother is still working through some things. You just take care of Prissy Pants, be true to her and make her happy. That's all the commitment we need."

"Thanks, guys. I plan to."

CHAPTER 40

It's hard to believe that I've just passed my first trimester. Twelve weeks, even if I do look more like twenty thanks to these two growing so quickly. Judd and Ryder completely painted the inside of the house and we have everything set up the way we want it. The only room not finished is the nursery, I just had them paint it a neutral color, that way we don't have to repaint. We can't wait to find out if we are having boys, girls, or one of each. I'm kinda glad that we aren't having identical twins. Something about two people looking so much alike freaks me out. I know that even though the babies are fraternal, they could still look a lot alike, but not identical.

It's Thanksgiving break and I volunteered to do some extra time in the ER. They are always shorthanded during the holidays. The good thing about the nursing program I'm in is I have the same advisor all the way through. After telling her about the twins, she suggested that while I'm feeling up to it, I could do some extra hours. She would save them for next semester in case I have to go out early or go on bed rest.

The week of Thanksgiving break is crazy at a hospital. College students are celebrating being home or just being on a break. Alcohol poisoning, drug overdose and DUI wrecks top the lists.

I was just sitting down to eat my granola bar when a young blonde girl was being brought in the wrong ER doors by a brunette girl. One of the guards was about to send them back out when I made my way over to them. Something drew me to this girl.

I look at the security guard. "It's okay, I've got it."

I turn to the girls. "Girls, what's going on? What's your names?"

The brunette looks at me. "I'm Jenna and this is my cousin Becca. We think someone put something in her drink. We were at a party in Column Heights. We were talking to these really nice guys and they were giving her drinks."

"What about you?"

"I don't drink. I was drinking bottled water."

I pull the girls into a small exam room. "Did anything else happen?"

Becca still isn't speaking. "Jenna, did something else happen to her?"

She nods her head. "I'm not sure how far it went, but the blonde guy kicked her out of the room when she threw up on him."

I touch Becca's shoulder. "Okay, Becca. I need you to put on this gown and put your clothes in this bag. I will be back with a doctor soon to check on you." Becca nods and I look at Jenna. "Jenna, could you step outside with me for a minute?"

I had a sinking feeling about just who had thrown this party. I know Column Heights. I know the Wilson's live out there and a bunch of others who think their money buys them everything. "Jenna, it's policy that I have to file a police report on this. Do you know the address where the party was at?"

She nods. "Yes."

"I know Becca isn't talking much right now, but will you be able to talk to the police?"

"Yes. Who in the hell do these guys think they are? How could somebody do that to someone? I thought she quit breathing on the way here. When her father gets word on this, he'll kill someone. We weren't even supposed to go out tonight."

I pull my phone from my pocket. Call it my new found mothering instincts, but I did some social media investigating on Patrick and his friends. I pull up some pictures of them.

"Jenna. Were any of the guys in this picture at the party?"

She nods and starts pointing. "That's the asshole who kept giving her drinks and the blonde asshole is the one who took her to the room. They kept trying to get me to drink something other than my water. When I wouldn't, they just ignored me and tried to separate us."

She had just pointed to Patrick as the blonde and the other was the guy who'd drugged me.

"Jenna, I think you should call her dad. This is about to get ugly."

She sighs. "He's out of town." She lowers her voice. "Her father is Senator Brooklyn."

"When is he due back?"

"Tomorrow, he's coming in for Thanksgiving. We just got in a couple of days early."

"You need to go ahead and call him. He'll probably come on. The guys you just pointed to? Well, they do think they can get away with anything. She's going to need her father's support."

She nods and goes to make the phone call while I get Dr. Anders. We go in and do her exam. Dr. Anders said that even though I went against the admin policies for getting the girls in, one of the most important jobs as a nurse was to get as many details as I could.

A little while later, a deputy comes in from the sheriff's department. He's the same deputy that took my statement at Nana's.

"Well, it's nice to see you again, Ms. Garrett."

"Please, call me Annabelle."

"Annabelle, please call me Steve. Can you give me a heads up of what's going on before I go in there?"

I run down the story with him, letting him know that Jenna has contacted Senator Brooklyn and he's on his way as we speak. I show him the pictures on my phone of the guys Jenna pointed out. He's going to speak with the girls. I stop him before he goes in.

"Steve, I need to tell you something. The second guy in that picture slipped drugs in my drink a little over a year ago. The only difference is I didn't finish my drink and I left and called a friend before anything could happen. I wouldn't let my friend take me to the hospital to get a report. I should have, it might have stopped them. If she decides to go further with this, it will get ugly. I just hope more girls will come out and seal the fate of these assholes."

He puts his hand on my shoulder. "Annabelle, I've watched way too many girls go through something like this. I've been an officer for fifteen years, but my job doesn't get any easier. I know the two jerks in those pictures and you're right, they think they can get away with anything, but this time I doubt it. The Senator will be out for blood. He lost his wife when she gave birth to Becca. That little girl has been his life since she was born."

I nod. "If you need anything with the case or my statement, just let me know. If you could, keep this quiet until he's had a chance to get here and check on her. She's very shaken."

"She has every right to be and she also has every right to her privacy."

"Thank you, Steve."

He nods and walks into the exam room with Jenna and Becca.

CHAPTER 41

Even though it's Thanksgiving, the cows don't know that. I was up and getting ready for the day when my exhausted Princess came in. She took a shower and went straight to bed. She told me we needed to talk when she woke up for lunch.

As I make my way back home for lunch, I'm a little worried. I don't know what she wants to talk about but I'm kinda nervous. She's been working quite a bit trying to do some extra so next semester won't be so hard on her.

Pulling up to the house, I see a dark sedan pulling in at the same time. An older gentleman gets out and opens the rear door for another man. I do a double take when I realize it's Senator Brooklyn.

I walk over. "Sir, can I help you?"

He nods. "Are you Ms. Pearl's grandson?"

I shake my head. "Not by blood, but by love, yes. If you are looking for her, she passed away a few months ago."

"No, young man, I'm not. I just recognized the address when we arrived. I was friends with her son, Greer, back in our college years. I'm actually here to see Ms. Annabelle Garrett. The lady from the hospital told me I could find her here."

I nod. "Yes, she's my-." What do I call her, my baby momma? "She's my girl. She's sleeping from work last night. I'm about to go in and wake her up, though, for lunch." I motion for him to come in the house behind me. "If you'll have a seat, I'll get her."

He nods and takes a seat. "You're Nelson's boy, aren't you?"

I nod. "Yes, sir."

"You're right, you were her grandson by love."

I walk into our bedroom and see her sleeping so peacefully. I hate to wake her but she has to eat. Plus, I'm curious as hell to find out what's going on.

Sitting on the side of the bed, I rub her arm. "Princess."

She rolls a little. "Hmm?"

"Can you tell me why there is a Senator in our living room that wants to speak with you?'

She bolts up in the bed. "What?"

"Senator Brooklyn is in the living room. He asked to speak with you."

She shoves the covers off the bed and runs to the closet. "Tell him I'll be out in a minute. Offer him some coffee, tea or lemonade."

I chuckle. "Yes, ma'am."

Walking back into the living room, I motion down the hall. "She'll be out in a minute. Would you like some coffee, some sweet tea or lemonade?"

"No, thank you. I really need to get back to my daughter."

I nod. "Okay."

He looks at my small limp as I walk to the couch. "I heard about your injury. Is everything coming along alright?"

I shrug. "I have good days and bad days. Physically and mentally."

I knew the Senator had served in the Gulf War so he would understand.

He looked at me. "All I can tell you, son, is that it'll get better as time goes on. You learn how to deal with it."

"I hope so. I'm working on it." Beau gets up and flops his head in my lap. "Beau here is helping me, too."

He nods and smiles. "I've read the studies. You know, I remember how in tune my animals were to me when I got back from overseas. I always thought they could sense that I needed a sounding board or a friend."

"He's been great. Helps a lot at night."

We both look up when Princess enters the room. She smiles. "Senator Brooklyn, what can I do for you?"

"I just wanted to stop by personally and thank you for taking care of my daughter last night."

She shakes her head. "I'm just sorry she had to go through that. Is she doing okay this morning?"

"She's at home with my sister, Dawn, and my niece, Jenna. She's resting. I know we have a long road ahead of us, but I'm going to make sure those boys pay."

She smiles. "I'm glad. I told the officer, Steve, that I would be willing to give my statement. If it would even help. It's been over a year, but in any case, I'd be willing to give it."

I look at both of them. "Wait. What's going on? What statement?"

The Senator stands up. "I'm going to be going so you two can talk. I just really wanted to say how much I appreciate how nice and sensitive you were to the girls last night. They needed that nurturing." He points to her rounded stomach. "You are going to be a wonderful mother."

She stands and smiles, walking him to the door. She give him a hug. "Tell Becca if she wants to talk or anything to call me. I gave Jenna my personal number last night."

He nods and wishes us a happy holiday.

After the door is closed, I look at her. "Princess, are you going to explain this to me?"

She sighs and looks sad. "His daughter and niece were at a party last night in Column Heights. She had drugs put in her drink and well, it's possible that Patrick Wilson had sex with her. The girls came into the ER. They ID'ed the guys to the officer."

"How did they ID them?"

"I pulled up some social media pictures from Patrick's pages. It was him and the guy who drugged me. I told my story to the officer."

I flop back on the couch. "Whoa, this is going to get ugly."

She sits down with me and puts her head on my shoulder. "I know. I just feel so bad for his daughter. She just thought she'd sneak off to a party and have fun. Those assholes ruined it for her, they took so much from her in just a few hours."

She's crying now. This has been known to happen since she's gotten pregnant, but I know today the tears aren't for her. They are for that girl. I need to make her smile and my conversation with the Senator convinced me that I'm ready.

I get up to go to our bedroom. Beau hops up on the couch and lays his head protectively on her stomach.

When I return, she's wiping her eyes. "I'm sorry. I didn't mean to get so emotional. It just bothers me."

"Baby, you have every right to be upset about this. Now. Have a seat. I've been thinking."

I sit on the edge of the coffee table in front of her. "When the Senator pulled up and asked for you, I called you my girl because I wasn't really sure what to call you." I reach in my shirt pocket and pull out the box I have been hiding. "I'd like to start calling you my fiancé. That is, if you'll let me."

She starts sobbing and Beau barks at me. "Yes!"

I pull her up from the couch as I stand up and swing her around. "I love you, Annabelle."

CHAPTER 42

Thanksgiving Day was full of excitement. Scarlet and Naomi screamed when I showed them my engagement ring and went into planning mode. We decided that we'll have a small Christmas wedding at the farm. I want to be married when the babies are born. Plus, I know if I don't do it now, I'll never get the chance after the twins get here.

Normally, Scarlet and I would be getting ready to go Black Friday shopping, but I'm not in the mood this year. So I came home and went to sleep, still trying to catch up from the night shift I'd worked the day before.

My phone rang at eight o'clock. I answered it without looking. "Hello."

"Annabelle, I'm on my way down to your place now. You have to see the paper this morning." Scarlet screeches out.

"Okay. I'm getting up."

We hang up and I pull on some comfy lounge pants and a t-shirt of Judd's. He must already be out checking the cows. I've really got to go maternity clothes shopping. My scrubs do okay, but regular clothes are becoming less and less comfortable.

I hear her knocking on the door. As soon as I open it, she thrusts the paper into my hands. She's rambling and going on about something but I'm not sure what.

I read today's headline and cover my mouth.

Local Investment Firm Heirs Arrested

I look down and read about Patrick and his buddy Derek being arrested on rape and assault charges. The report filed by Becca Brooklyn has been made public. I laugh when I think of the police cars swooping into Column Heights to arrest them.

Of course, there is no comment from Patrick or Derek. They are trying to deny there was even a party at the house that night.

I'm proud, though, that Senator Brooklyn isn't backing down. Most politicians wouldn't like this kind of publicity, but he said his daughter's well-being comes first.

I look up and see Scarlet staring at me. "You knew this somehow, didn't you?"

"I was there when they brought Becca in. Once her cousin told me where the party was, I pulled up pictures of Patrick and his friends on my phone. They identified them to the police. The Senator stopped by to speak with me yesterday morning. I also told the officer about Derek drugging me. I volunteered my statement to help take them down."

She pulls me into a hug. "Oh my God. You just never cease to amaze me how strong you are."

~*~*~

It's been a few weeks since the arrest. The officer has been by and gotten an official statement from me. He also said that four other girls came into the station to make statements. Apparently my creepy vibes were spot on about Patrick. From the sounds of things, they make this a regular event.

I'm hoping they don't get away with this. I just think it's karma that they are battling someone with more money than them. They are accustomed to throwing money at a problem and making it go away. Well, this time that isn't the case.

They have come up with an entire list of charges for them, including contributing to the delinquency of minors, since Becca was only nineteen.

I've been trying to get all the extra hours I can at the hospital. So here I am, finishing up another double shift. The director of nursing has asked me to think about applying here after I graduate and have the twins. She'd really like to have me on staff. She says she feels guilty for all of the non-paid hours I've put in here.

Walking out into the cool Savannah air, a car pulls up to the curb. The back window rolls down and my parents appear.

"Annabelle. We need to speak with you." My father says.

"I'm not going anywhere with you. You can come join me in the coffee shop here or I can meet you at the Java Café just down the street."

To say I don't trust my parents is putting it very lightly.

My mother rolls her eyes and sits back, mumbling something. My father clears his throat. "We'll meet you just down the street then."

As soon as they pull off, I text Chris and ask him to come meet me. He lets me know he'll be there in five minutes, he's close by. I also text Judd to let him know what's going on. He plans to be at the café soon.

Pulling up to the café, I see my parents have already entered the building. I wait a couple of minutes until Chris pulls up. I get out of my car and meet him.

"Hey, Prissy Pants. Do you know what they want?"

"No, but I can't deal with them stressing me out. I just worked a double. I need to get off my feet, but I wanted to get whatever the hell this is over with."

He looks over at me as we walk. "When was the last time you talked to them?"

"The day I left their house after causing significant damage to Mom's yard."

He laughs remembering that day. "Alright, let's get this over with." He says as he grabs the door handle.

I sit down and Chris takes the seat beside me. My mother rolls her eyes. "Really, Annabelle, you couldn't come without your brother? Do you think we would cause a scene in public or something?"

I shake my head. "No. But I really don't need your stress right now."

My father looks down his nose at me. "Yes. I see you've gotten yourself in a situation." He snarls.

"My situation is that I'm having two babies with a wonderful man. One who I know will accept them for who they are, not try to mold them into some clone."

My father goes to raise his voice, but Chris gives him a death glare.

My mother clears her throat. "The purpose for this visit is to understand why you would lob such allegations at close friends of ours?"

"Excuse me?"

"We heard that you were one of the girls that came forward to make a complaint about poor Patrick and Derek."

I grit my teeth. "First of all, I didn't come forward soon enough. A young girl ended up in the ER because of them. They are despicable trash. Derek drugged me over a year ago. The only difference is he didn't succeed when it came to me. I hope they both rot in hell. While they are in prison waiting to go to hell, I pray they get fucked in the ass everyday by some guy named Spike."

My mother puts her hand over her mouth. My father glares at me. "You watch your mouth, young lady."

I feel a strong hand on my shoulder and then a strong voice behind me. "Or what? Are you going to slap your pregnant daughter around right here in public?"

"Excuse me, young man, this is a private conversation." My mother says, acting as if she has no clue why he's standing there.

Judd sits down beside me. "Oh, when my Princess and those babies are involved, it's all my business."

My father sits up straight. "Oh, so you are the cause of the mess she's in?"

Judd keeps his cool. "Oh, she's not in any mess. She's happy and healthy. The babies are doing great and she's already been offered a job at the hospital when she graduates. She has a wonderful supportive family *now*. So I think overall, she's doing great."

"She had a family before you came along." My mother scoffs.

Chris speaks up. "No, she was living with fucking vultures. She has an awesome supportive family now, along with Vic and me. You guys need to go back to your little gated community." He chuckles. "If you can still afford to live there and stay out of our lives. Go keep controlling Shane and Gregory, they've never minded. Stay away from us."

My father ignores him. "Annabelle, you need to drop your complaint against Derek."

I sit up in my chair. "No. I'm the one who helped the girls identify them and I volunteered my statement. So no. I'm just glad I was never left alone in a room with Patrick."

My mother exaggerates a sigh. "Really, Annabelle."

Judd sits forward. "You two should be ashamed of yourselves. I picked your daughter up that night, I took care of her while she was puking her guts up. Most parents would be like Senator Brooklyn, they would be irate at these people. You people, though? You want your daughter to be weak and retreat. Give these guys a free pass to hurt women. Well, she's not doing it." He stands up beside me. "Come on, Princess. You've had a long day. Let's get you home."

CHAPTER 43

Chris is walking Princess out to her car. Her parents stand up from the table and her father looks at me. "Young man, you would be wise to watch yourself. I have friends."

I lean across the table close to his face and speak through gritted teeth. "Do you seriously think you are intimidating me? Let's clear something up. You don't have friends, you have people that would drop you in a second if it suits them. Don't fuck with me, old man. I've stared the enemy down face to face. I've lived through things that you couldn't imagine. If you ever come near her or lay your hands on her again, I'll kill you and no one will find the body. You might have friends but I do too, and unlike yours, mine like me for me. Not because I drop to my knees and suck their dick every chance I get."

I hear her mother gasp at my crass tone.

I turn and walk out of the café. Princess looks at me. "Judd, what did you do?"

I shake my head. "Nothing, I just told them how it was going to be."

Chris laughs. "Ha. I'm sure they liked that."

I shrug. "I don't give a shit what they do or don't like."

I take Princess's hand. "Let's go grab a bite to eat and relax for a few minutes. Then we'll come back to get the car. Chris, why don't you call Angie and ask her to join us?"

Chris looks at me. "Wish I could, man, but I have class in the morning and I have to study tonight. Being back in school sucks ass sometimes."

I slap him on the shoulder. "Hey, man, it will be worth it in the end. Maybe you, Vic and Princess will all work at the same hospital."

They both laugh and Princess nods. "We've talked about that. I told them I'm not taking orders from them."

I laugh. "You would say that. Come on, let's go so he can study."

After we get in my truck, she looks over at me. "Judd, I'm sorry I ever doubted your ability to control your rage. I know you just did a really good job of it in there."

"Honest truth, Princess. I was scared I'd never be able to control it, too. I'm proud of myself." I put the truck in gear and drive to our favorite little diner.

~*~*~

It's our wedding day, yesterday was Christmas. Time has flown since Thanksgiving. Princess finished up Nana's memoirs and gave everyone a copy from Nana just like she wanted. We all sat around laughing and crying at the stories.

For the wedding, we set up out back just like we did for Ryder and Scarlet, but the crowd is much smaller. Plus, there is definitely a presence missing, but I'm sure Nana is watching over us.

Ryder slaps me on the back. "You ready to go, man?"

"Yep."

Ryder and I make our way to the front with the preacher. We both give my mom a kiss as we pass by her.

Standing up front waiting for Princess to make her way down the aisle is killing me. Finally, Scarlet starts down in her true to name scarlet red dress. Next, Chris and Vic appear with a very beautifully pregnant Princess tucked between them.

She takes my breath away every time I see her. She worries that she's too fat because of the babies. I tell her it's beautiful because she's making room for our little boy and girl.

Yep, we found out on our last ultrasound that we are getting one of each. She and Scarlet have went crazy in the nursery. The ladies from Nana's quilting group are planning a baby shower for her. They've already started on baby quilts. We are both definitely missing Nana right now.

Once she's up front, she smiles and her brothers both give her a kiss on each cheek.

I stare into her eyes as we repeat the standard vows. Neither one of us really wanted to write something to share with the world, so we decided to wait until after and tell each other in private.

The next thing I know, the preacher is telling me to kiss her and introducing us. "Ladies and gentlemen, Mr. and Mrs. Judd Hughes."

I smile. "Come on, Princess."

She smiles at me. "Sure."

After we get to the end of the aisle, I lean down to her ear. "So, do you think we can have sex in the barn again tonight? You know, relive the moment?"

She bursts out laughing. "Yeah, I don't think so. How about we just have some plain Jane sex in our house, in the bed? I'm not sure if I got down on the hay, I could get back up."

I smile. "Whatever you say."

"I'm sure you're thinking you should have run."

I shake my head and nuzzle her neck. "Nope, I'm thinking I'm one lucky SOB to have landed myself a Princess."

EPILOGUE

SIX MONTHS LATER...

Sitting by the pool with Scarlet, it's a hot freaking day at the end of May. I'm a miserable thirty-six weeks pregnant and I feel like I may burst into flames at any time.

On the plus side, I did graduate with my degree in nursing. I also was hired at the hospital I've been doing clinicals in. As soon as these babies get here and I'm ready, I'll be going to work.

I'm lucky that Naomi is going to keep them for me to work. Finding sitters that can juggle my shifts flip flopping and Judd's early hours is hard. Plus, this way they can be at home and Judd can peak in on them. Nelson will get plenty of time with them, too, I'm sure.

Naomi walks out of the house. "Here you go, sweetie, a tall glass of lemonade."

I shake my head. "Thank you so much."

Everyone has been watching me like a hawk because the doctor has been saying ever since I was at thirty-two weeks that I could go at any time. This little girl and boy are ready. But they must not be too damn ready because here I am fat, hot, sweaty, swollen and miserable.

Scarlet looks at me with sympathy. "Sweetie, have you tried the things the doctor told you to do?"

"Not to get too graphic in front of Naomi, but Judd has definitely done his part in trying to get me to have these babies. Plus, I've probably walked the entire state of Georgia by now."

About that time, Judd and Ryder come chasing each other like kids through the fence.

Naomi stands up. "You two stop before you get hurt. You aren't teenagers anymore."

"Fuck this, I'm hot. I gotta go inside. Scar, help me up."

Scarlet reaches for my hands and I stand up. As soon as I stand up, I feel a whoosh of water running down my legs. "Shit."

Scarlet's face lights up and she turns to our husbands who are still chasing each other. "Dip shits, stop running! Annabelle's water just broke."

Naomi drops the tray of glasses she was carrying back inside. "Shit." Then she covers her mouth, embarrassed.

Judd runs over to me, trying to pick my big ass up. "Stop, Judd. I can walk. Someone get me a towel, I don't want to mess up the seats in my new Tahoe."

"Jesus, baby, don't worry about the damn seats. I'll have them cleaned, or I'll clean them myself."

I look at Ryder who is staring at me like I may turn into an alien or something. "Ryder, get me a damn towel now."

He runs in the house and grabs a couple of towels as I make my way to the vehicle. I look at him and smile. "Thank you."

Scarlet helps me latch my seat belt. "Okay. We will wait here for a little bit and I'll call your brothers. Once you guys get checked in and settled, let me know. We will be there with bells on."

Twelve hours and one C-section later, Victoria and Grayton are here.

We never really told anyone about the names we chose, but we did make sure it wouldn't offend Ryder and Scarlet if we used the names.

Once the entire crew is at the hospital, I tell Judd to let them in. My brothers and their girlfriends are among the first. Naomi, Nelson, Ryder and Scarlet are next.

Ryder looks at Judd holding Vicky. "So my dad and Sarah will be here tomorrow."

Judd nods and smiles. "That's great."

Naomi smiles with tears in her eyes. "What are the names?"

I hold up Grayton. "This is Grayton Christopher, after my brother, Ryder and the original Grayton. We are going to call him Gray."

Judd holds up Vicky. "This little princess is Victoria Pearl, after Nana and my mom and Victor." He looks at everyone else. "Victoria is my mom's middle name. We are going to call her Vicky."

His dad comes over to us. "Annabelle, you did good, kid. These babies are beautiful and I know they didn't get that from me and him."

I smile. "Awe, I think y'all are pretty handsome guys."

Naomi hugs me tight. "Nana would be so proud." She whispers in my ear. "Your momma and daddy are fools for not seeing how wonderful you are."

I nod and look at my babies. "Well, I can't say I disagree with you on the fools' part. I'm just glad that when Dad's firm went under, they moved to California. The only thing better would have been Alaska. The further the better as far as I'm concerned." I shrug. "It's their loss."

Naomi smiles nodding and looks around the room. "Alright, well let's all get out of here and give them some time to be mommy and daddy. Them and the babies need some rest."

Ryder walks over to Judd. "So man, was the C-section cool?"

Scarlet rolls her eyes and smacks him. "Let's go. He can tell you about it later or you can ask Gable if you can be in the room when Ivie has their baby."

I laugh. "Oh yeah, how many weeks is she now?"

Scarlet smiles. "Sixteen. They are finally going to make it public. Next week they are doing an interview with People. They are going to let everyone know how long they've been married and about the baby on the way."

I smile. "Good for them. They deserve happiness."

After everyone leaves the room, I look at Judd who is swaying back and forth with our daughter. "You are the most beautiful man on this planet, Judd Hughes."

He leans down and kisses me. "You, my Princess, are the most beautiful woman on this planet. And this little girl right here is the most beautiful girl on the planet. Yes, she is."

He puts her down in the bassinet, followed by Gray. Finally, he sits beside me on the bed. "Princess, I think today is the happiest day of my life."

I yawn and smile. "Really? Me, too."

He smiles. "For me it's been an uphill battle, but you've been with me all the way."

"That's what I'm here for. It's like the old song, *Love is a Battlefield.*"

He chuckles and brushes my hair from my face. "Yep, the drugs are working great, you are quoting eighties music. I love you, Princess, get some rest." He kisses my forehead.

I shut my eyes. "I love you, too."

Acknowledgments

Thank you to my readers. Without you I would not be having this awesome adventure. You have helped make my dreams come true and for that I'm truly blessed and grateful.

I need to give a big **Thank You to Chelly Peeler**. She's not only my editor but my friend. She always listens to my random crazy thoughts. She loves my characters and understands my craziness. Thank you again.

To my husband, thank you for standing behind me for all of these years and always pushing me in your own way. To my son Bailey, thank you for trying to understand why mom is on her computer so much.

To my Mom for listening to my random story ideas and telling me to go for it. To my sisters, thank you for always supporting me. You guys always have my back. Daddy, I miss you every day and I know you're watching over me.

To my BETA readers you are awesome.

Thanks to all of the book bloggers out there who spend so much time helping us promote books and everyone who leaves a review, you are all awesome.

To my Author friends, thank you for being supportive and inspirational all at the same time.

I hope you've all enjoyed this series as much as the Temptation Series. If you haven't had the pleasure of reading it you can grab up that Box set also at all eBook retailers.

About the Author

S.M. Donaldson is a born and raised Southern girl. She grew up in a small rural town on Florida's Gulf Coast, the kind of place where everyone knows your business before you do, especially when your Daddy is a cop and your Mom works for the school system. She married one of her best friends at the age of 20 and has one son. She is a proud military wife, has always had a soft spot for a good story, and is known to have a potty mouth. At the age of 31, she decided there was no time like the present to attempt her first book. Sam's Choice was born and she hasn't stopped since. If you are looking for a good, steamy, Southern set romance with true Southern dialect, she's your girl.

My Links:

www.smdonaldson.com

www.facebook.com/s.m.donaldson.author

www.goodreads.com/AuthorSMDonaldson

Twitter: @SMDonaldson1

Instagram: SMDONALDSON1981

Other titles by S.M. Donaldson

The Sam Series
Sam's Choice

Sam's Fight for Freedom

The Temptation Series
Lying with Temptation

Acting on Temptation

Fighting Temptation

(The Temptation Box Set)

The Secrets of Savannah Series
Secrets Behind Those Eyes

Secrets in The Lyrics

Secrets in Battle

Secrets of Savannah (The Entire Series)

Novellas
Just the Other Sister Series (E-book only)

Seasons of Change Novella Series
Summer of Forgiveness

Falling for Autumn

Holiday with Holli

Camellia In Bloom (Coming Soon)

Marco's MMA Boys
Letting Lox In

In Sly's Eyes (Coming Soon)

Made in the USA
Middletown, DE
08 September 2021